Volume One

THE HERO DISCOVERED

BY
MATT WAGNER

COLORS
JEROMY COX
JAMES ROCHELLE

IMAGE COMICS, INC.

Robert Kirkman, Chief Operating Officer • **Erik Larsen**, Chief Financial Officer • **Todd McFarlane**, President • **Marc Silvestri**, Chief Executive Officer • **Jim Valentino**, Vice-President • **Eric Stephenson**, Publisher • **Corey Murphy**, Director of Sales • **Jeff Boison**, Director of Publishing Planning & Book Trade Sales • **Chris Ross**, Director of Digital Sales • **Jeff Stang**, Director of Specialty Sales • **Kat Salazar**, Director of PR & Marketing • **Branwyn Bigglestone**, Controller • **Sue Korpela**, Accounts Manager • **Drew Gill**, Art Director • **Brett Warnock**, Production Manager • **Leigh Thomas**, Print Manager • **Tricia Ramos**, Traffic Manager • **Briah Skelly**, Publicist • **Aly Hoffman**, Events & Conventions Coordinator • **Sasha Head**, Sales & Marketing Production Designer • **David Brothers**, Branding Manager • **Melissa Gifford**, Content Manager • **Drew Fitzgerald**, Publicity Assistant • **Vincent Kukua**, Production Artist • **Erika Schnatz**, Production Artist • **Ryan Brewer**, Production Artist • **Shanna Matuszak**, Production Artist • **Carey Hall**, Production Artist • **Esther Kim**, Direct Market Sales Representative • **Emilio Bautista**, Digital Sales Representative • **Leanna Caunter**, Accounting Assistant • **Chloe Ramos-Peterson**, Library Market Sales Representative • **Marla Eizik**, Administrative Assistant

IMAGECOMICS.COM

THE HERO DISCOVERED

MAGE

Chapter 01

Outrageous Slings and Arrows

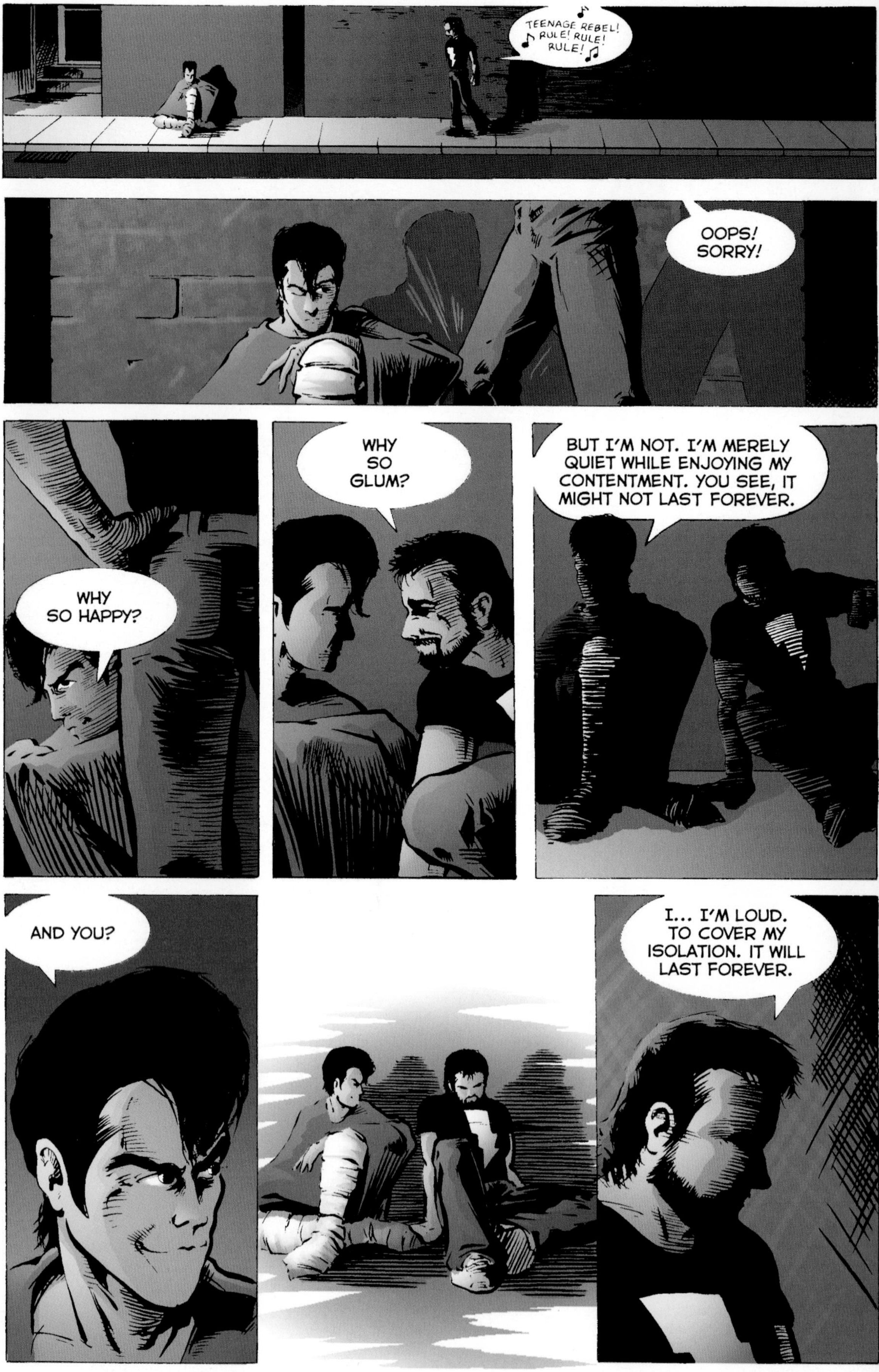
TEENAGE REBEL! RULE! RULE! RULE!
OOPS! SORRY!
WHY SO HAPPY?
WHY SO GLUM?
BUT I'M NOT. I'M MERELY QUIET WHILE ENJOYING MY CONTENTMENT. YOU SEE, IT MIGHT NOT LAST FOREVER.
AND YOU?
I... I'M LOUD. TO COVER MY ISOLATION. IT WILL LAST FOREVER.

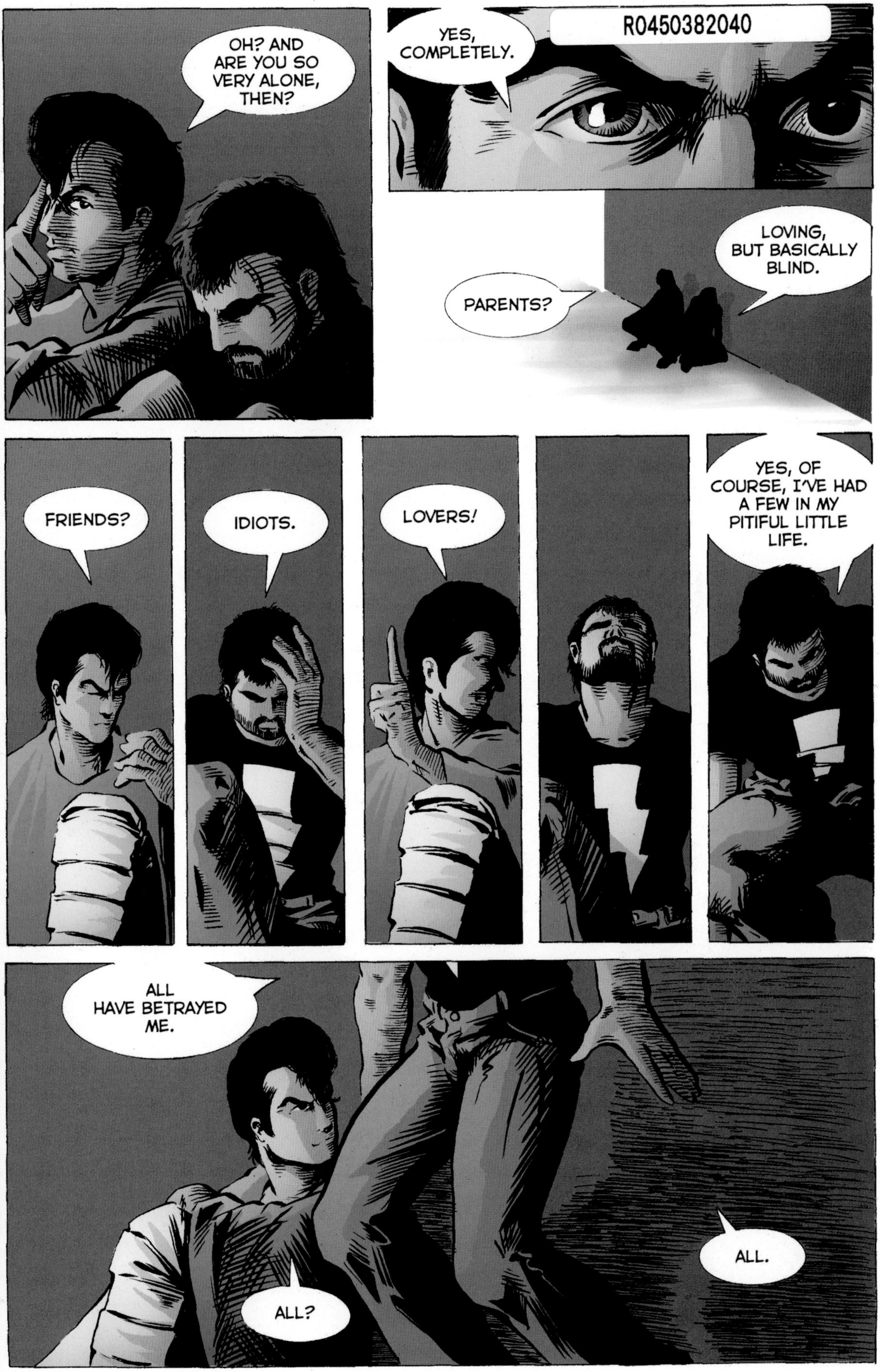
OH? AND ARE YOU SO VERY ALONE, THEN?
YES, COMPLETELY.
PARENTS?
LOVING, BUT BASICALLY BLIND.
FRIENDS?
IDIOTS.
LOVERS!
YES, OF COURSE, I'VE HAD A FEW IN MY PITIFUL LITTLE LIFE.
ALL HAVE BETRAYED ME.
ALL?
ALL.

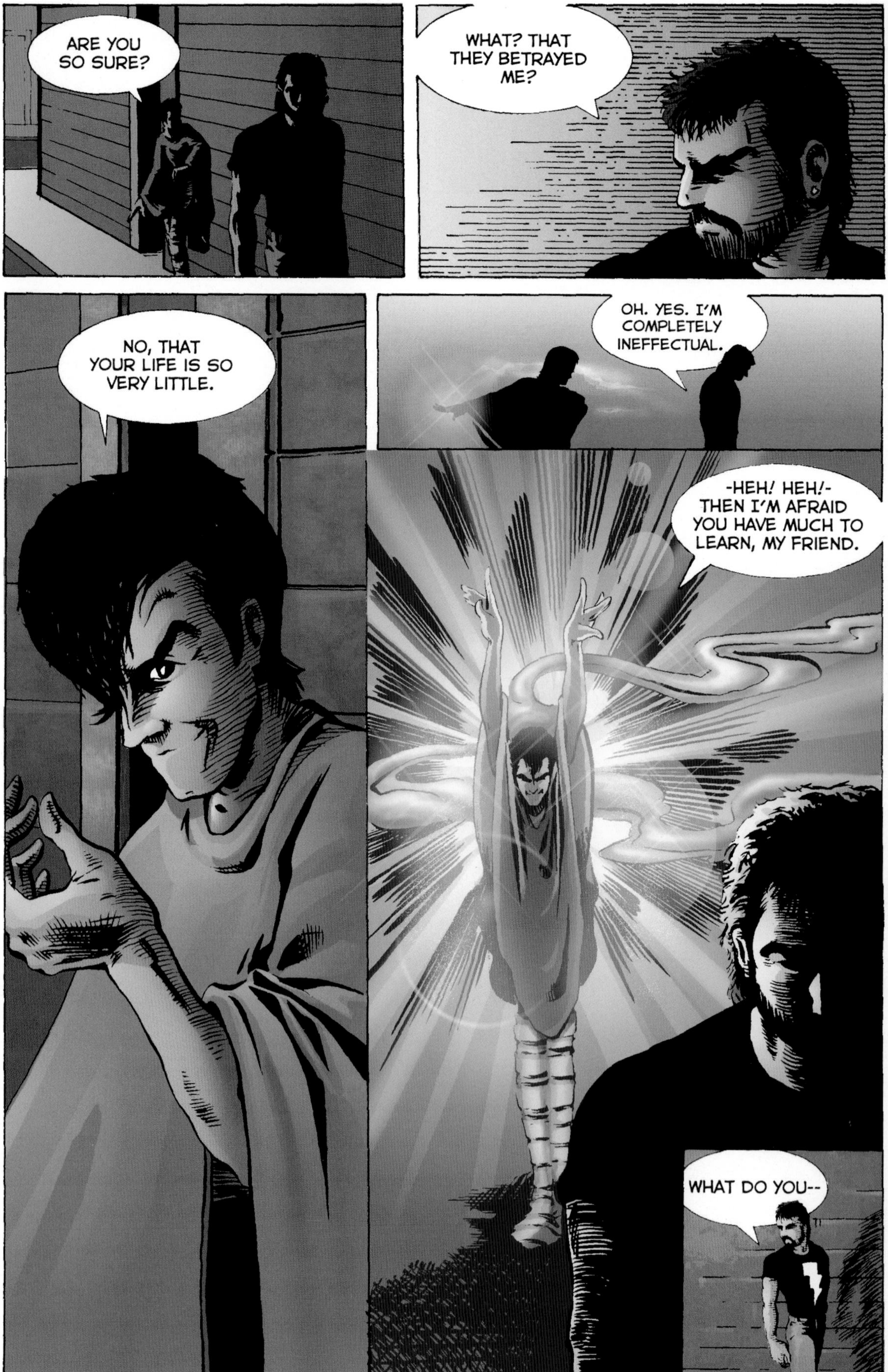
ARE YOU SO SURE?
WHAT? THAT THEY BETRAYED ME?
NO, THAT YOUR LIFE IS SO VERY LITTLE.
OH. YES. I'M COMPLETELY INEFFECTUAL.
-HEH! HEH!- THEN I'M AFRAID YOU HAVE MUCH TO LEARN, MY FRIEND.
WHAT DO YOU--

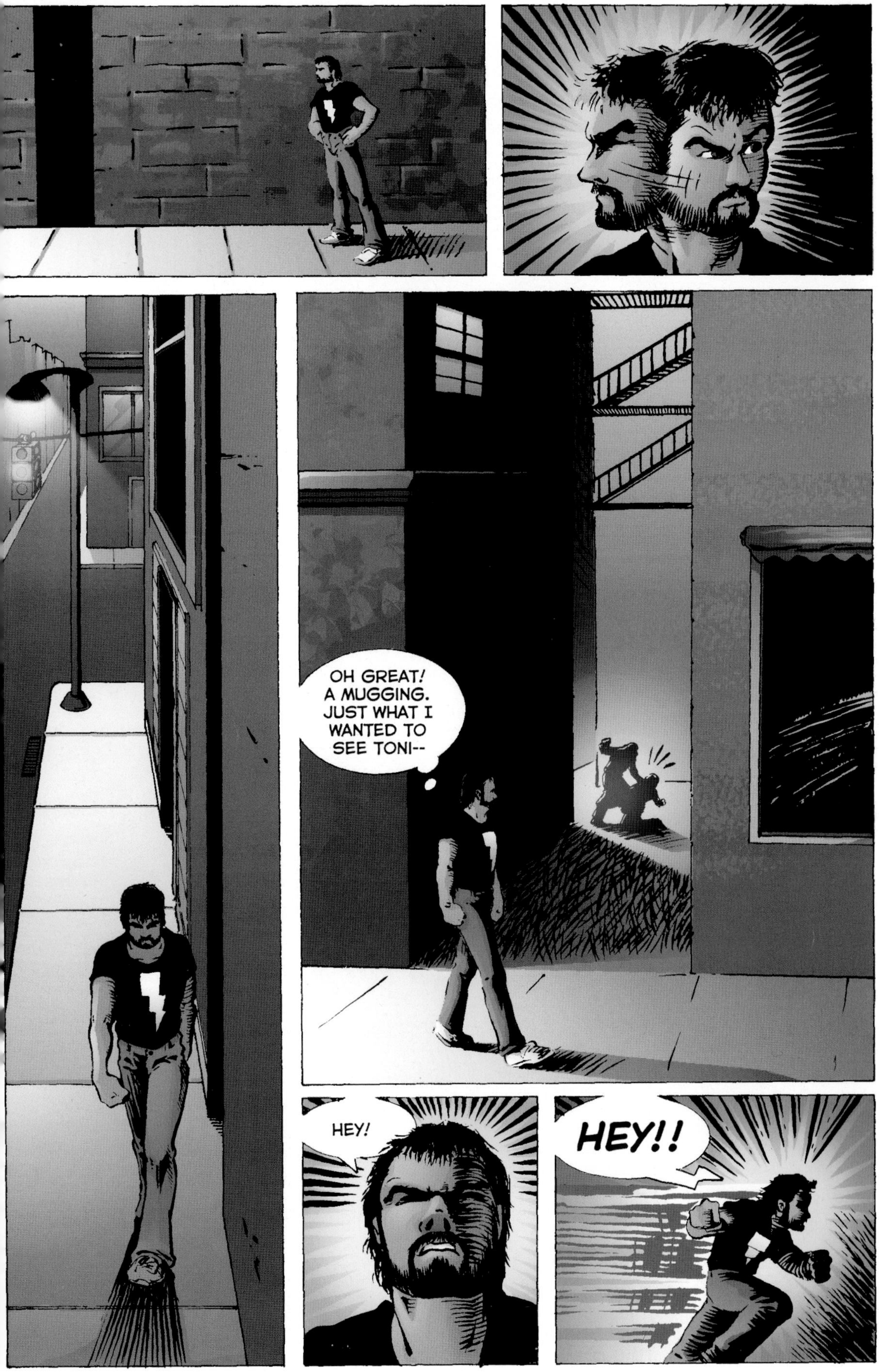
OH GREAT! A MUGGING. JUST WHAT I WANTED TO SEE TONI--
HEY!
HEY!!

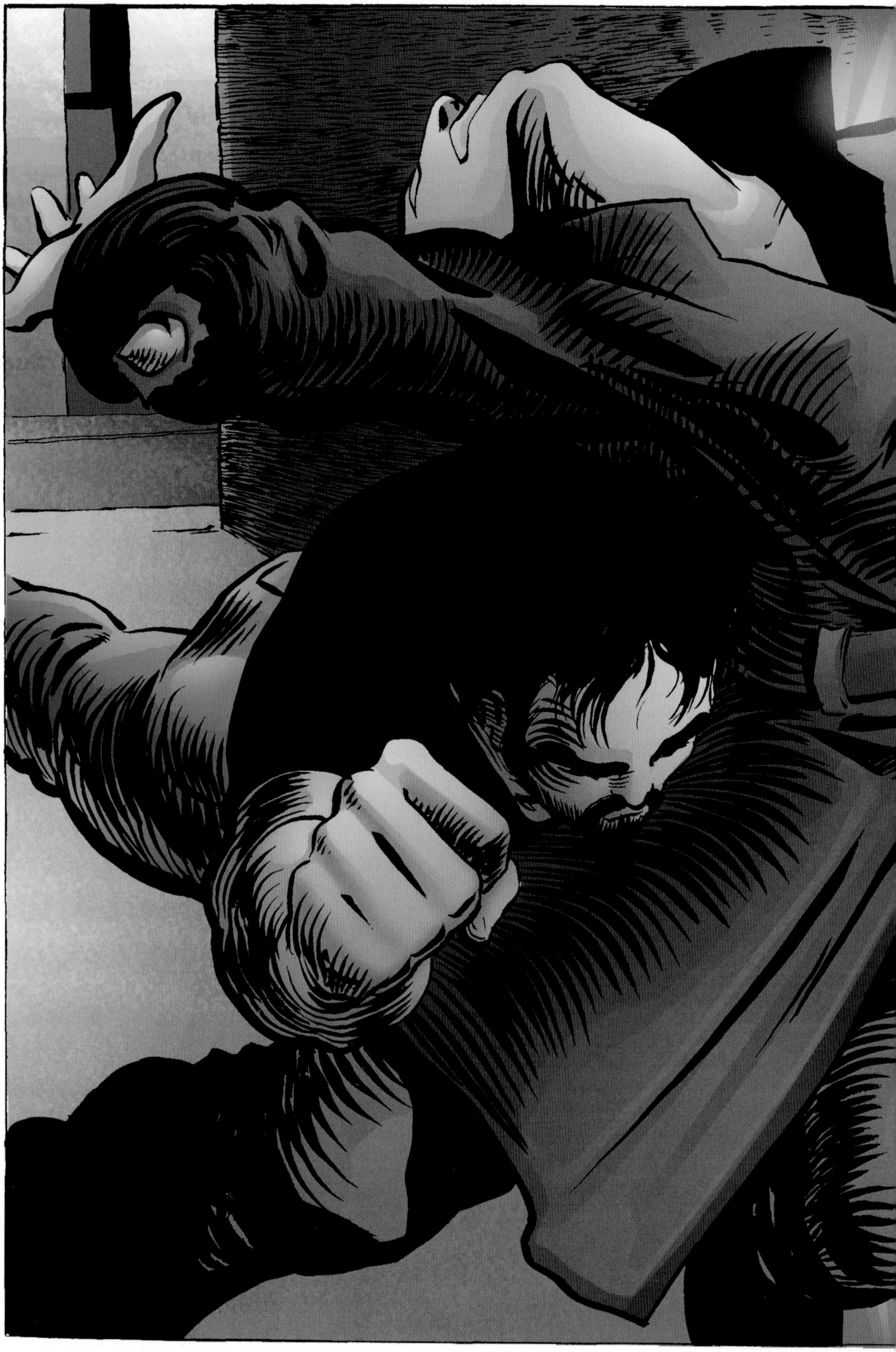

THUMP!

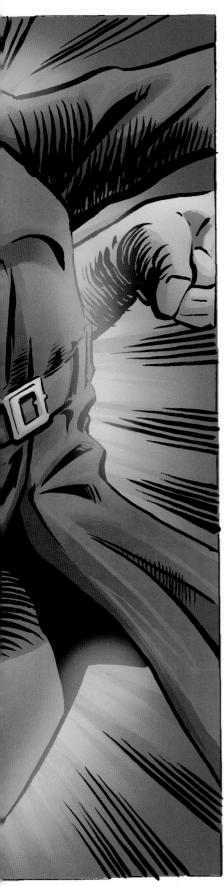

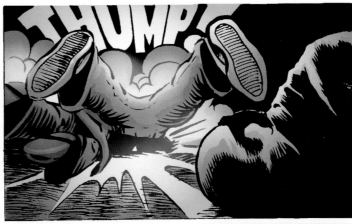

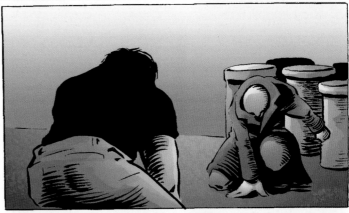

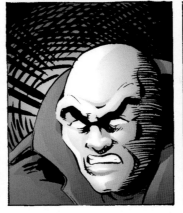

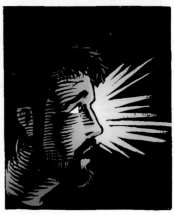

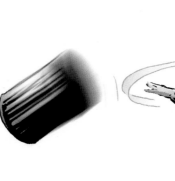

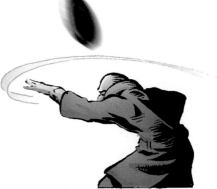

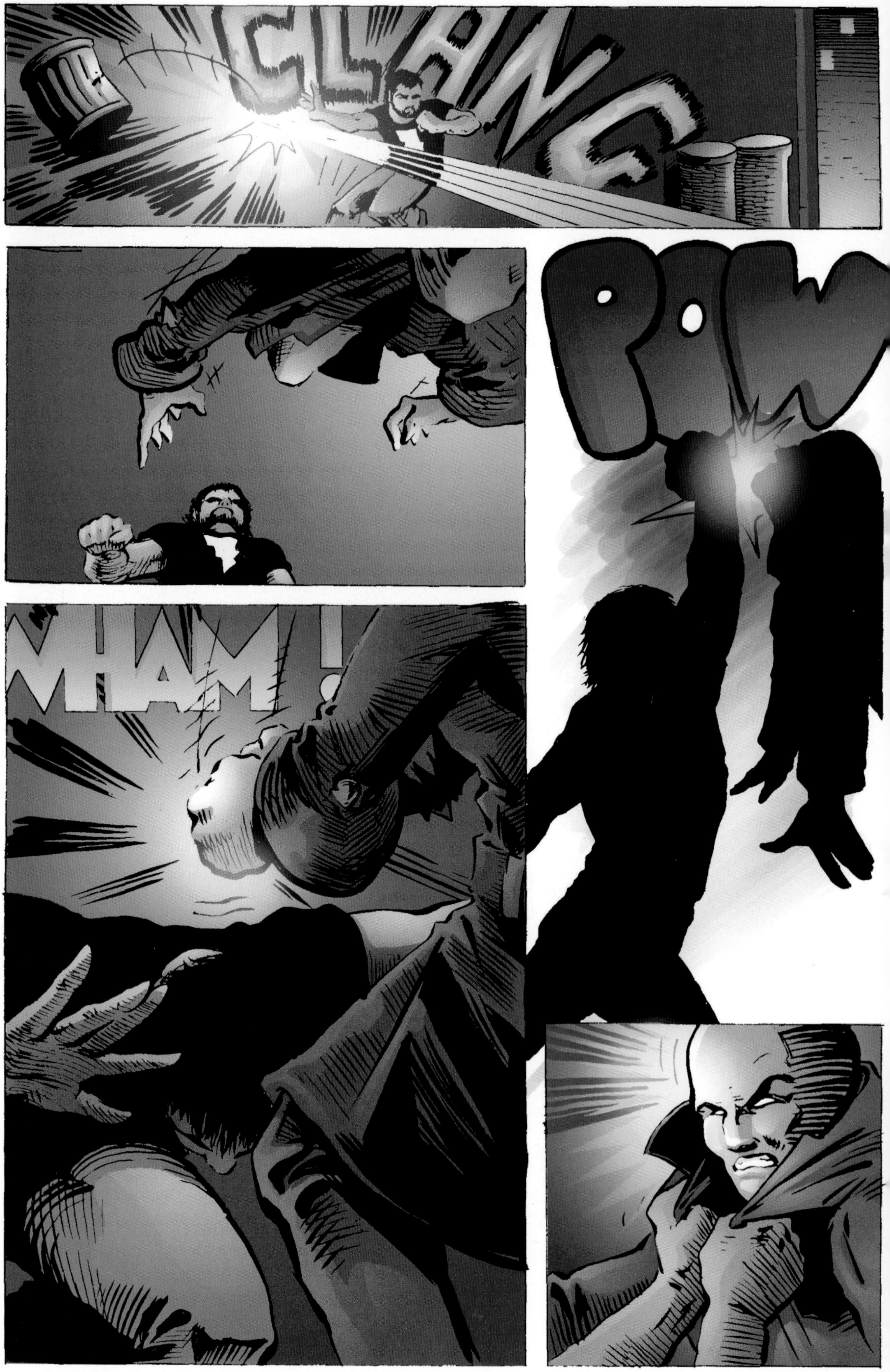
CLANG
POW
WHAM!

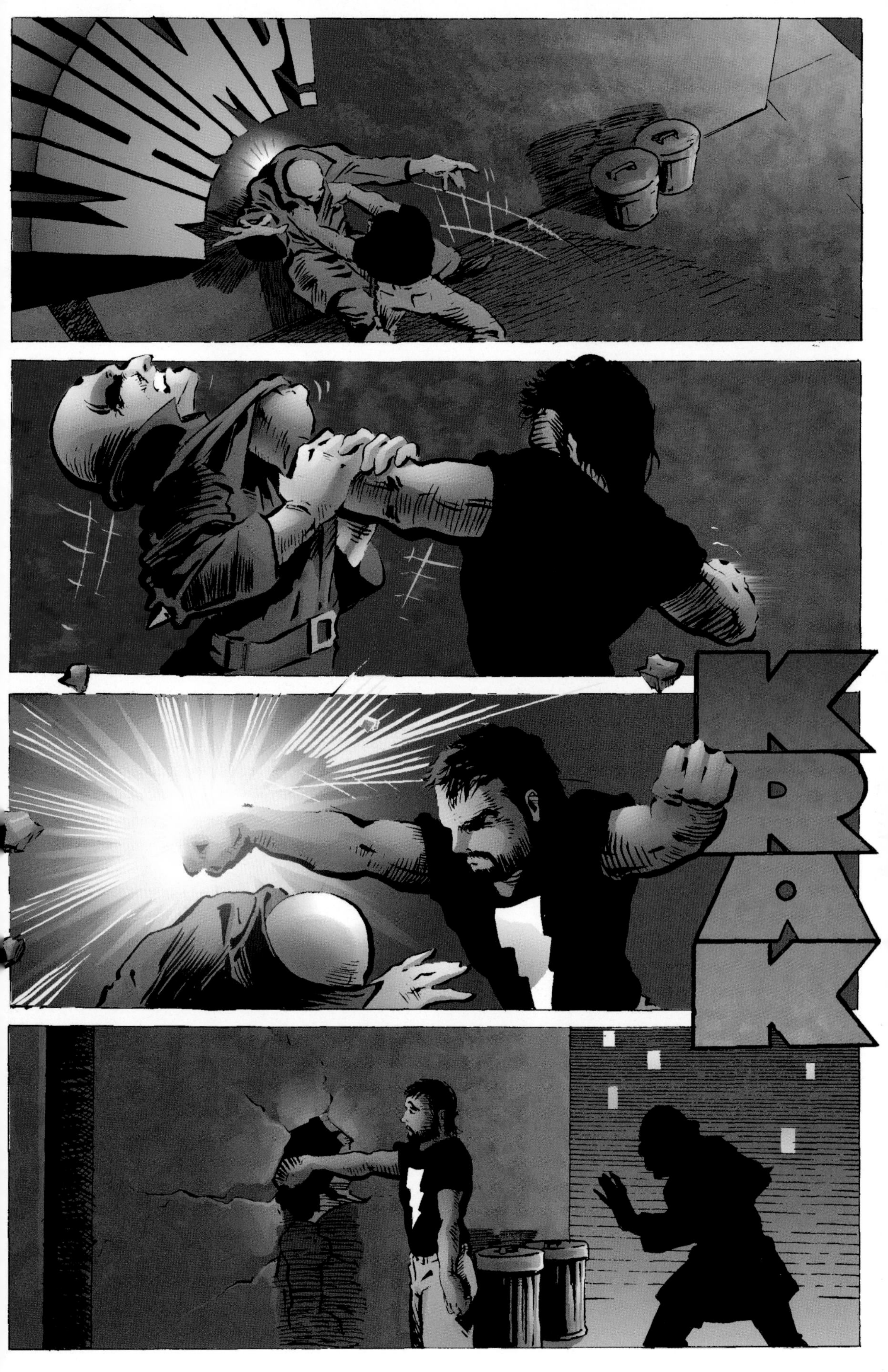
WHUMP!
KRAK

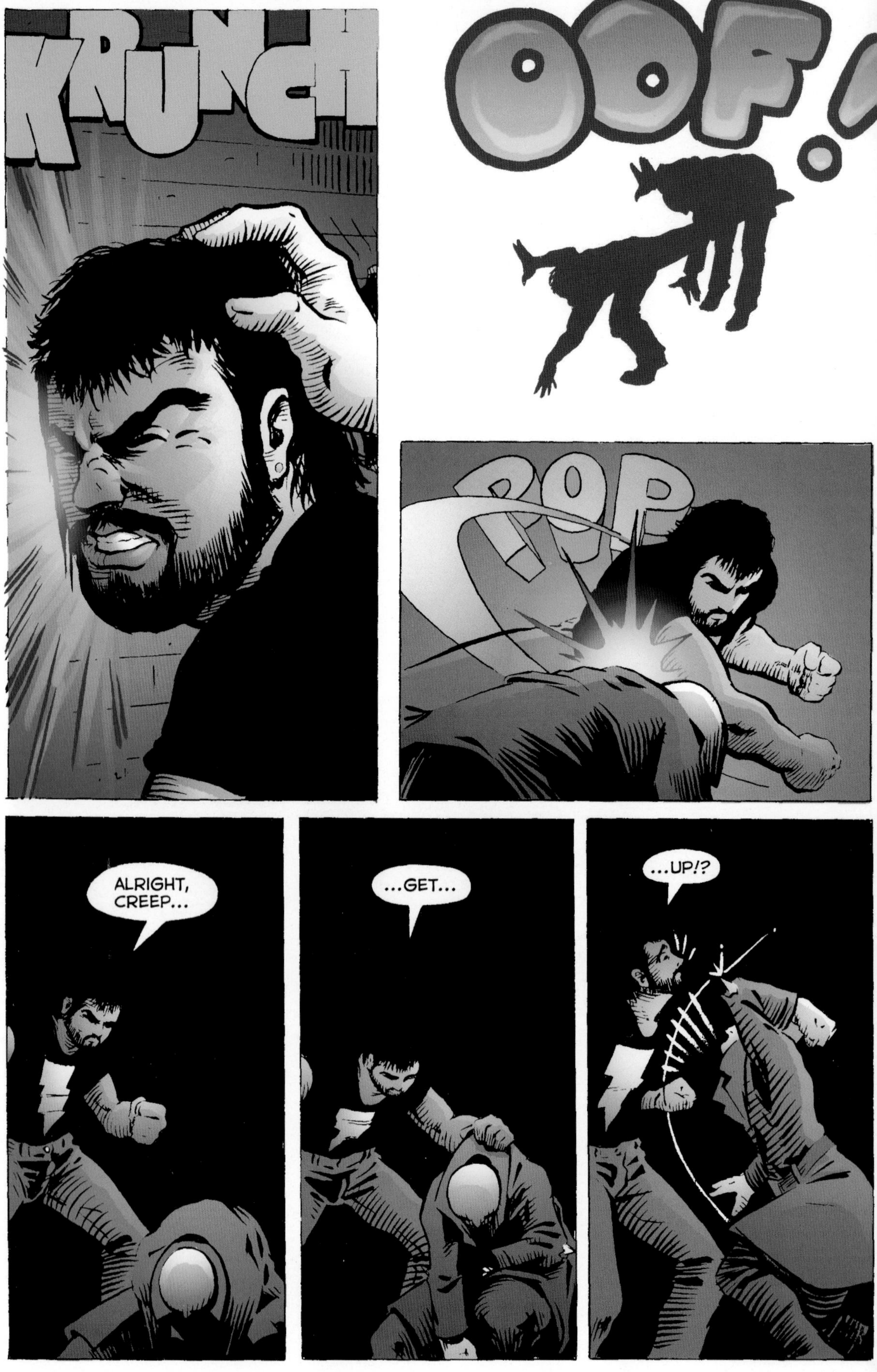
KRUNCH
OOF!
POP
ALRIGHT, CREEP...
...GET...
...UP!?

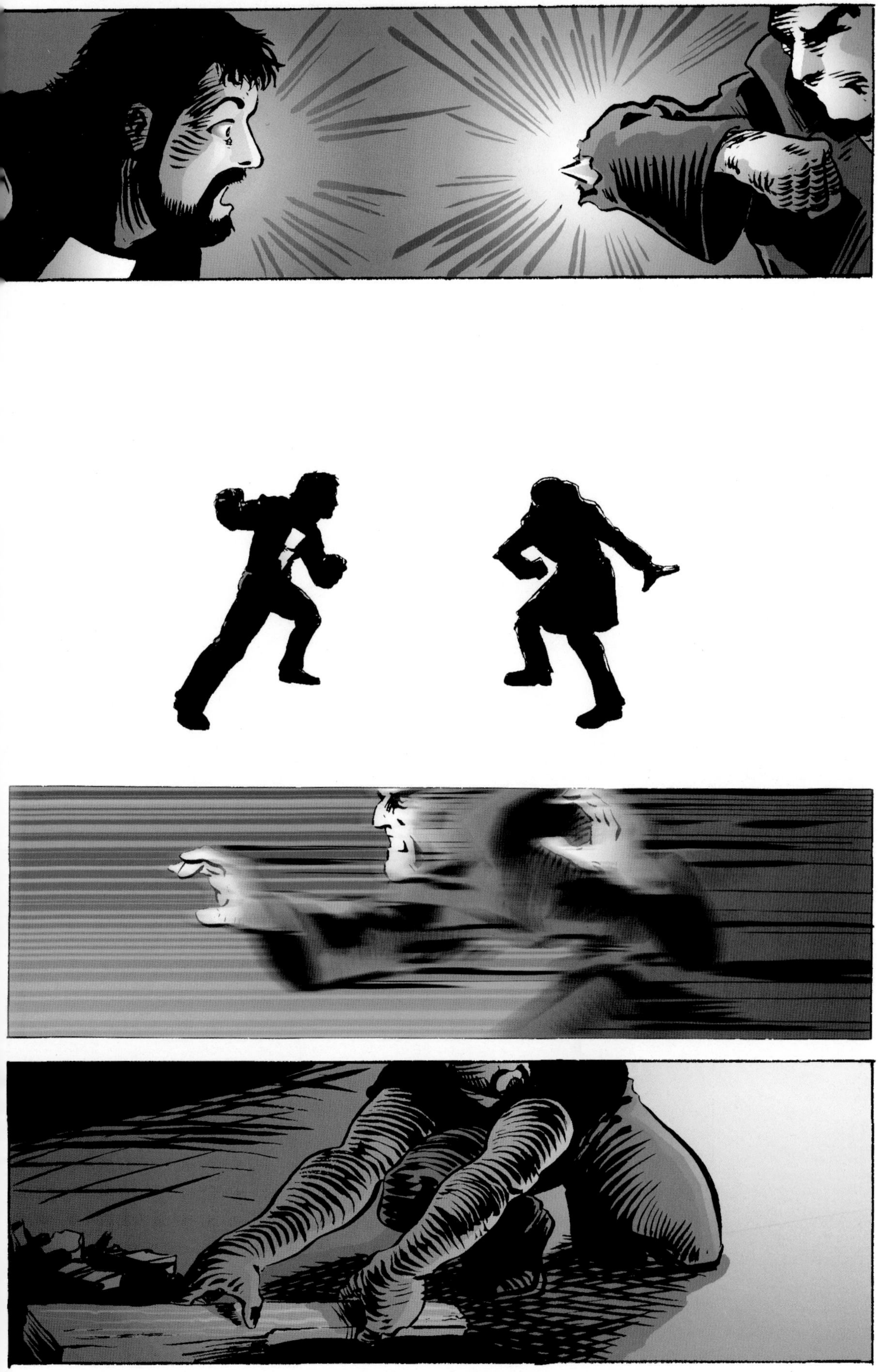

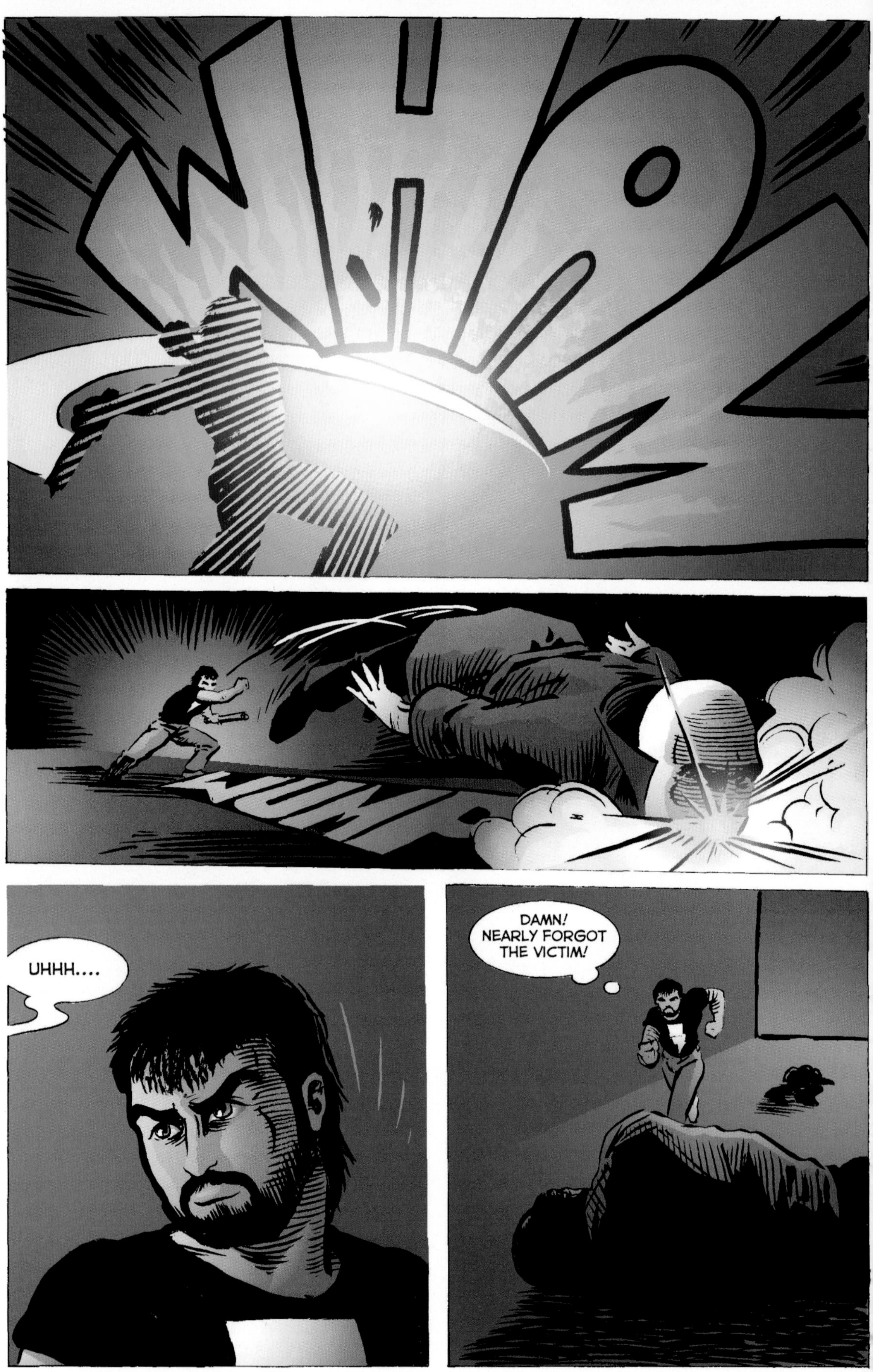
WHOOM
WUMP
UHHH....
DAMN! NEARLY FORGOT THE VICTIM!

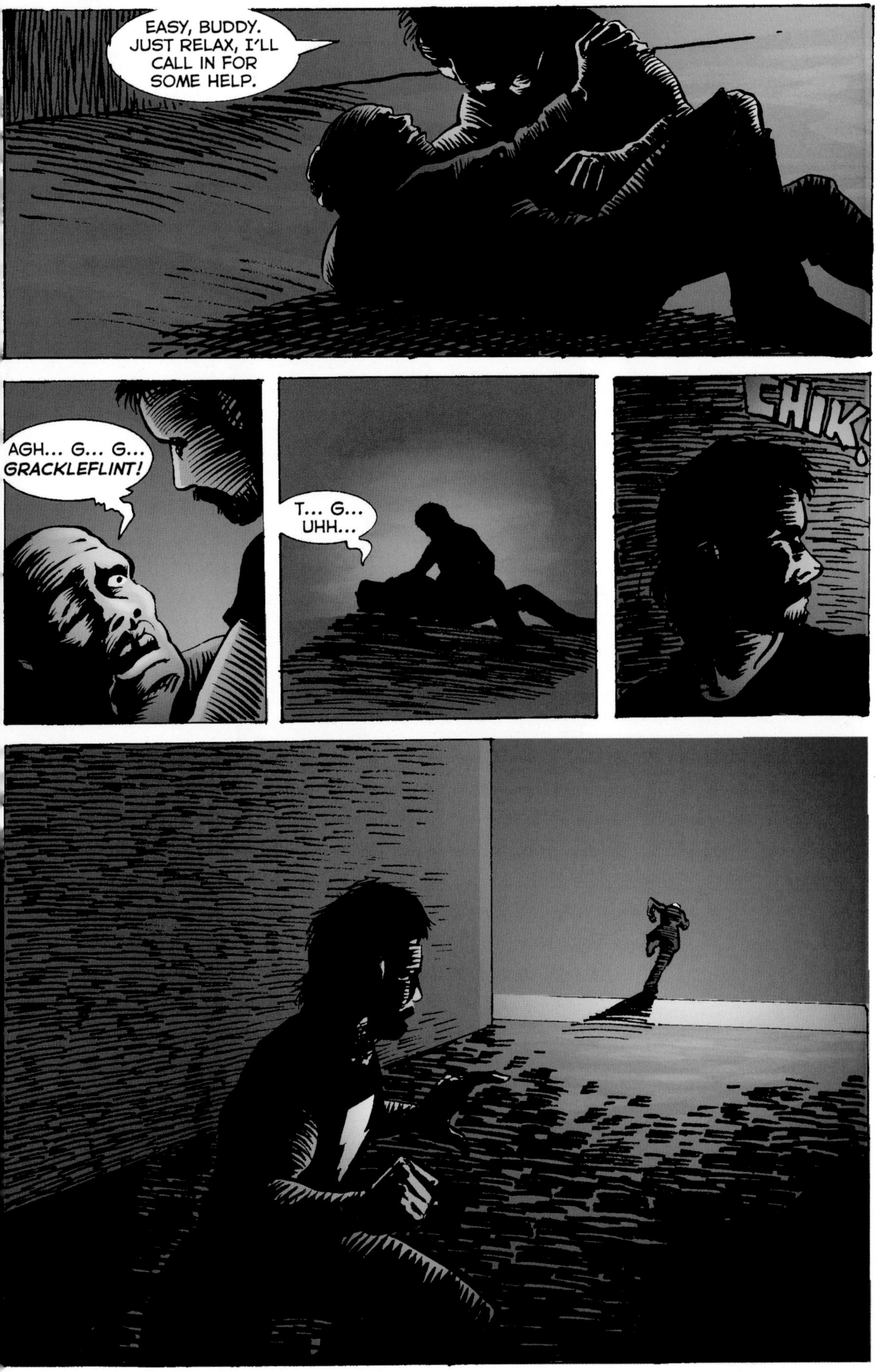
EASY, BUDDY. JUST RELAX, I'LL CALL IN FOR SOME HELP.
AGH... G... G... GRACKLEFLINT!
T... G... UHH...
CHIK!

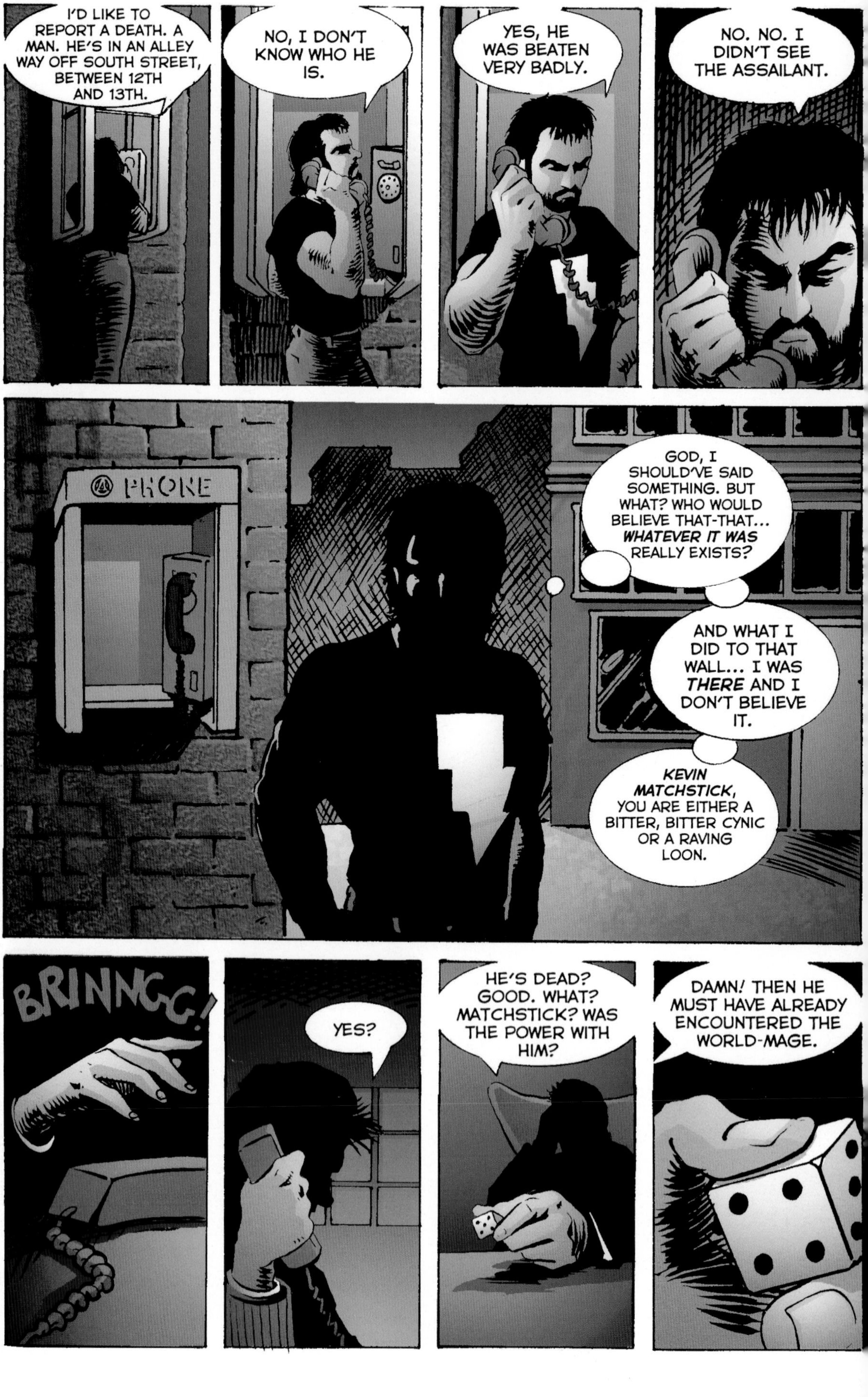
I'D LIKE TO REPORT A DEATH. A MAN. HE'S IN AN ALLEY WAY OFF SOUTH STREET, BETWEEN 12TH AND 13TH.
NO, I DON'T KNOW WHO HE IS.
YES, HE WAS BEATEN VERY BADLY.
NO. NO. I DIDN'T SEE THE ASSAILANT.
PHONE
GOD, I SHOULD'VE SAID SOMETHING. BUT WHAT? WHO WOULD BELIEVE THAT-THAT... WHATEVER IT WAS REALLY EXISTS?
AND WHAT I DID TO THAT WALL... I WAS THERE AND I DON'T BELIEVE IT.
KEVIN MATCHSTICK, YOU ARE EITHER A BITTER, BITTER CYNIC OR A RAVING LOON.
BRINNGG!
YES?
HE'S DEAD? GOOD. WHAT? MATCHSTICK? WAS THE POWER WITH HIM?
DAMN! THEN HE MUST HAVE ALREADY ENCOUNTERED THE WORLD-MAGE.

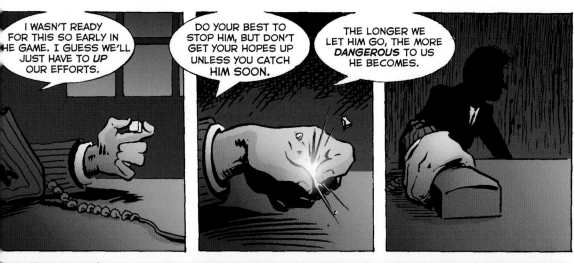

I WASN'T READY FOR THIS SO EARLY IN HE GAME. I GUESS WE'LL JUST HAVE TO *UP* OUR EFFORTS.

DO YOUR BEST TO STOP HIM, BUT DON'T GET YOUR HOPES UP UNLESS YOU CATCH HIM SOON.

THE LONGER WE LET HIM GO, THE MORE *DANGEROUS* TO US HE BECOMES.

AND WHAT ABOUT THAT BUM ON THE STREET?

WHAT THE HELL COMPELLED ME TO OPEN UP TO HIM LIKE THAT?

AND THEN THE MUGGING...

ONE MOMENT I'M MERELY A SPECTATOR AND THE NEXT I'M PLAYING *CAPTAIN MARVEL*.

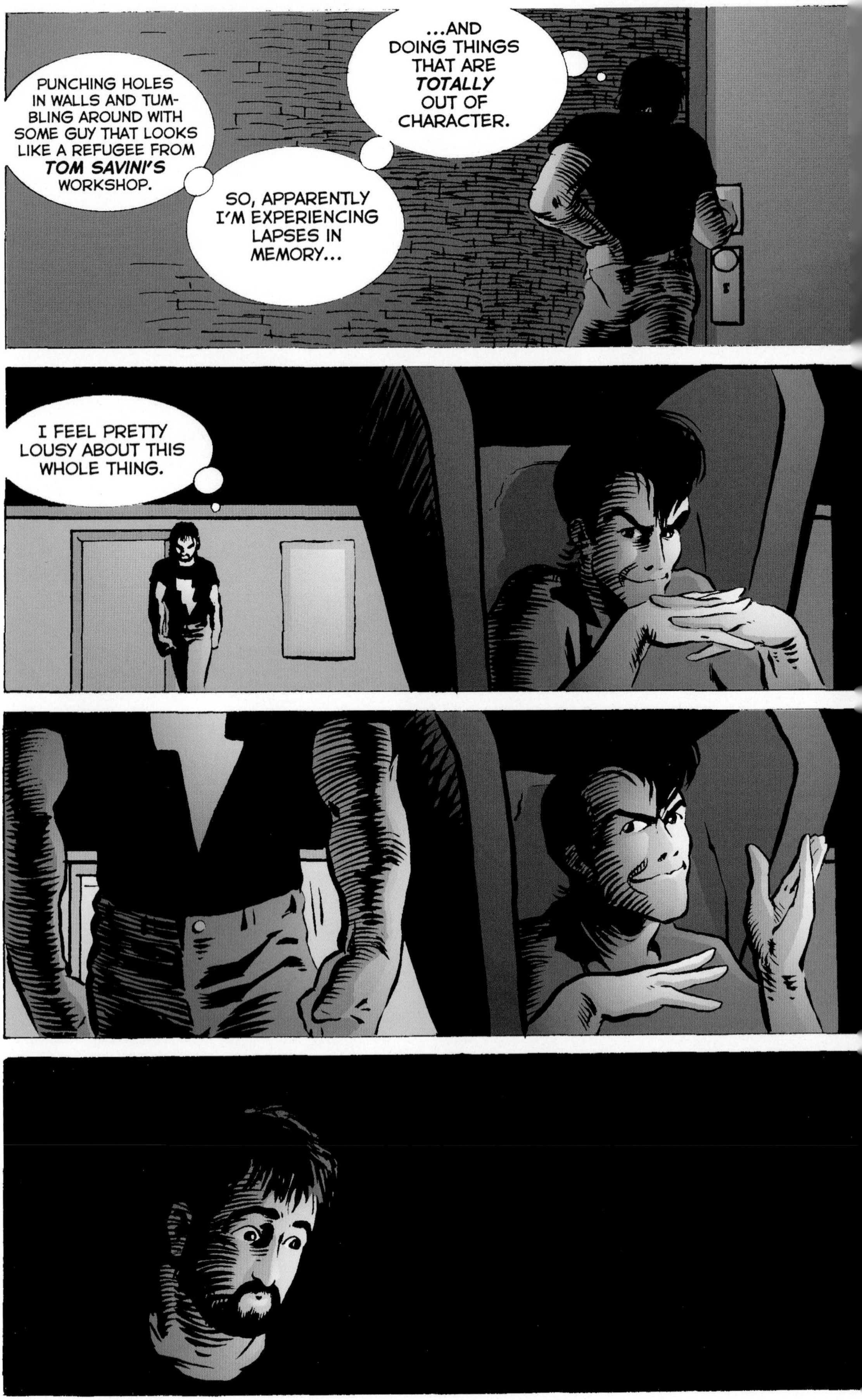
PUNCHING HOLES IN WALLS AND TUMBLING AROUND WITH SOME GUY THAT LOOKS LIKE A REFUGEE FROM TOM SAVINI'S WORKSHOP.
...AND DOING THINGS THAT ARE TOTALLY OUT OF CHARACTER.
SO, APPARENTLY I'M EXPERIENCING LAPSES IN MEMORY...
I FEEL PRETTY LOUSY ABOUT THIS WHOLE THING.

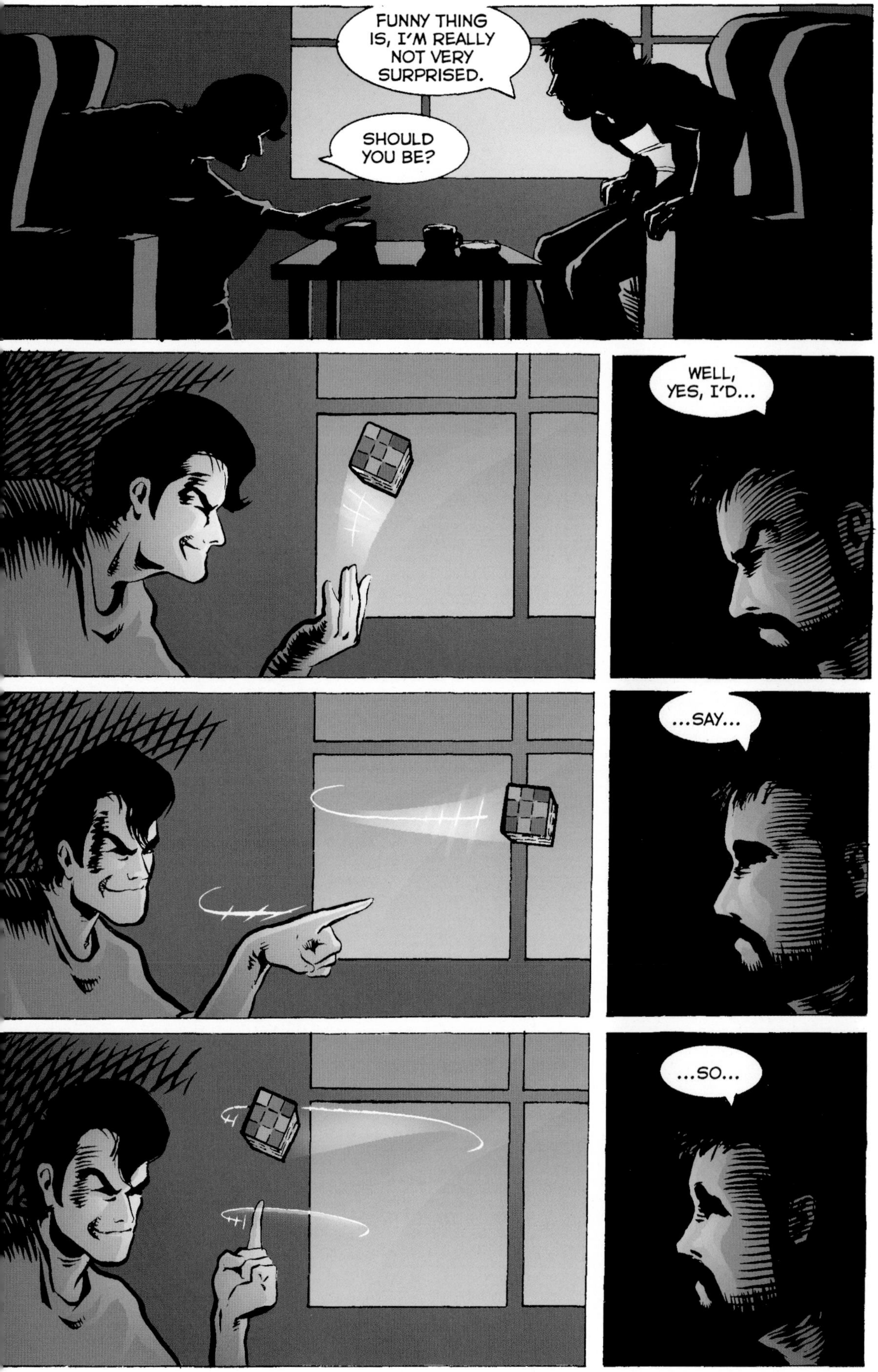
FUNNY THING IS, I'M REALLY NOT VERY SURPRISED.
SHOULD YOU BE?
WELL, YES, I'D...
...SAY...
...SO...

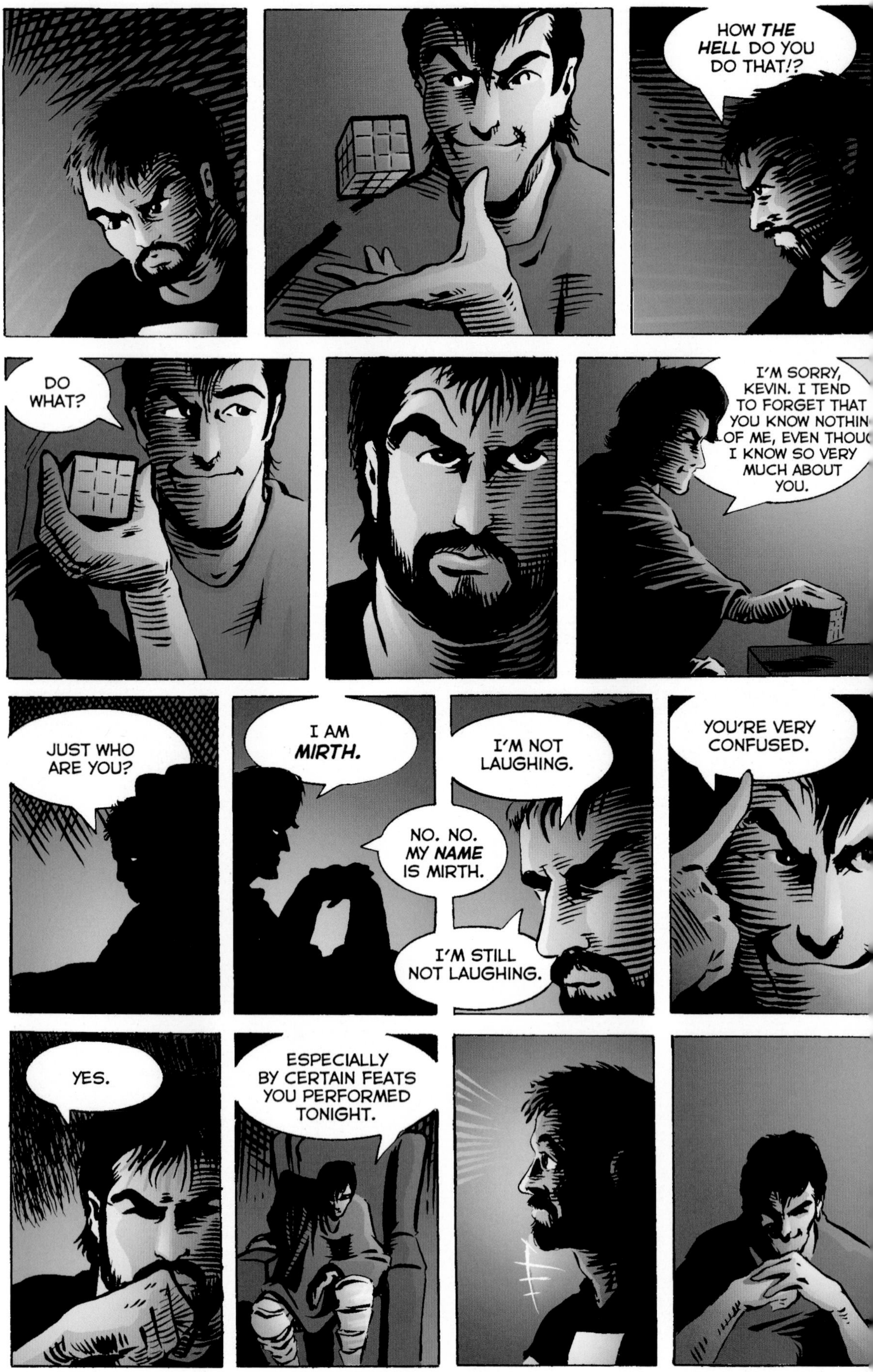
HOW *THE HELL* DO YOU DO THAT!?
DO WHAT?
I'M SORRY, KEVIN. I TEND TO FORGET THAT YOU KNOW NOTHIN OF ME, EVEN THOU I KNOW SO VERY MUCH ABOUT YOU.
JUST WHO ARE YOU?
I AM *MIRTH.*
I'M NOT LAUGHING.
NO. NO. *MY NAME* IS MIRTH.
I'M STILL NOT LAUGHING.
YOU'RE VERY CONFUSED.
YES.
ESPECIALLY BY CERTAIN FEATS YOU PERFORMED TONIGHT.

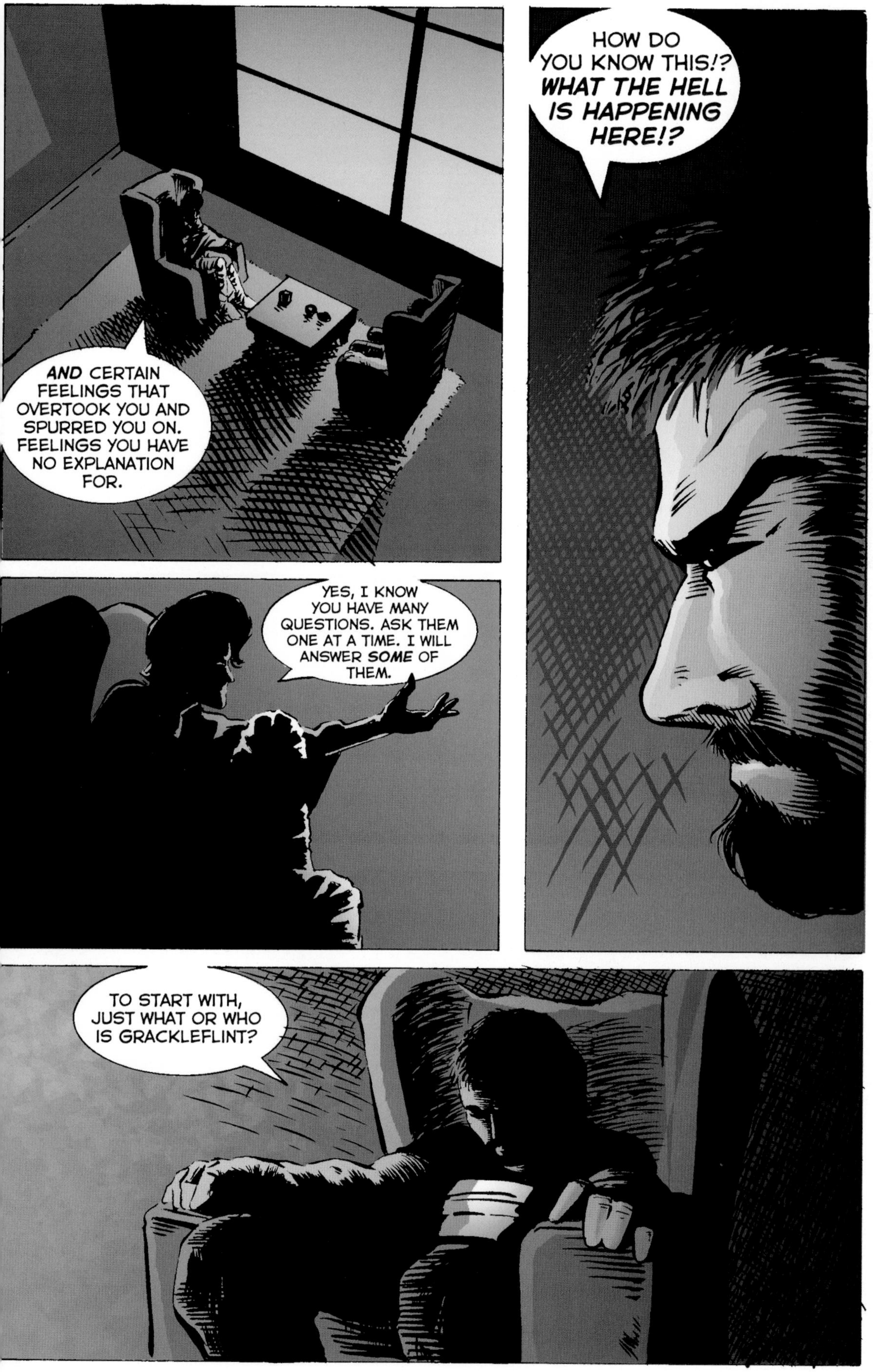
AND CERTAIN FEELINGS THAT OVERTOOK YOU AND SPURRED YOU ON. FEELINGS YOU HAVE NO EXPLANATION FOR.
HOW DO YOU KNOW THIS!? WHAT THE HELL IS HAPPENING HERE!?
YES, I KNOW YOU HAVE MANY QUESTIONS. ASK THEM ONE AT A TIME. I WILL ANSWER SOME OF THEM.
TO START WITH, JUST WHAT OR WHO IS GRACKLEFLINT?

WELL, YOU SEE, MY FRIEND, A *GRACKLEFLINT* IS A WHAT *AND* A WHO.

OH BOY.

YOU FOUGHT ONE NOT TWO HOURS AGO.

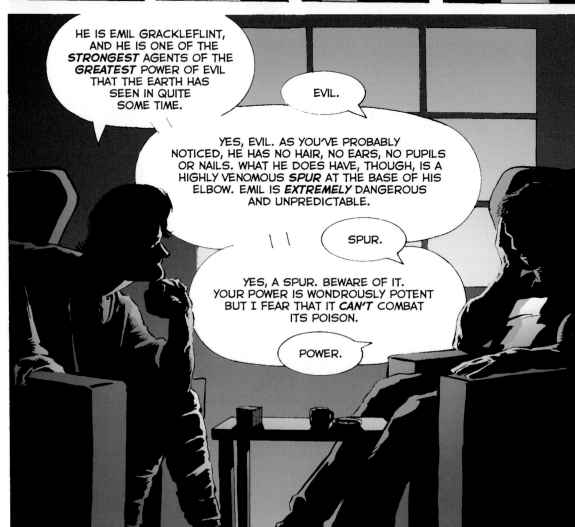

HE IS EMIL GRACKLEFLINT, AND HE IS ONE OF THE *STRONGEST* AGENTS OF THE *GREATEST* POWER OF EVIL THAT THE EARTH HAS SEEN IN QUITE SOME TIME.

EVIL.

YES, EVIL. AS YOU'VE PROBABLY NOTICED, HE HAS NO HAIR, NO EARS, NO PUPILS OR NAILS. WHAT HE DOES HAVE, THOUGH, IS A HIGHLY VENOMOUS *SPUR* AT THE BASE OF HIS ELBOW. EMIL IS *EXTREMELY* DANGEROUS AND UNPREDICTABLE.

SPUR.

YES, A SPUR. BEWARE OF IT. YOUR POWER IS WONDROUSLY POTENT BUT I FEAR THAT IT *CAN'T* COMBAT ITS POISON.

POWER.

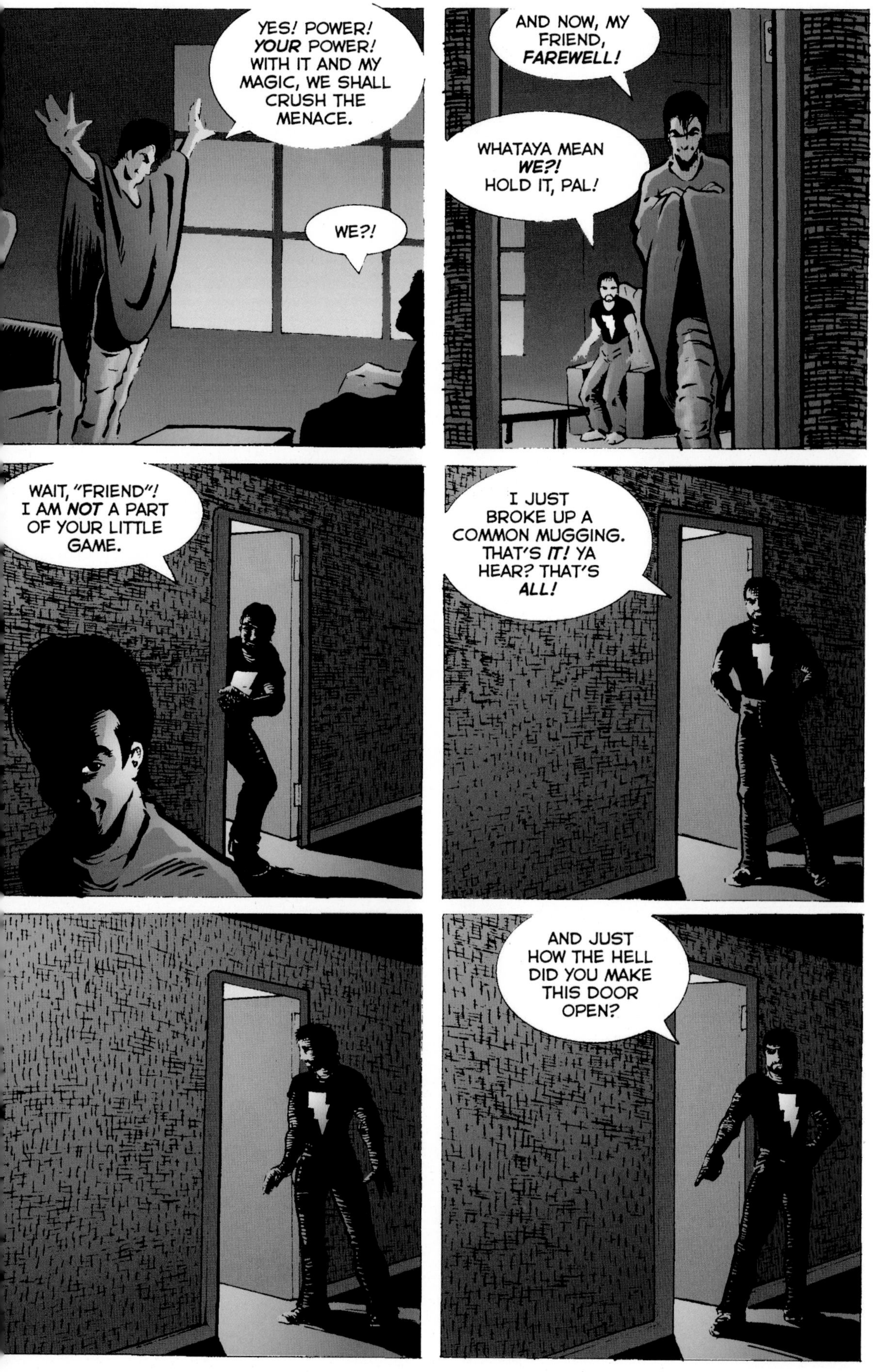
YES! POWER! YOUR POWER! WITH IT AND MY MAGIC, WE SHALL CRUSH THE MENACE.
WE?!
AND NOW, MY FRIEND, FAREWELL!
WHATAYA MEAN WE?! HOLD IT, PAL!
WAIT, "FRIEND"! I AM NOT A PART OF YOUR LITTLE GAME.
I JUST BROKE UP A COMMON MUGGING. THAT'S IT! YA HEAR? THAT'S ALL!
AND JUST HOW THE HELL DID YOU MAKE THIS DOOR OPEN?

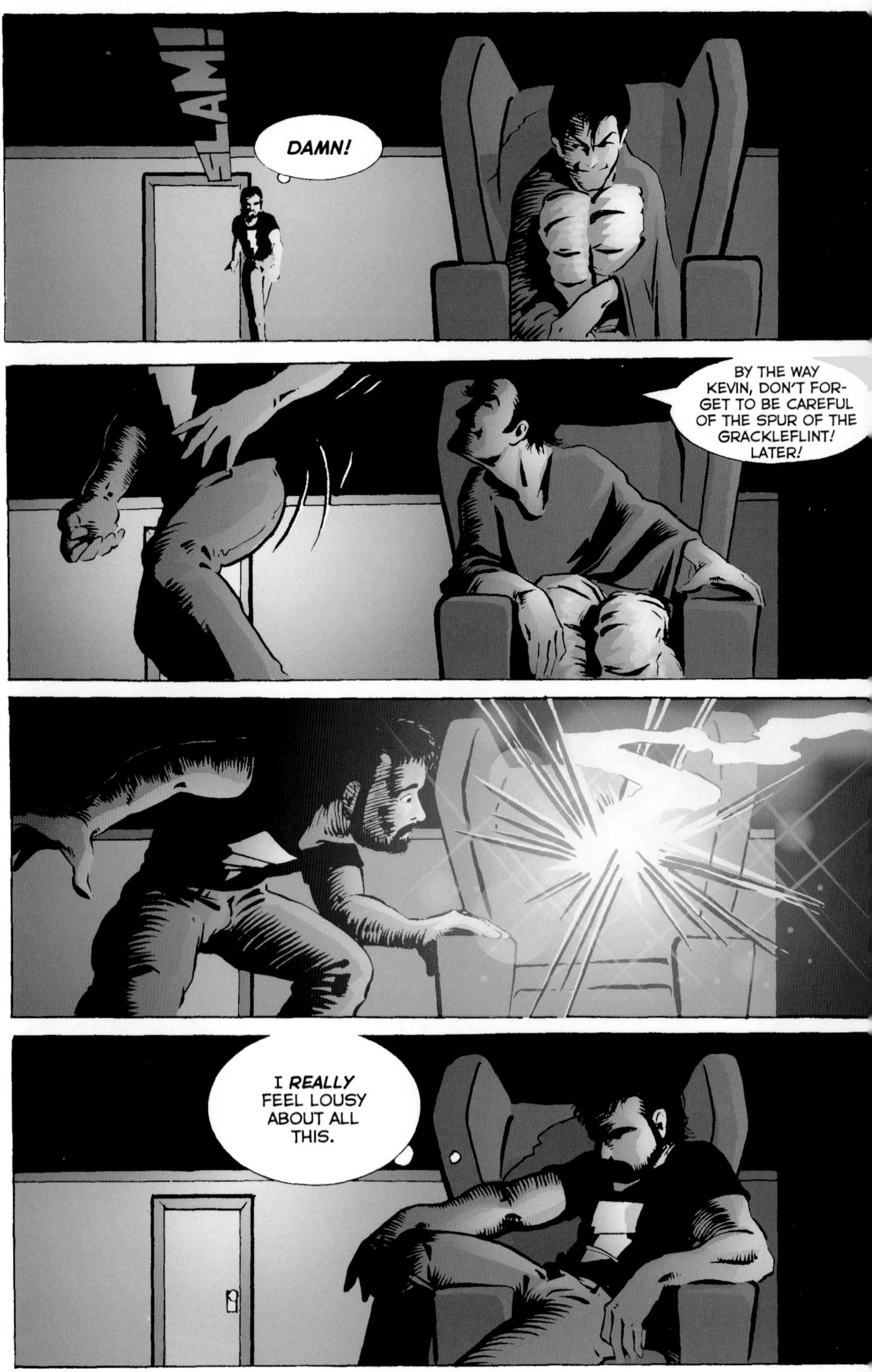
SLAM!
DAMN!
BY THE WAY KEVIN, DON'T FOR-GET TO BE CAREFUL OF THE SPUR OF THE GRACKLEFLINT! LATER!
I REALLY FEEL LOUSY ABOUT ALL THIS.

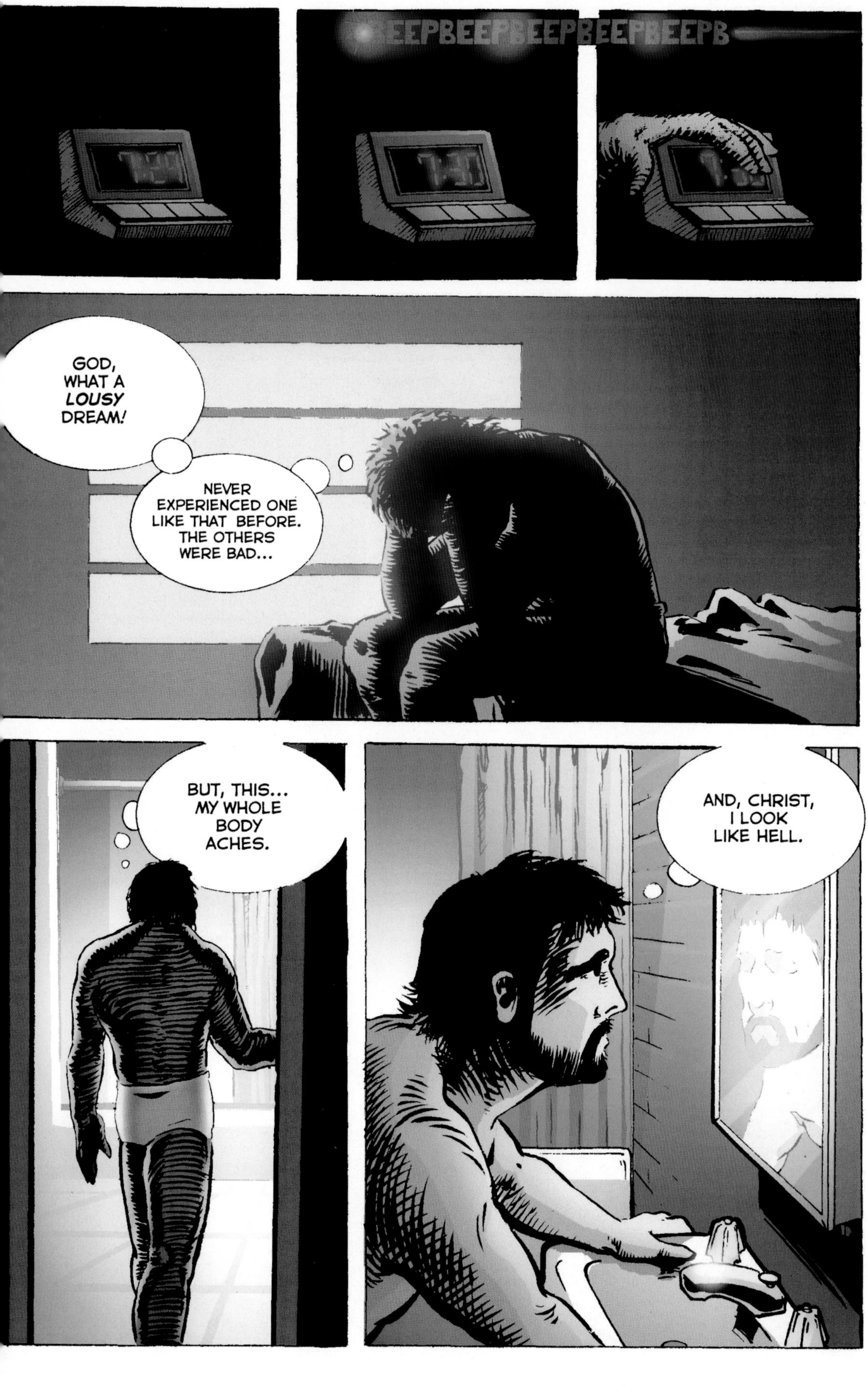
BEEPBEEPBEEPBEEPBEEPB
GOD, WHAT A *LOUSY* DREAM!
NEVER EXPERIENCED ONE LIKE THAT BEFORE. THE OTHERS WERE BAD...
BUT, THIS... MY WHOLE BODY ACHES.
AND, CHRIST, I LOOK LIKE HELL.

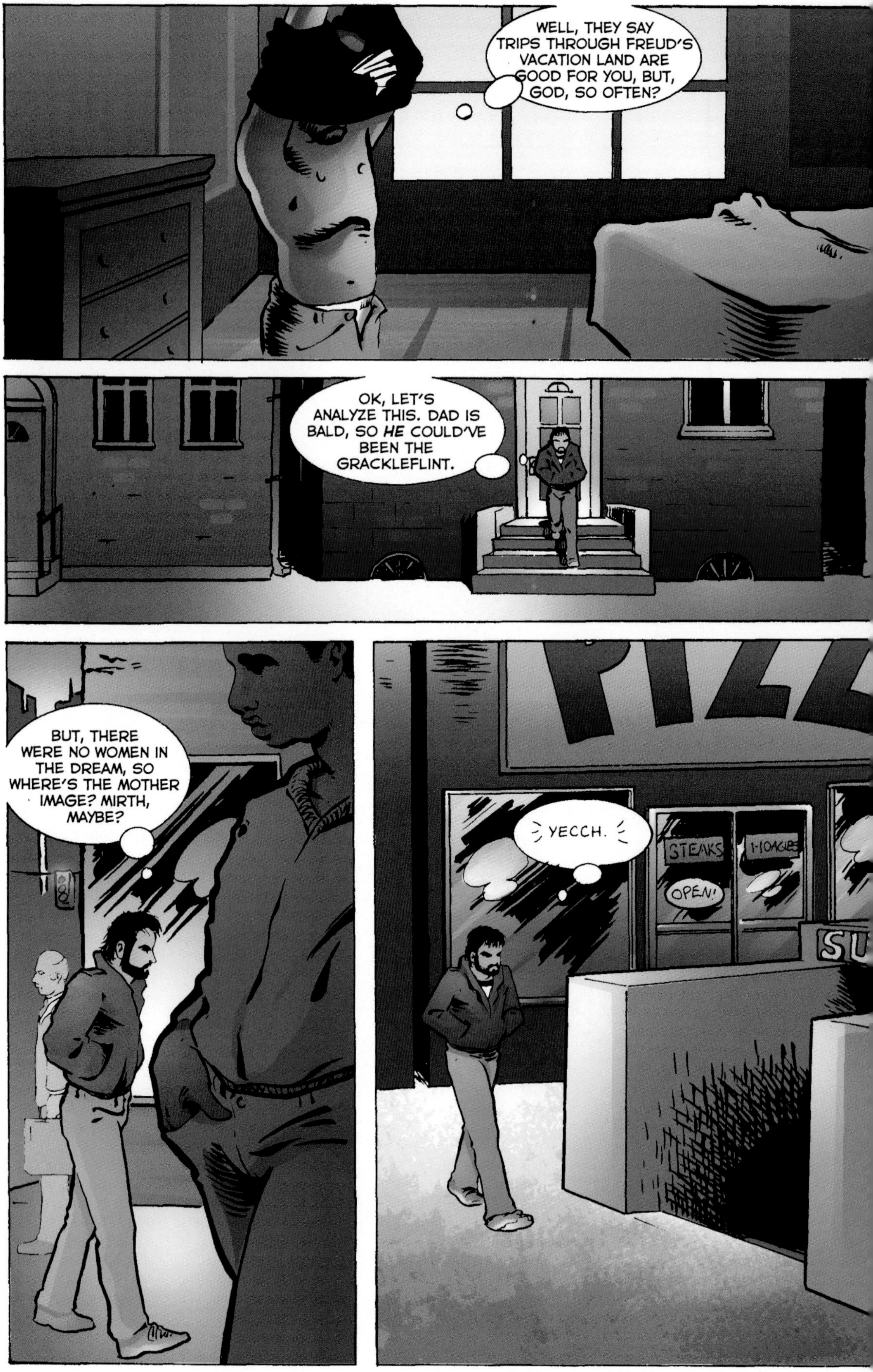
WELL, THEY SAY TRIPS THROUGH FREUD'S VACATION LAND ARE GOOD FOR YOU, BUT, GOD, SO OFTEN?
OK, LET'S ANALYZE THIS. DAD IS BALD, SO *HE* COULD'VE BEEN THE GRACKLEFLINT.
BUT, THERE WERE NO WOMEN IN THE DREAM, SO WHERE'S THE MOTHER IMAGE? MIRTH, MAYBE?
YECCH.
STEAKS
OPEN!

JEEZ, THAT'S ALL I NEED. DREAMING UP SUPPORT AND GUIDANCE FROM SOME RAGGED-OUT STREET MONKEY.

YOU'RE A SICK PUP, *MATCHSTICK.*

WOW, THIS IS WEIRD. NEVER SEEN THE SUBWAY SO DESERTED BEFORE. KINDA CREEPY.

SKREECH

THANKS, GET ME OUTTA HERE.

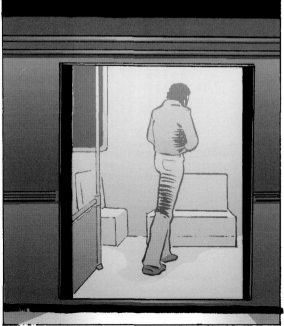

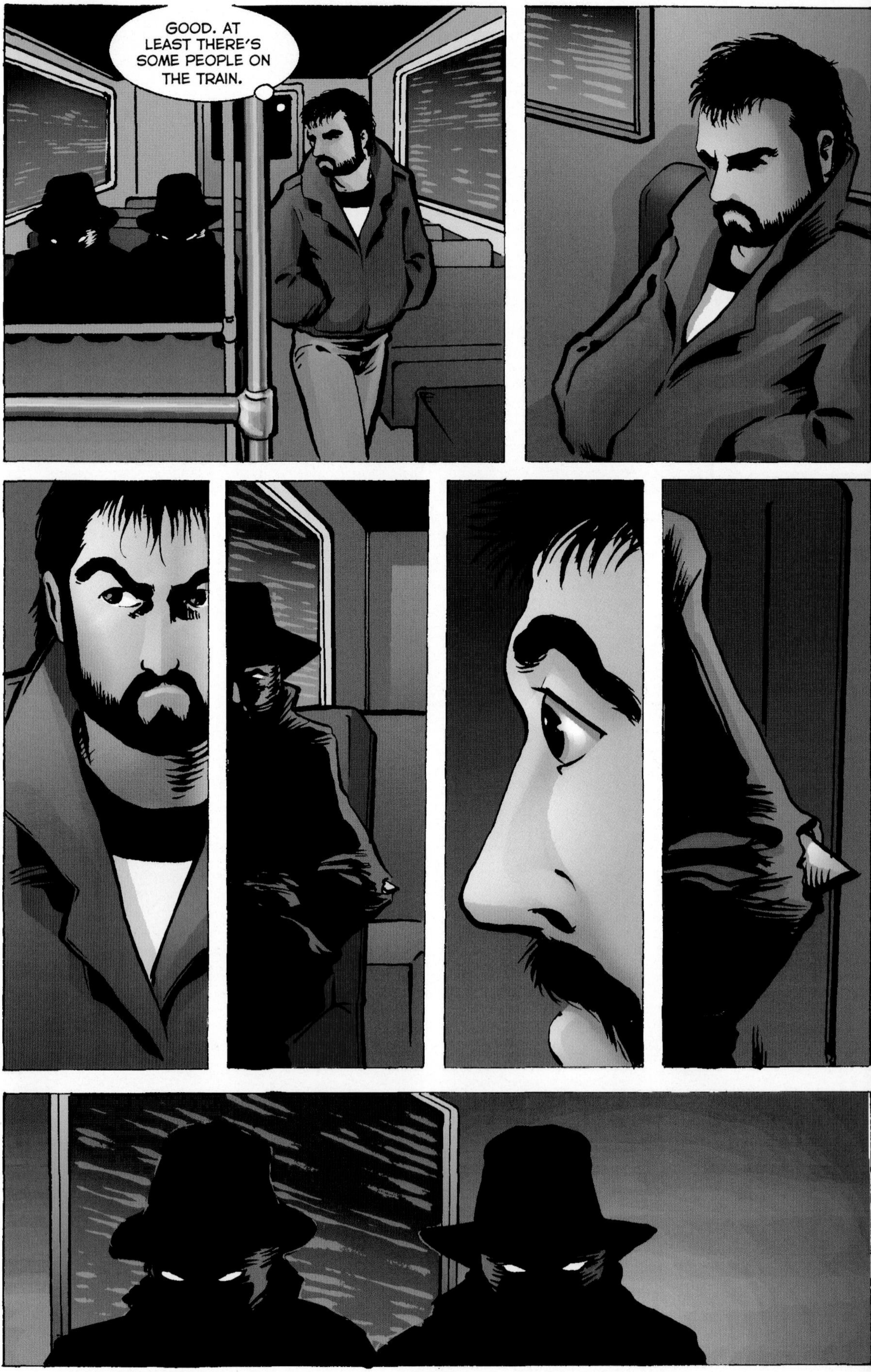
GOOD. AT LEAST THERE'S SOME PEOPLE ON THE TRAIN.

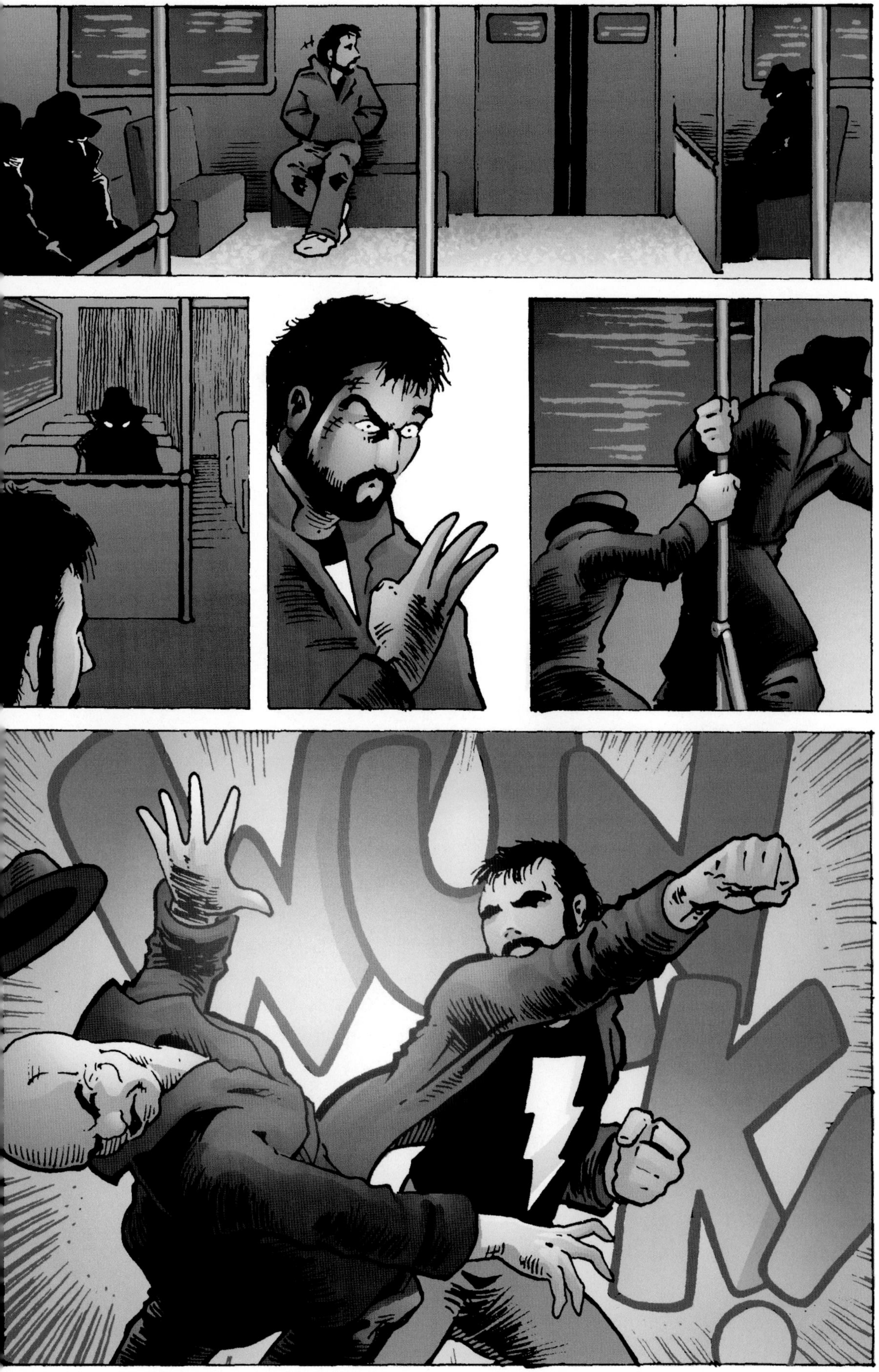

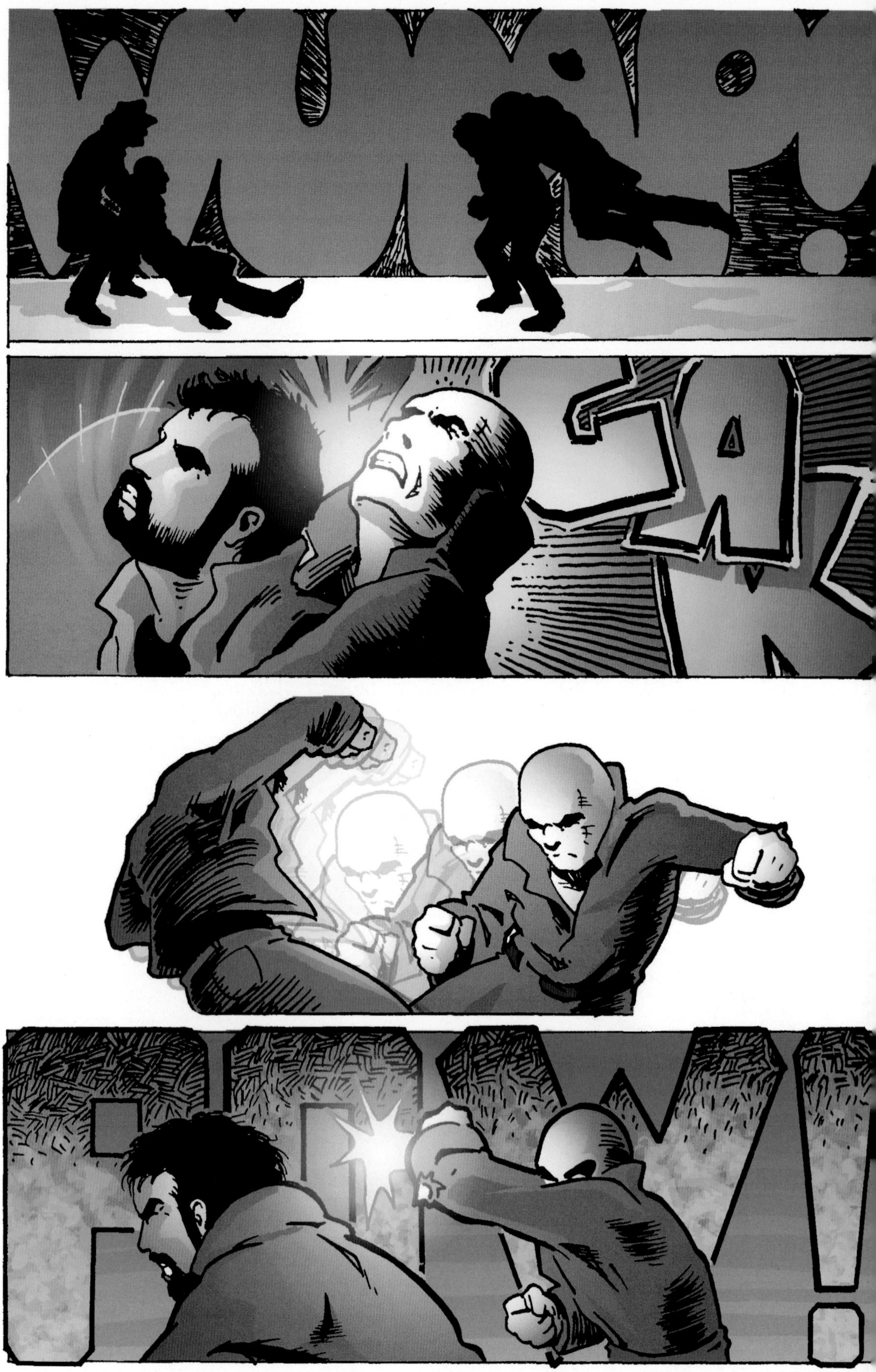
POW!

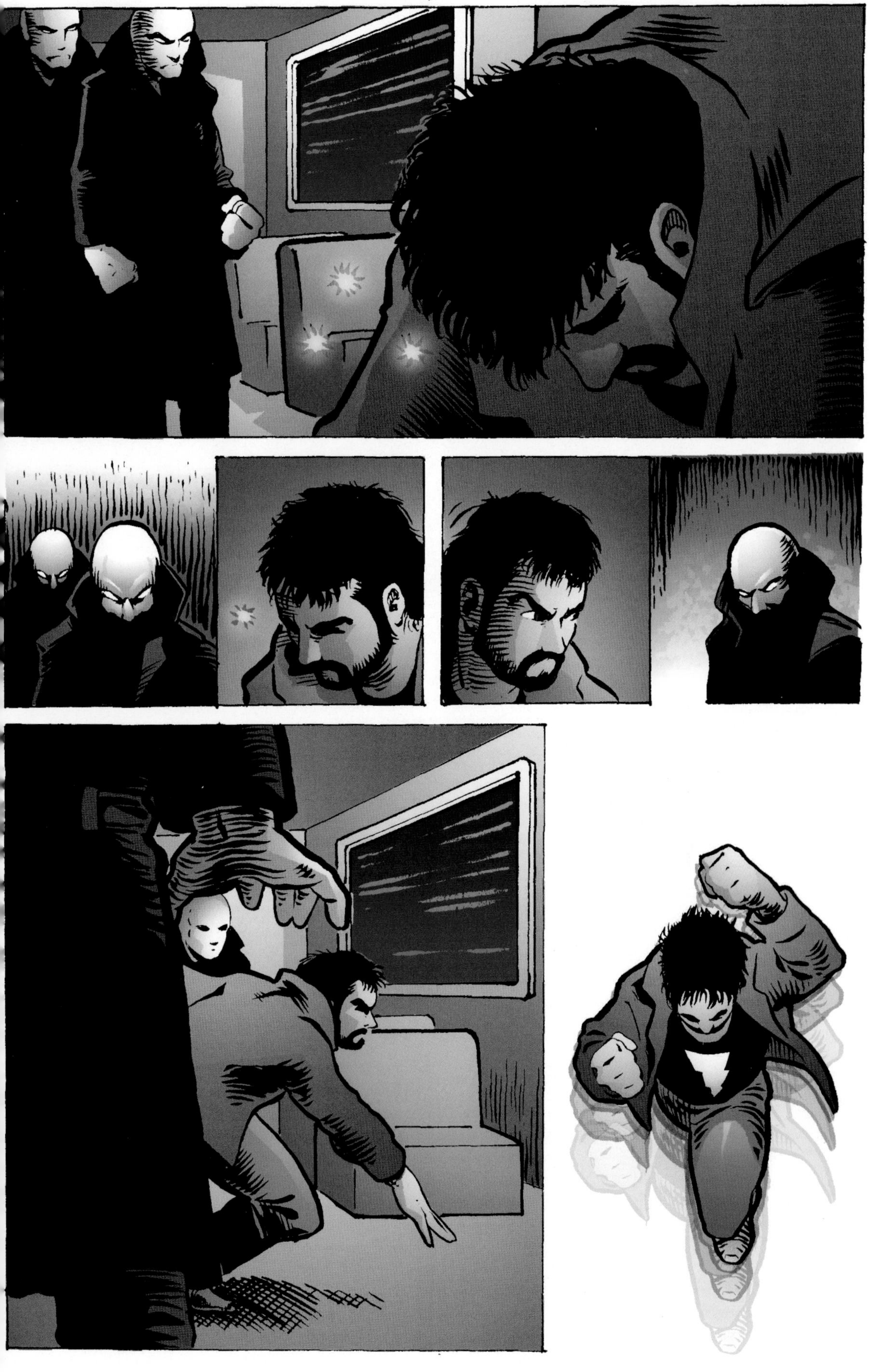

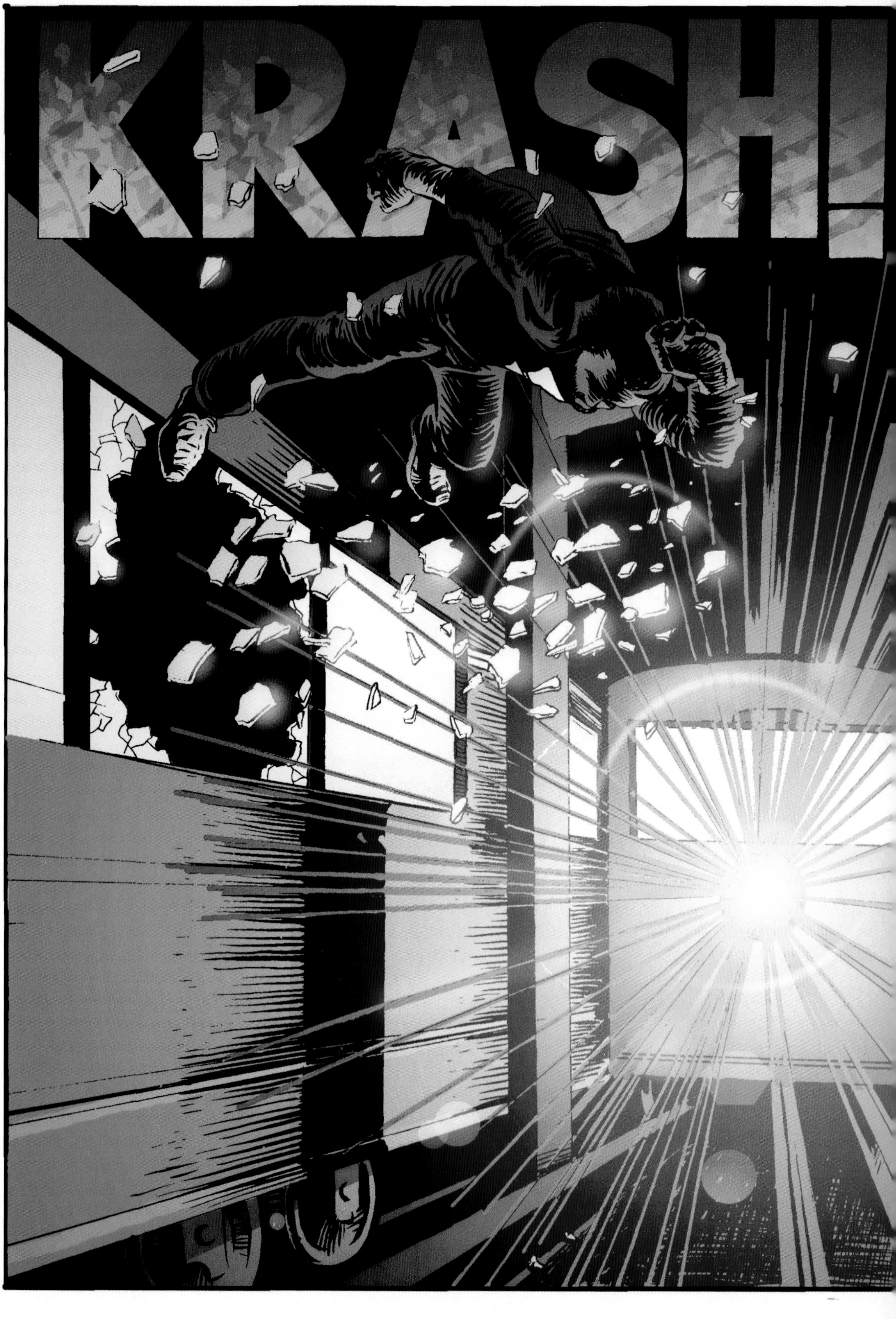
KRASH!

THE HERO DISCOVERED

MAGE

Chapter 02

Too Too Solid Flesh

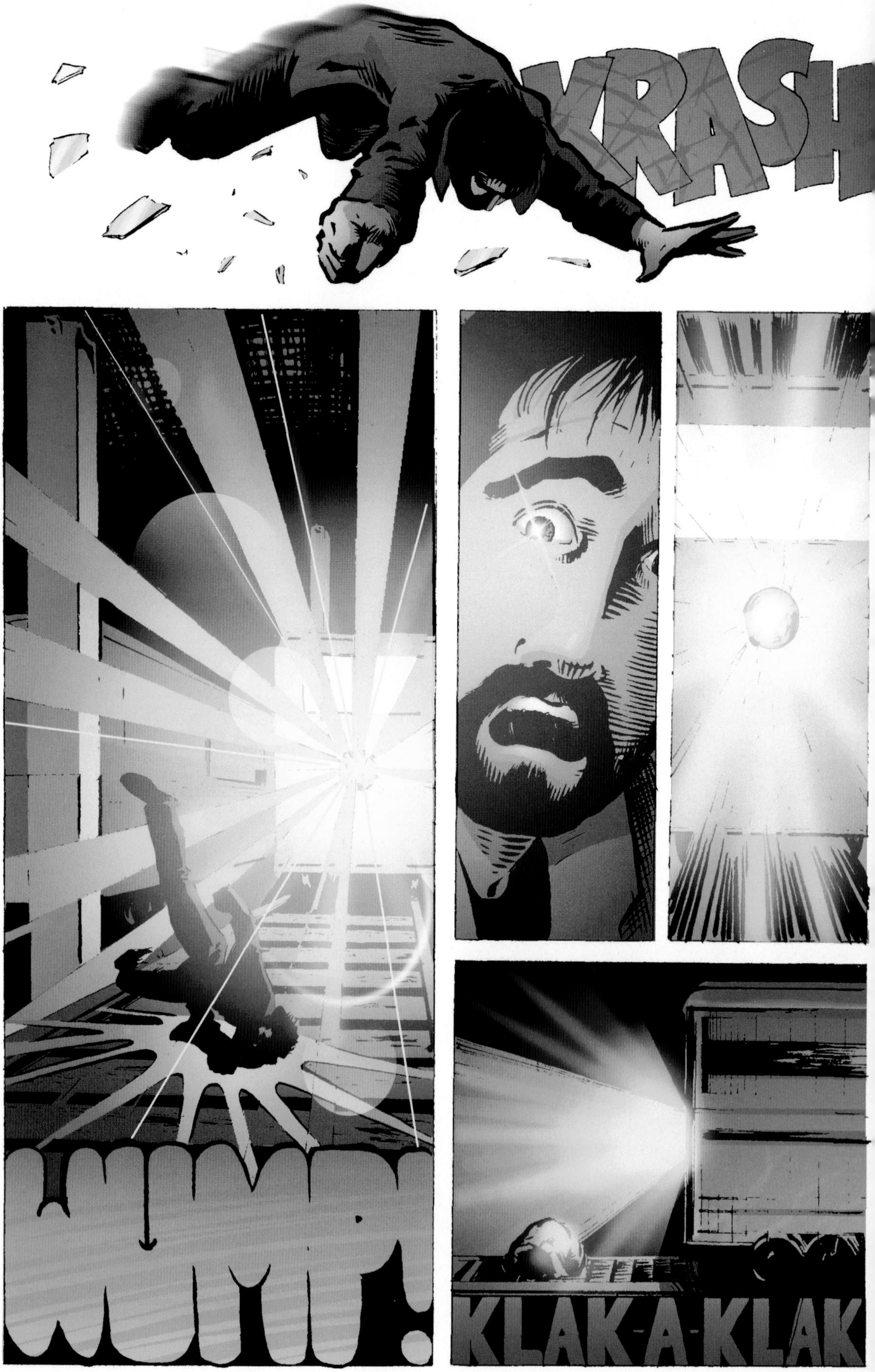
KRASH
WUMP!
KLAK-A-KLAK

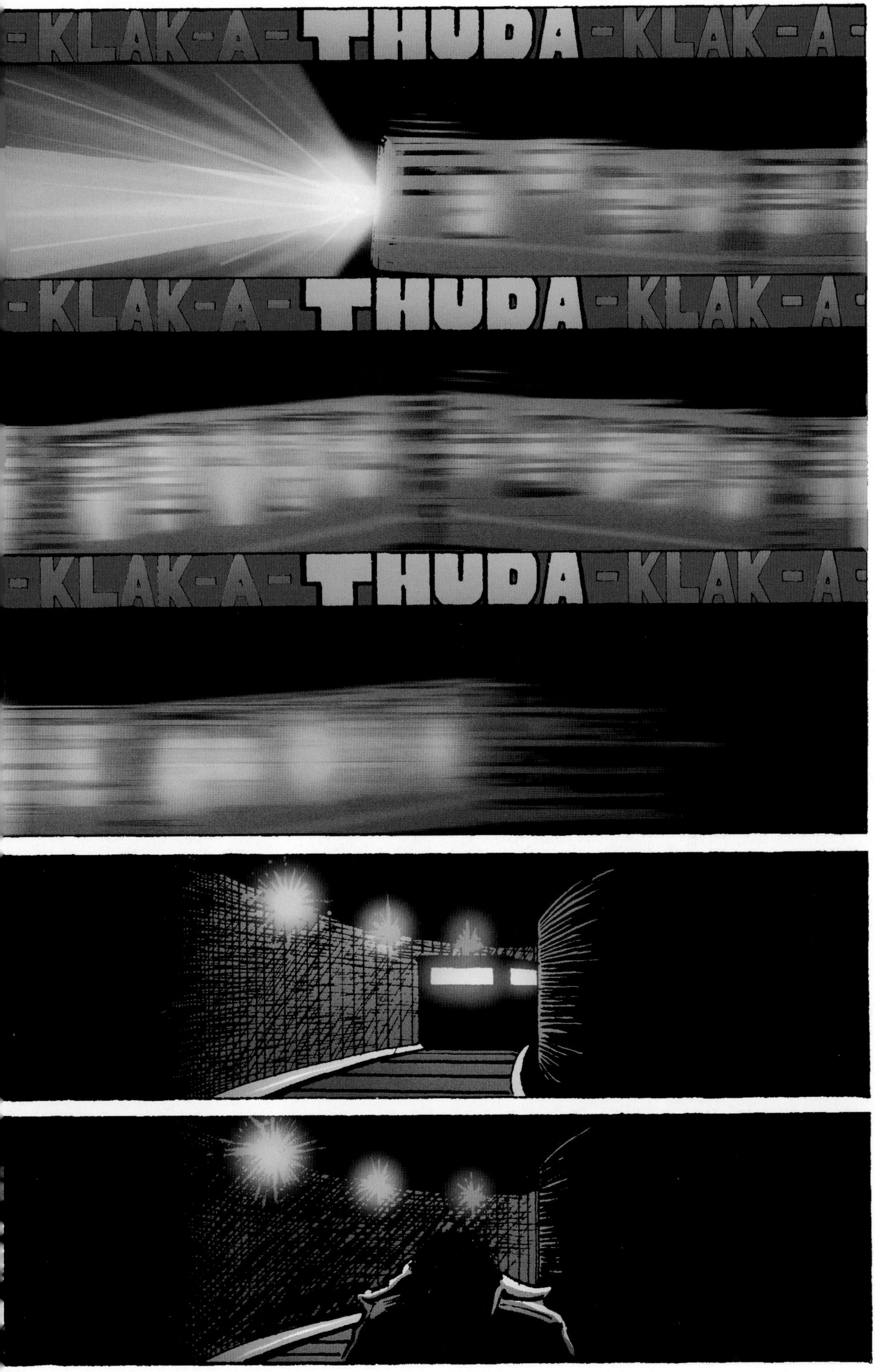

-KLAK-A-THUDA-KLAK-A-
-KLAK-A-THUDA-KLAK-A-
-KLAK-A-THUDA-KLAK-A-

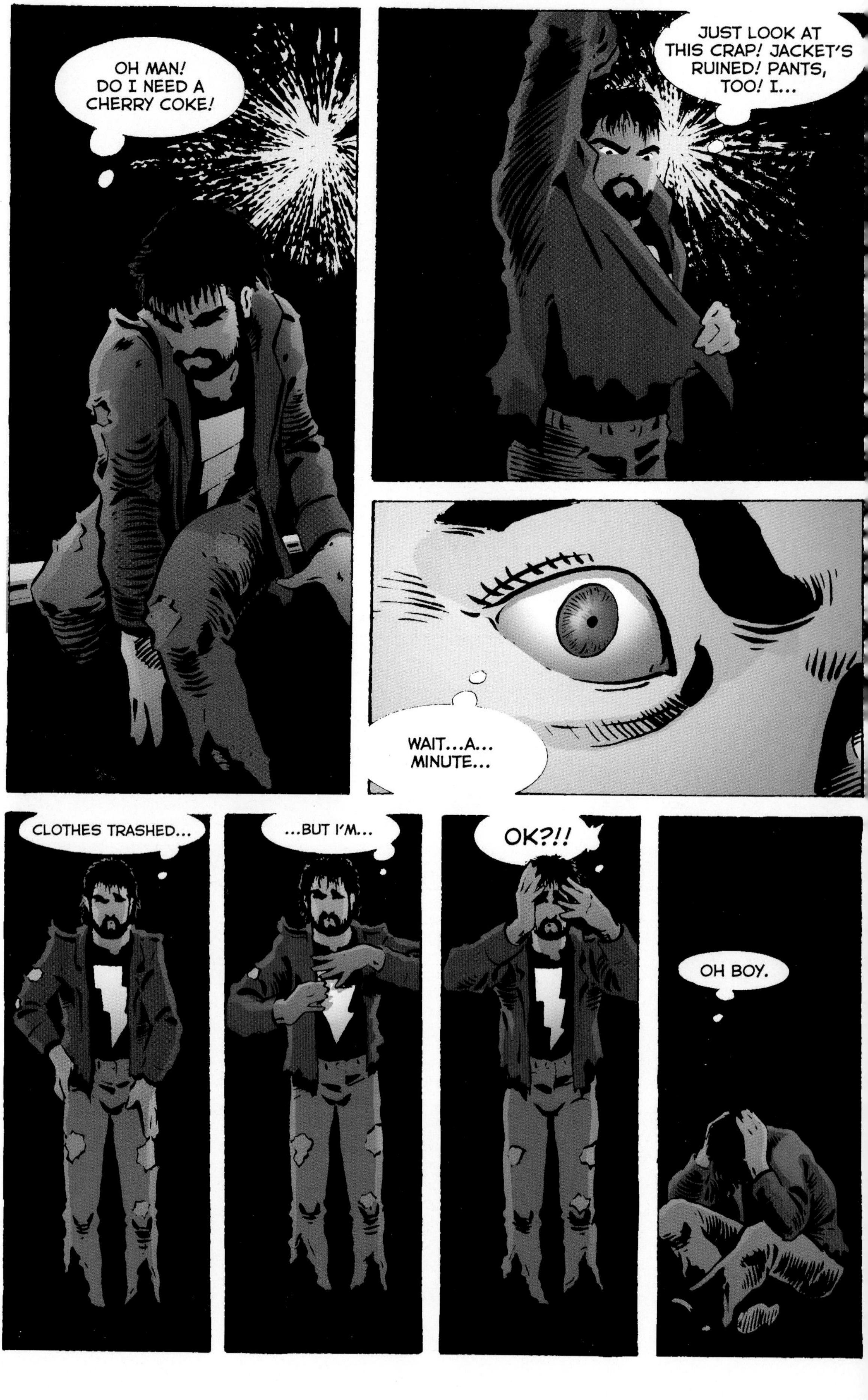
OH MAN! DO I NEED A CHERRY COKE!
JUST LOOK AT THIS CRAP! JACKET'S RUINED! PANTS, TOO! I...
WAIT...A... MINUTE...
CLOTHES TRASHED...
...BUT I'M...
OK?!!
OH BOY.

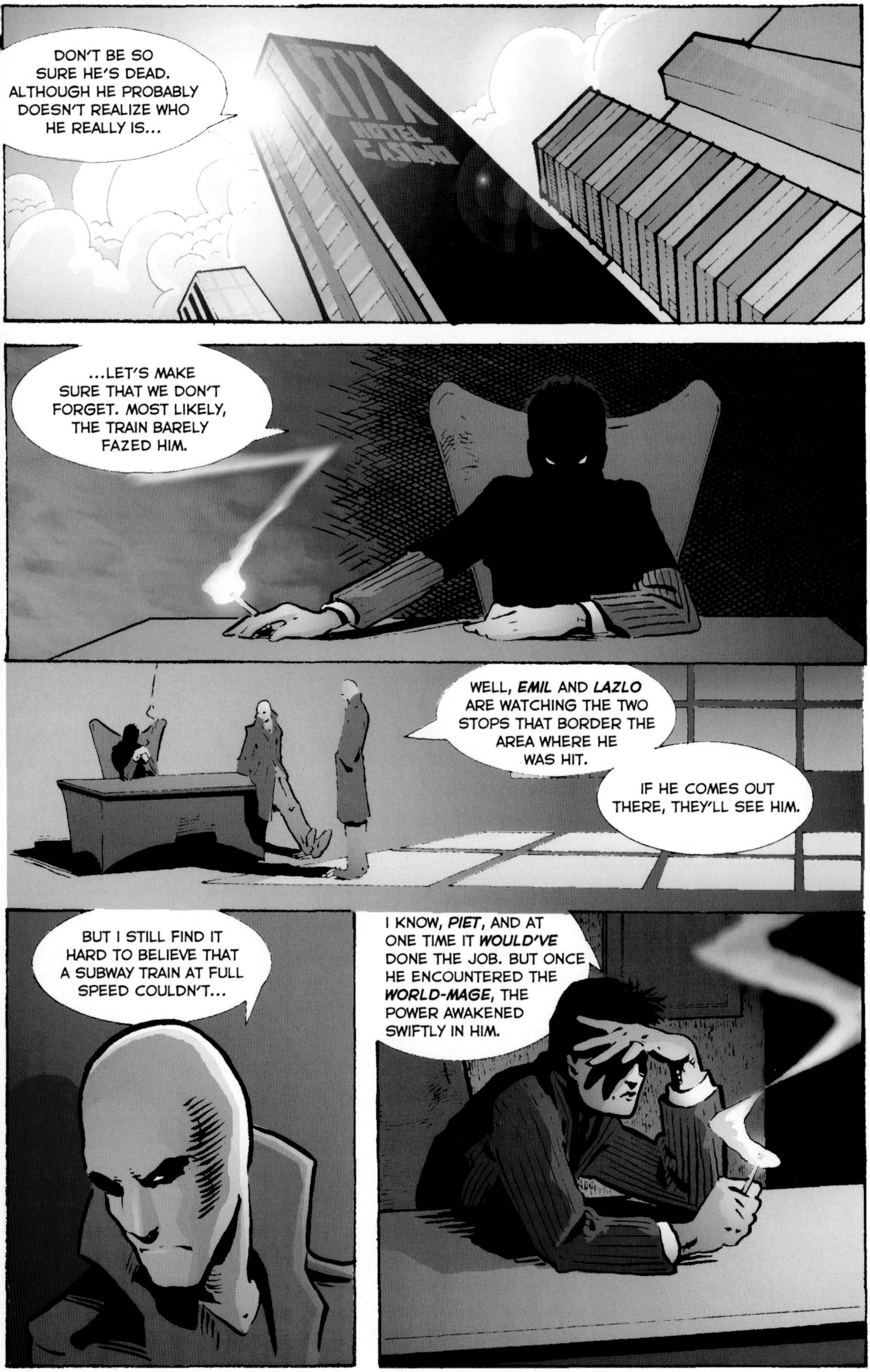
DON'T BE SO SURE HE'S DEAD. ALTHOUGH HE PROBABLY DOESN'T REALIZE WHO HE REALLY IS...
...LET'S MAKE SURE THAT WE DON'T FORGET. MOST LIKELY, THE TRAIN BARELY FAZED HIM.
WELL, *EMIL* AND *LAZLO* ARE WATCHING THE TWO STOPS THAT BORDER THE AREA WHERE HE WAS HIT.
IF HE COMES OUT THERE, THEY'LL SEE HIM.
BUT I STILL FIND IT HARD TO BELIEVE THAT A SUBWAY TRAIN AT FULL SPEED COULDN'T...
I KNOW, *PIET*, AND AT ONE TIME IT *WOULD'VE* DONE THE JOB. BUT ONCE HE ENCOUNTERED THE *WORLD-MAGE*, THE POWER AWAKENED SWIFTLY IN HIM.

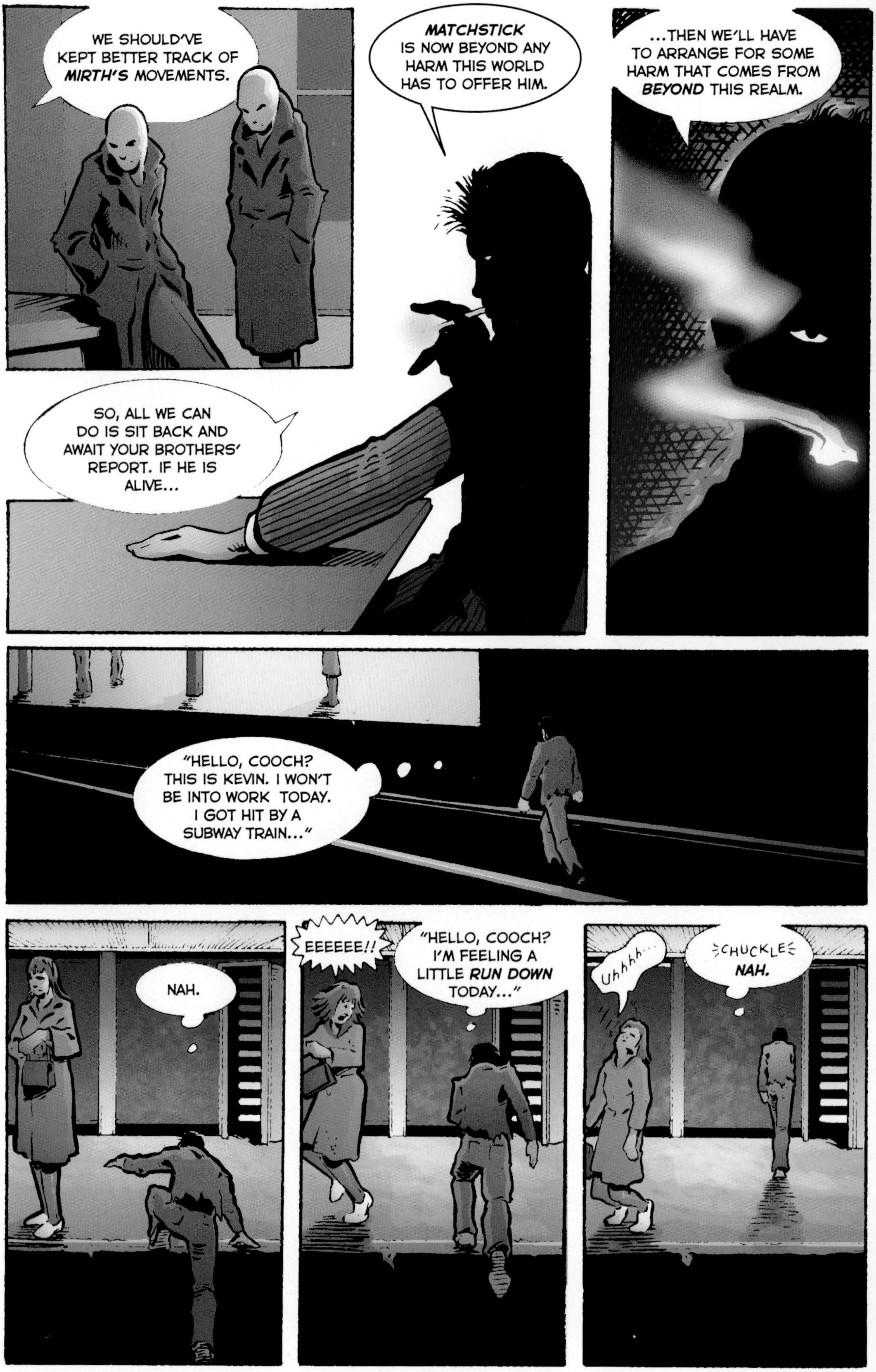
WE SHOULD'VE KEPT BETTER TRACK OF MIRTH'S MOVEMENTS.
MATCHSTICK IS NOW BEYOND ANY HARM THIS WORLD HAS TO OFFER HIM.
...THEN WE'LL HAVE TO ARRANGE FOR SOME HARM THAT COMES FROM BEYOND THIS REALM.
SO, ALL WE CAN DO IS SIT BACK AND AWAIT YOUR BROTHERS' REPORT. IF HE IS ALIVE...
"HELLO, COOCH? THIS IS KEVIN. I WON'T BE INTO WORK TODAY. I GOT HIT BY A SUBWAY TRAIN..."
NAH.
EEEEEE!!
"HELLO, COOCH? I'M FEELING A LITTLE RUN DOWN TODAY..."
Uhhhh...
CHUCKLE
NAH.

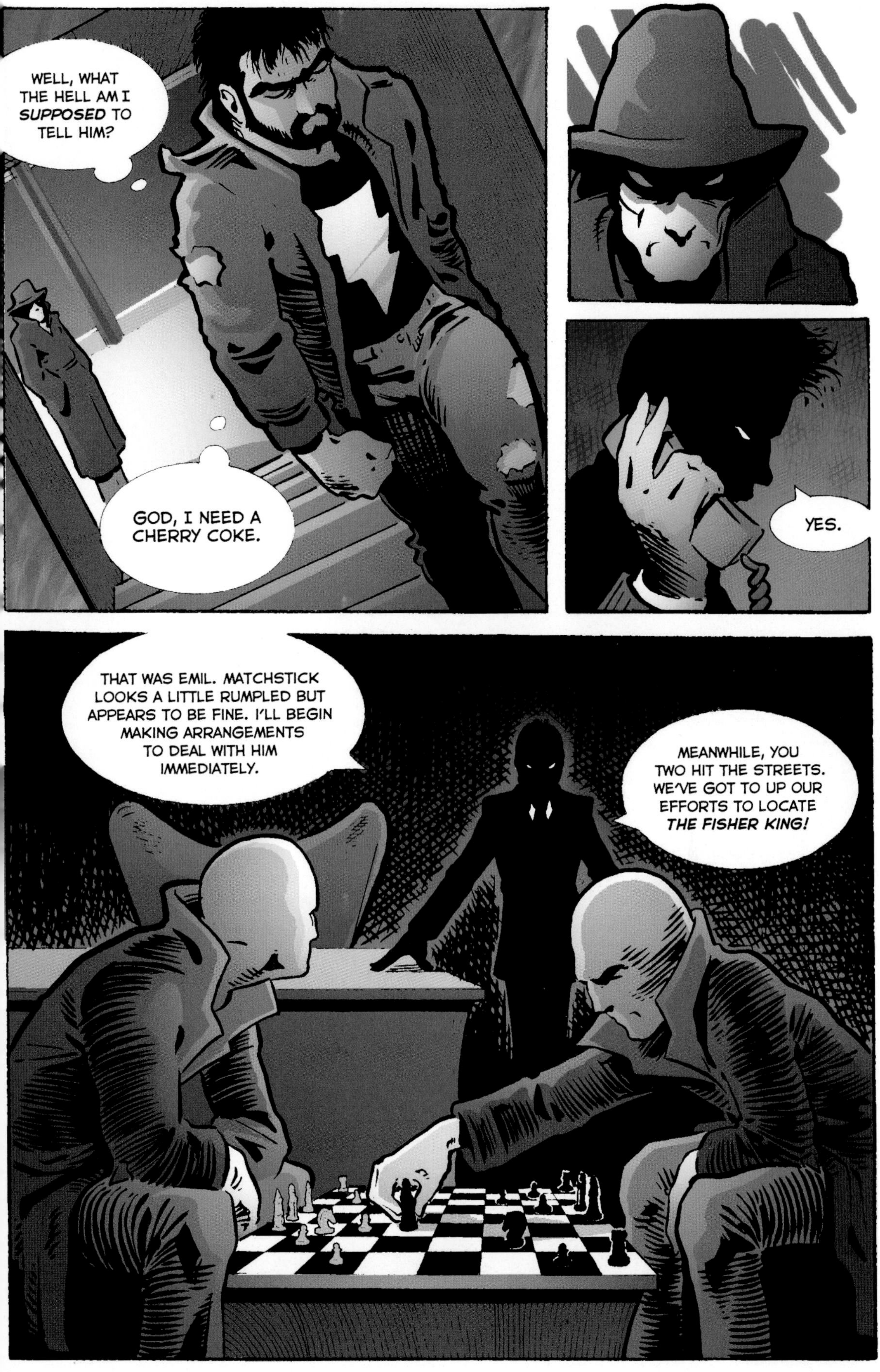
WELL, WHAT THE HELL AM I *SUPPOSED* TO TELL HIM?
GOD, I NEED A CHERRY COKE.
YES.
THAT WAS EMIL. MATCHSTICK LOOKS A LITTLE RUMPLED BUT APPEARS TO BE FINE. I'LL BEGIN MAKING ARRANGEMENTS TO DEAL WITH HIM IMMEDIATELY.
MEANWHILE, YOU TWO HIT THE STREETS. WE'VE GOT TO UP OUR EFFORTS TO LOCATE ***THE FISHER KING!***

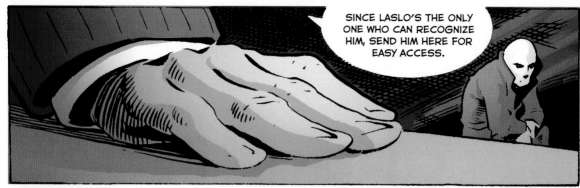

SINCE LASLO'S THE ONLY ONE WHO CAN RECOGNIZE HIM, SEND HIM HERE FOR EASY ACCESS.

TELL OUR STREET AGENTS TO BE *EXTRA* ALERT AND REPORT *ANY* NEW CHARACTERS IN THEIR AREAS.

WE'LL PAY *DOUBLE* FOR THEIR EFFORTS.

HIS SHAPE-CHANGING ABILITY MAKES IT DIFFICULT FOR US.

BUT NO MATTER WHAT FORM HE TAKES...

...*THE KING* WILL ALWAYS...

...BE *LAME*.

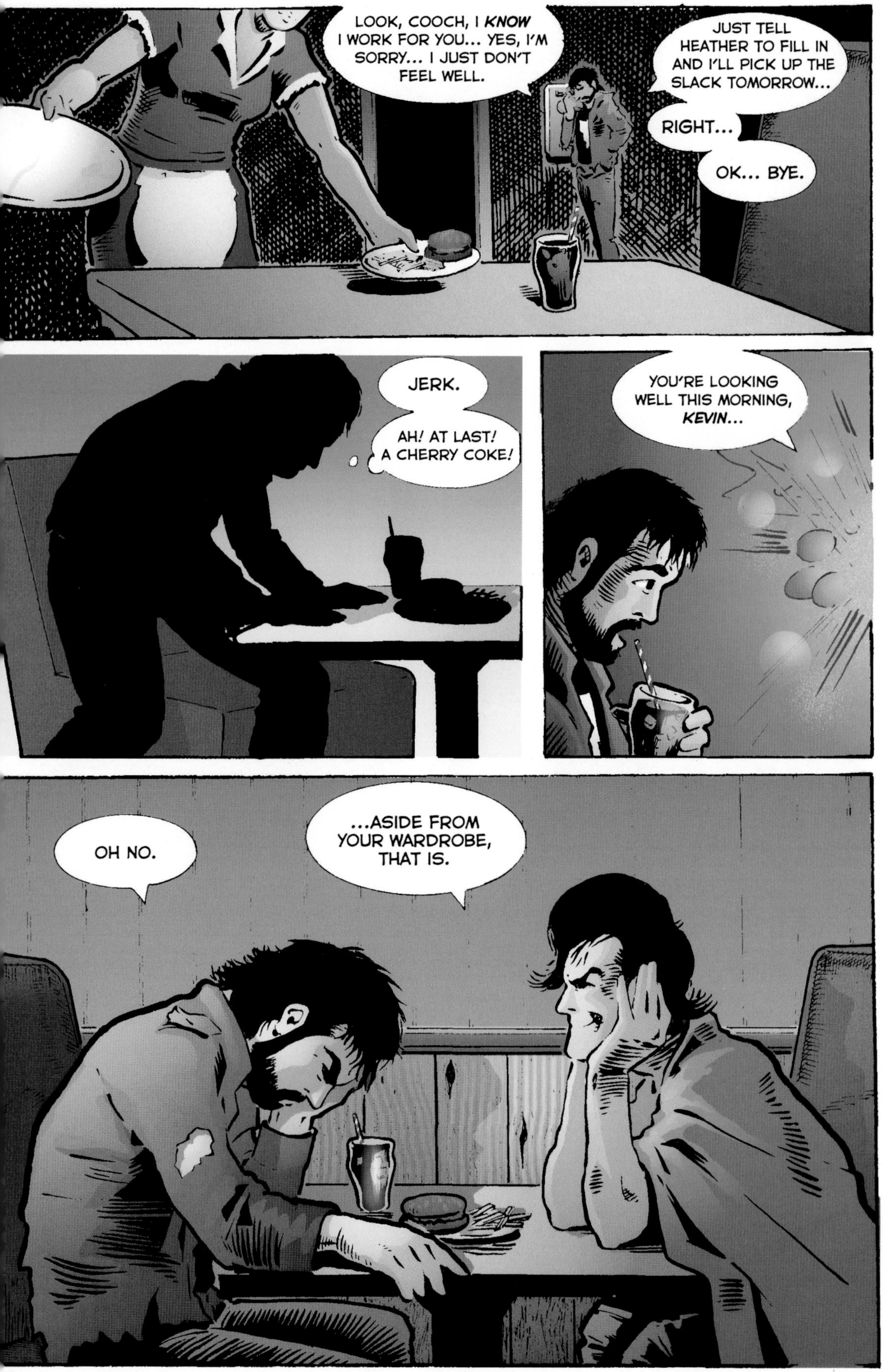
LOOK, COOCH, I KNOW I WORK FOR YOU... YES, I'M SORRY... I JUST DON'T FEEL WELL.
JUST TELL HEATHER TO FILL IN AND I'LL PICK UP THE SLACK TOMORROW...
RIGHT...
OK... BYE.
JERK.
AH! AT LAST! A CHERRY COKE!
YOU'RE LOOKING WELL THIS MORNING, KEVIN...
OH NO.
...ASIDE FROM YOUR WARDROBE, THAT IS.

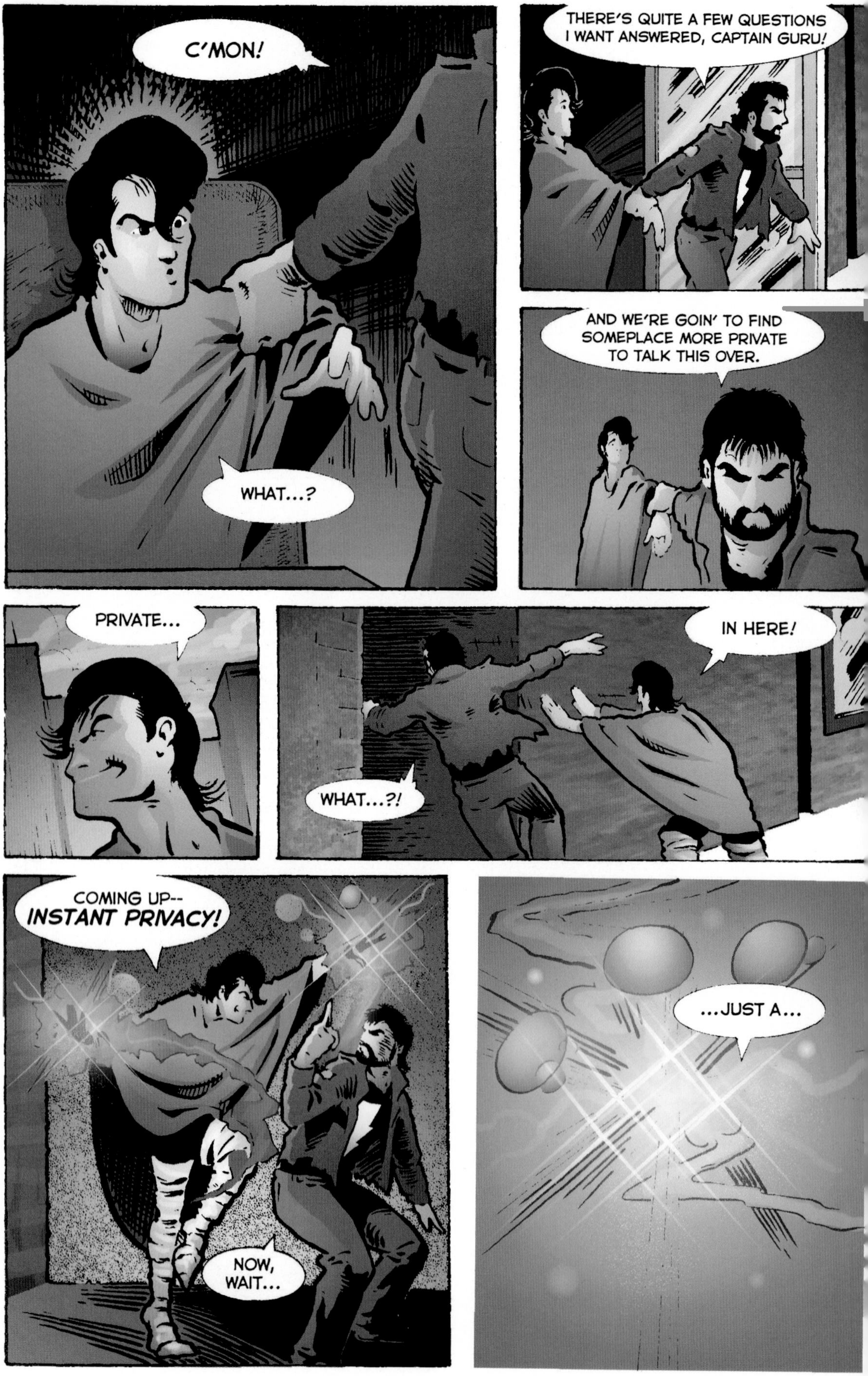
C'MON!
WHAT...?
THERE'S QUITE A FEW QUESTIONS I WANT ANSWERED, CAPTAIN GURU!
AND WE'RE GOIN' TO FIND SOMEPLACE MORE PRIVATE TO TALK THIS OVER.
PRIVATE...
IN HERE!
WHAT...?!
COMING UP-- INSTANT PRIVACY!
NOW, WAIT...
...JUST A...

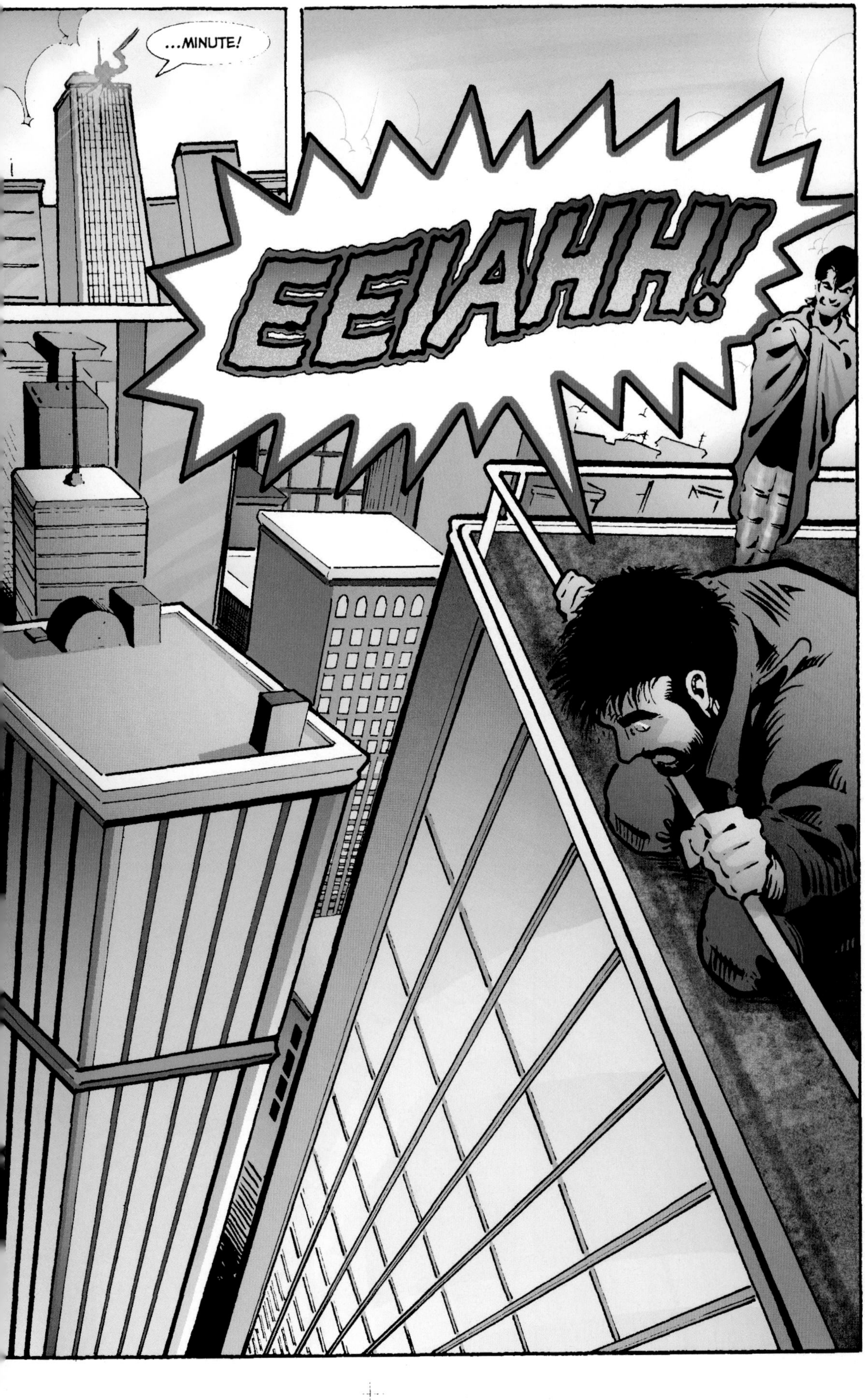
...MINUTE!
EEIAHH!

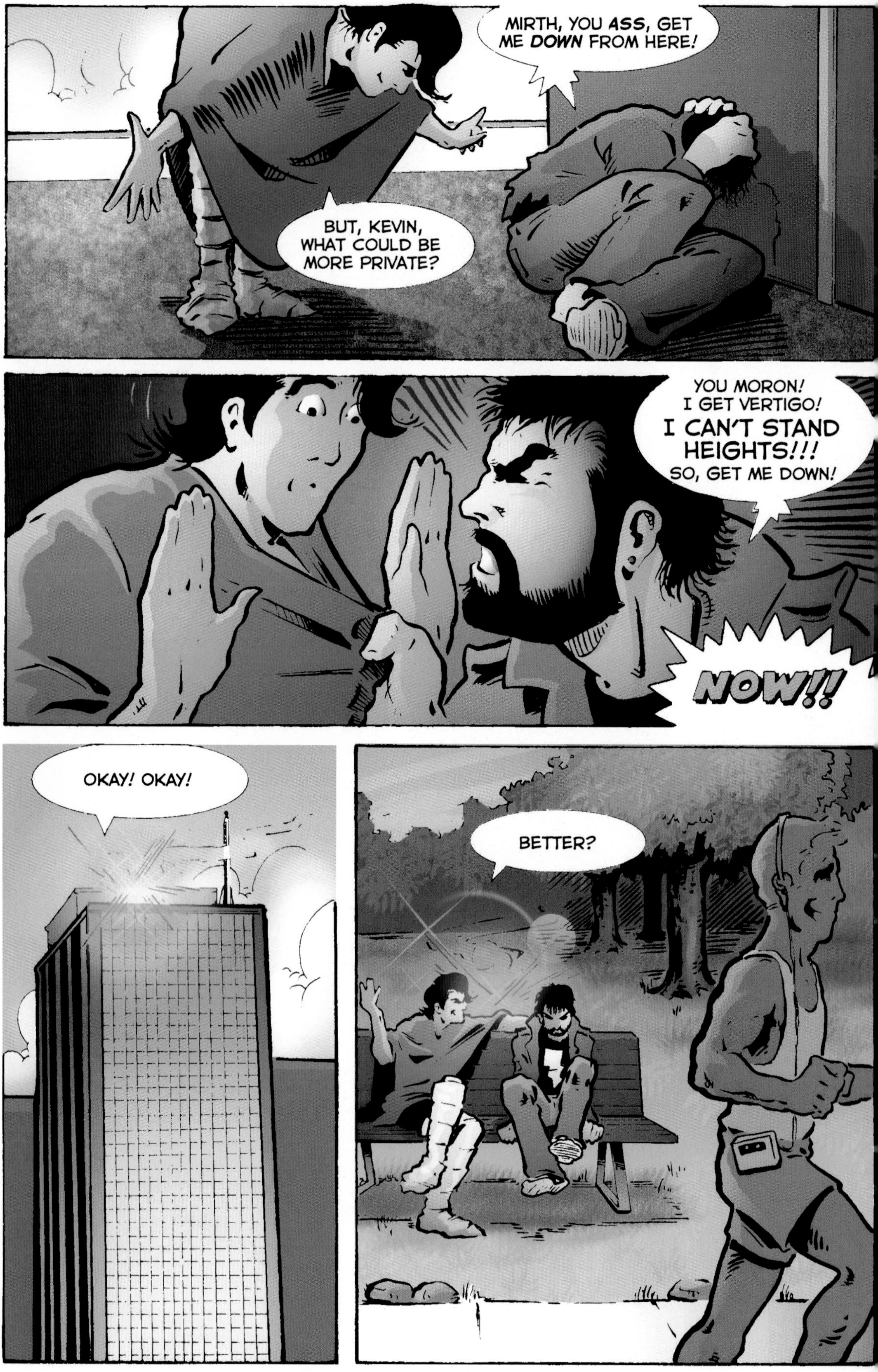
MIRTH, YOU **ASS**, GET ME ***DOWN*** FROM HERE!
BUT, KEVIN, WHAT COULD BE MORE PRIVATE?
YOU MORON! I GET VERTIGO! I CAN'T STAND HEIGHTS!!! SO, GET ME DOWN!
NOW!!
OKAY! OKAY!
BETTER?

WELL... NOT *TOTALLY* PRIVATE, BUT IT'LL DO. NOW...

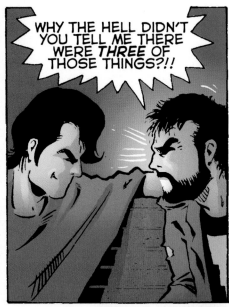

WHY THE HELL DIDN'T YOU TELL ME THERE WERE *THREE* OF THOSE THINGS?!!

BUT THERE AREN'T.

WHAT DO YOU MEAN THERE AREN'T?! I...

THERE'RE FIVE!

OH BOY.

AND THEY ARE THE DEADLY ENEMIES OF MANKIND IN GENERAL AND *YOU* IN PARTICULAR.

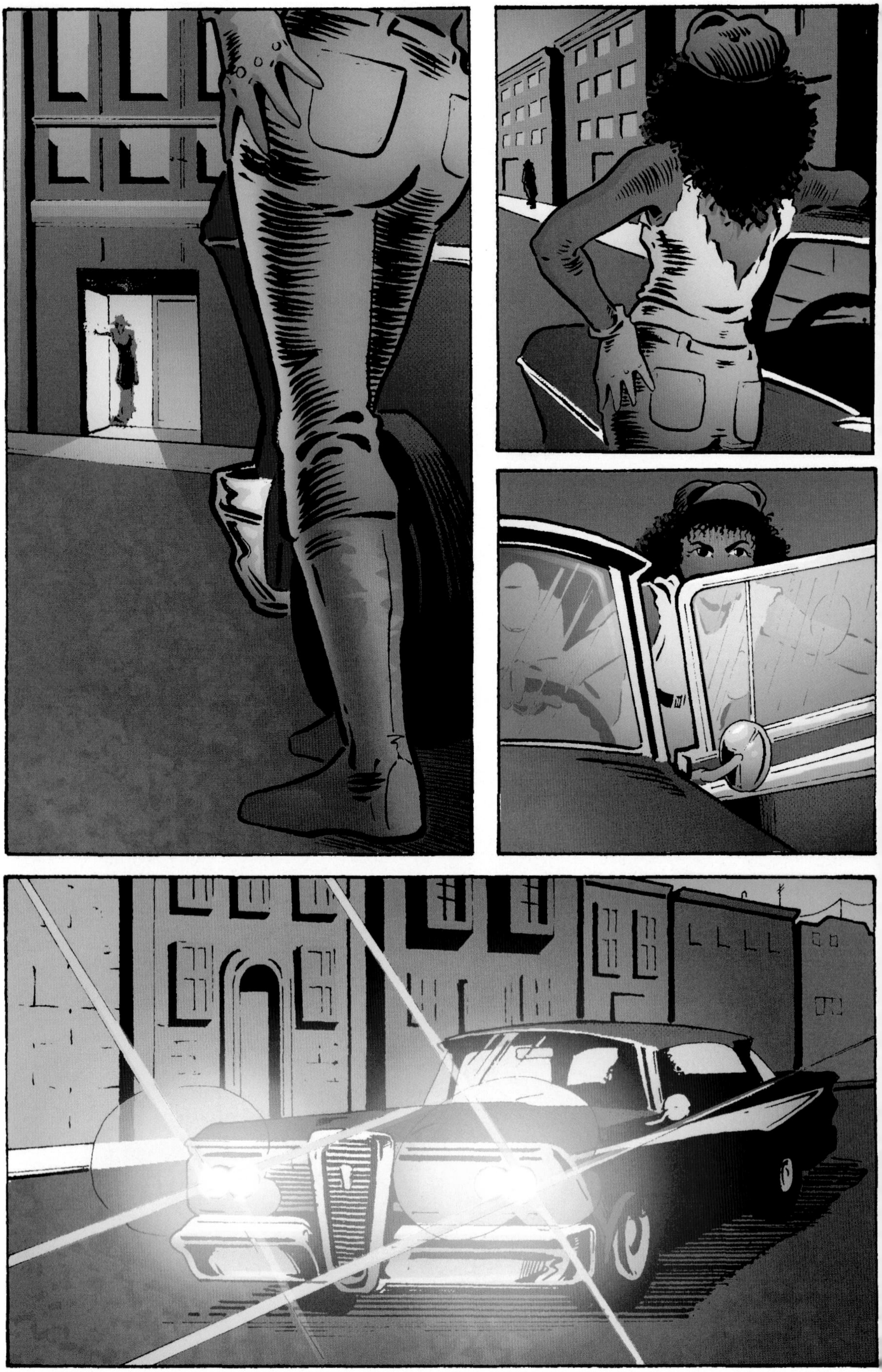

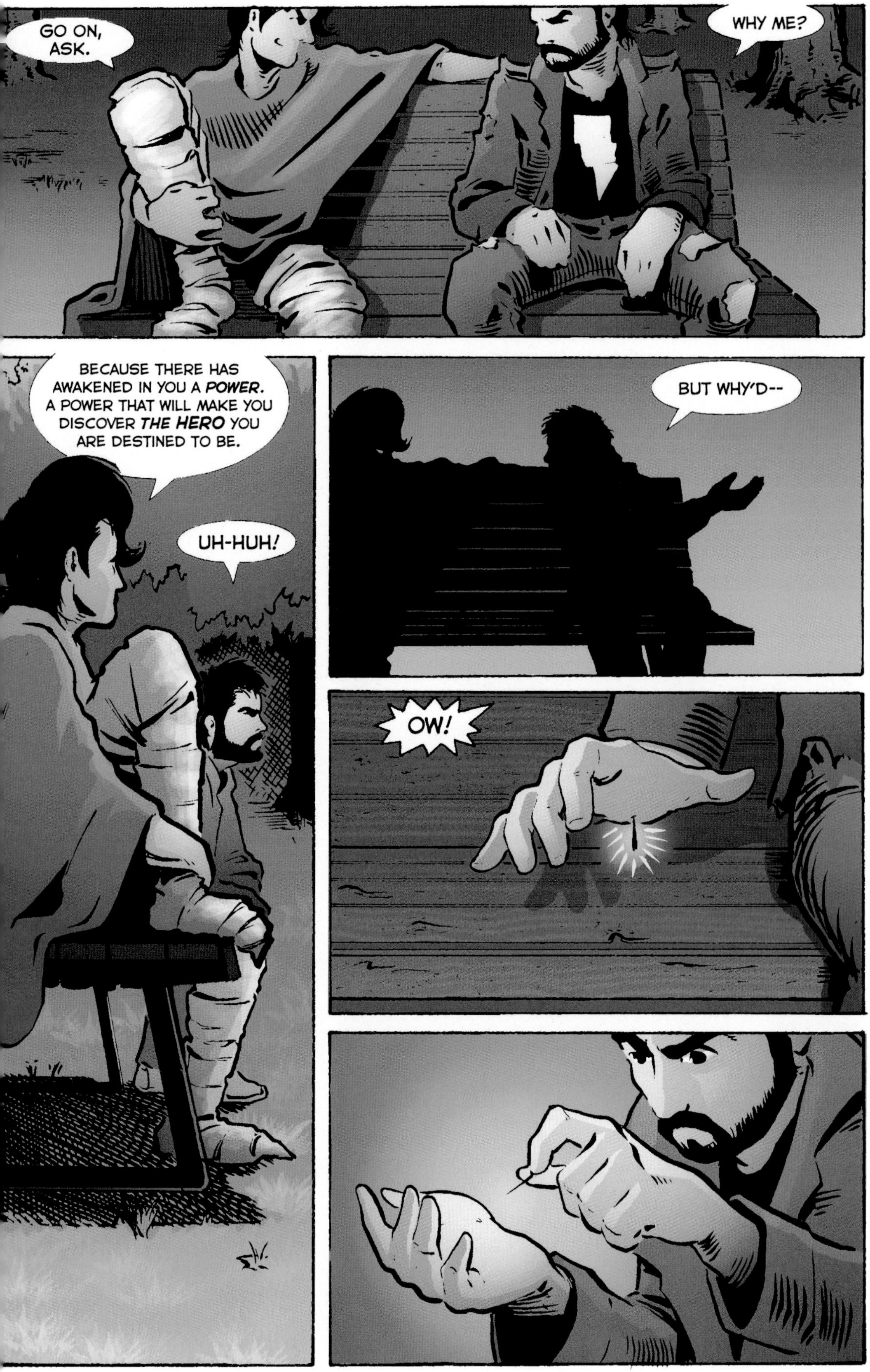
GO ON, ASK.
WHY ME?
BECAUSE THERE HAS AWAKENED IN YOU A *POWER.* A POWER THAT WILL MAKE YOU DISCOVER ***THE HERO*** YOU ARE DESTINED TO BE.
UH-HUH!
BUT WHY'D--
OW!

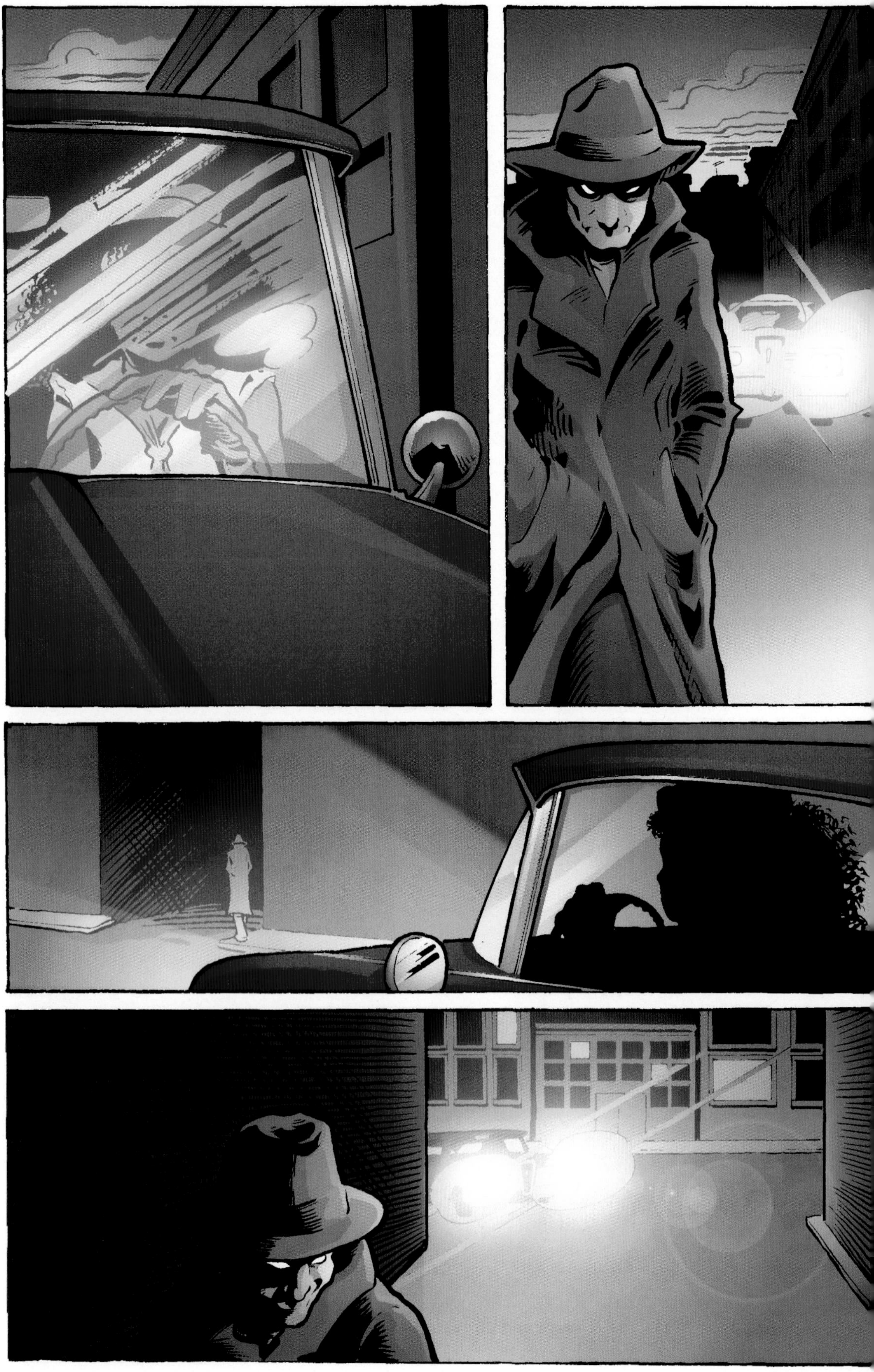

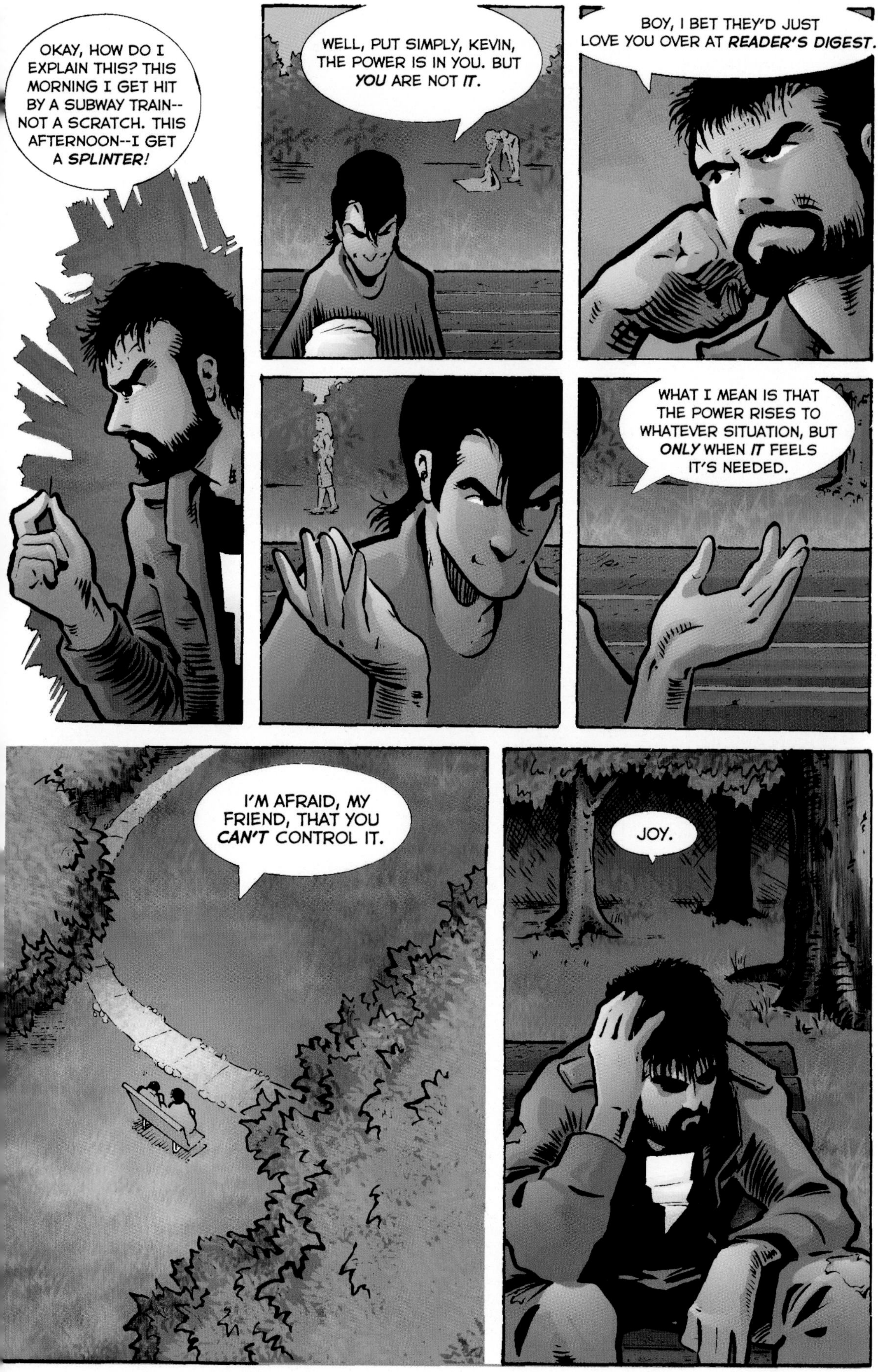
OKAY, HOW DO I EXPLAIN THIS? THIS MORNING I GET HIT BY A SUBWAY TRAIN--NOT A SCRATCH. THIS AFTERNOON--I GET A SPLINTER!
WELL, PUT SIMPLY, KEVIN, THE POWER IS IN YOU. BUT YOU ARE NOT IT.
BOY, I BET THEY'D JUST LOVE YOU OVER AT READER'S DIGEST.
WHAT I MEAN IS THAT THE POWER RISES TO WHATEVER SITUATION, BUT ONLY WHEN IT FEELS IT'S NEEDED.
I'M AFRAID, MY FRIEND, THAT YOU CAN'T CONTROL IT.
JOY.

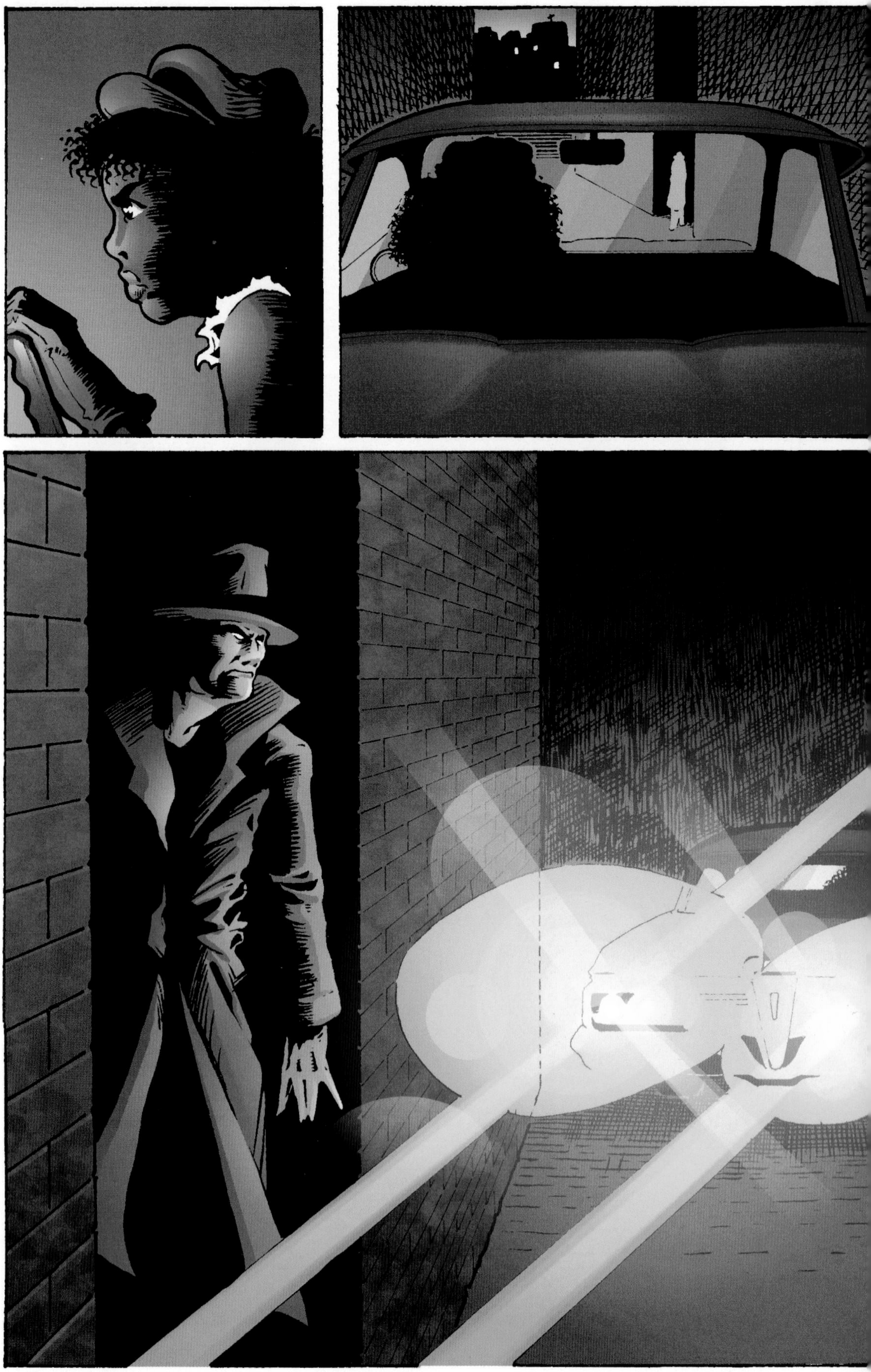

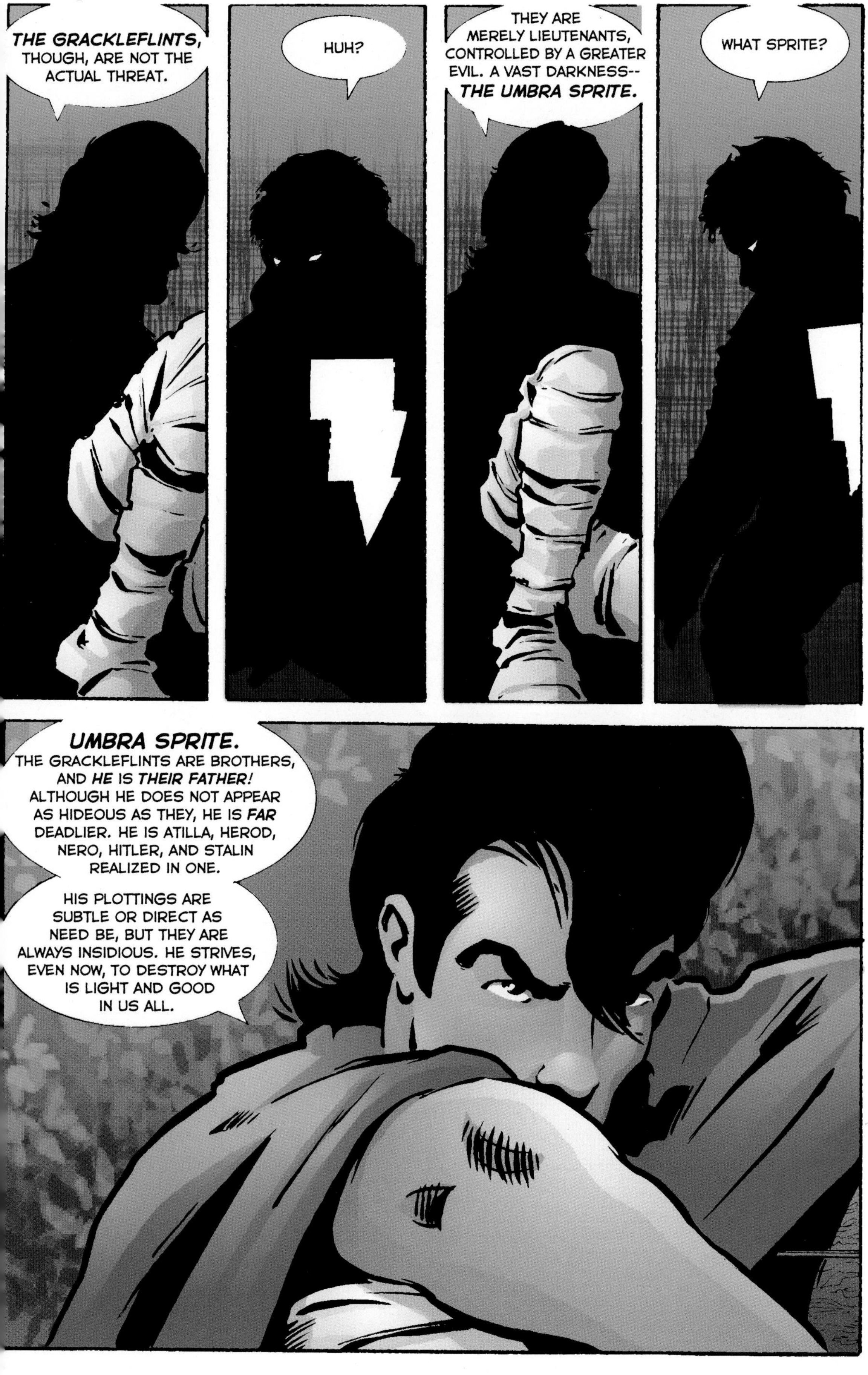
THE GRACKLEFLINTS, THOUGH, ARE NOT THE ACTUAL THREAT.
HUH?
THEY ARE MERELY LIEUTENANTS, CONTROLLED BY A GREATER EVIL. A VAST DARKNESS-- THE UMBRA SPRITE.
WHAT SPRITE?
UMBRA SPRITE. THE GRACKLEFLINTS ARE BROTHERS, AND HE IS THEIR FATHER! ALTHOUGH HE DOES NOT APPEAR AS HIDEOUS AS THEY, HE IS FAR DEADLIER. HE IS ATILLA, HEROD, NERO, HITLER, AND STALIN REALIZED IN ONE.
HIS PLOTTINGS ARE SUBTLE OR DIRECT AS NEED BE, BUT THEY ARE ALWAYS INSIDIOUS. HE STRIVES, EVEN NOW, TO DESTROY WHAT IS LIGHT AND GOOD IN US ALL.

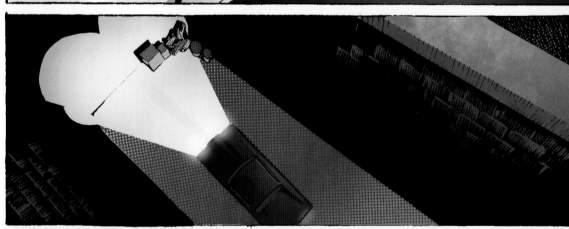

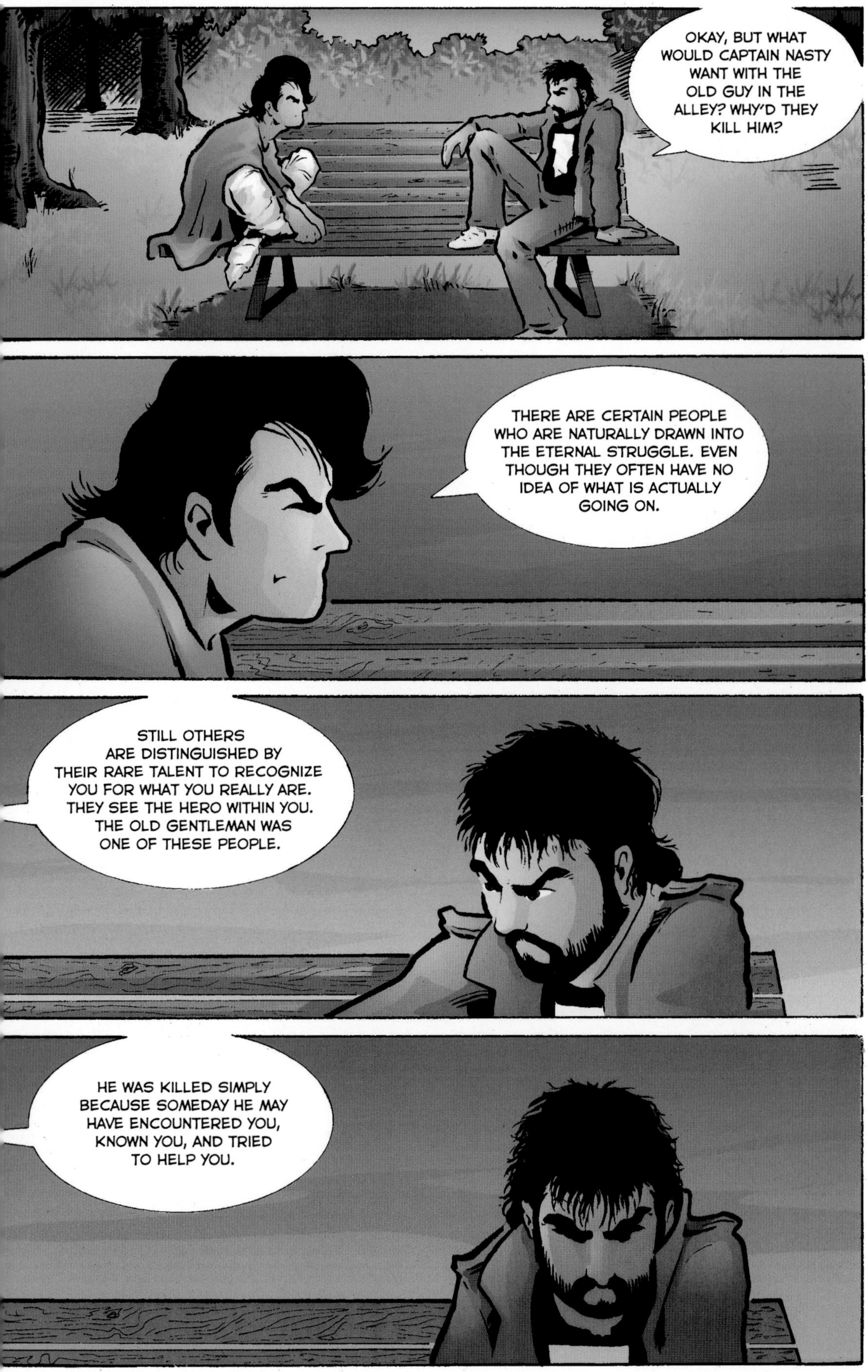
OKAY, BUT WHAT WOULD CAPTAIN NASTY WANT WITH THE OLD GUY IN THE ALLEY? WHY'D THEY KILL HIM?
THERE ARE CERTAIN PEOPLE WHO ARE NATURALLY DRAWN INTO THE ETERNAL STRUGGLE. EVEN THOUGH THEY OFTEN HAVE NO IDEA OF WHAT IS ACTUALLY GOING ON.
STILL OTHERS ARE DISTINGUISHED BY THEIR RARE TALENT TO RECOGNIZE YOU FOR WHAT YOU REALLY ARE. THEY SEE THE HERO WITHIN YOU. THE OLD GENTLEMAN WAS ONE OF THESE PEOPLE.
HE WAS KILLED SIMPLY BECAUSE SOMEDAY HE MAY HAVE ENCOUNTERED YOU, KNOWN YOU, AND TRIED TO HELP YOU.

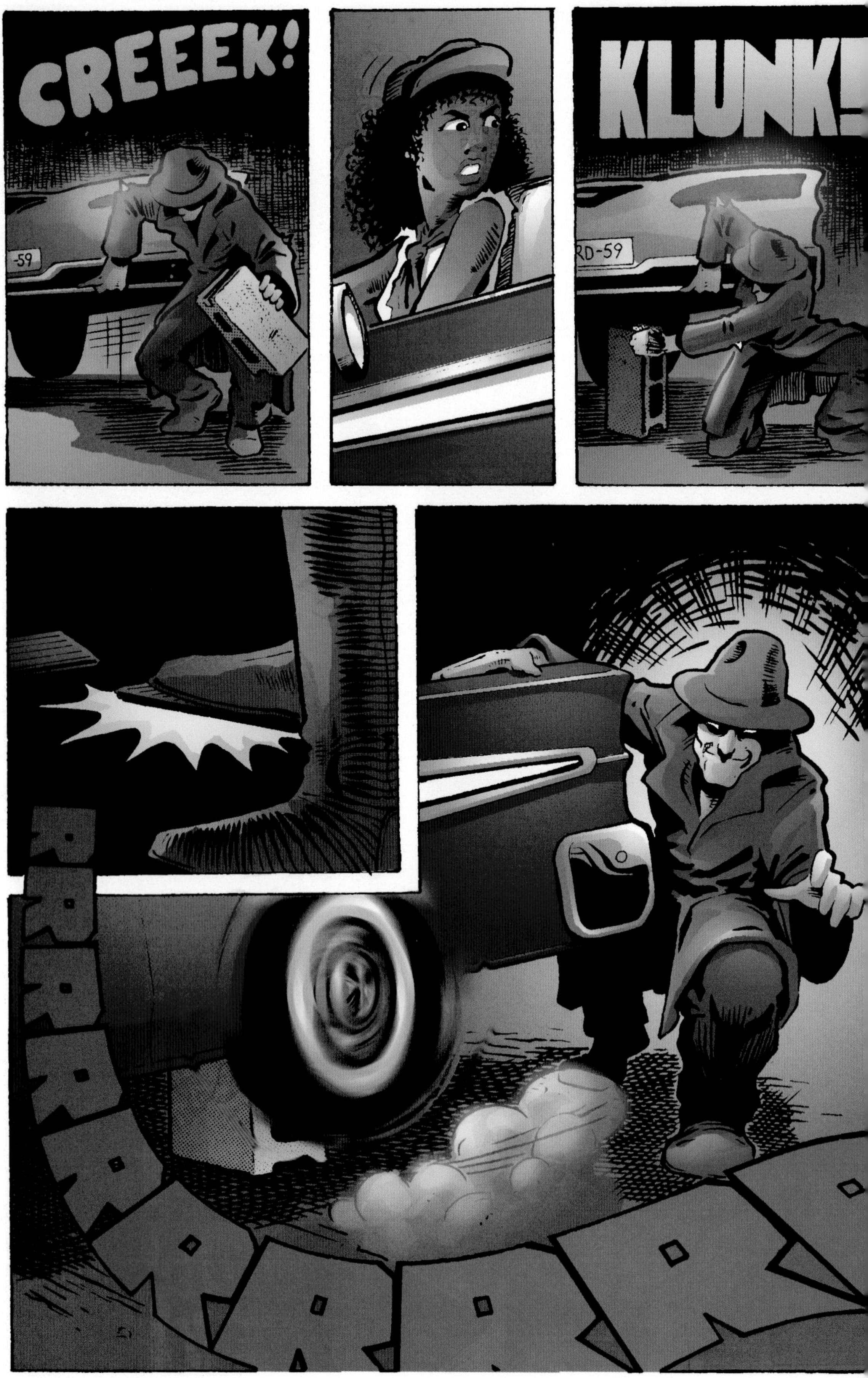
CREEEK!
KLUNK!

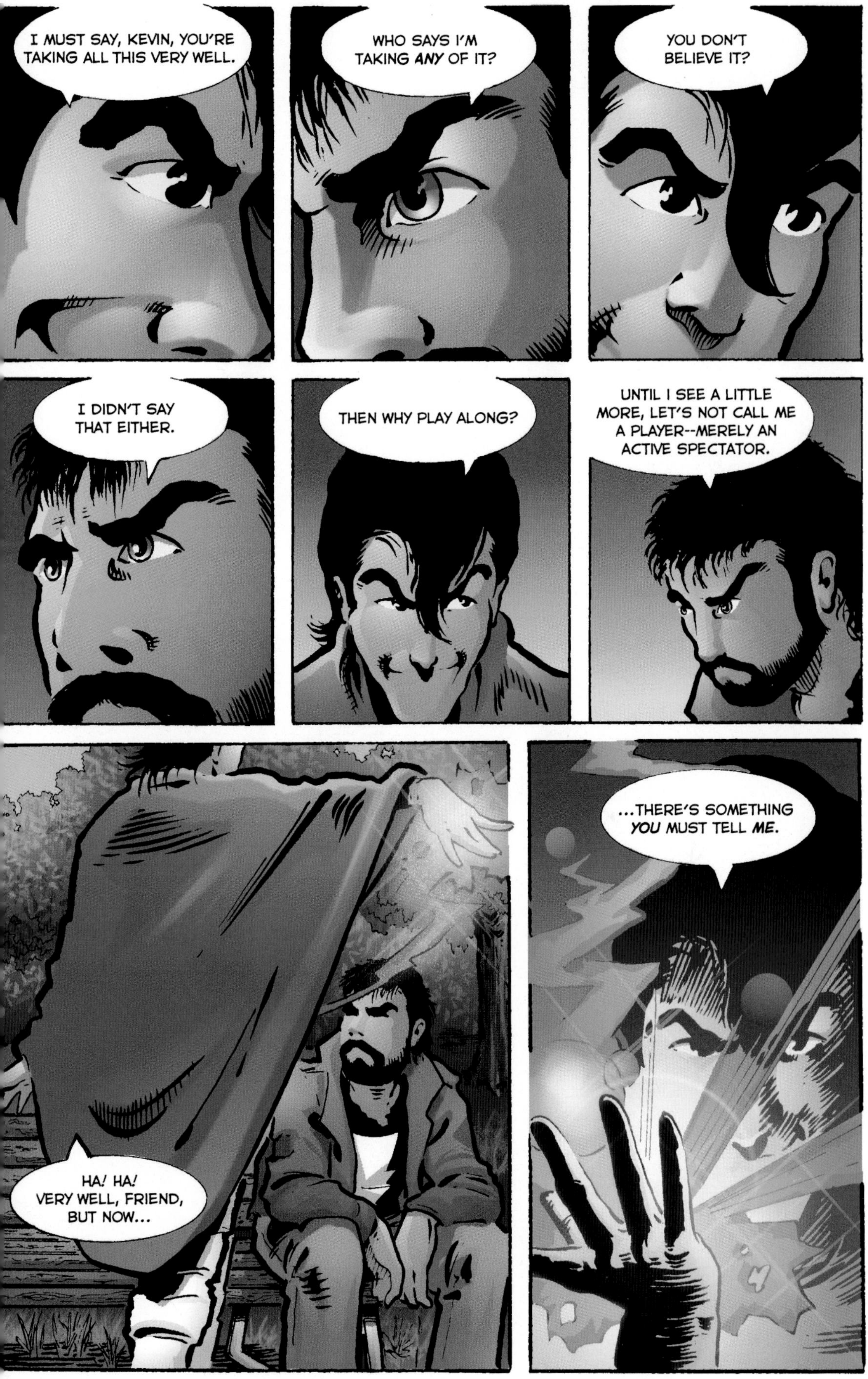
I MUST SAY, KEVIN, YOU'RE TAKING ALL THIS VERY WELL.
WHO SAYS I'M TAKING *ANY* OF IT?
YOU DON'T BELIEVE IT?
I DIDN'T SAY THAT EITHER.
THEN WHY PLAY ALONG?
UNTIL I SEE A LITTLE MORE, LET'S NOT CALL ME A PLAYER--MERELY AN ACTIVE SPECTATOR.
HA! HA! VERY WELL, FRIEND, BUT NOW...
...THERE'S SOMETHING *YOU* MUST TELL *ME*.

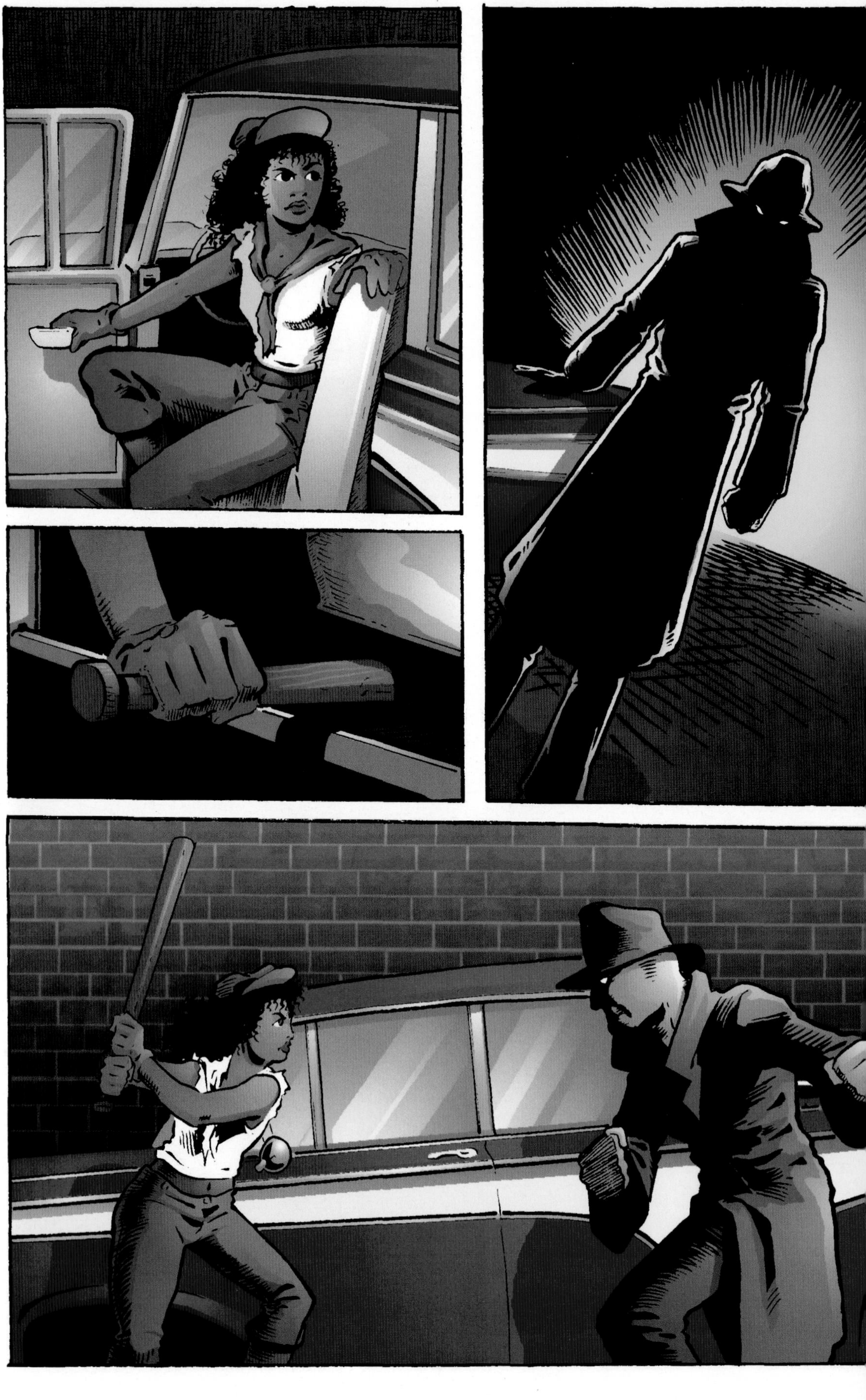

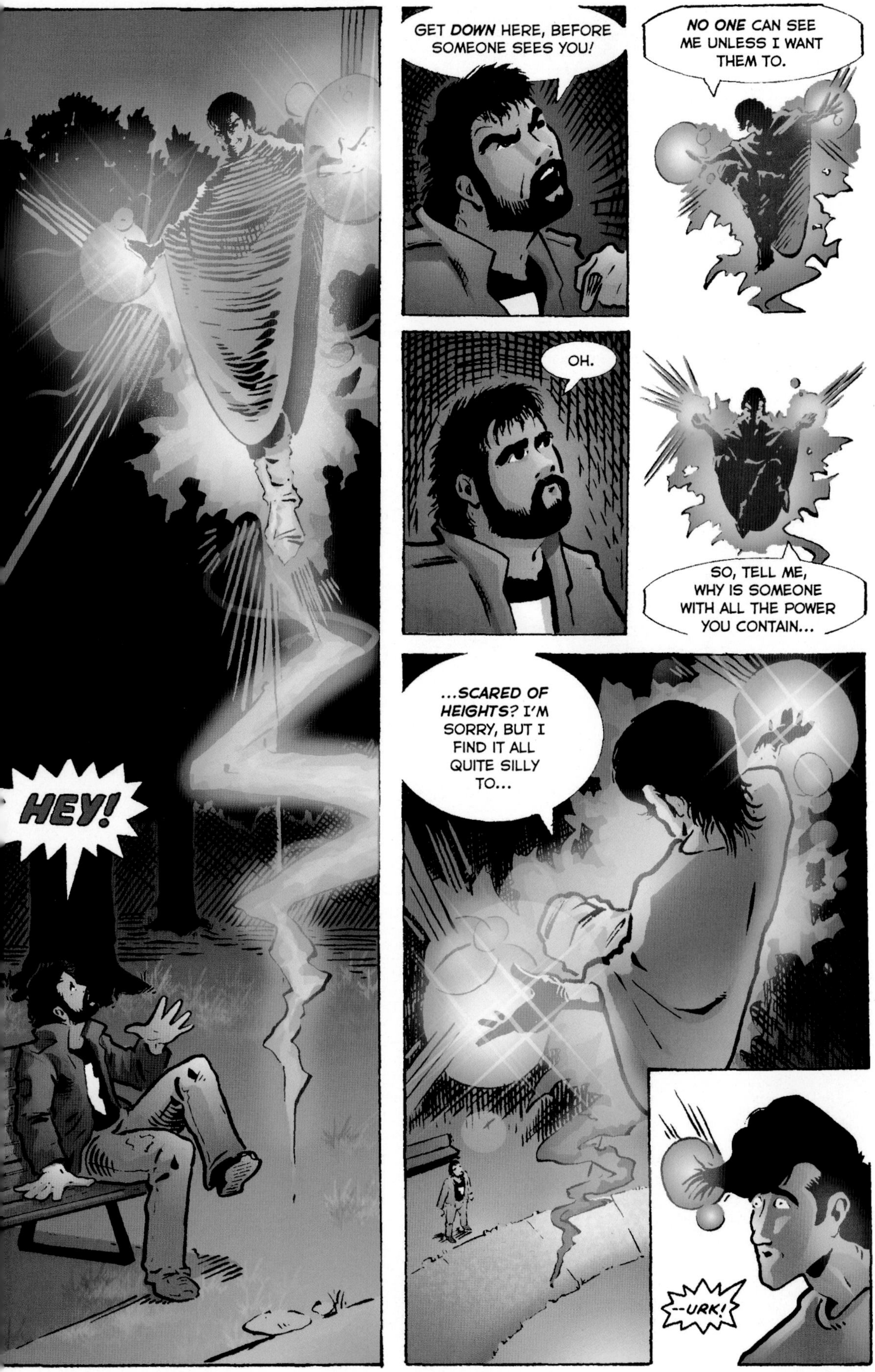
HEY!
GET *DOWN* HERE, BEFORE SOMEONE SEES YOU!
NO ONE CAN SEE ME UNLESS I WANT THEM TO.
OH.
SO, TELL ME, WHY IS SOMEONE WITH ALL THE POWER YOU CONTAIN...
...*SCARED OF HEIGHTS?* I'M SORRY, BUT I FIND IT ALL QUITE SILLY TO...
--URK!

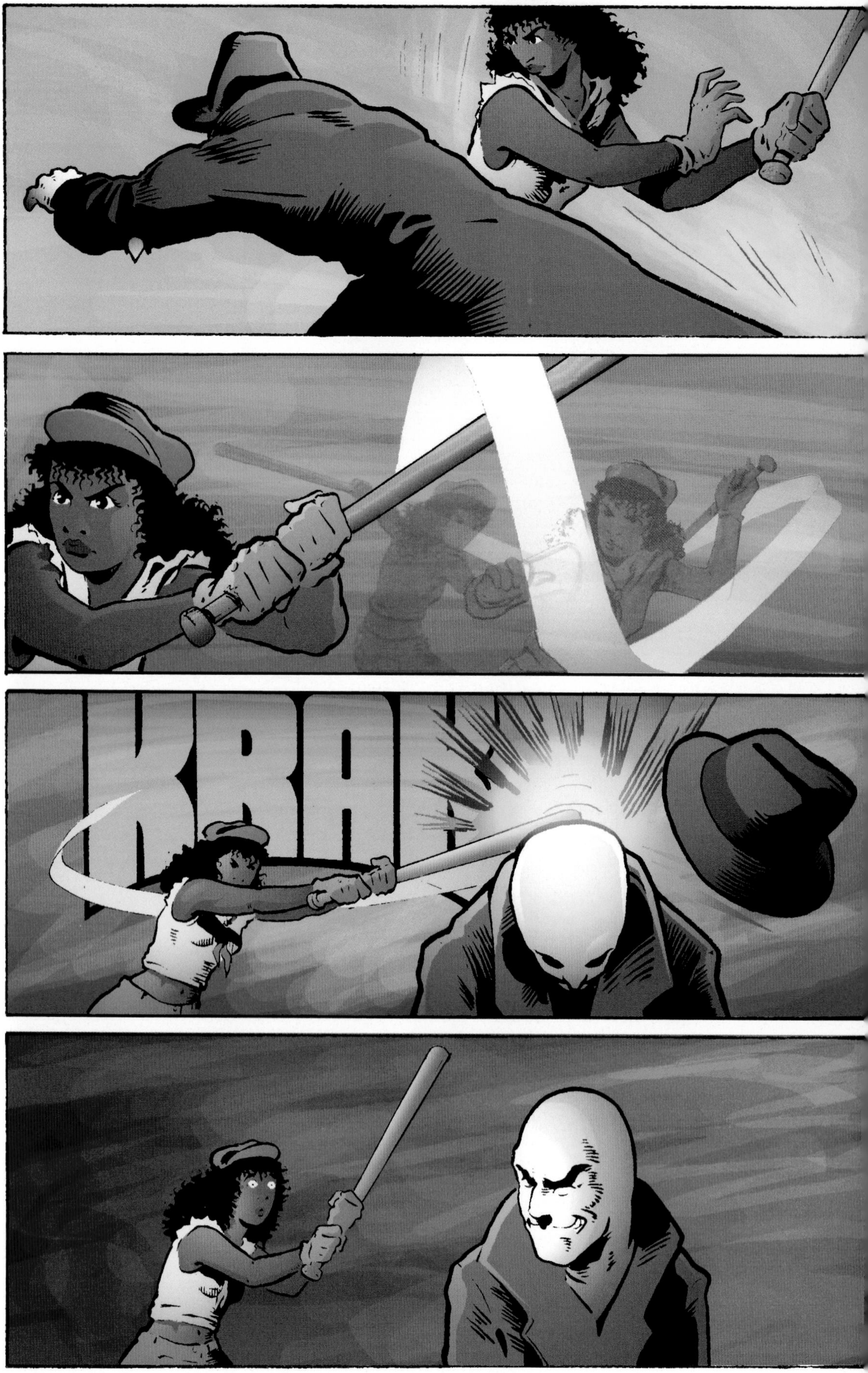
KRA

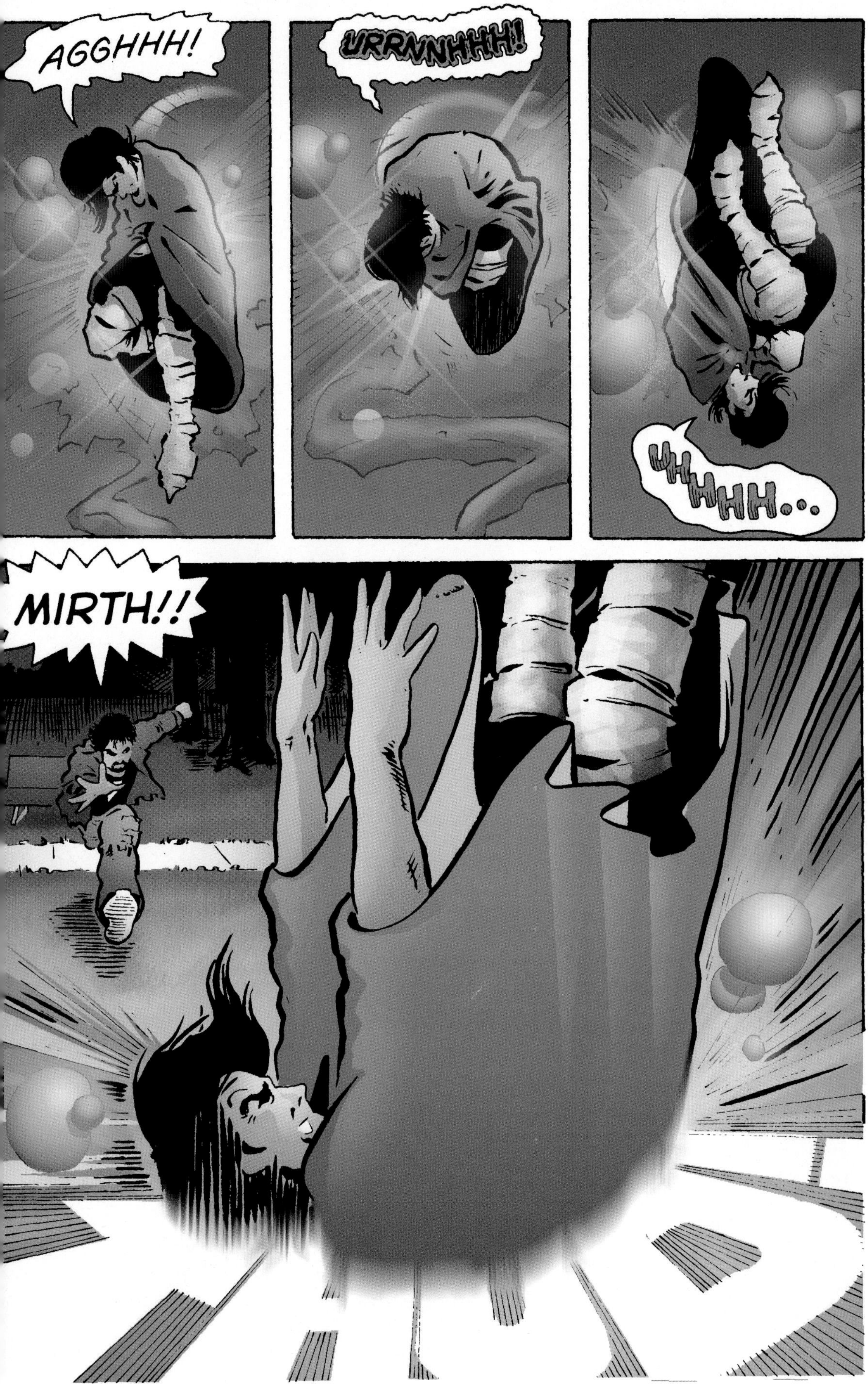

AGGHHH!
URRNNHHH!
UHHHHH...
MIRTH!!

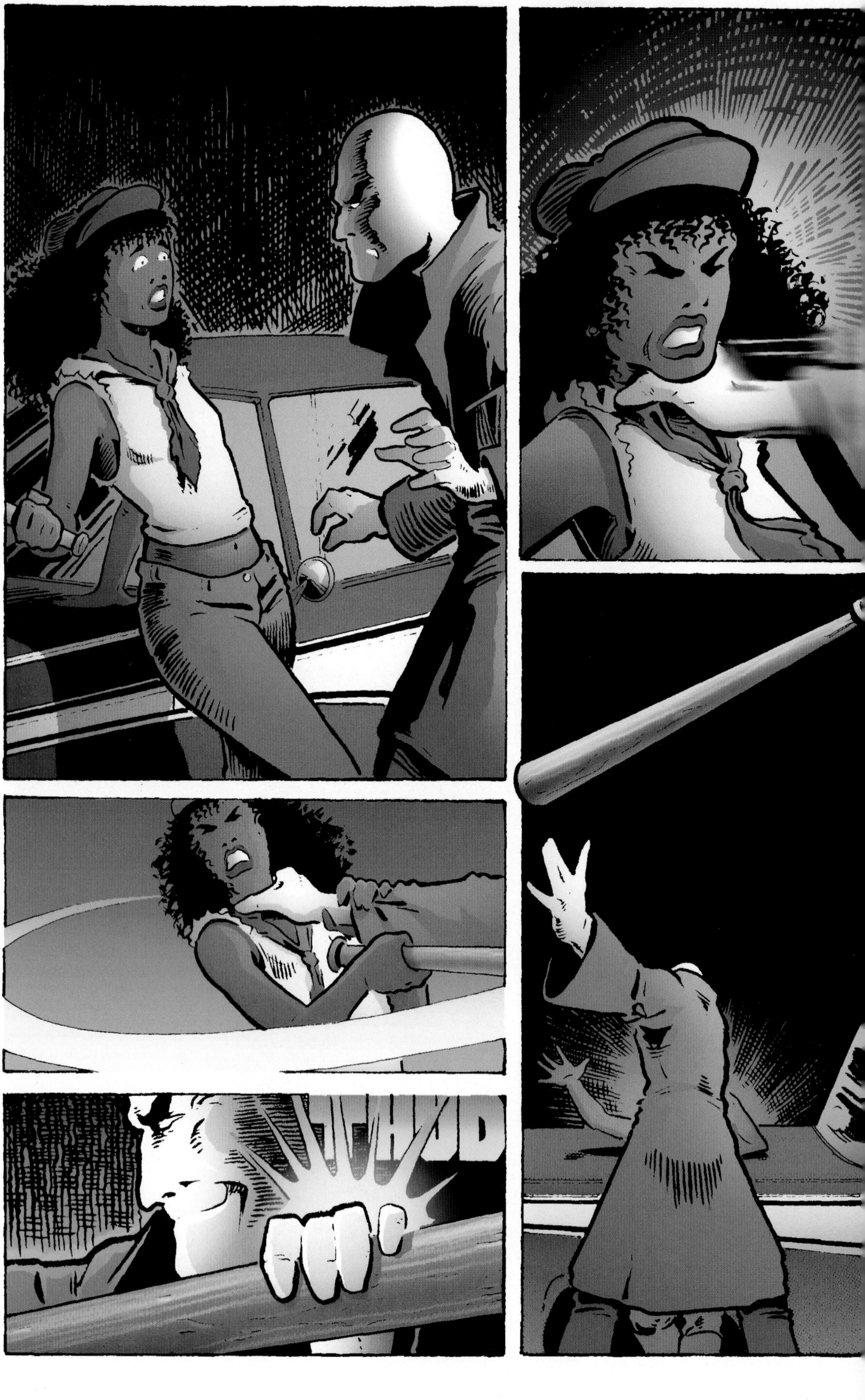
THUD

MIRTH? WHAT'S WRONG!? ARE YOU--
I'M ALRIGHT, KEVIN. IT'S JUST THE SIGHT.
IT COMES ON ME UNEXPECTEDLY AND THE BEGINNING IS PAINFUL.
BUT NOW THE PAIN CLEARS, AND I BEGIN TO SEE...
NO!
IT HAPPENS AGAIN! ONE OF THOSE I SPOKE TO YOU OF--THOSE WHO WILL KNOW YOU AND JOIN YOU--IS AGAIN AT THE MERCY OF A GRACKLEFLINT!!

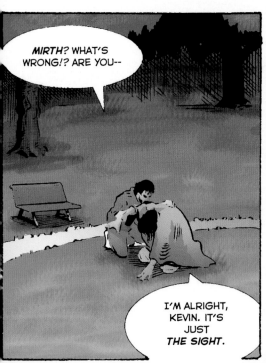

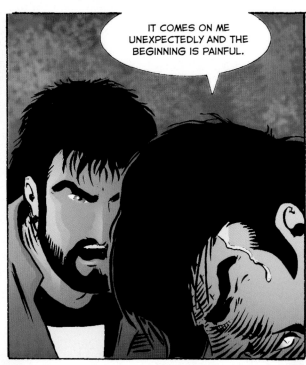

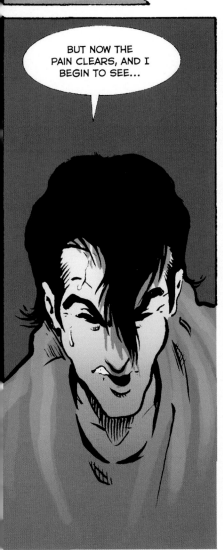

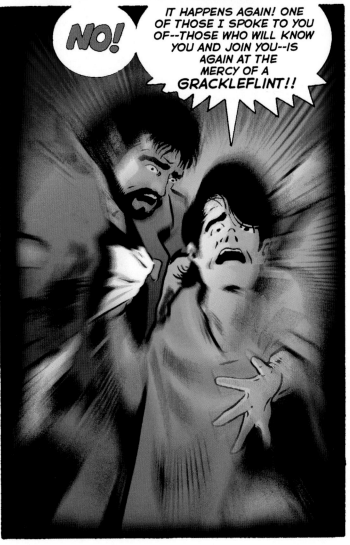

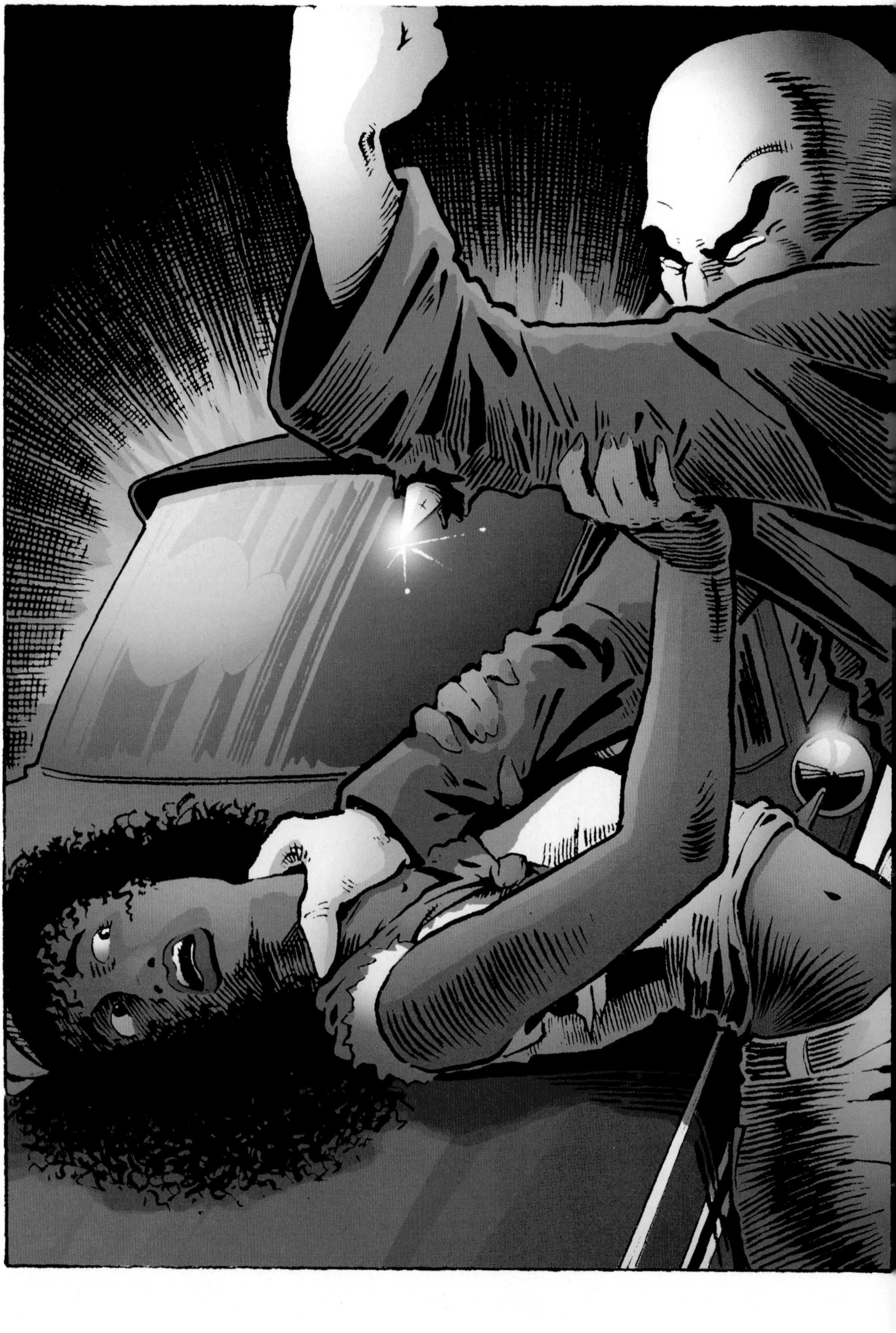

THE HERO DISCOVERED

MAGE

Chapter 03

The Mousetrap

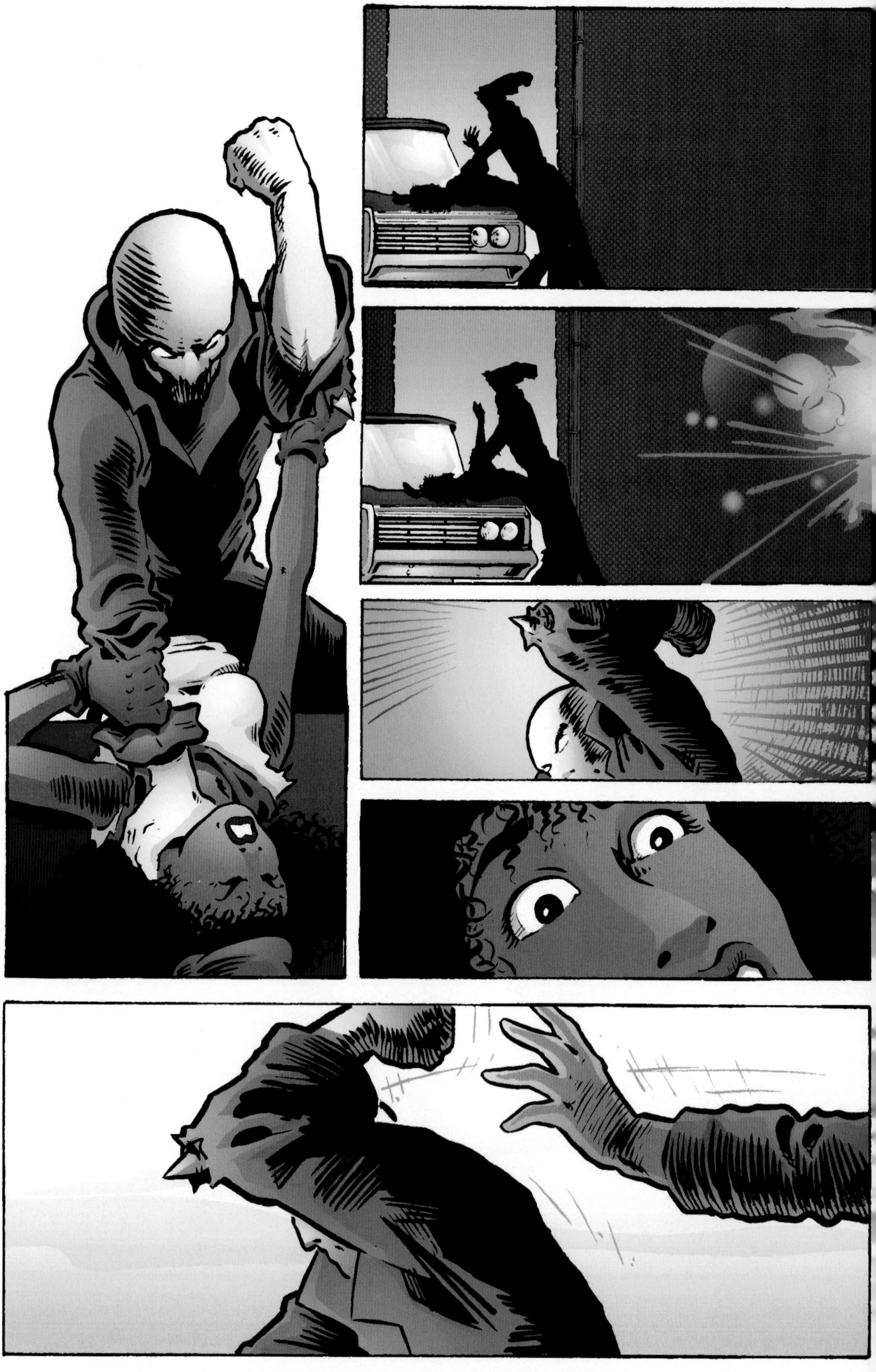

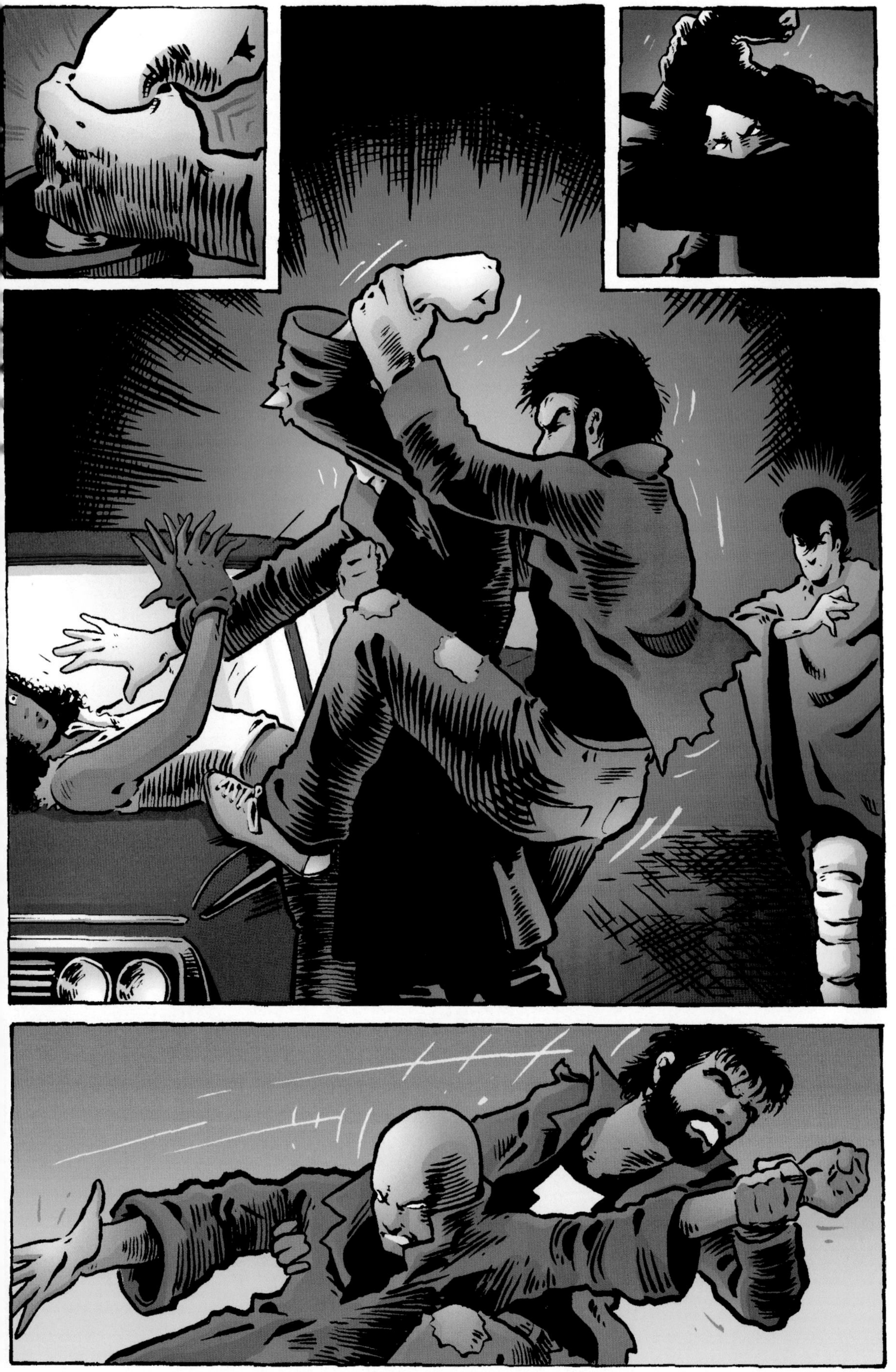

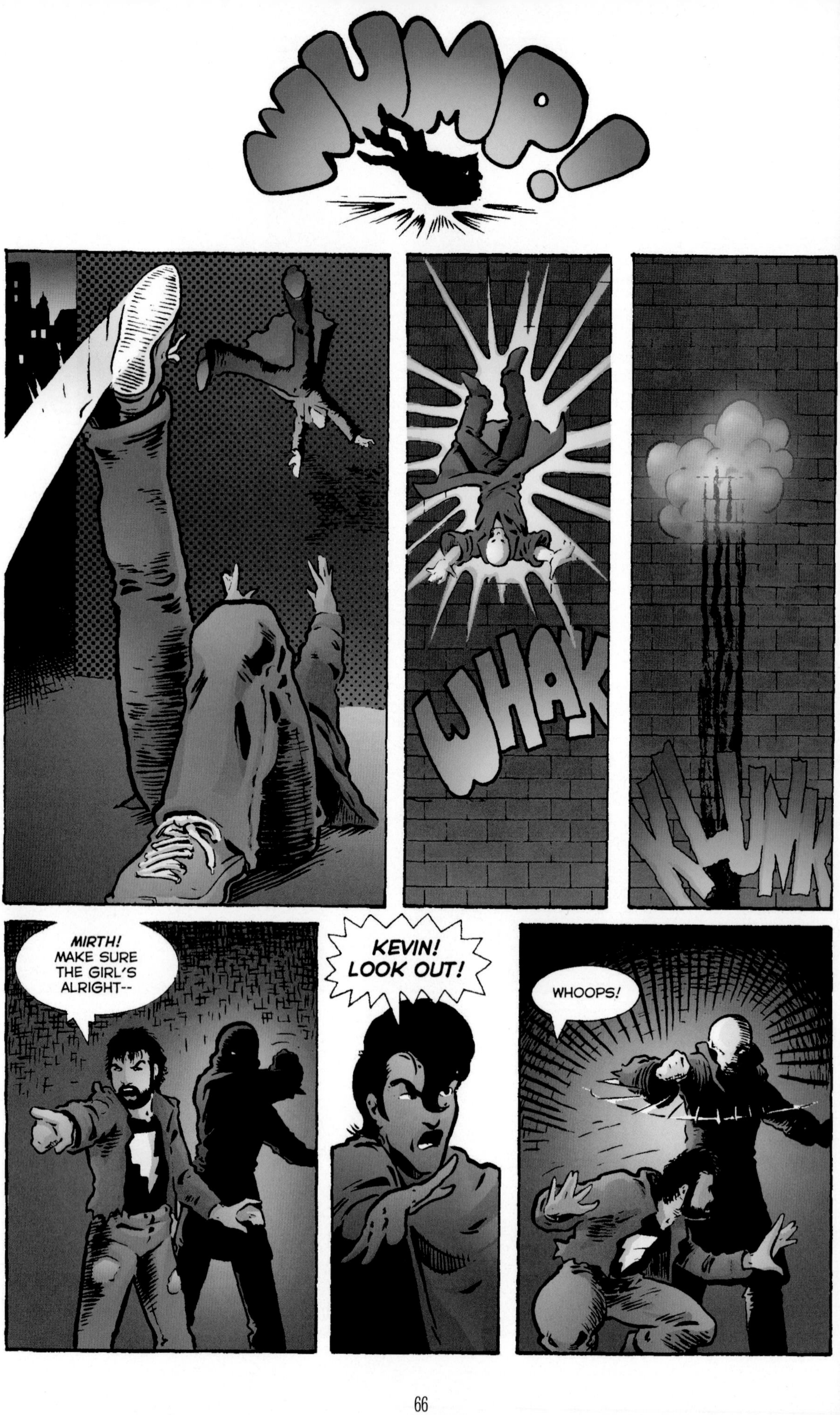
WHUMP!!
WHAK
KLUNK
MIRTH! MAKE SURE THE GIRL'S ALRIGHT--
KEVIN! LOOK OUT!
WHOOPS!

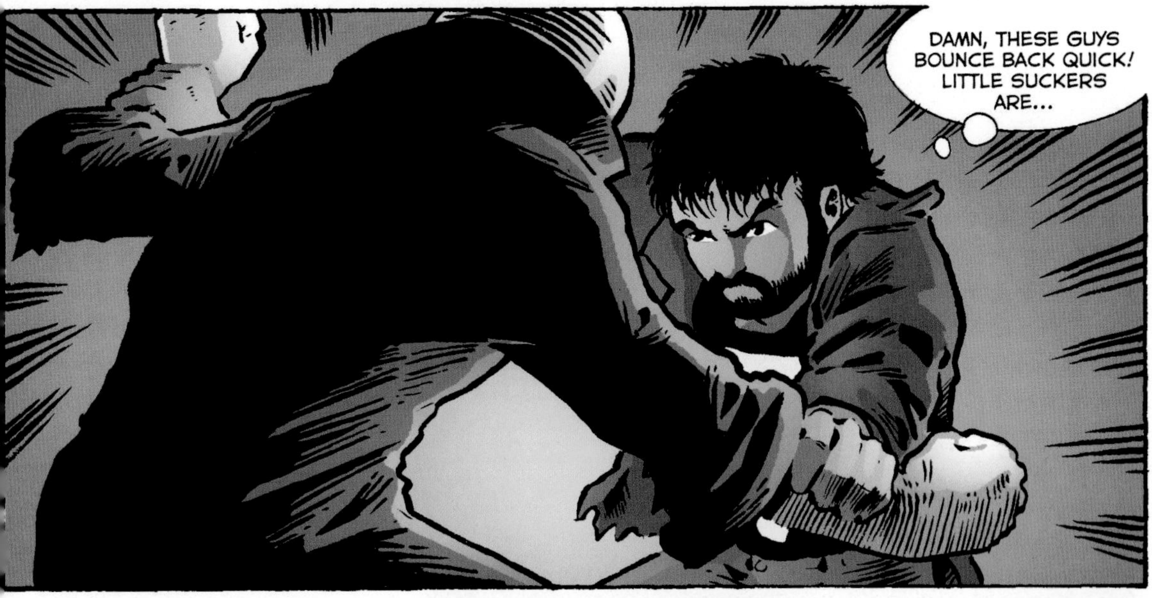
DAMN, THESE GUYS BOUNCE BACK QUICK! LITTLE SUCKERS ARE...

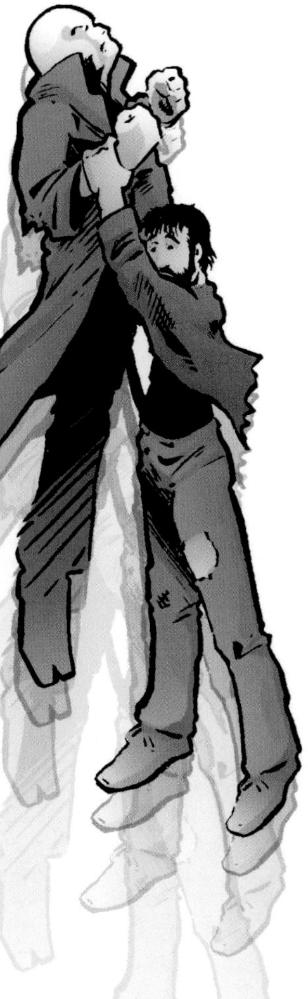

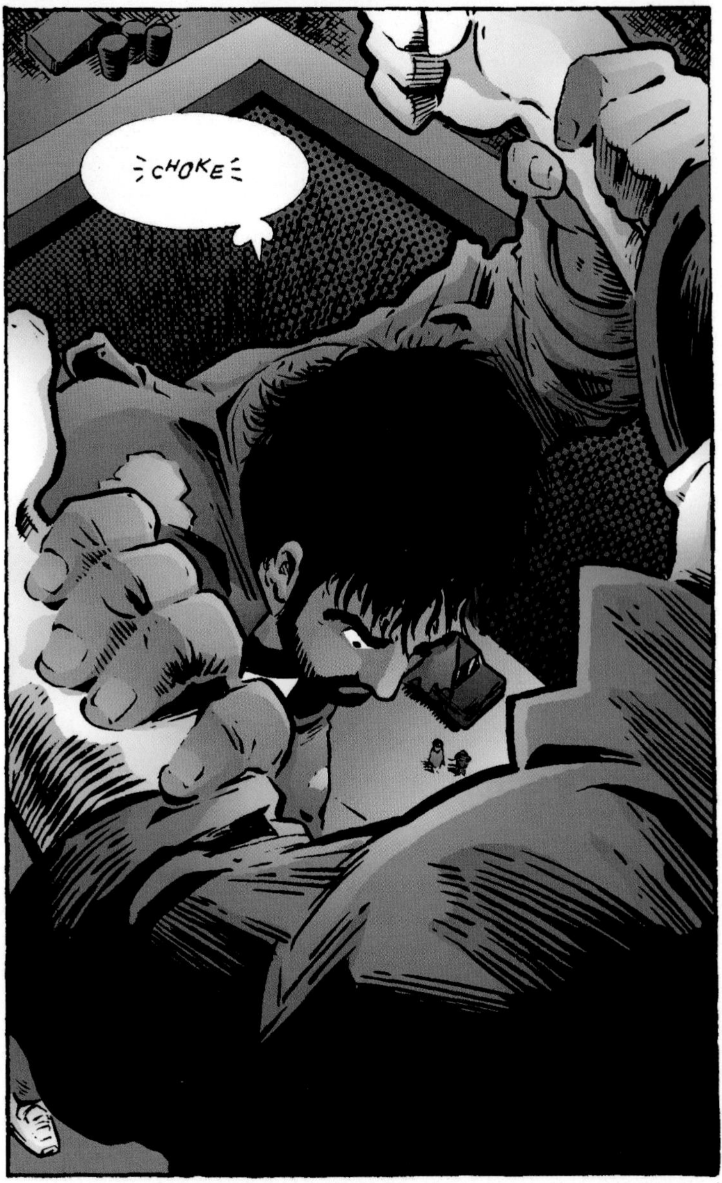
CHOKE

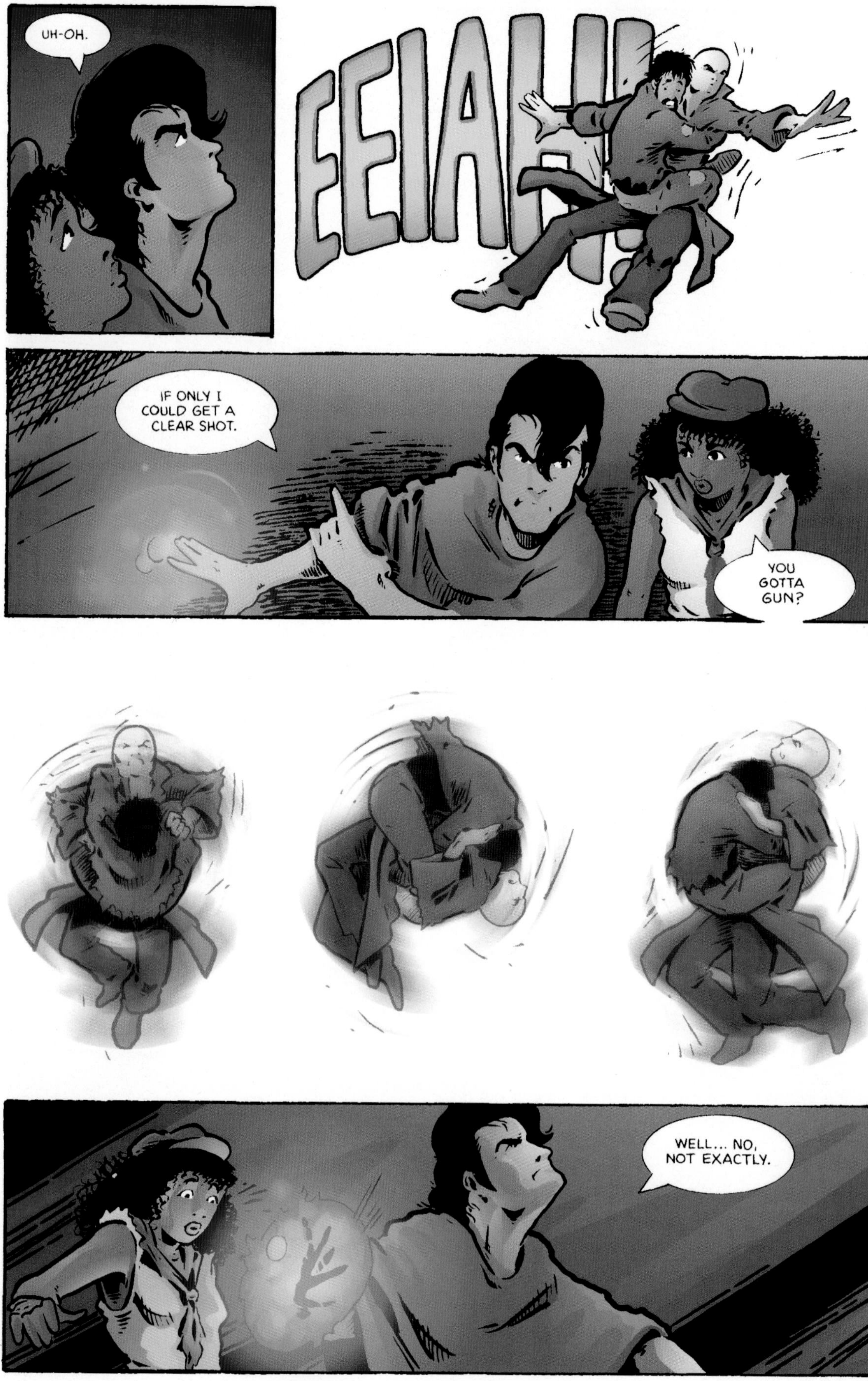

UH-OH.
EEIAH!!
IF ONLY I COULD GET A CLEAR SHOT.
YOU GOTTA GUN?
WELL... NO, NOT EXACTLY.

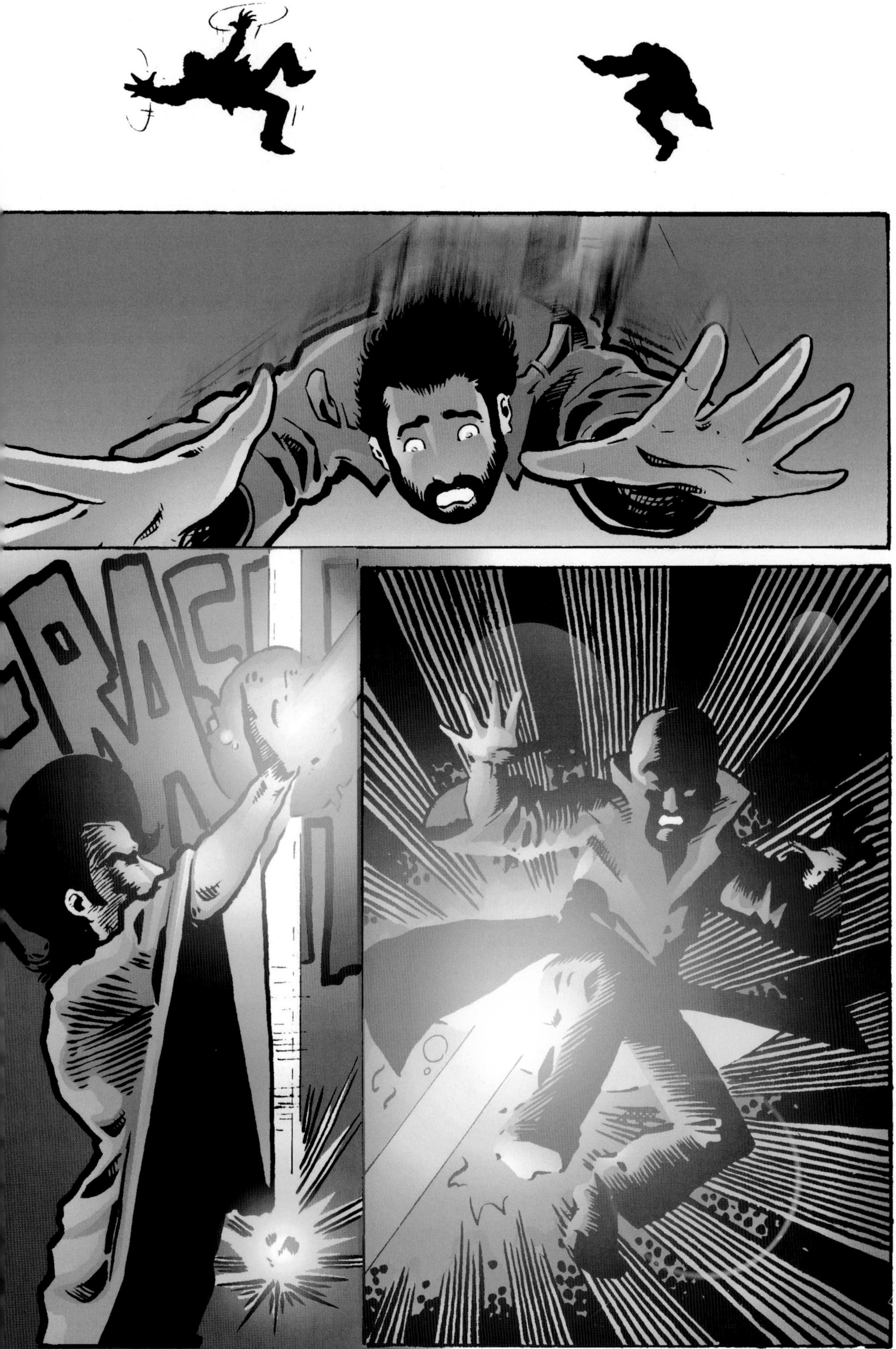

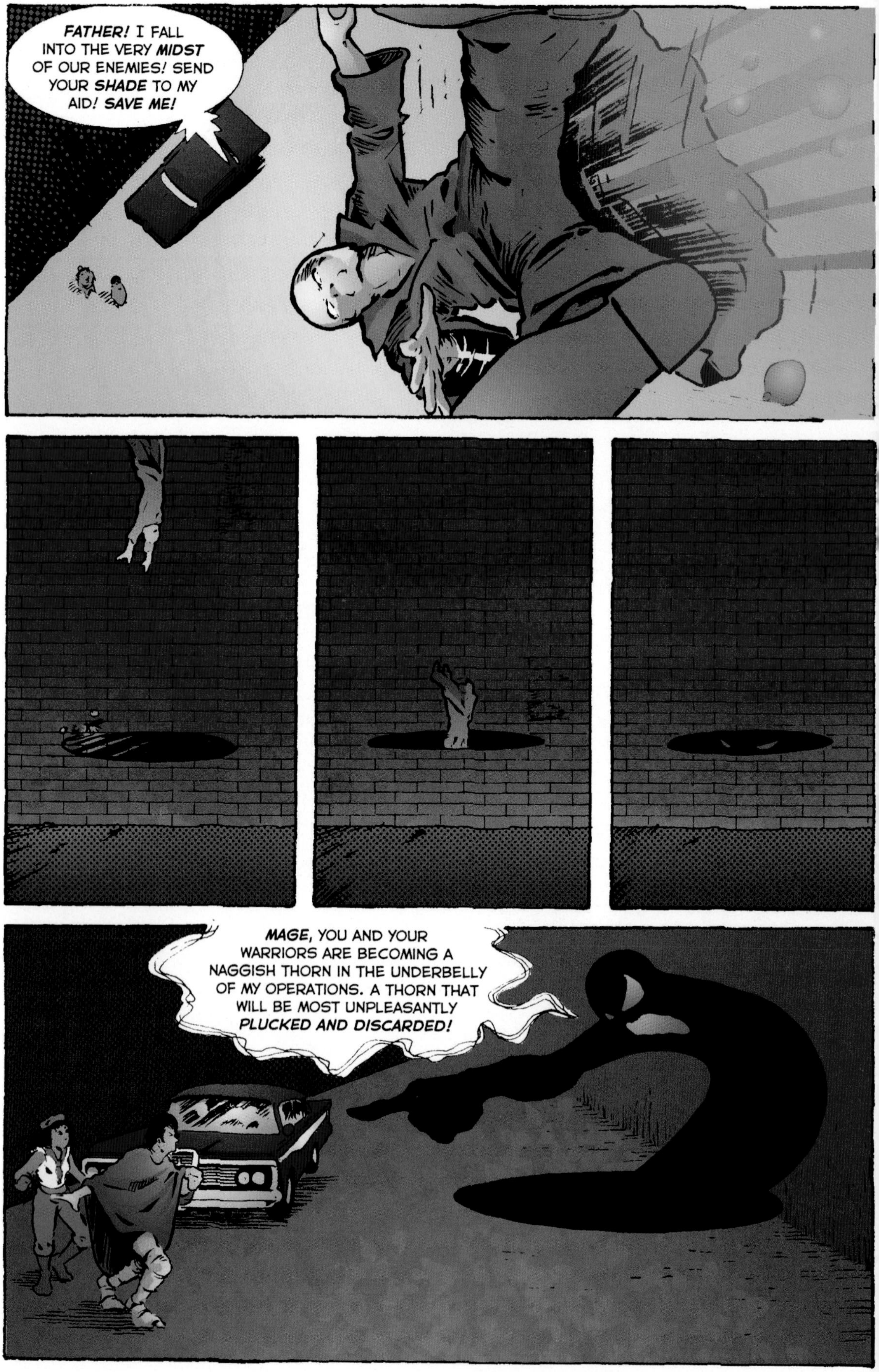
FATHER! I FALL INTO THE VERY MIDST OF OUR ENEMIES! SEND YOUR SHADE TO MY AID! SAVE ME!
MAGE, YOU AND YOUR WARRIORS ARE BECOMING A NAGGISH THORN IN THE UNDERBELLY OF MY OPERATIONS. A THORN THAT WILL BE MOST UNPLEASANTLY PLUCKED AND DISCARDED!

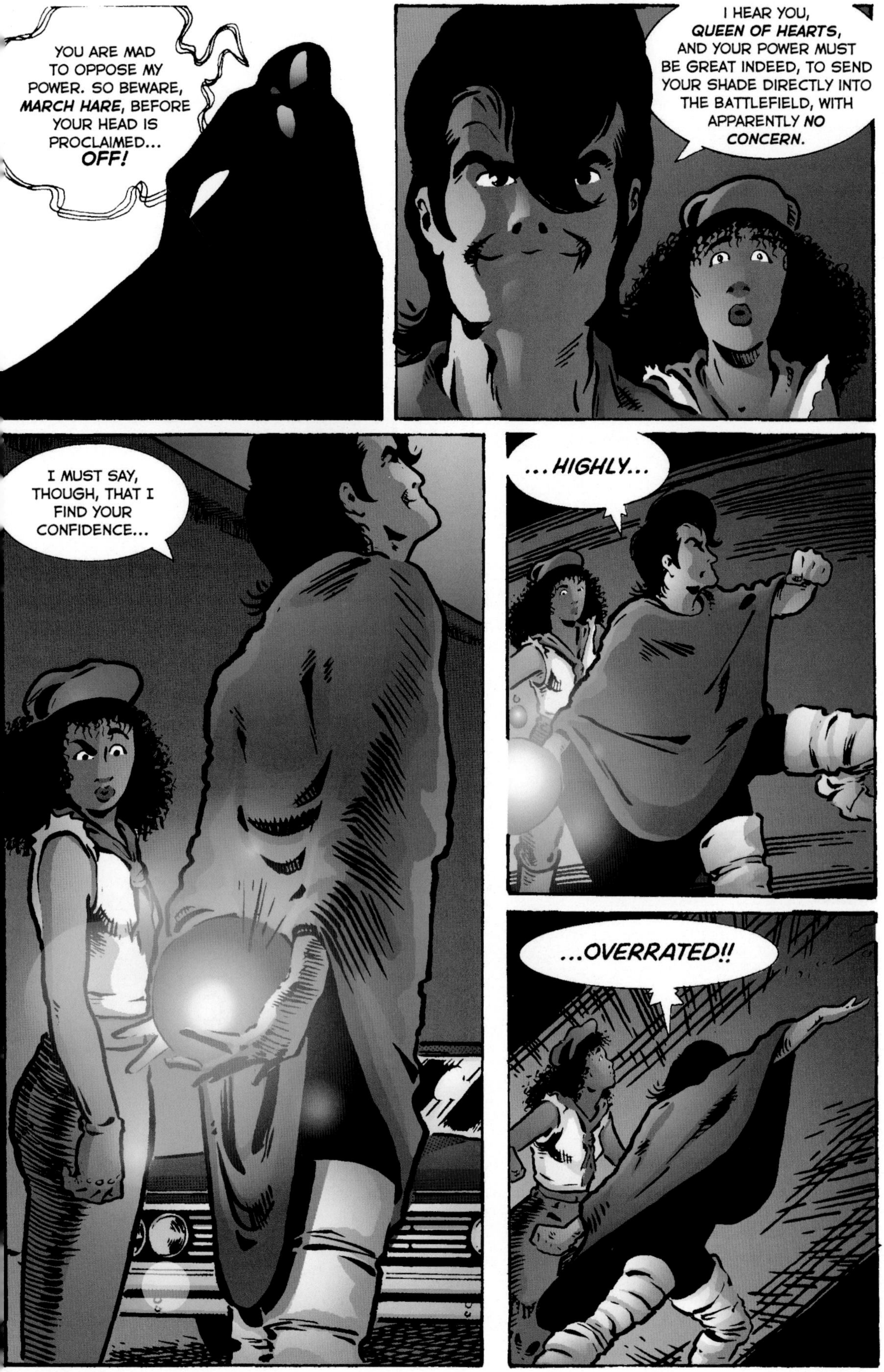

YOU ARE MAD TO OPPOSE MY POWER. SO BEWARE, MARCH HARE, BEFORE YOUR HEAD IS PROCLAIMED... OFF!
I HEAR YOU, QUEEN OF HEARTS, AND YOUR POWER MUST BE GREAT INDEED, TO SEND YOUR SHADE DIRECTLY INTO THE BATTLEFIELD, WITH APPARENTLY NO CONCERN.
I MUST SAY, THOUGH, THAT I FIND YOUR CONFIDENCE...
...HIGHLY...
...OVERRATED!!

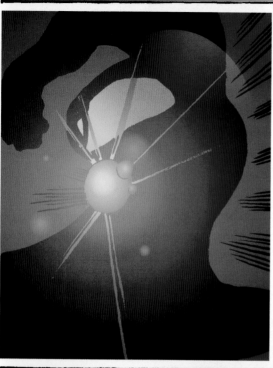

HEY, DRAPES...

THAT WAS A CUTE LITTLE TRICK, BUT AREN'T YOU FORGETTING THE *STAR OF OUR SHOW* OVER HERE?

OH, HE'S ALRIGHT.

OH, RIGHT! I'M SURE HE'S JUST GREAT! HE ONLY FELL ABOUT *FIVE OR SIX* STORIES!

YOUNG LADY, I *ASSURE* YOU, HE'S JUST *FINE!*

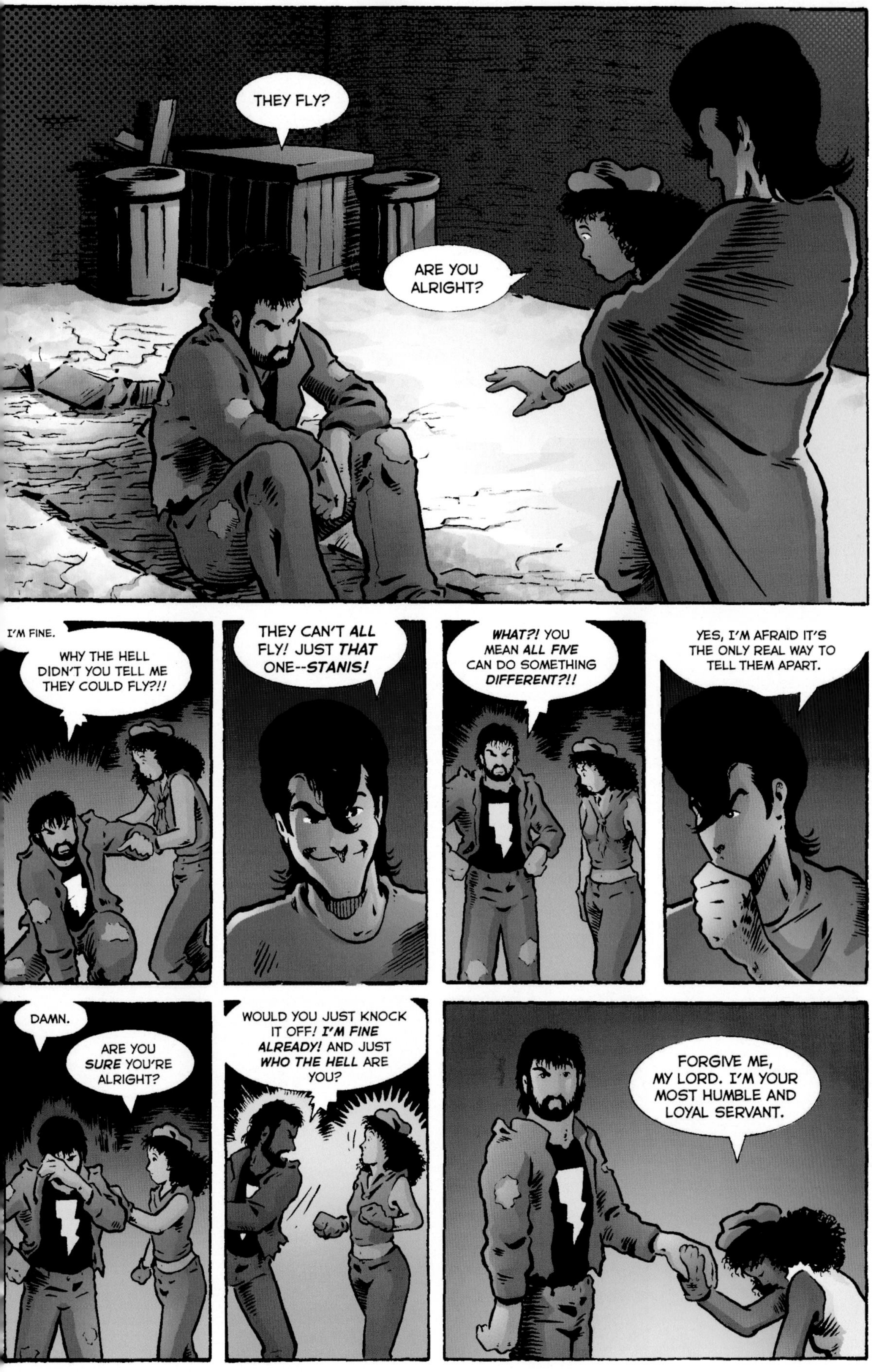
THEY FLY?
ARE YOU ALRIGHT?
I'M FINE.
WHY THE HELL DIDN'T YOU TELL ME THEY COULD FLY?!!
THEY CAN'T ALL FLY! JUST THAT ONE--STANIS!
WHAT?! YOU MEAN ALL FIVE CAN DO SOMETHING DIFFERENT?!!
YES, I'M AFRAID IT'S THE ONLY REAL WAY TO TELL THEM APART.
DAMN.
ARE YOU SURE YOU'RE ALRIGHT?
WOULD YOU JUST KNOCK IT OFF! I'M FINE ALREADY! AND JUST WHO THE HELL ARE YOU?
FORGIVE ME, MY LORD. I'M YOUR MOST HUMBLE AND LOYAL SERVANT.

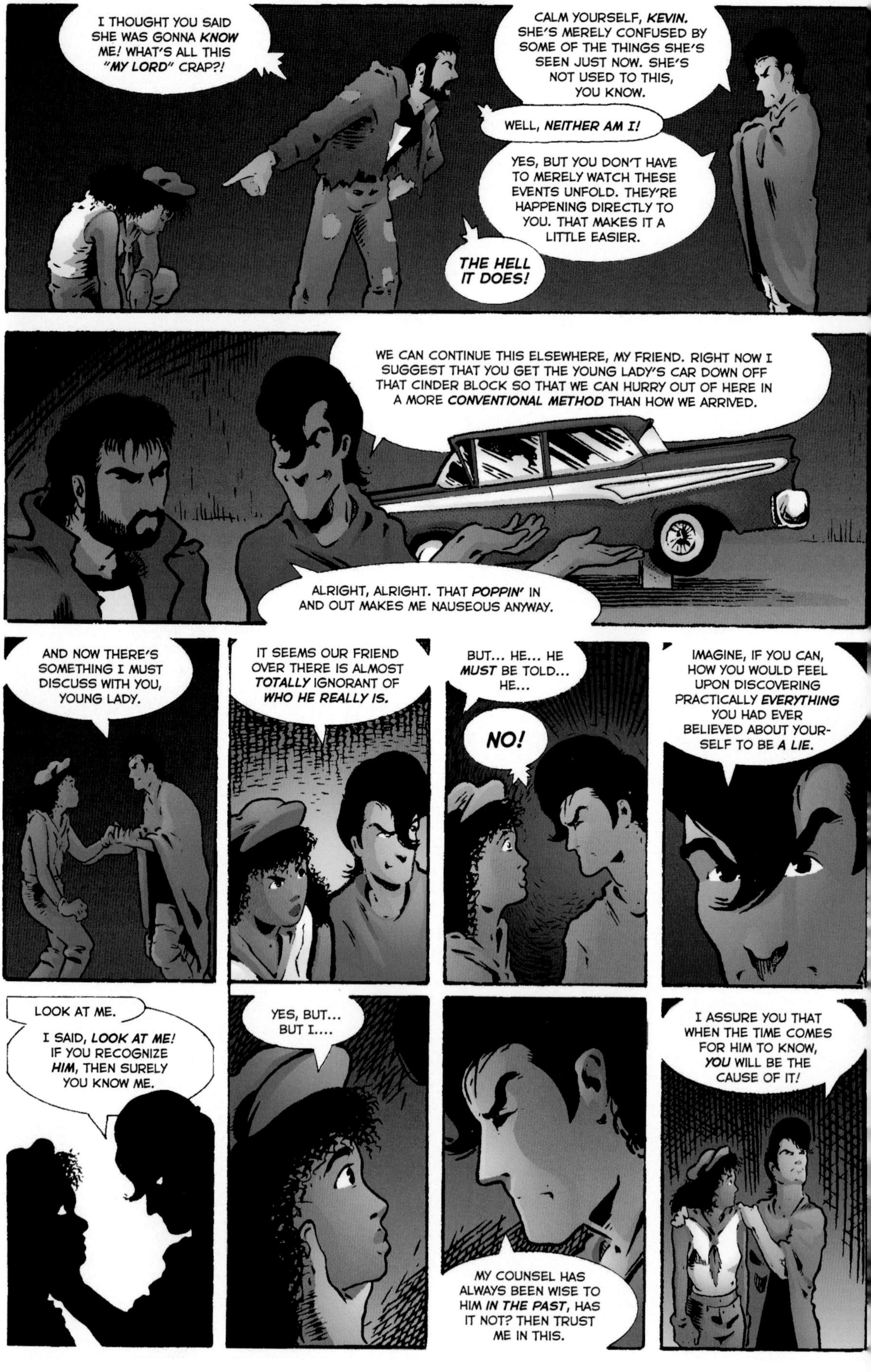

I THOUGHT YOU SAID SHE WAS GONNA KNOW ME! WHAT'S ALL THIS "MY LORD" CRAP?!
CALM YOURSELF, KEVIN. SHE'S MERELY CONFUSED BY SOME OF THE THINGS SHE'S SEEN JUST NOW. SHE'S NOT USED TO THIS, YOU KNOW.
WELL, NEITHER AM I!
YES, BUT YOU DON'T HAVE TO MERELY WATCH THESE EVENTS UNFOLD. THEY'RE HAPPENING DIRECTLY TO YOU. THAT MAKES IT A LITTLE EASIER.
THE HELL IT DOES!
WE CAN CONTINUE THIS ELSEWHERE, MY FRIEND. RIGHT NOW I SUGGEST THAT YOU GET THE YOUNG LADY'S CAR DOWN OFF THAT CINDER BLOCK SO THAT WE CAN HURRY OUT OF HERE IN A MORE CONVENTIONAL METHOD THAN HOW WE ARRIVED.
ALRIGHT, ALRIGHT. THAT POPPIN' IN AND OUT MAKES ME NAUSEOUS ANYWAY.
AND NOW THERE'S SOMETHING I MUST DISCUSS WITH YOU, YOUNG LADY.
IT SEEMS OUR FRIEND OVER THERE IS ALMOST TOTALLY IGNORANT OF WHO HE REALLY IS.
BUT... HE... HE MUST BE TOLD... HE...
NO!
IMAGINE, IF YOU CAN, HOW YOU WOULD FEEL UPON DISCOVERING PRACTICALLY EVERYTHING YOU HAD EVER BELIEVED ABOUT YOURSELF TO BE A LIE.
LOOK AT ME.
I SAID, LOOK AT ME! IF YOU RECOGNIZE HIM, THEN SURELY YOU KNOW ME.
YES, BUT... BUT I....
MY COUNSEL HAS ALWAYS BEEN WISE TO HIM IN THE PAST, HAS IT NOT? THEN TRUST ME IN THIS.
I ASSURE YOU THAT WHEN THE TIME COMES FOR HIM TO KNOW, YOU WILL BE THE CAUSE OF IT!

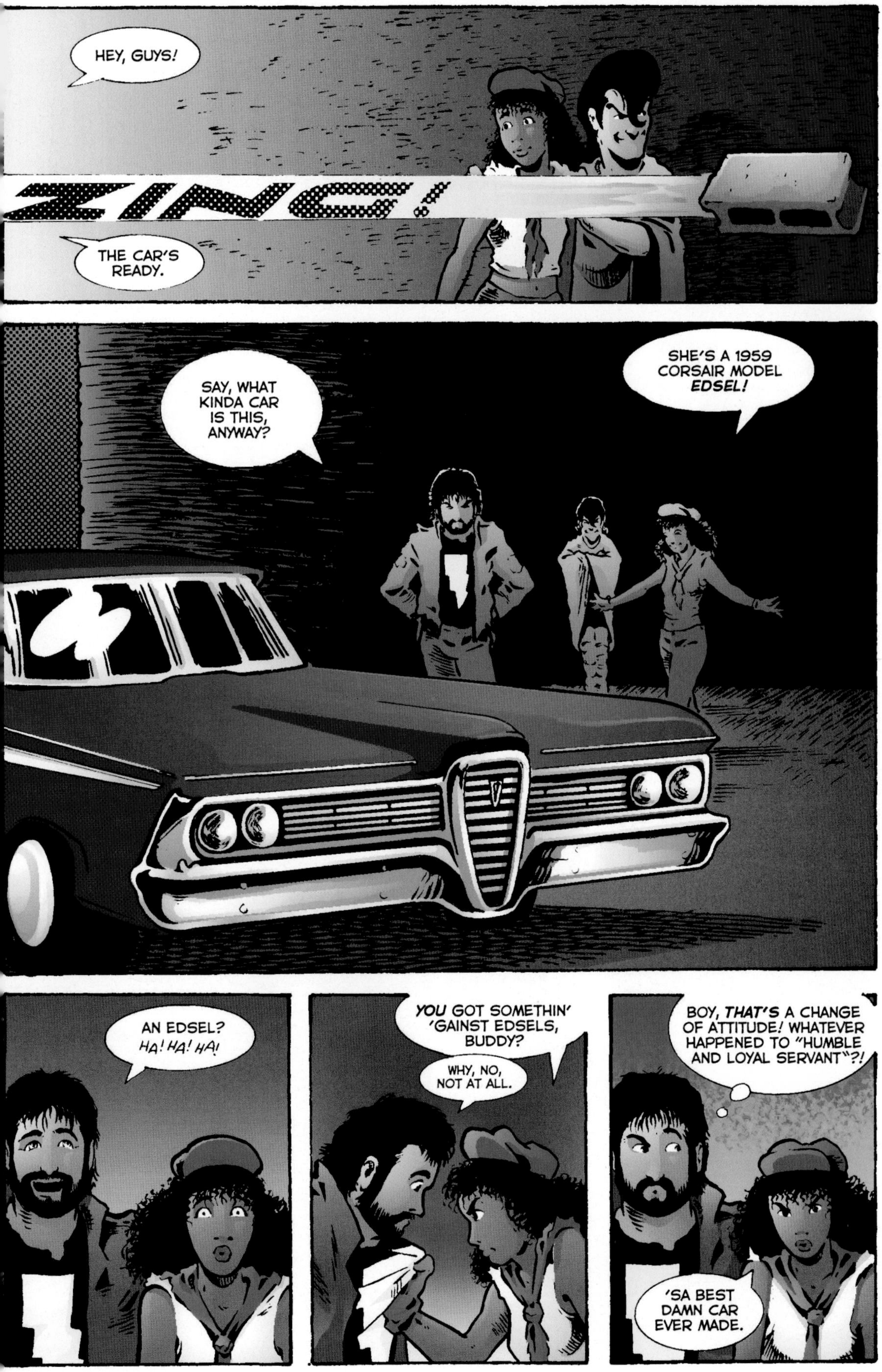
HEY, GUYS!
ZING!
THE CAR'S READY.
SAY, WHAT KINDA CAR IS THIS, ANYWAY?
SHE'S A 1959 CORSAIR MODEL EDSEL!
AN EDSEL? HA! HA! HA!
YOU GOT SOMETHIN' 'GAINST EDSELS, BUDDY?
WHY, NO, NOT AT ALL.
BOY, THAT'S A CHANGE OF ATTITUDE! WHATEVER HAPPENED TO "HUMBLE AND LOYAL SERVANT"?!
'SA BEST DAMN CAR EVER MADE.

13

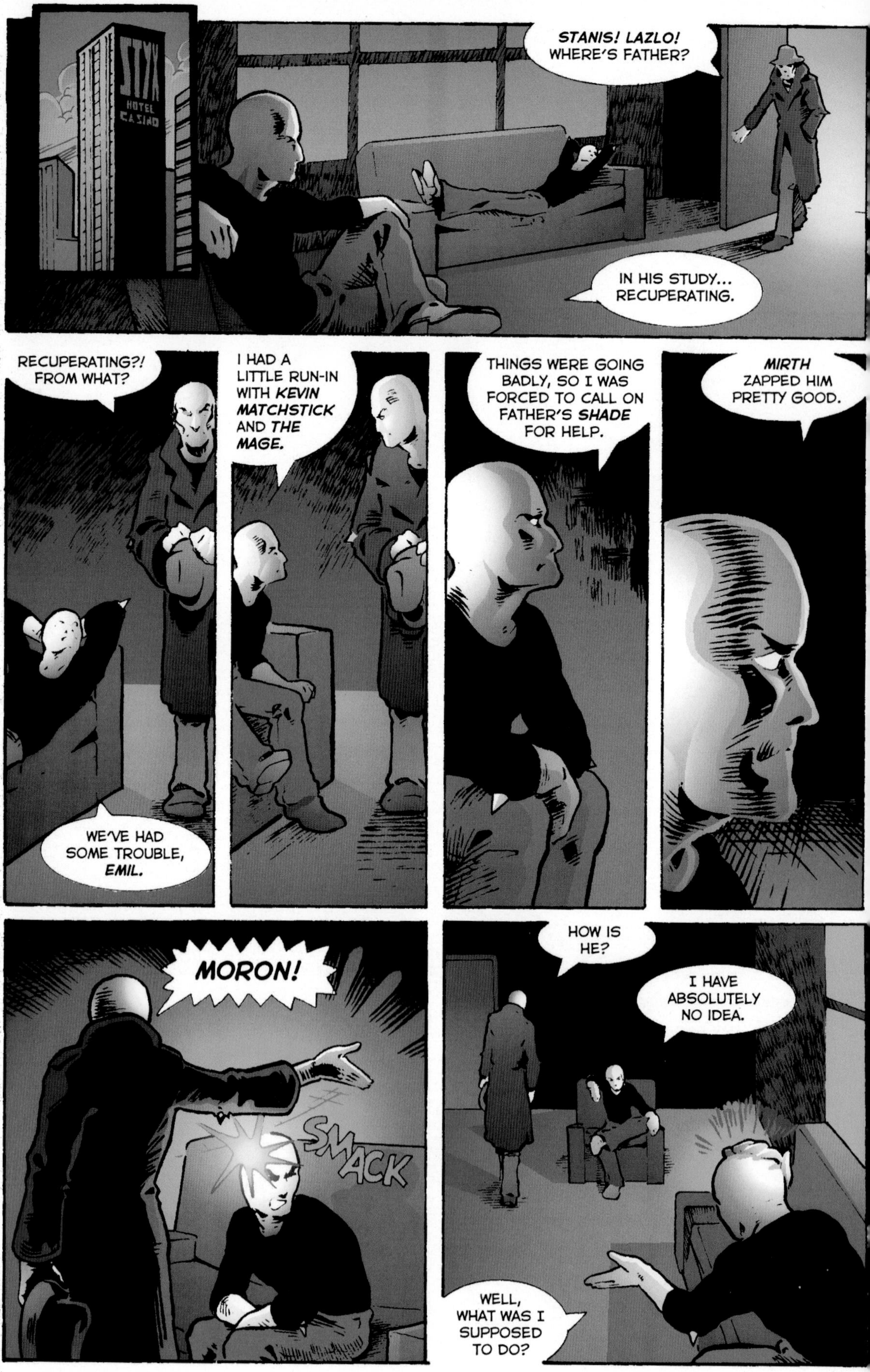
STYX HOTEL CASINO
STANIS! LAZLO! WHERE'S FATHER?
IN HIS STUDY... RECUPERATING.
RECUPERATING?! FROM WHAT?
WE'VE HAD SOME TROUBLE, EMIL.
I HAD A LITTLE RUN-IN WITH KEVIN MATCHSTICK AND THE MAGE.
THINGS WERE GOING BADLY, SO I WAS FORCED TO CALL ON FATHER'S SHADE FOR HELP.
MIRTH ZAPPED HIM PRETTY GOOD.
MORON!
SMACK
HOW IS HE?
I HAVE ABSOLUTELY NO IDEA.
WELL, WHAT WAS I SUPPOSED TO DO?

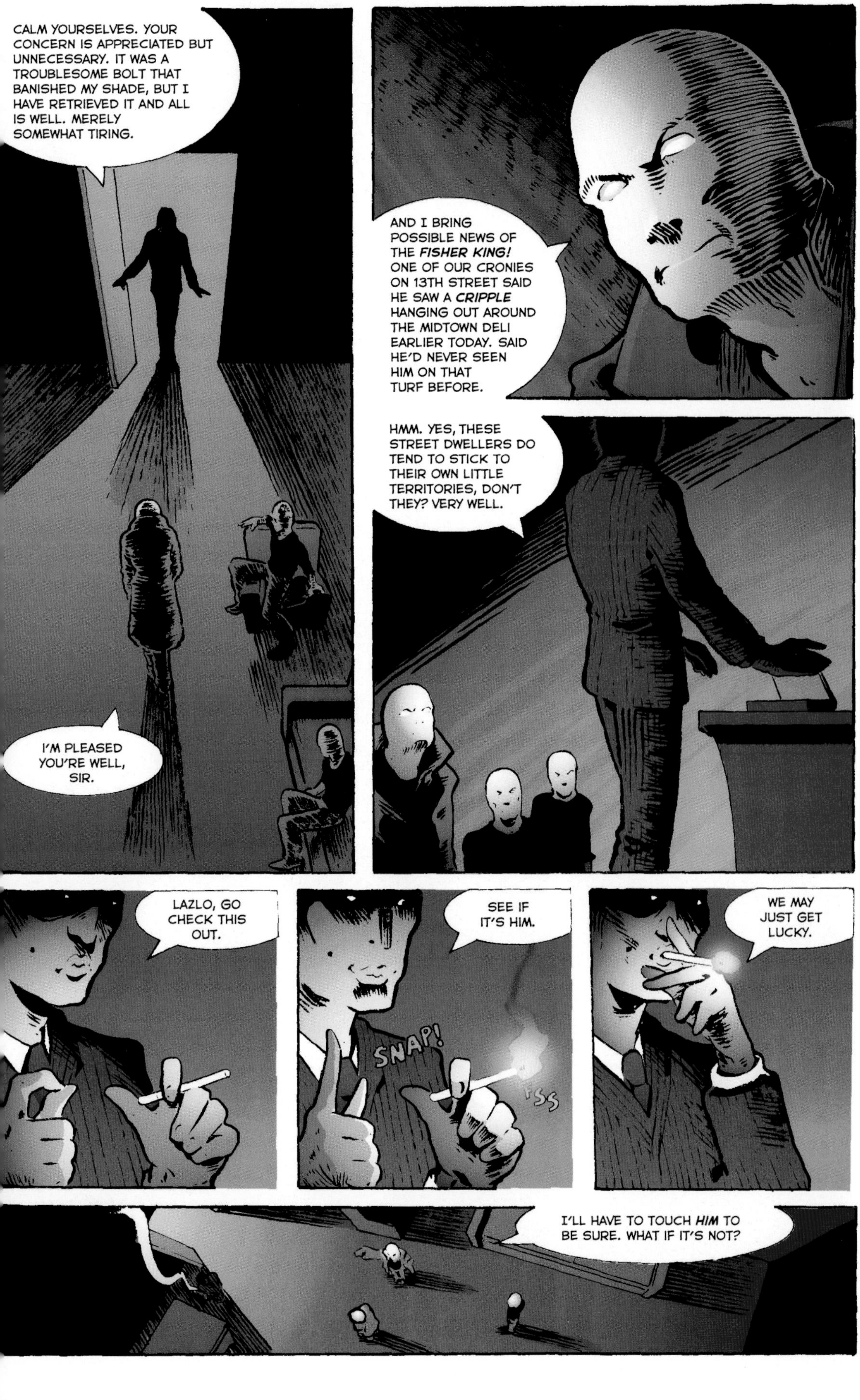
CALM YOURSELVES. YOUR CONCERN IS APPRECIATED BUT UNNECESSARY. IT WAS A TROUBLESOME BOLT THAT BANISHED MY SHADE, BUT I HAVE RETRIEVED IT AND ALL IS WELL. MERELY SOMEWHAT TIRING.
I'M PLEASED YOU'RE WELL, SIR.
AND I BRING POSSIBLE NEWS OF THE *FISHER KING!* ONE OF OUR CRONIES ON 13TH STREET SAID HE SAW A *CRIPPLE* HANGING OUT AROUND THE MIDTOWN DELI EARLIER TODAY. SAID HE'D NEVER SEEN HIM ON THAT TURF BEFORE.
HMM. YES, THESE STREET DWELLERS DO TEND TO STICK TO THEIR OWN LITTLE TERRITORIES, DON'T THEY? VERY WELL.
LAZLO, GO CHECK THIS OUT.
SEE IF IT'S HIM.
SNAP!
FSS
WE MAY JUST GET LUCKY.
I'LL HAVE TO TOUCH *HIM* TO BE SURE. WHAT IF IT'S NOT?

KILL HIM ANYWAY.

IF HE IS JUST A BEGGAR, NO ONE WILL MISS HIM.

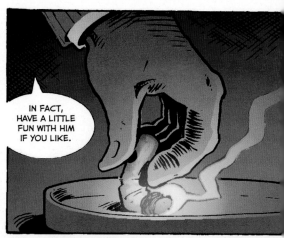

IN FACT, HAVE A LITTLE FUN WITH HIM IF YOU LIKE.

AND NOW, I MUST RETIRE AGAIN AND CONTINUE THE SUMMONING OF THE *MARHAULT OGRE*.

EMIL, YOU AND STANIS REMAIN HERE. I MAY NEED YOUR ASSISTANCE LATER.

YOU REMEMBER HOW UNPLEASANT IT WAS *TRAVELLING* TO THIS WRETCHED LITTLE PLANE?

WELL, SUMMONING SOMETHING TO IT IS MUCH, *MUCH WORSE!*

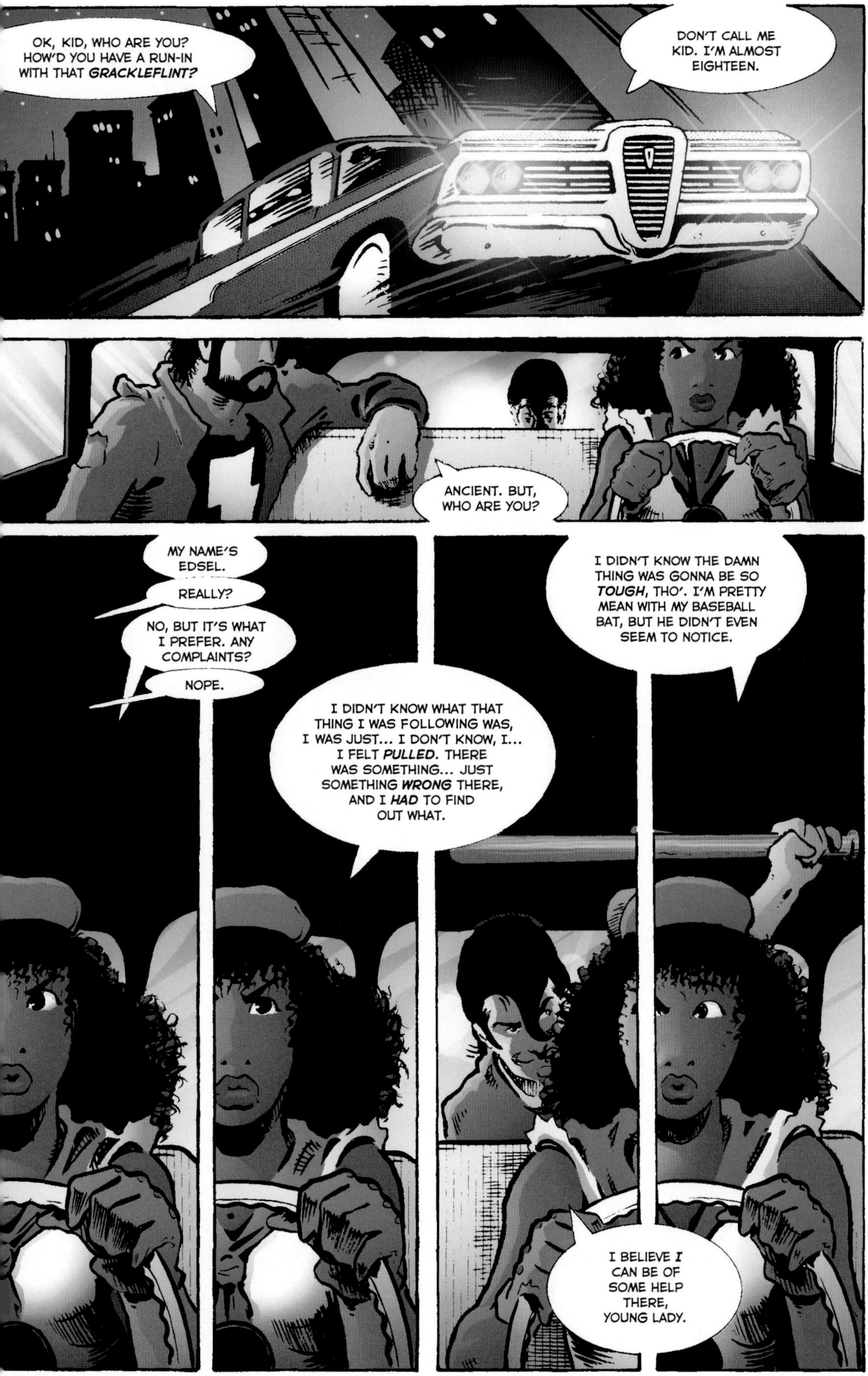
OK, KID, WHO ARE YOU? HOW'D YOU HAVE A RUN-IN WITH THAT *GRACKLEFLINT?*
DON'T CALL ME KID. I'M ALMOST EIGHTEEN.
ANCIENT. BUT, WHO ARE YOU?
MY NAME'S EDSEL.
REALLY?
NO, BUT IT'S WHAT I PREFER. ANY COMPLAINTS?
NOPE.
I DIDN'T KNOW WHAT THAT THING I WAS FOLLOWING WAS, I WAS JUST... I DON'T KNOW, I... I FELT *PULLED*. THERE WAS SOMETHING... JUST SOMETHING *WRONG* THERE, AND I *HAD* TO FIND OUT WHAT.
I DIDN'T KNOW THE DAMN THING WAS GONNA BE SO *TOUGH*, THO'. I'M PRETTY MEAN WITH MY BASEBALL BAT, BUT HE DIDN'T EVEN SEEM TO NOTICE.
I BELIEVE *I* CAN BE OF SOME HELP THERE, YOUNG LADY.

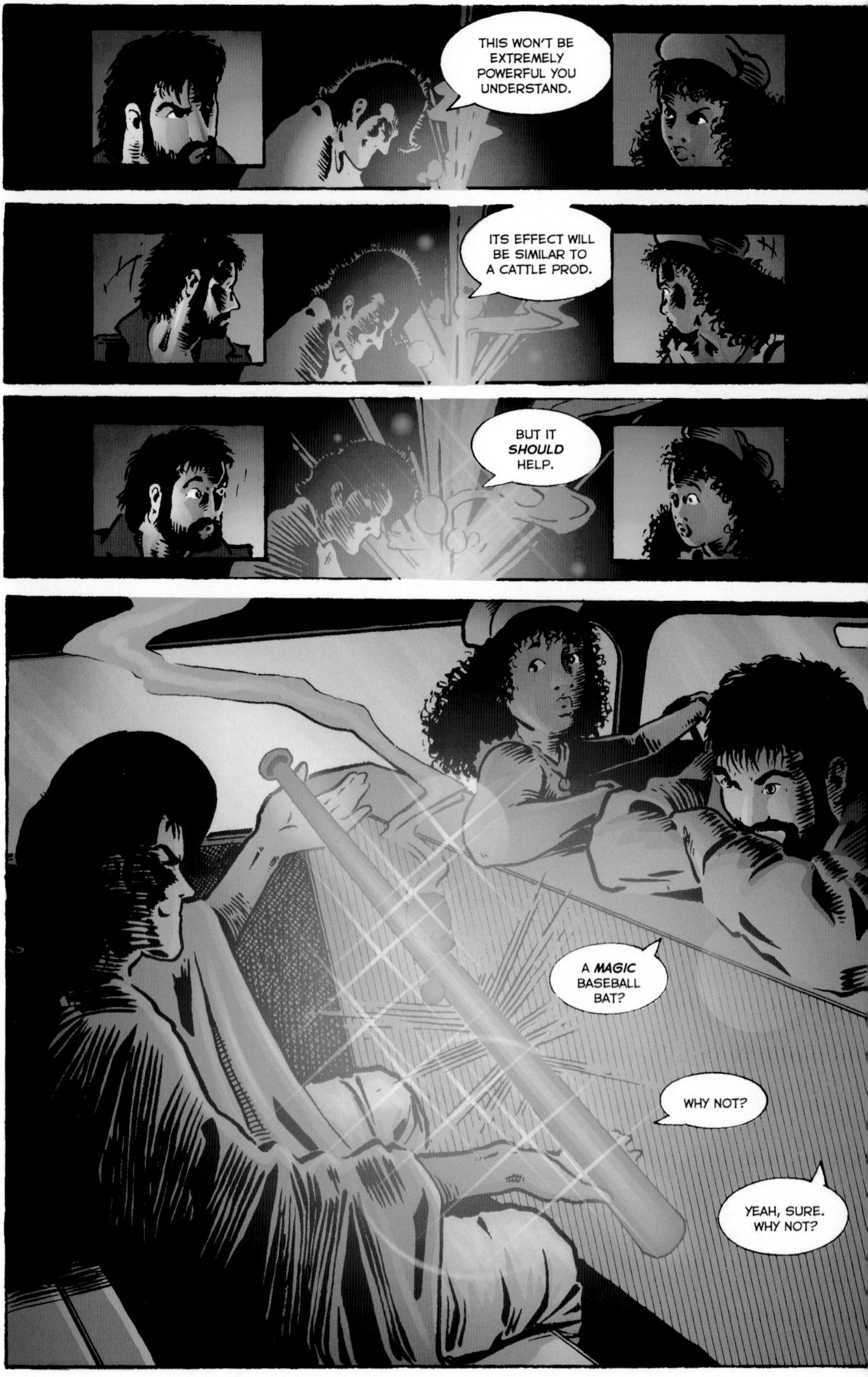
THIS WON'T BE EXTREMELY POWERFUL YOU UNDERSTAND.
ITS EFFECT WILL BE SIMILAR TO A CATTLE PROD.
BUT IT *SHOULD* HELP.
A *MAGIC* BASEBALL BAT?
WHY NOT?
YEAH, SURE. WHY NOT?

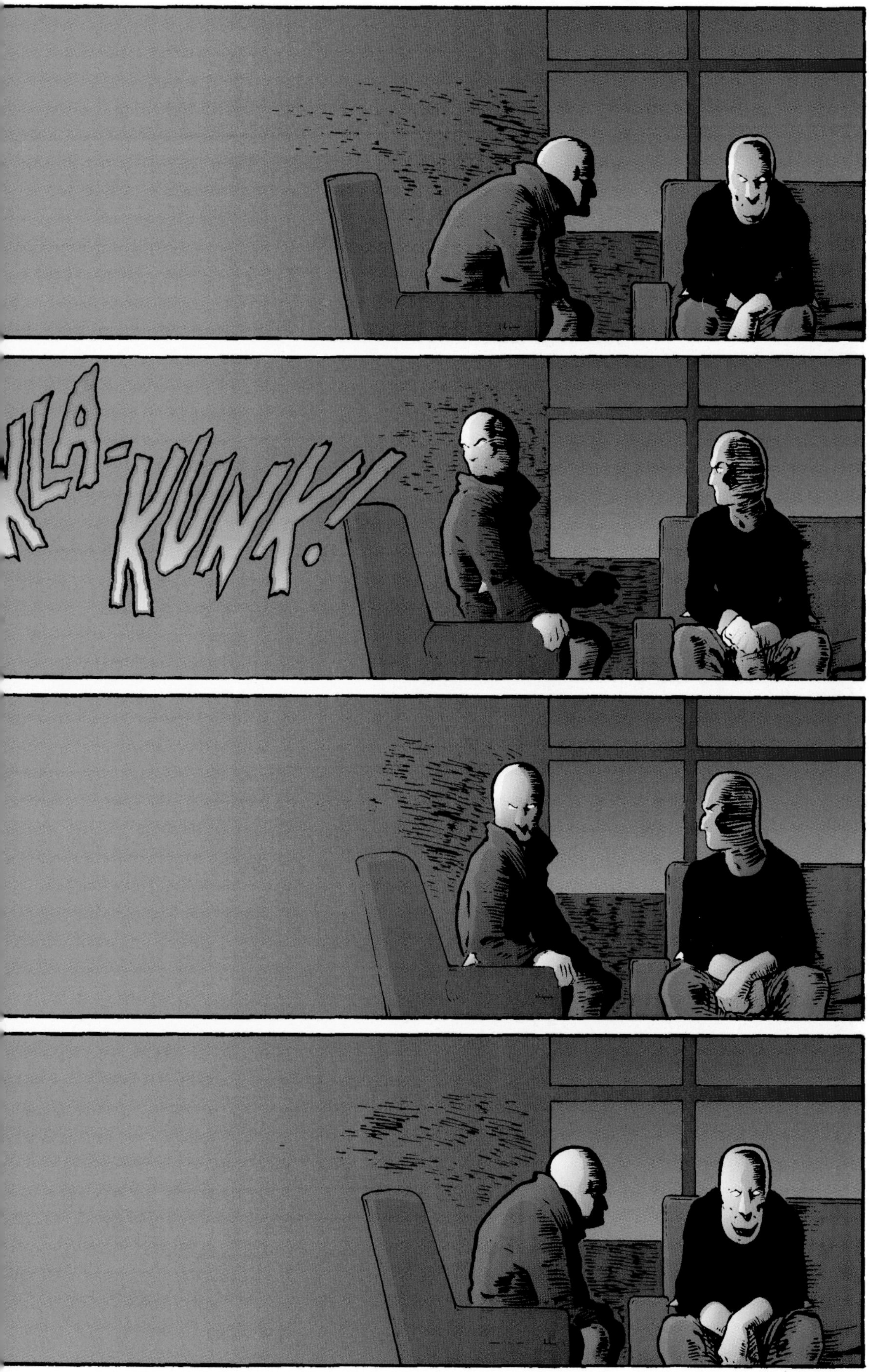
KLLA-KUNK!!

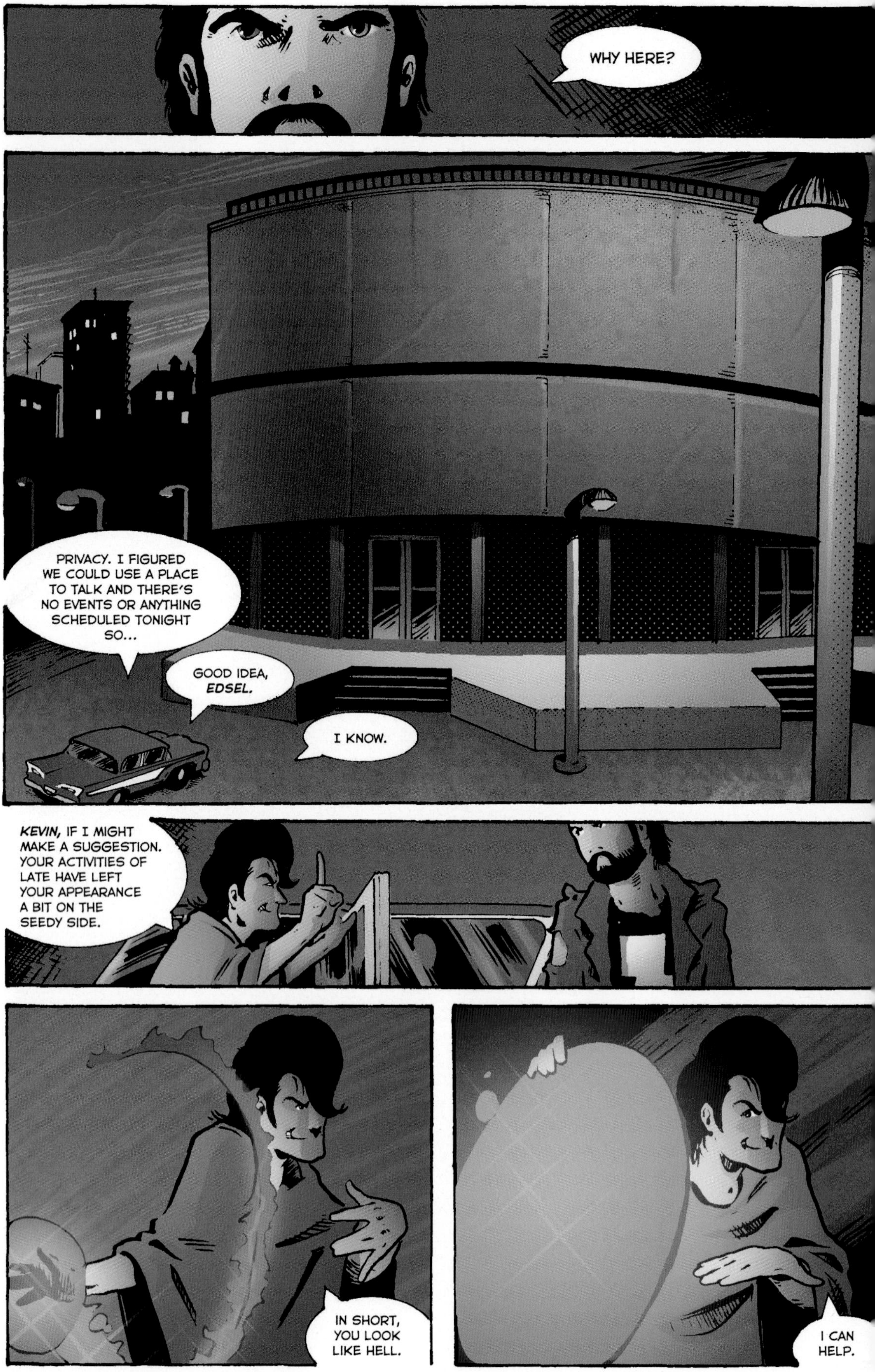
WHY HERE?
PRIVACY. I FIGURED WE COULD USE A PLACE TO TALK AND THERE'S NO EVENTS OR ANYTHING SCHEDULED TONIGHT SO...
GOOD IDEA, EDSEL.
I KNOW.
KEVIN, IF I MIGHT MAKE A SUGGESTION. YOUR ACTIVITIES OF LATE HAVE LEFT YOUR APPEARANCE A BIT ON THE SEEDY SIDE.
IN SHORT, YOU LOOK LIKE HELL.
I CAN HELP.

NOW, OBSERVE.

INSTANT...

FIX-IT!

WOW! THAT'S NEAT!

EVER THOUGHT OF SHOWING THAT THING TO *RONCO* OR *K-TEL?* THEY'D *LOVE* IT!

NAH, DAMN THING CAN'T DO *JULIENNE FRIES!*

AND, NOW, MY FRIENDS, WE MUST DISCUSS THE EVENTS THAT HAVE LED TO THE FORMATION OF THIS LITTLE COMPANIONSHIP.

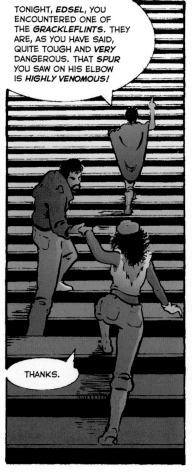

TONIGHT, *EDSEL*, YOU ENCOUNTERED ONE OF THE *GRACKLEFLINTS.* THEY ARE, AS YOU HAVE SAID, QUITE TOUGH AND *VERY* DANGEROUS. THAT *SPUR* YOU SAW ON HIS ELBOW IS *HIGHLY VENOMOUS!*

THANKS.

THERE ARE *FIVE* SUCH CREATURES IN THIS WORLD AND THEY ARE LED BY THEIR FATHER, THE *UMBRA SPRITE.*

MMM-- NICE NIGHT.

WELL, WHAT DO THEY WANT?

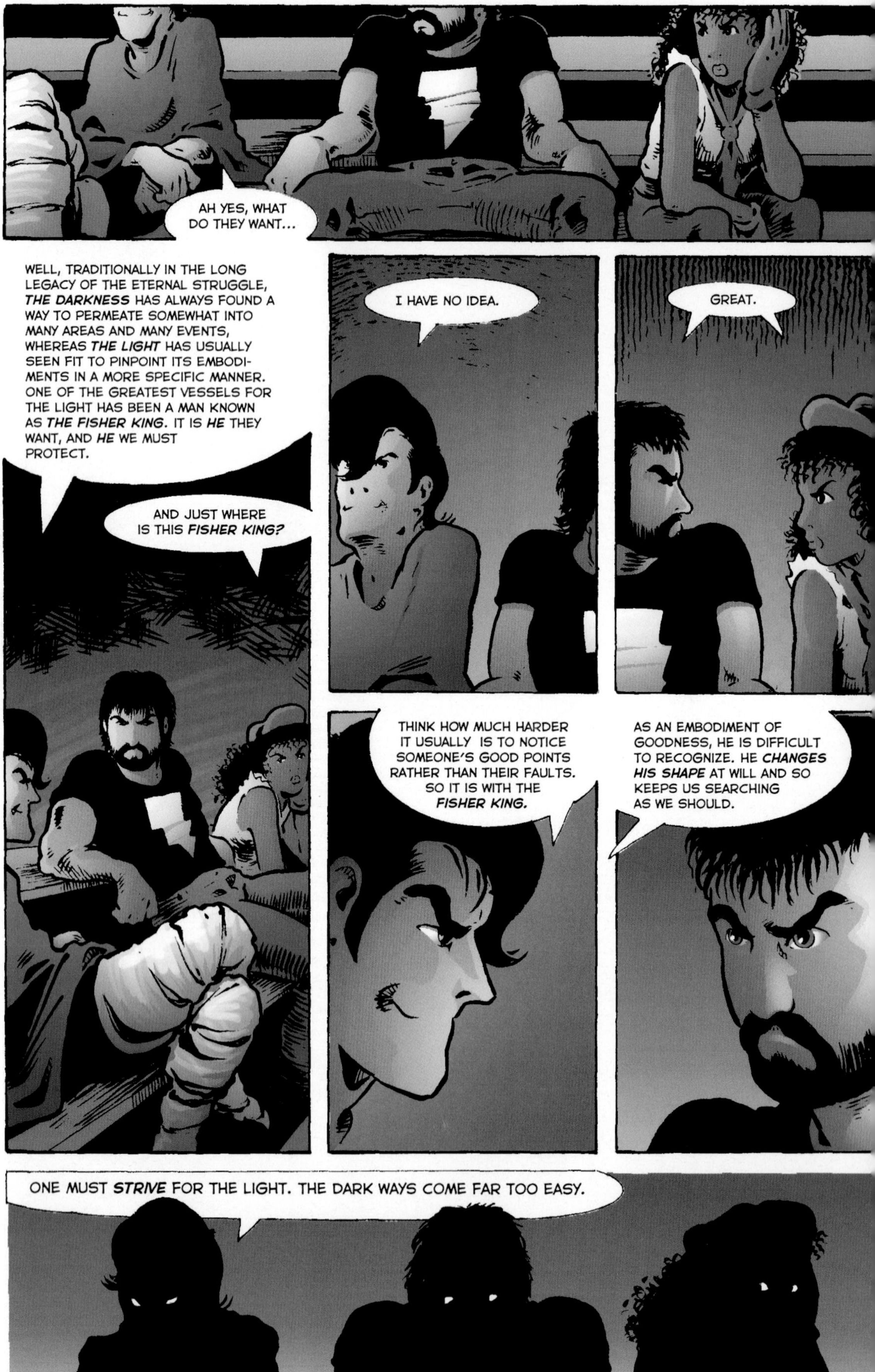
AH YES, WHAT DO THEY WANT...
WELL, TRADITIONALLY IN THE LONG LEGACY OF THE ETERNAL STRUGGLE, THE DARKNESS HAS ALWAYS FOUND A WAY TO PERMEATE SOMEWHAT INTO MANY AREAS AND MANY EVENTS, WHEREAS THE LIGHT HAS USUALLY SEEN FIT TO PINPOINT ITS EMBODIMENTS IN A MORE SPECIFIC MANNER. ONE OF THE GREATEST VESSELS FOR THE LIGHT HAS BEEN A MAN KNOWN AS THE FISHER KING. IT IS HE THEY WANT, AND HE WE MUST PROTECT.
AND JUST WHERE IS THIS FISHER KING?
I HAVE NO IDEA.
GREAT.
THINK HOW MUCH HARDER IT USUALLY IS TO NOTICE SOMEONE'S GOOD POINTS RATHER THAN THEIR FAULTS. SO IT IS WITH THE FISHER KING.
AS AN EMBODIMENT OF GOODNESS, HE IS DIFFICULT TO RECOGNIZE. HE CHANGES HIS SHAPE AT WILL AND SO KEEPS US SEARCHING AS WE SHOULD.
ONE MUST STRIVE FOR THE LIGHT. THE DARK WAYS COME FAR TOO EASY.

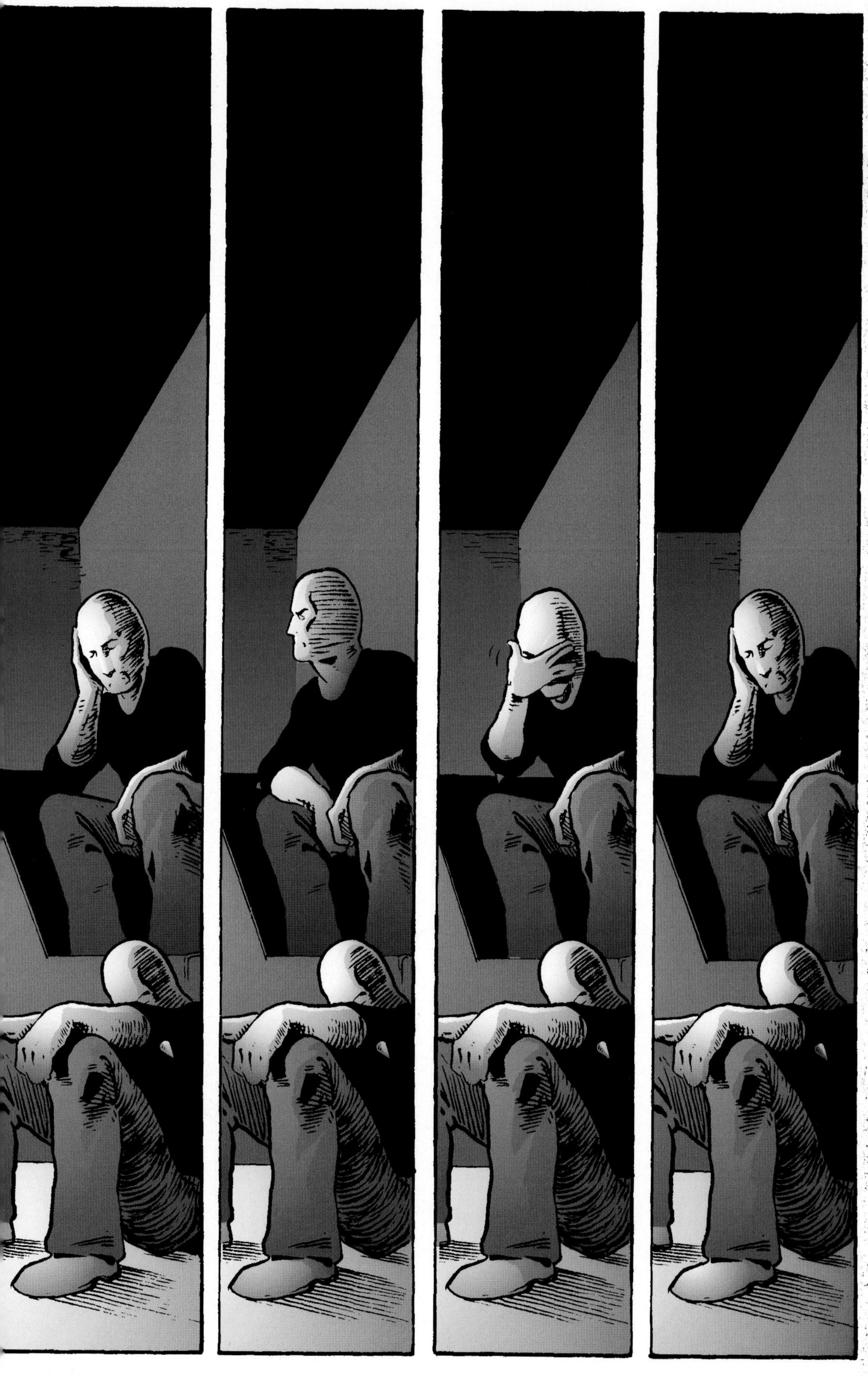

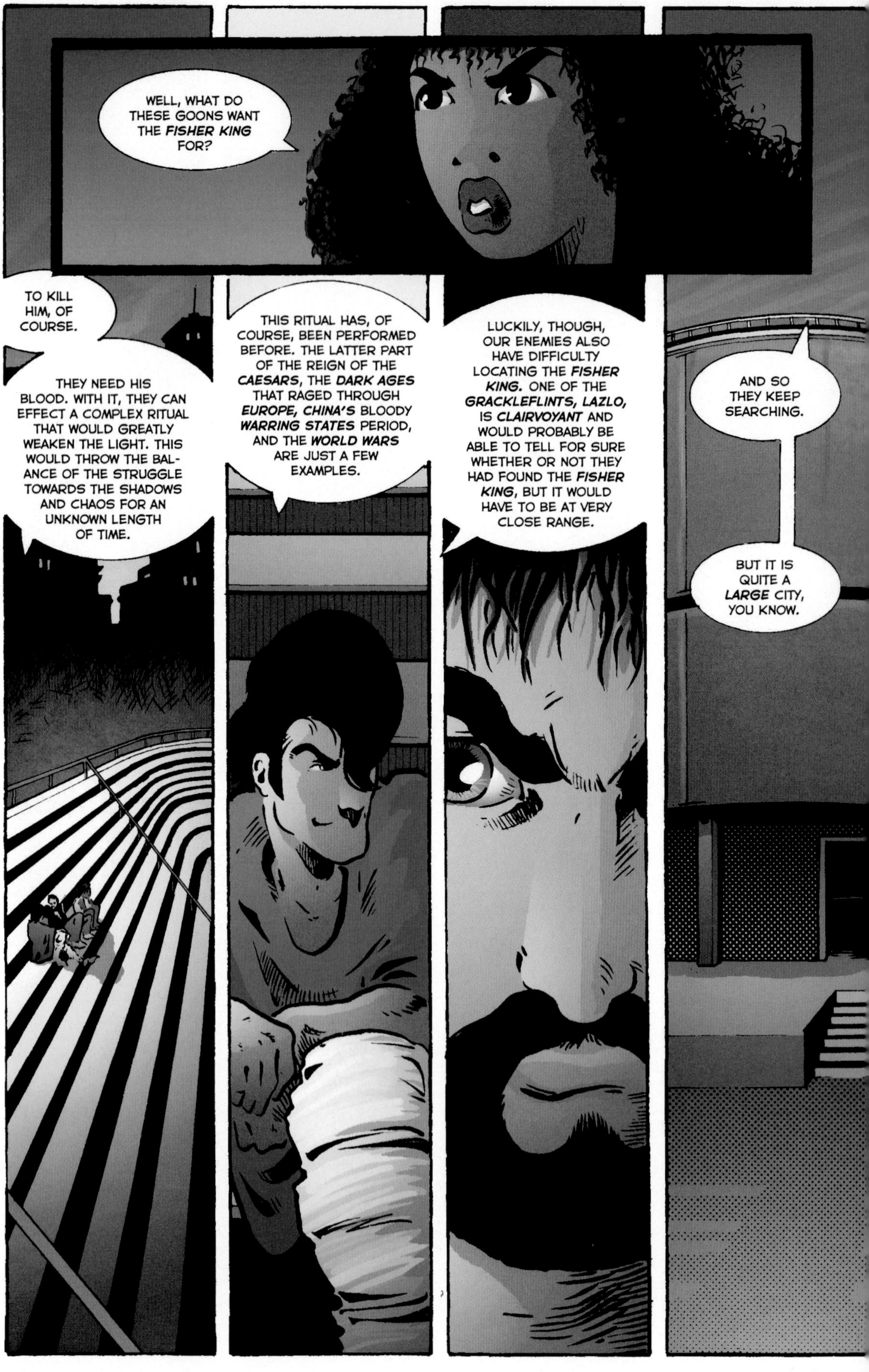
WELL, WHAT DO THESE GOONS WANT THE *FISHER KING* FOR?
TO KILL HIM, OF COURSE.
THEY NEED HIS BLOOD. WITH IT, THEY CAN EFFECT A COMPLEX RITUAL THAT WOULD GREATLY WEAKEN THE LIGHT. THIS WOULD THROW THE BALANCE OF THE STRUGGLE TOWARDS THE SHADOWS AND CHAOS FOR AN UNKNOWN LENGTH OF TIME.
THIS RITUAL HAS, OF COURSE, BEEN PERFORMED BEFORE. THE LATTER PART OF THE REIGN OF THE *CAESARS*, THE *DARK AGES* THAT RAGED THROUGH *EUROPE, CHINA'S* BLOODY *WARRING STATES* PERIOD, AND THE *WORLD WARS* ARE JUST A FEW EXAMPLES.
LUCKILY, THOUGH, OUR ENEMIES ALSO HAVE DIFFICULTY LOCATING THE *FISHER KING.* ONE OF THE *GRACKLEFLINTS, LAZLO,* IS *CLAIRVOYANT* AND WOULD PROBABLY BE ABLE TO TELL FOR SURE WHETHER OR NOT THEY HAD FOUND THE *FISHER KING,* BUT IT WOULD HAVE TO BE AT VERY CLOSE RANGE.
AND SO THEY KEEP SEARCHING.
BUT IT IS QUITE A *LARGE* CITY, YOU KNOW.

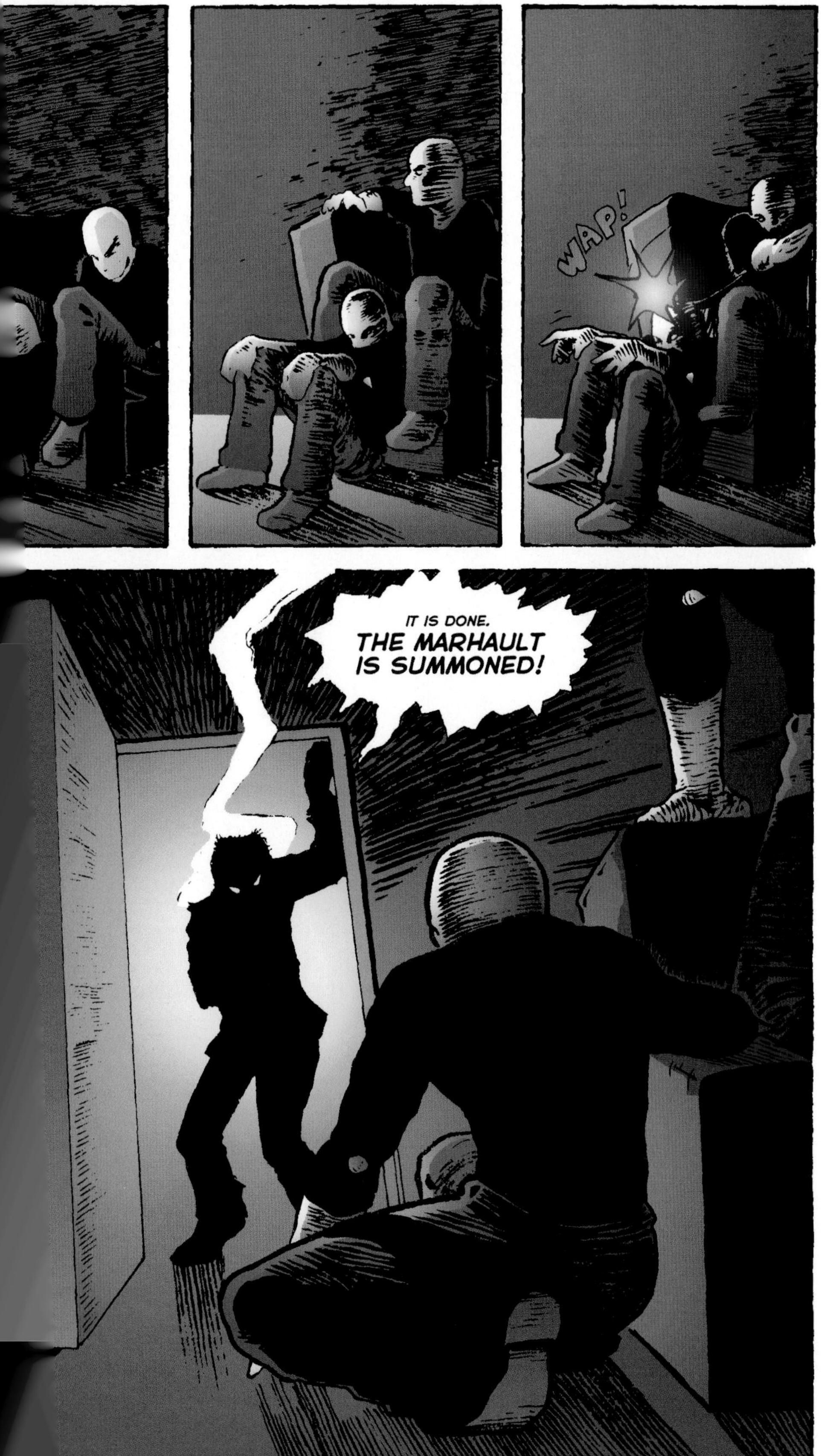
WAP!
IT IS DONE.
THE MARHAULT IS SUMMONED!

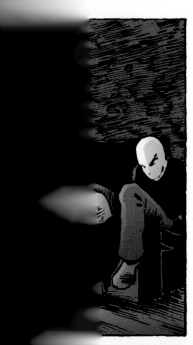

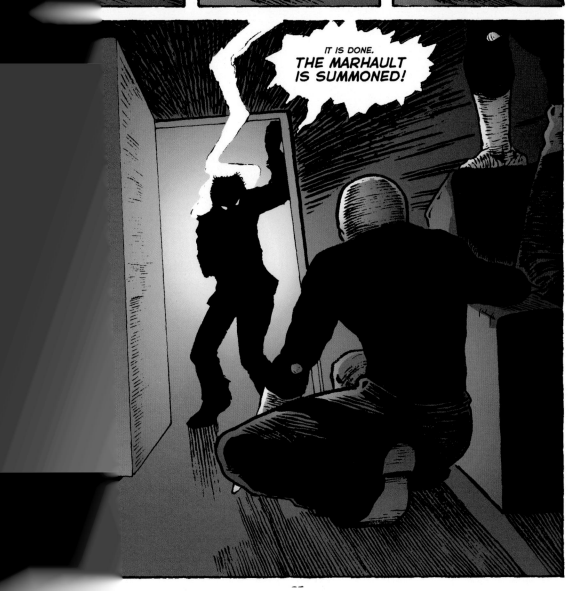

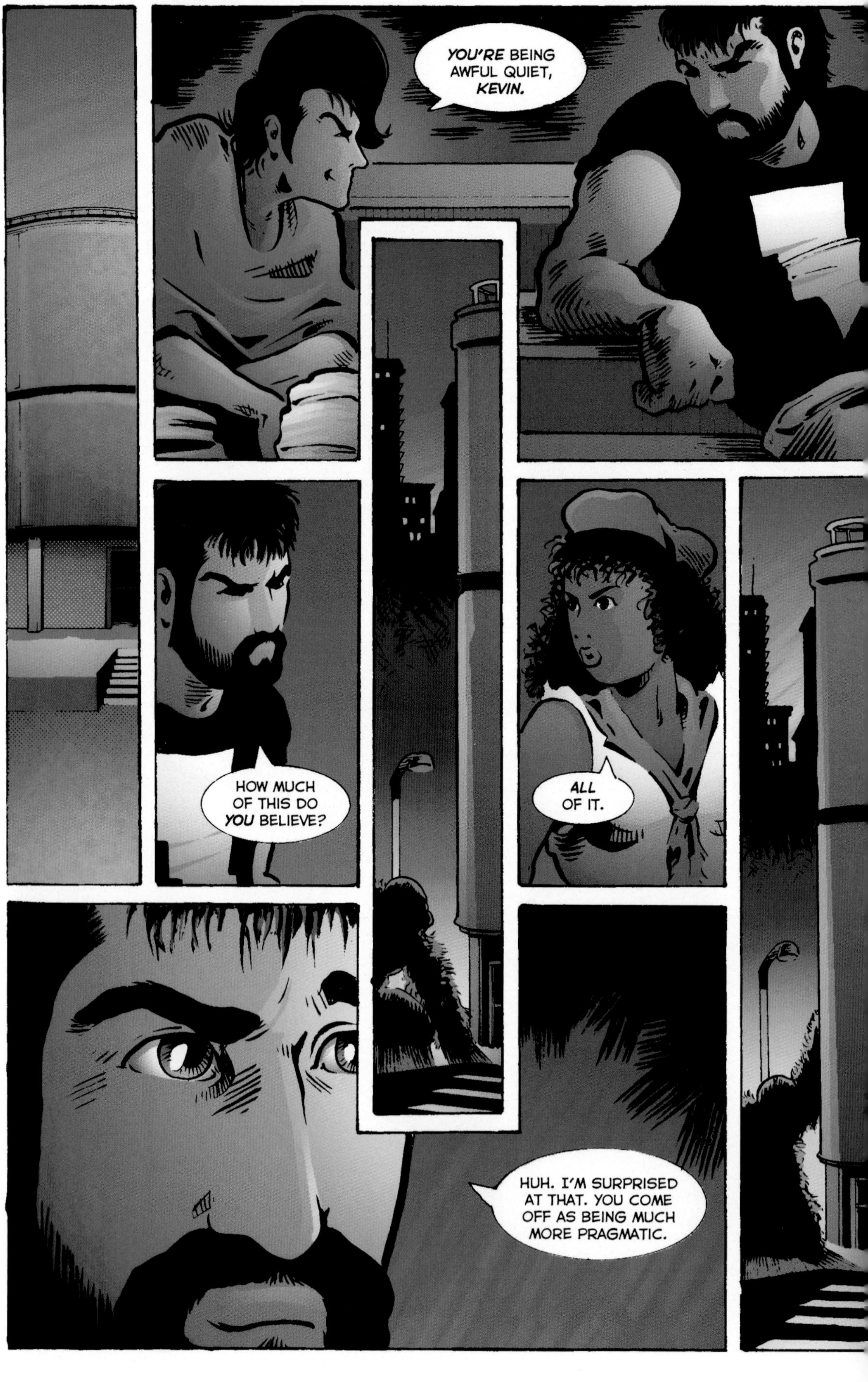
YOU'RE BEING AWFUL QUIET, KEVIN.
HOW MUCH OF THIS DO YOU BELIEVE?
ALL OF IT.
HUH. I'M SURPRISED AT THAT. YOU COME OFF AS BEING MUCH MORE PRAGMATIC.

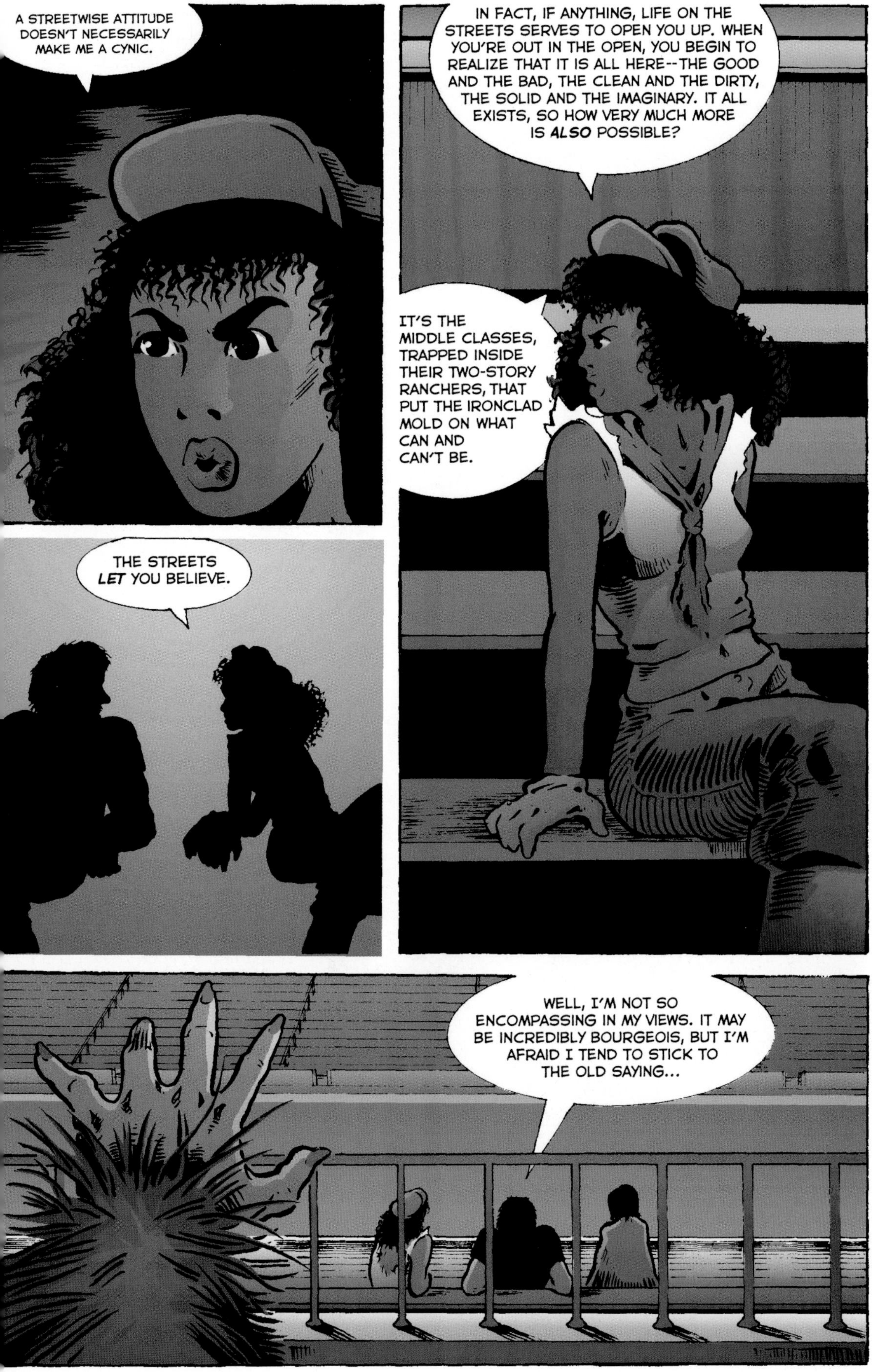
A STREETWISE ATTITUDE DOESN'T NECESSARILY MAKE ME A CYNIC.
IN FACT, IF ANYTHING, LIFE ON THE STREETS SERVES TO OPEN YOU UP. WHEN YOU'RE OUT IN THE OPEN, YOU BEGIN TO REALIZE THAT IT IS ALL HERE--THE GOOD AND THE BAD, THE CLEAN AND THE DIRTY, THE SOLID AND THE IMAGINARY. IT ALL EXISTS, SO HOW VERY MUCH MORE IS ALSO POSSIBLE?
IT'S THE MIDDLE CLASSES, TRAPPED INSIDE THEIR TWO-STORY RANCHERS, THAT PUT THE IRONCLAD MOLD ON WHAT CAN AND CAN'T BE.
THE STREETS LET YOU BELIEVE.
WELL, I'M NOT SO ENCOMPASSING IN MY VIEWS. IT MAY BE INCREDIBLY BOURGEOIS, BUT I'M AFRAID I TEND TO STICK TO THE OLD SAYING...

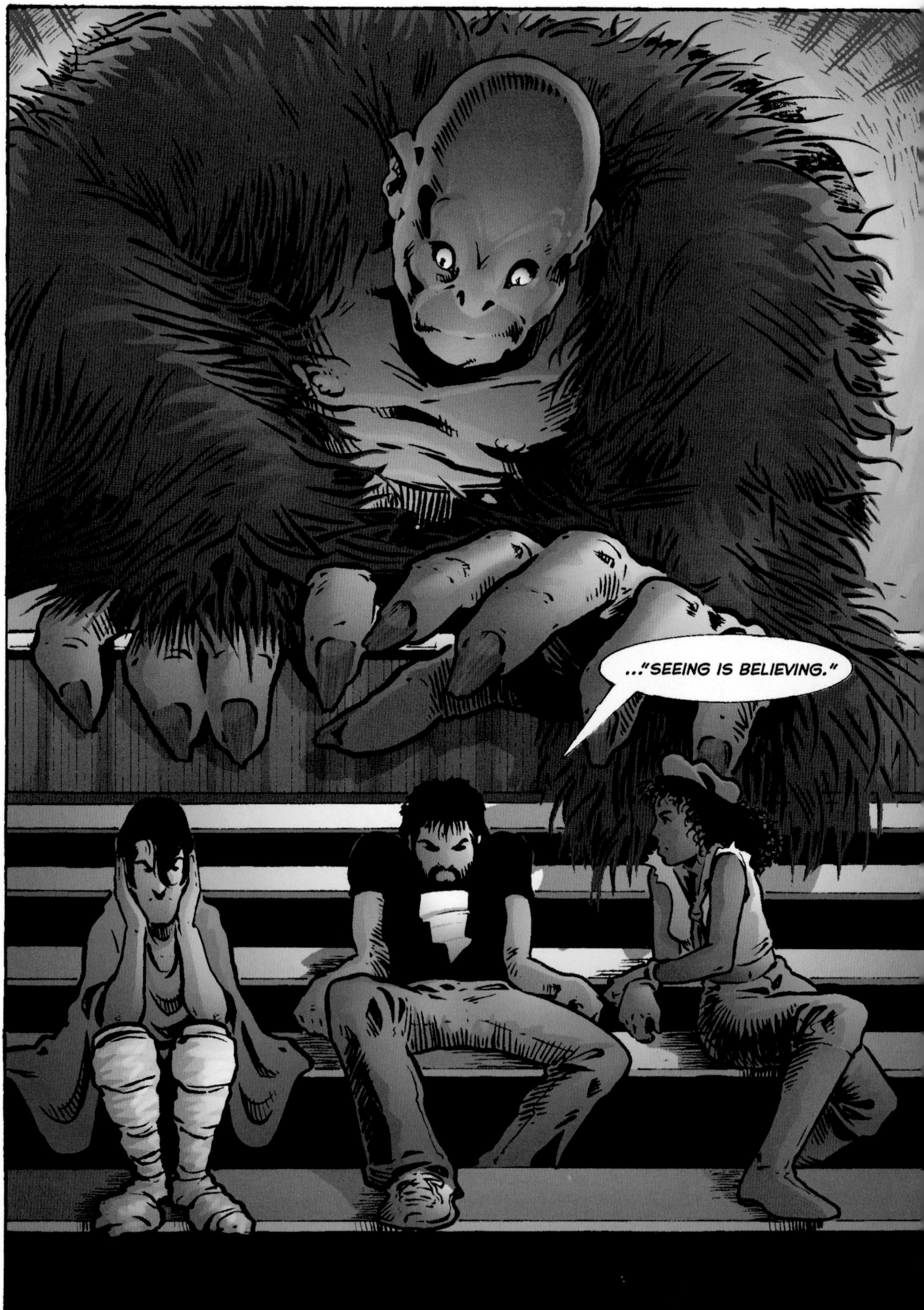
..."SEEING IS BELIEVING."

THE HERO DISCOVERED

Chapter 04

O, What A Rash And
Bloody Deed

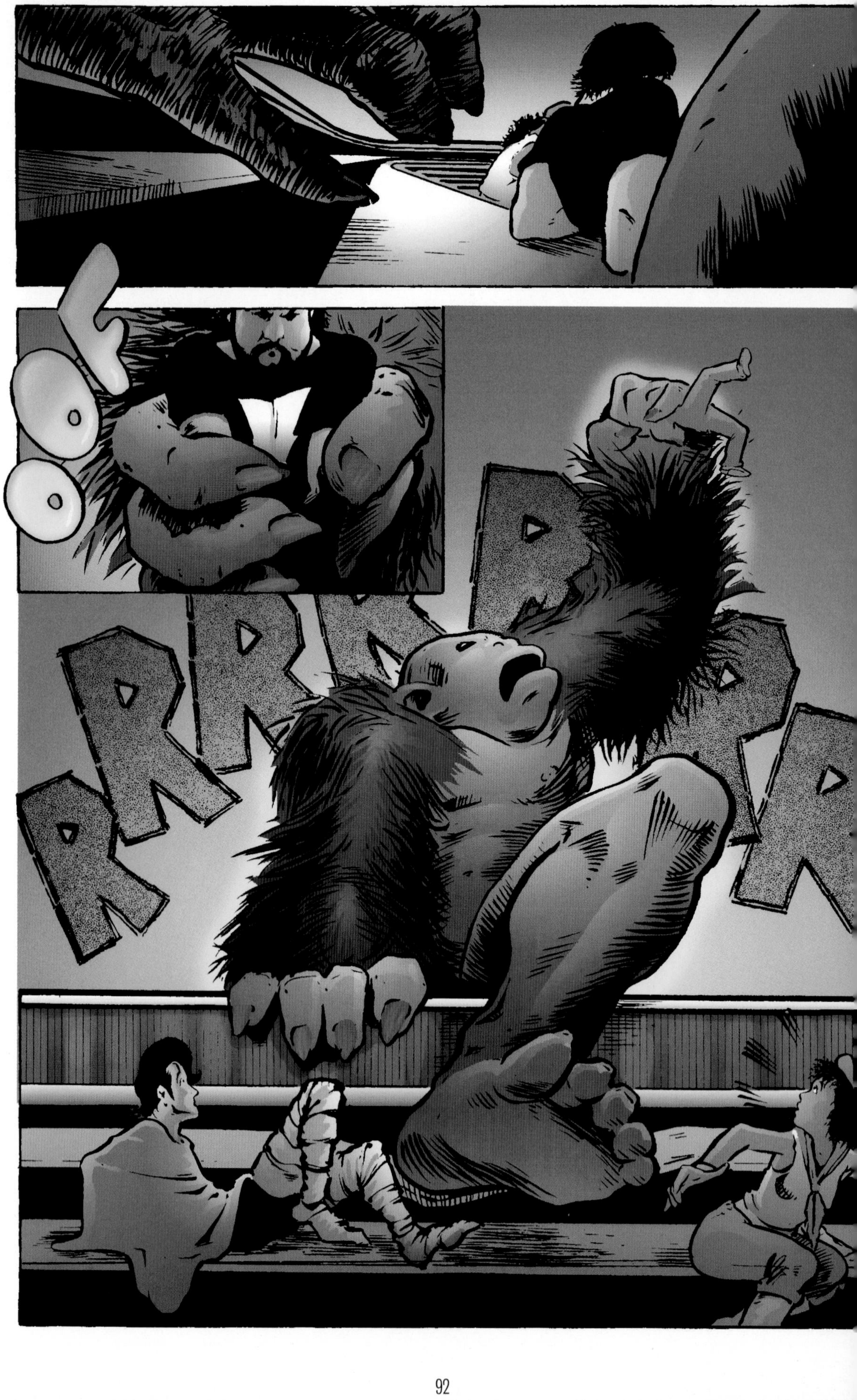
OOF
RRRRRR

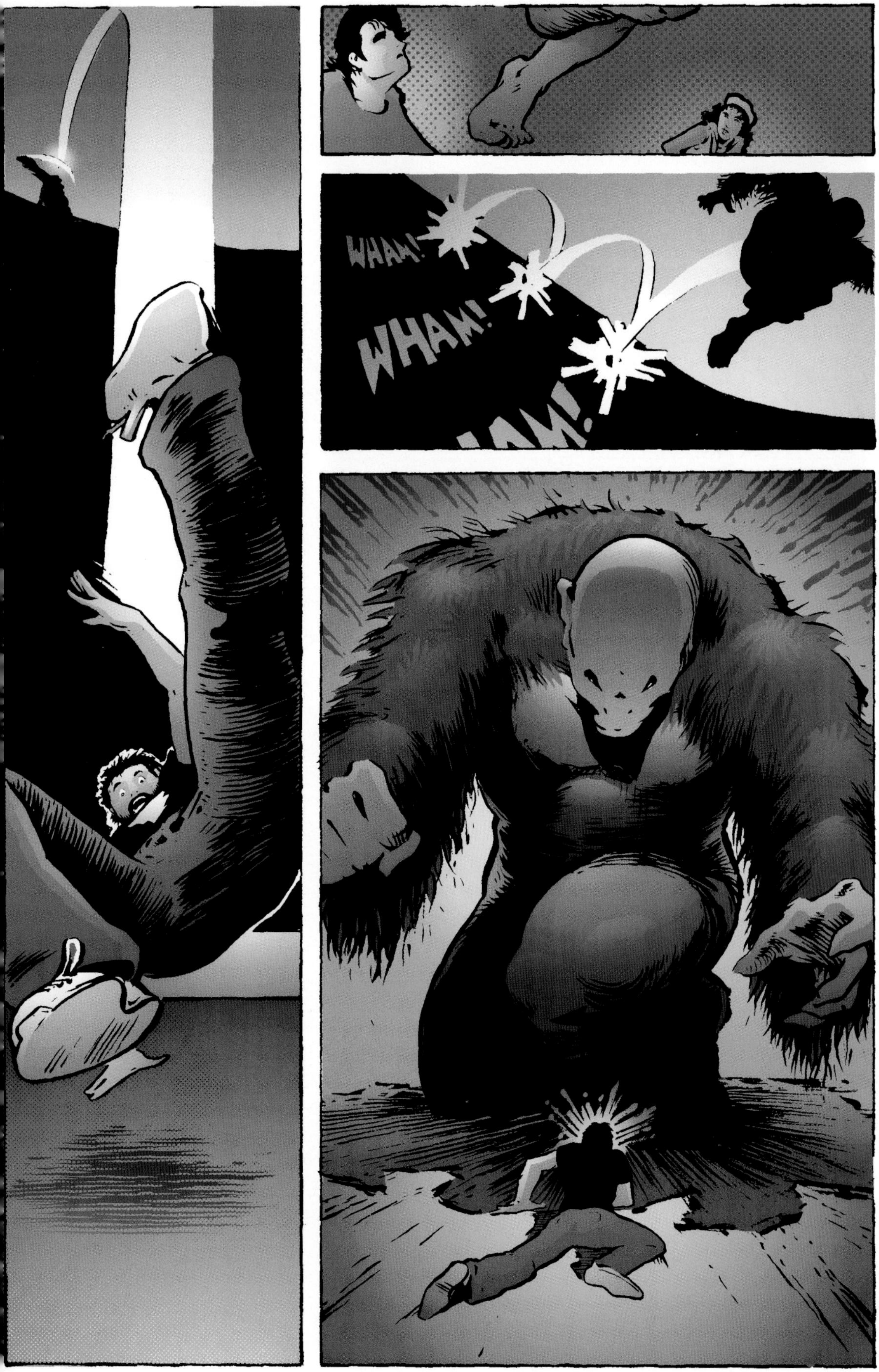
WHAM!
WHAM!

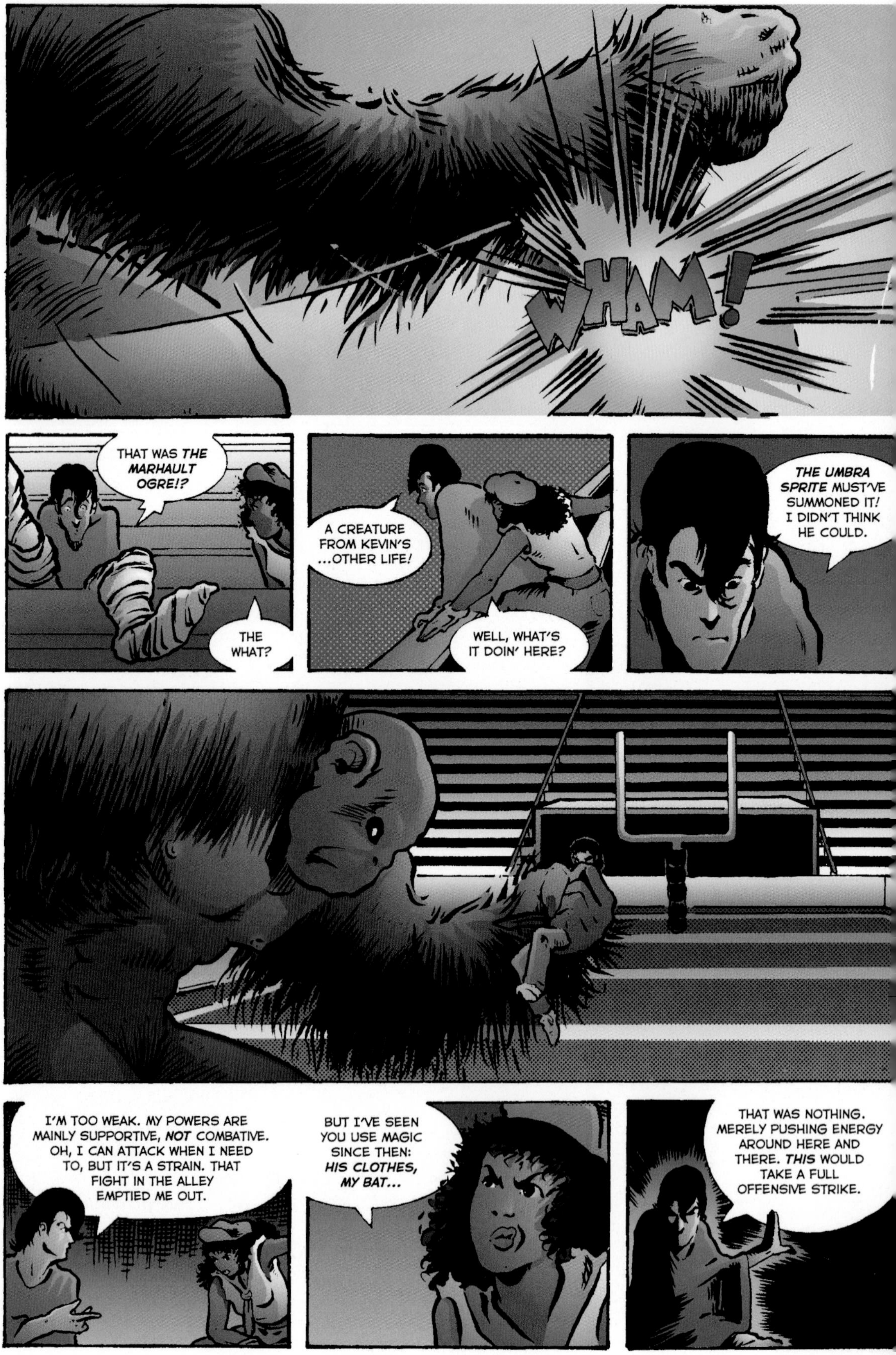
WHAM!
THAT WAS THE MARHAULT OGRE!?
THE WHAT?
A CREATURE FROM KEVIN'S ...OTHER LIFE!
WELL, WHAT'S IT DOIN' HERE?
THE UMBRA SPRITE MUST'VE SUMMONED IT! I DIDN'T THINK HE COULD.
I'M TOO WEAK. MY POWERS ARE MAINLY SUPPORTIVE, NOT COMBATIVE. OH, I CAN ATTACK WHEN I NEED TO, BUT IT'S A STRAIN. THAT FIGHT IN THE ALLEY EMPTIED ME OUT.
BUT I'VE SEEN YOU USE MAGIC SINCE THEN: HIS CLOTHES, MY BAT...
THAT WAS NOTHING. MERELY PUSHING ENERGY AROUND HERE AND THERE. THIS WOULD TAKE A FULL OFFENSIVE STRIKE.

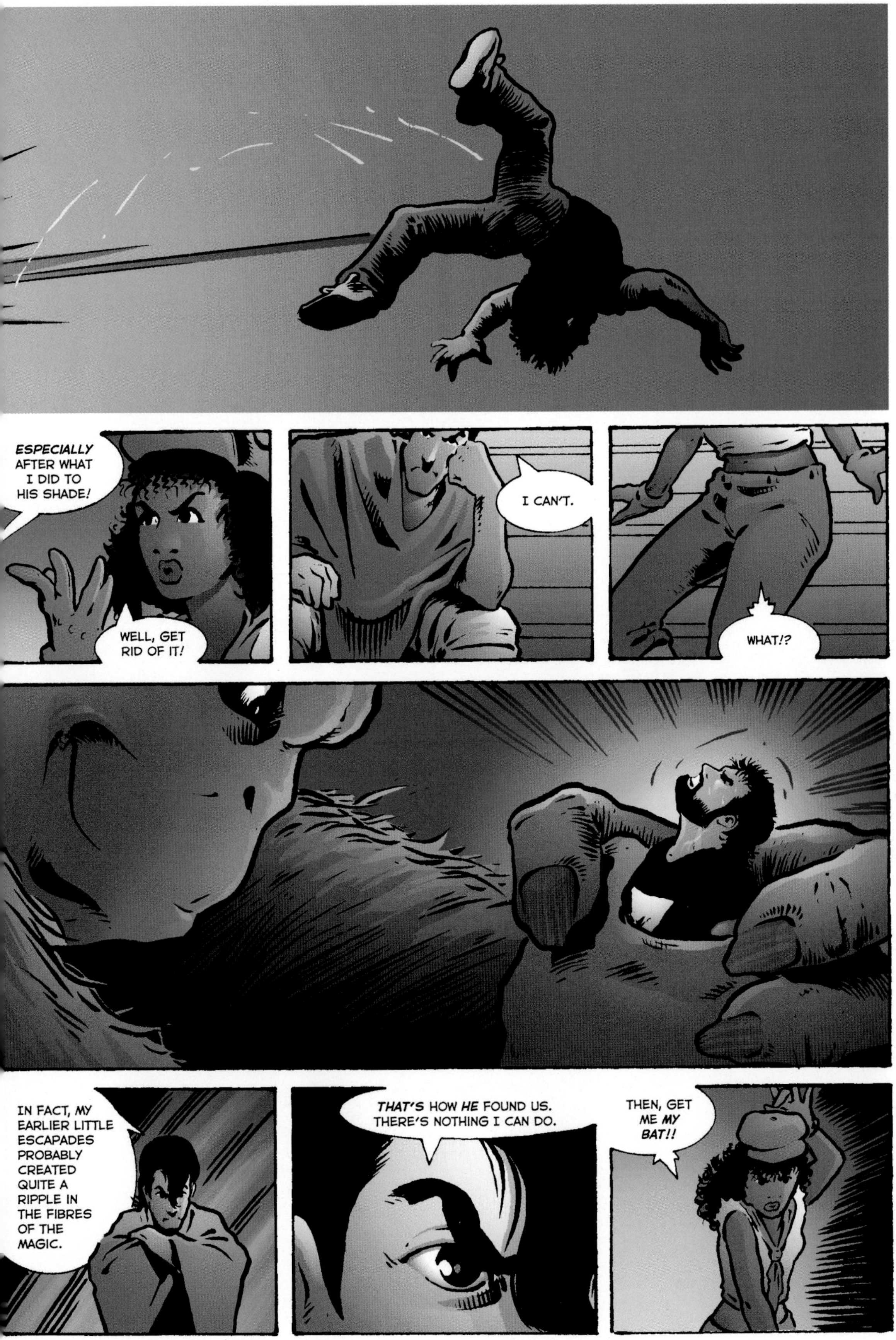
ESPECIALLY AFTER WHAT I DID TO HIS SHADE!
WELL, GET RID OF IT!
I CAN'T.
WHAT!?
IN FACT, MY EARLIER LITTLE ESCAPADES PROBABLY CREATED QUITE A RIPPLE IN THE FIBRES OF THE MAGIC.
THAT'S HOW HE FOUND US. THERE'S NOTHING I CAN DO.
THEN, GET ME MY BAT!!

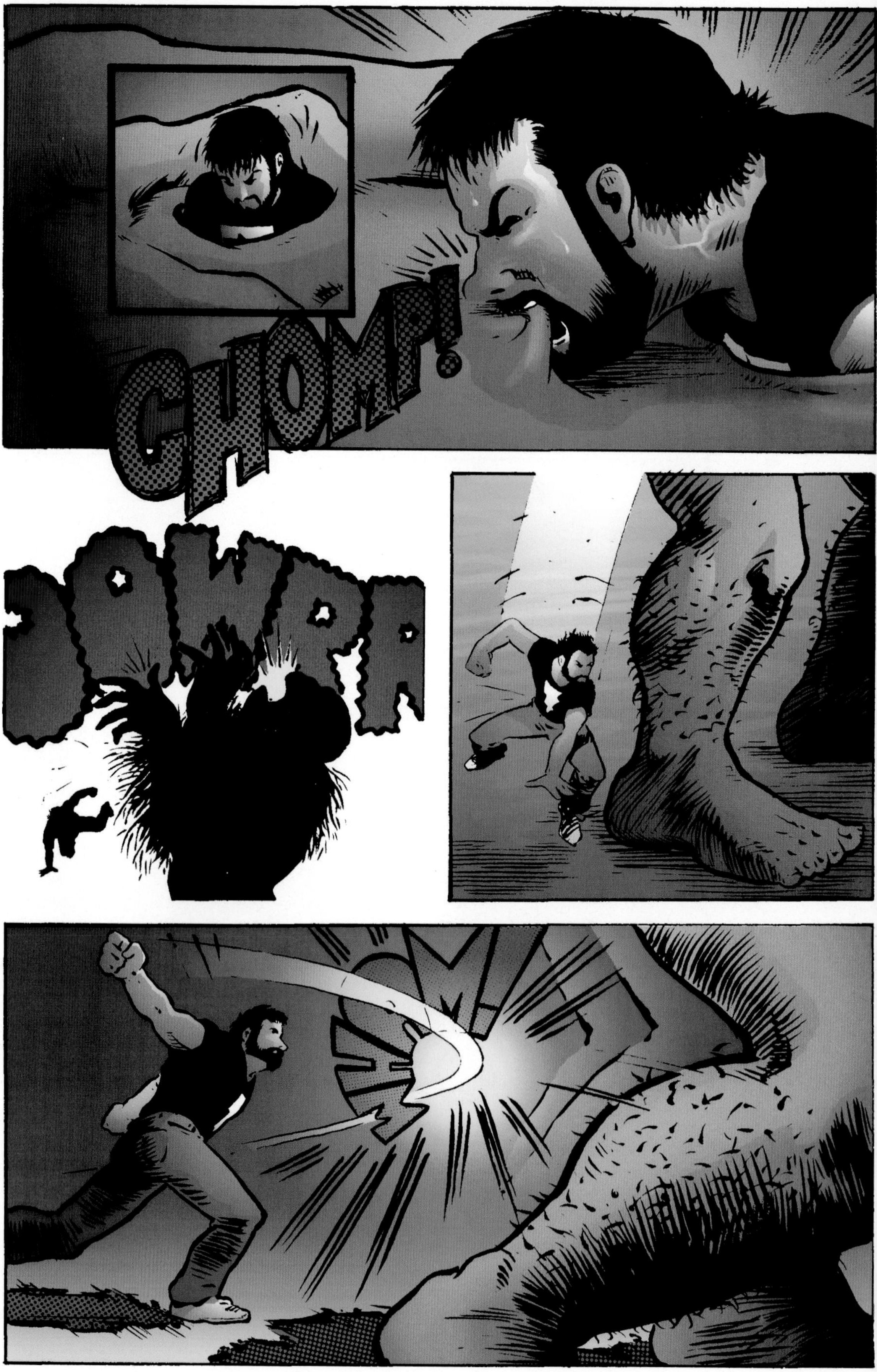
CHOMP!
WHOM!

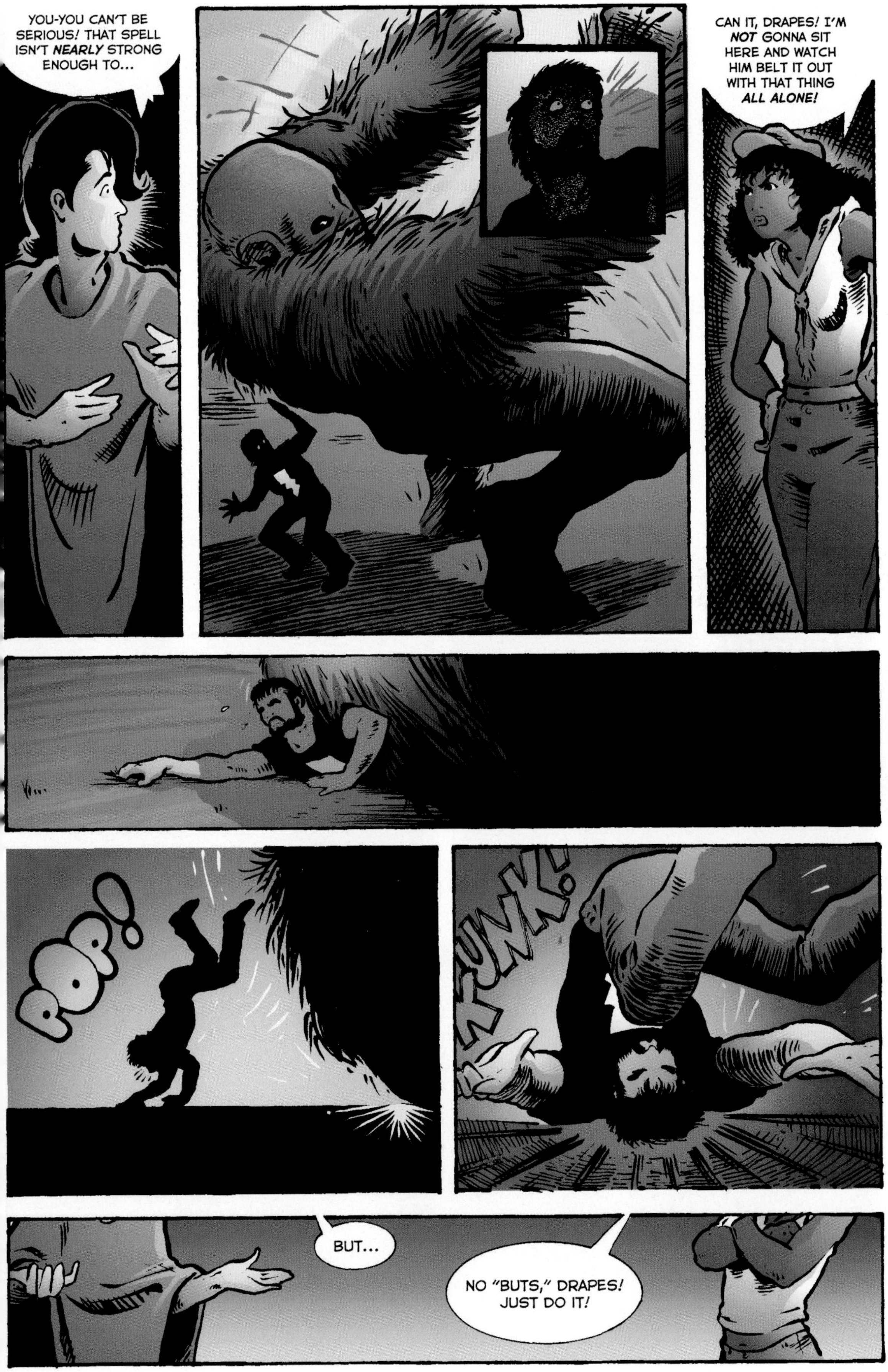
YOU-YOU CAN'T BE SERIOUS! THAT SPELL ISN'T NEARLY STRONG ENOUGH TO...
CAN IT, DRAPES! I'M NOT GONNA SIT HERE AND WATCH HIM BELT IT OUT WITH THAT THING ALL ALONE!
POP!
THUNK!
BUT...
NO "BUTS," DRAPES! JUST DO IT!

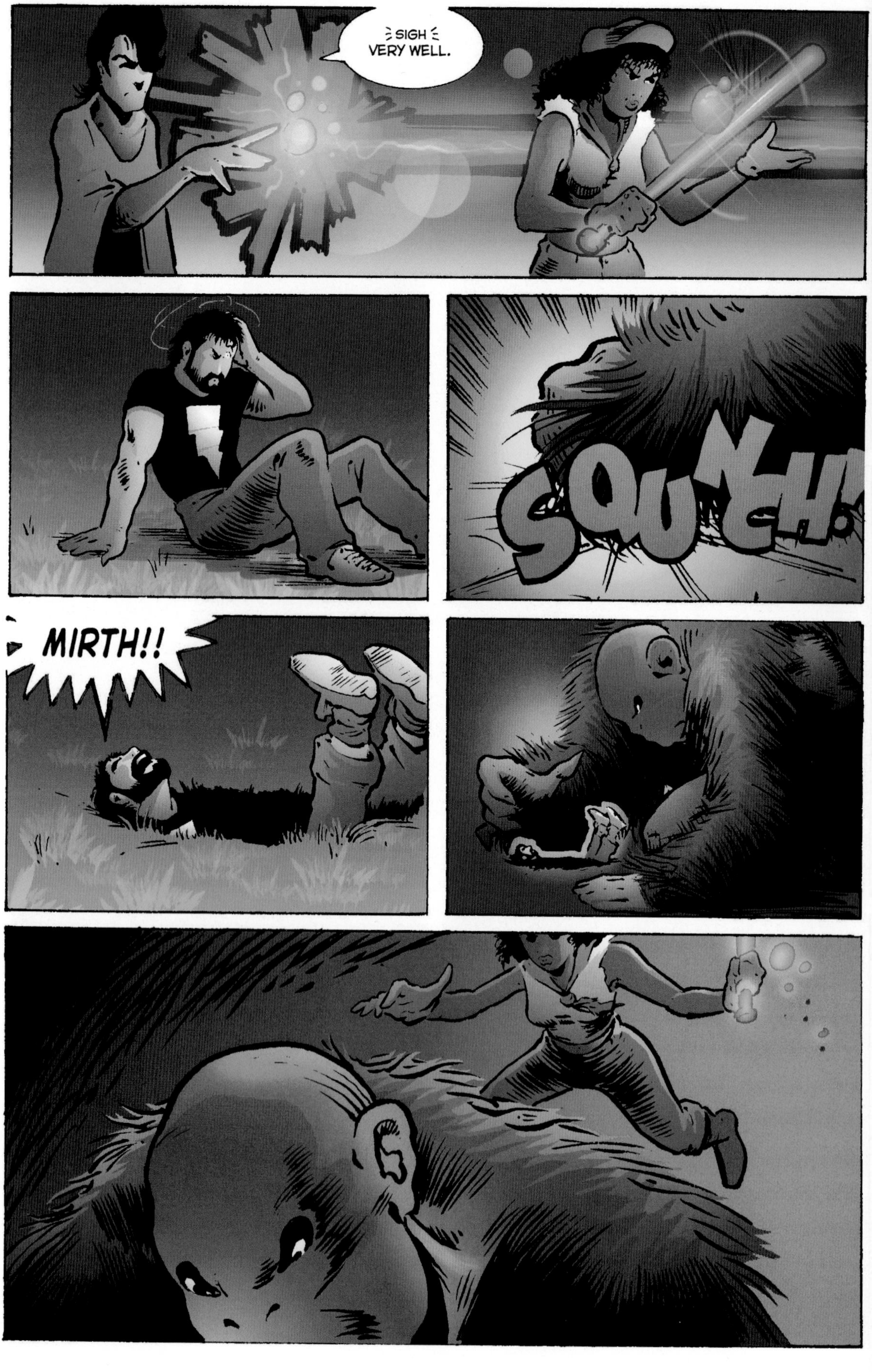
SIGH
VERY WELL.
SQUNCH!
MIRTH!!

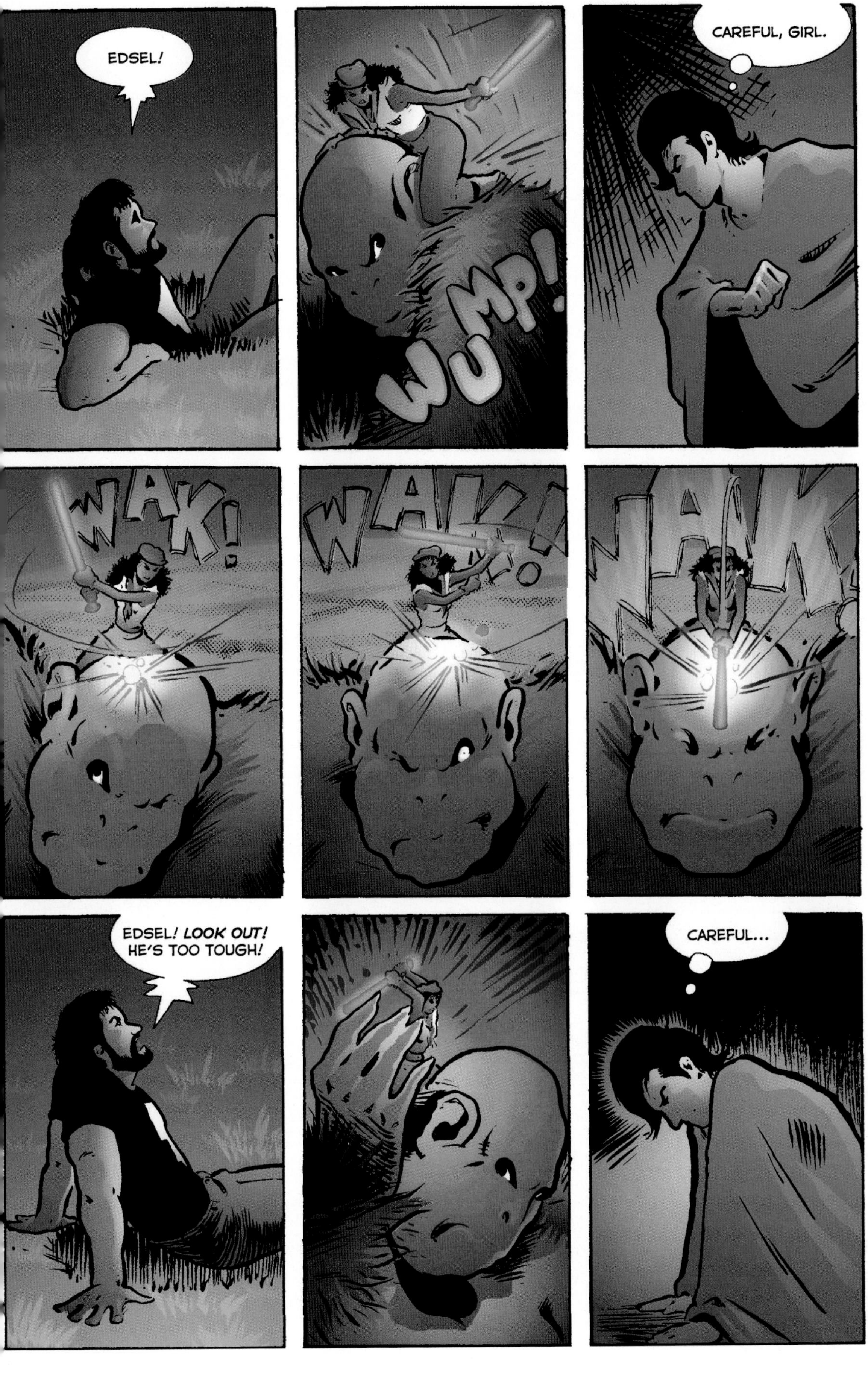
EDSEL!
WUMP!
CAREFUL, GIRL.
WAK!
WAK!
EDSEL! *LOOK OUT!*
HE'S TOO TOUGH!
CAREFUL...

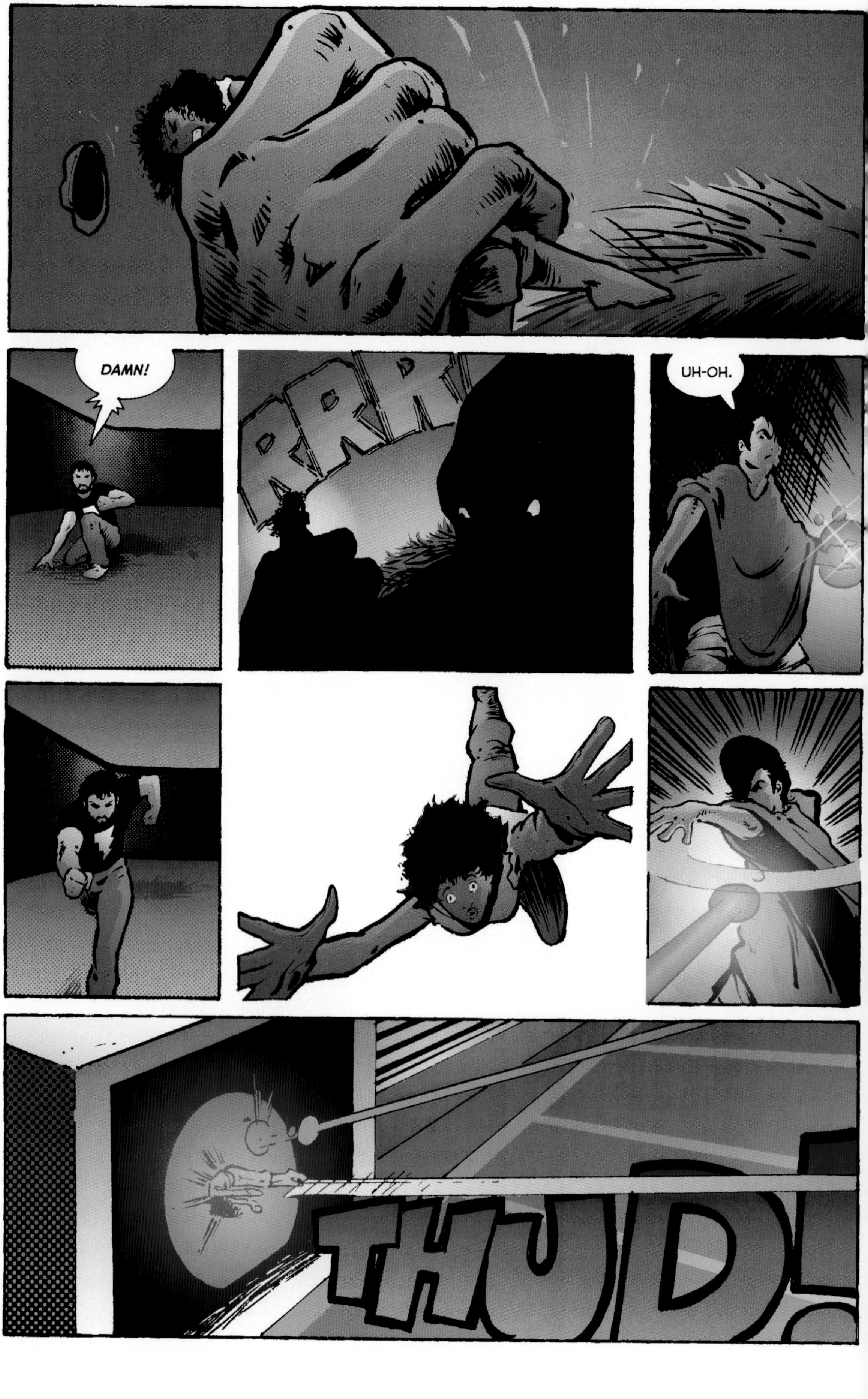
DAMN!
RRR
UH-OH.
THUD!

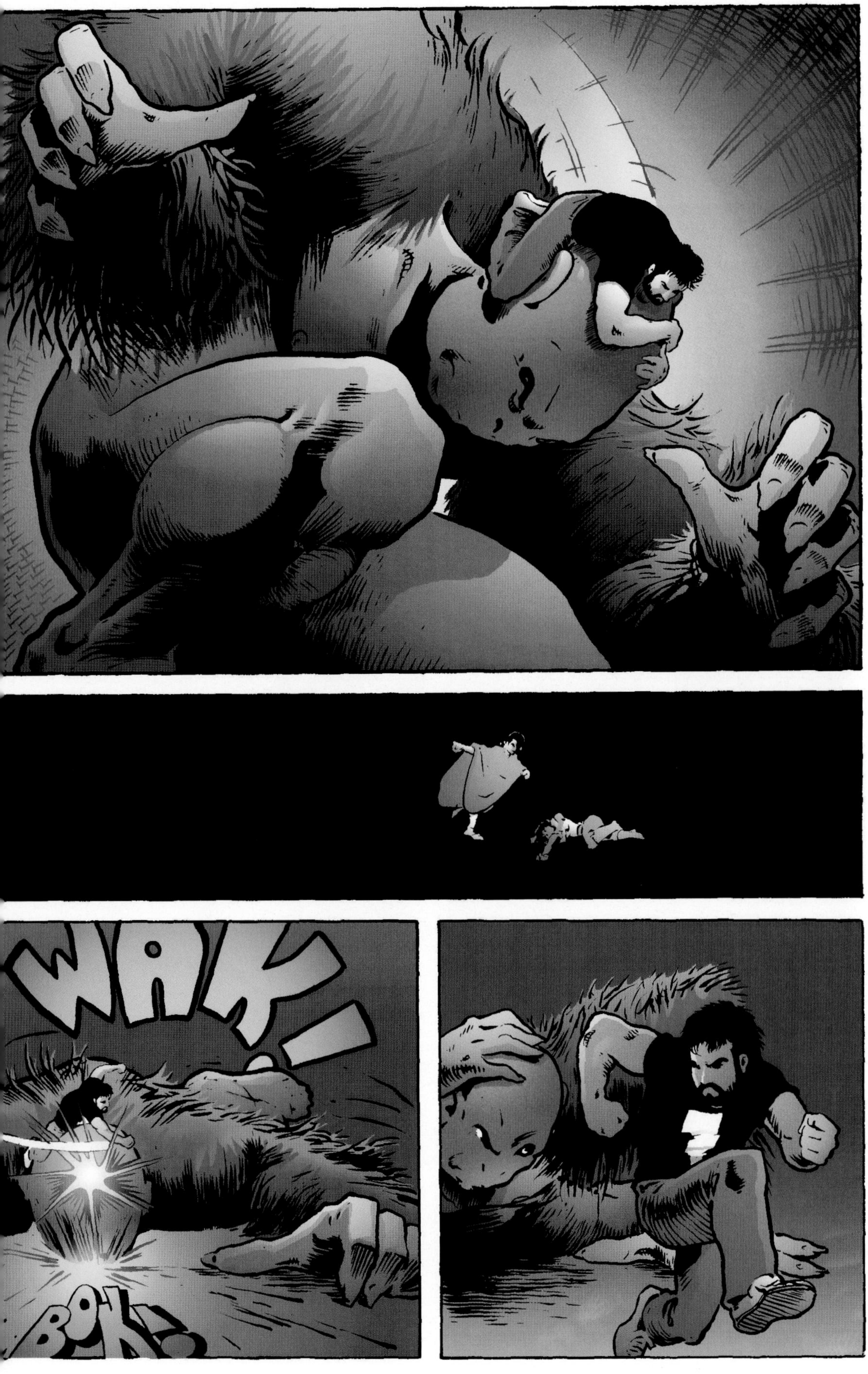
WAK!

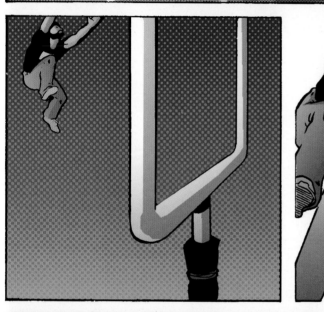

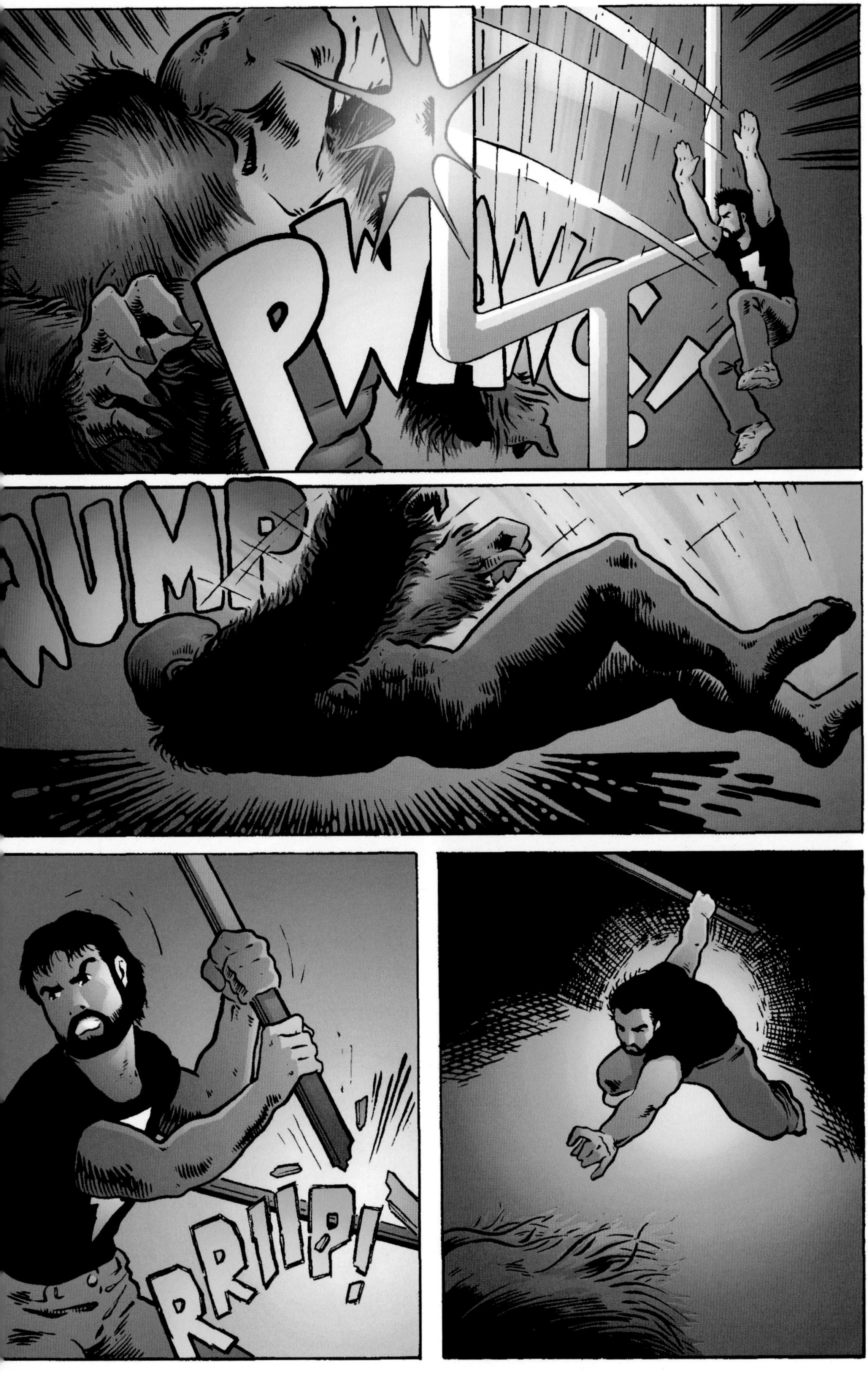
RRIIP!

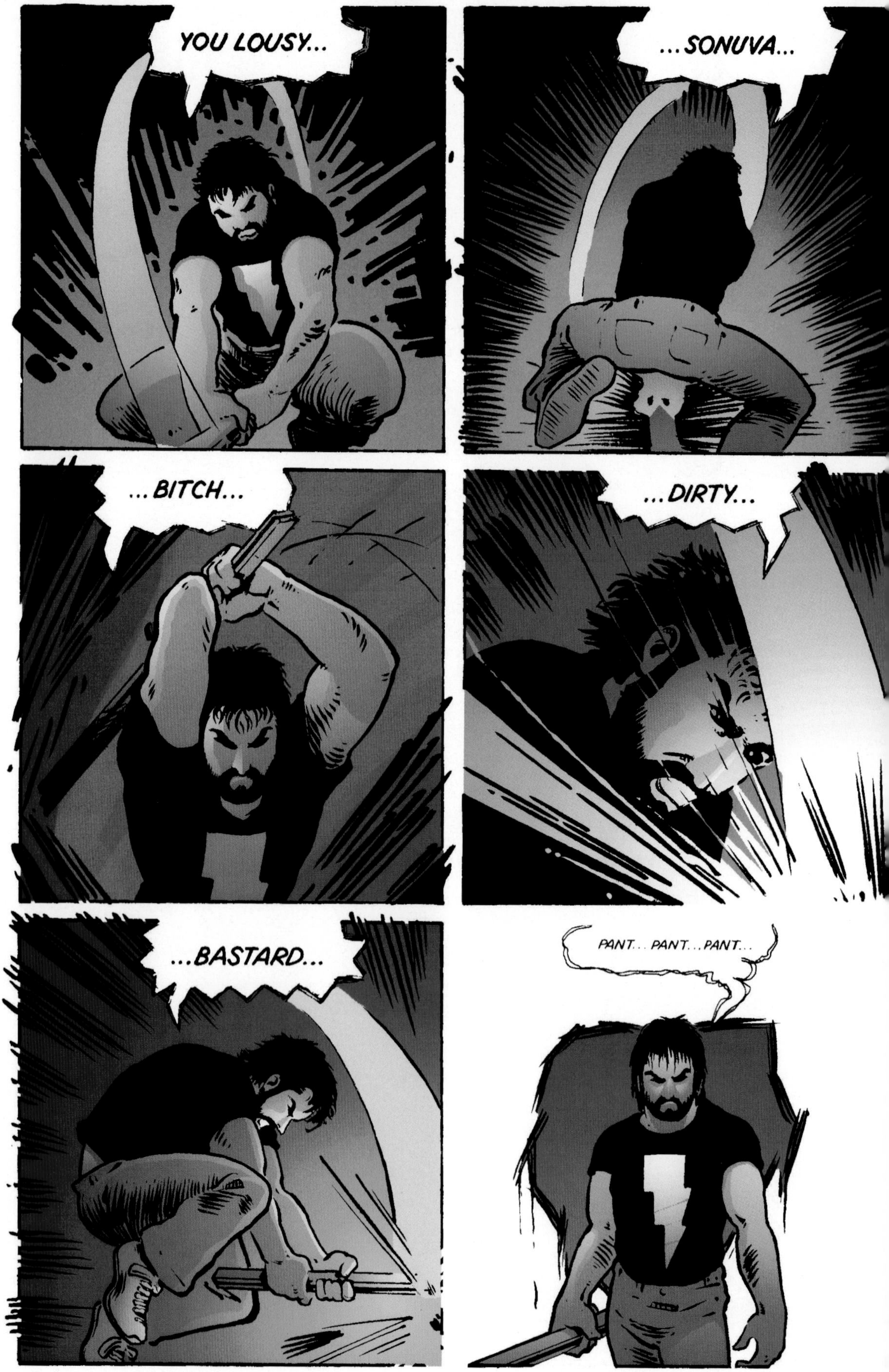
YOU LOUSY...
...SONUVA...
...BITCH...
...DIRTY...
...BASTARD...
PANT... PANT... PANT...

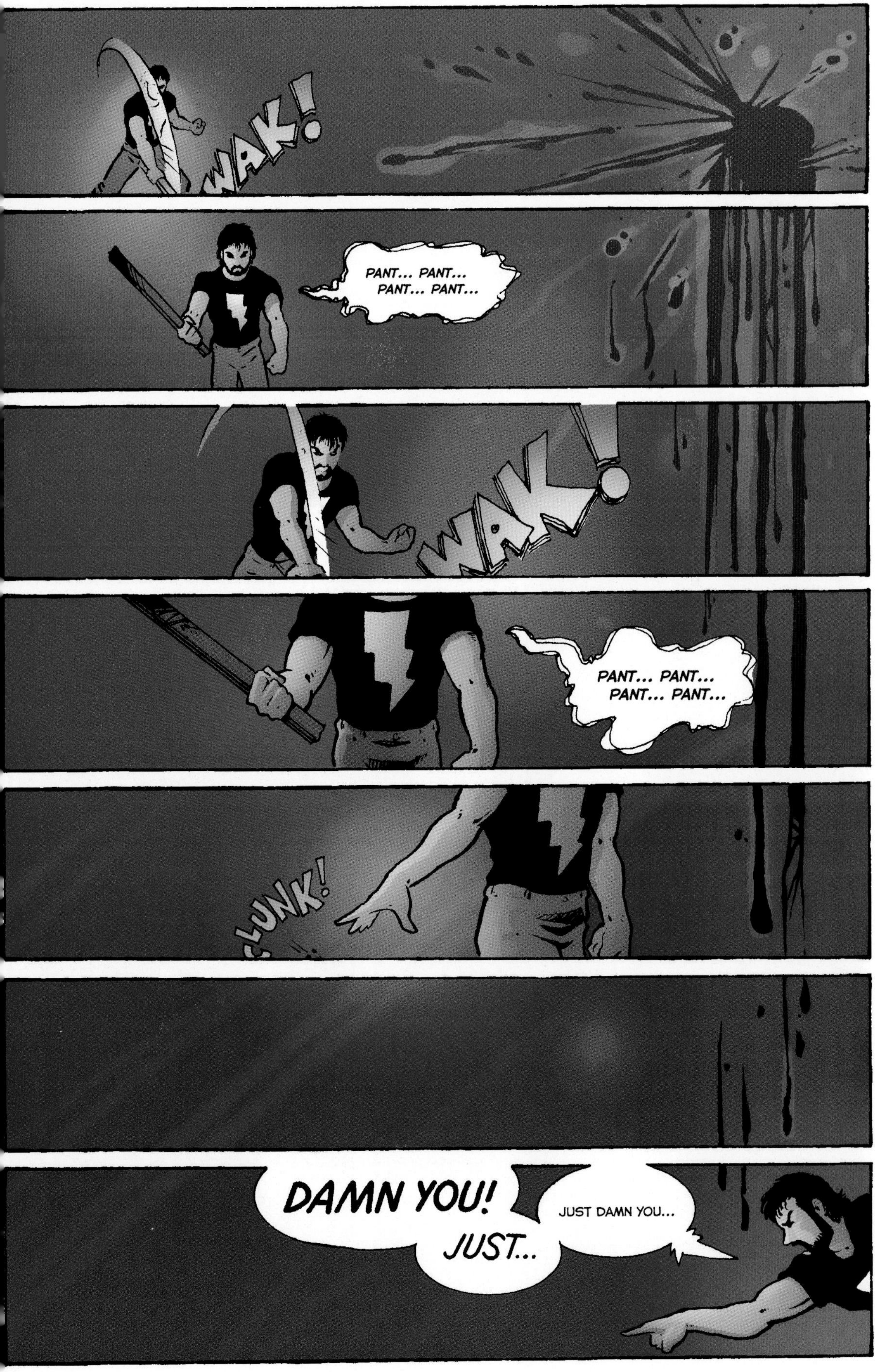
WAK!
PANT... PANT...
PANT... PANT...
WAK!
PANT... PANT...
PANT... PANT...
CLUNK!
DAMN YOU!
JUST...
JUST DAMN YOU...

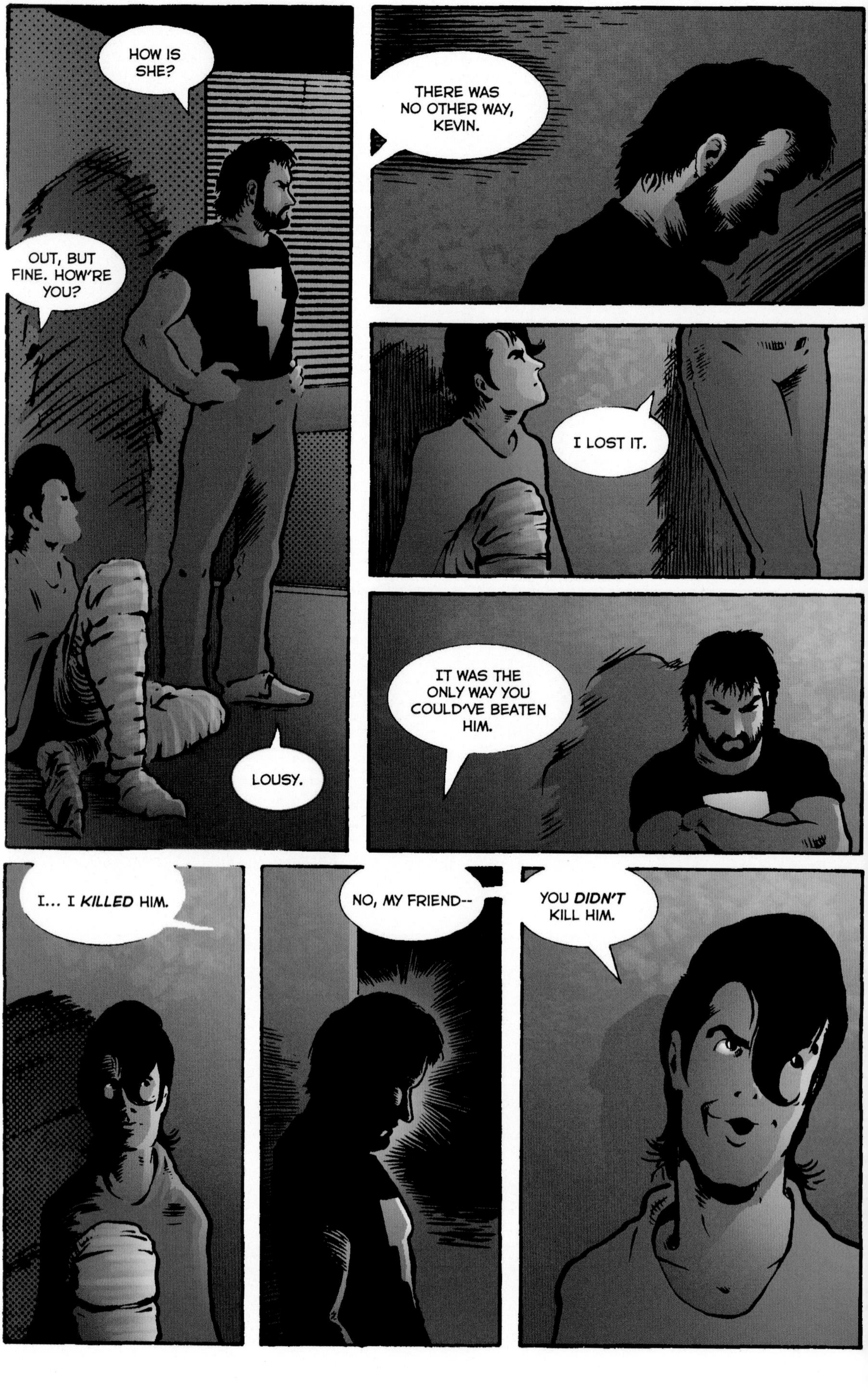

HOW IS SHE?
OUT, BUT FINE. HOW'RE YOU?
LOUSY.
THERE WAS NO OTHER WAY, KEVIN.
I LOST IT.
IT WAS THE ONLY WAY YOU COULD'VE BEATEN HIM.
I... I *KILLED* HIM.
NO, MY FRIEND--
YOU *DIDN'T* KILL HIM.

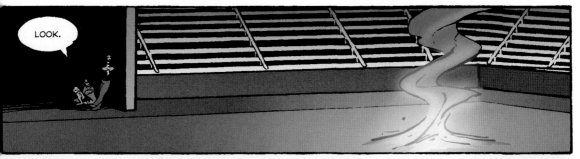

LOOK.

IT'S GONE!

JUST RETURNED TO HIS REALM.

IT'S VERY DIFFICULT TO KILL ONE FROM *THE FAERIE LANDS*, KEVIN. YOU MERELY BROKE THE SPELL THAT BOUND HIM TO THIS PLANE.

THAT WAS A FAERIE?!

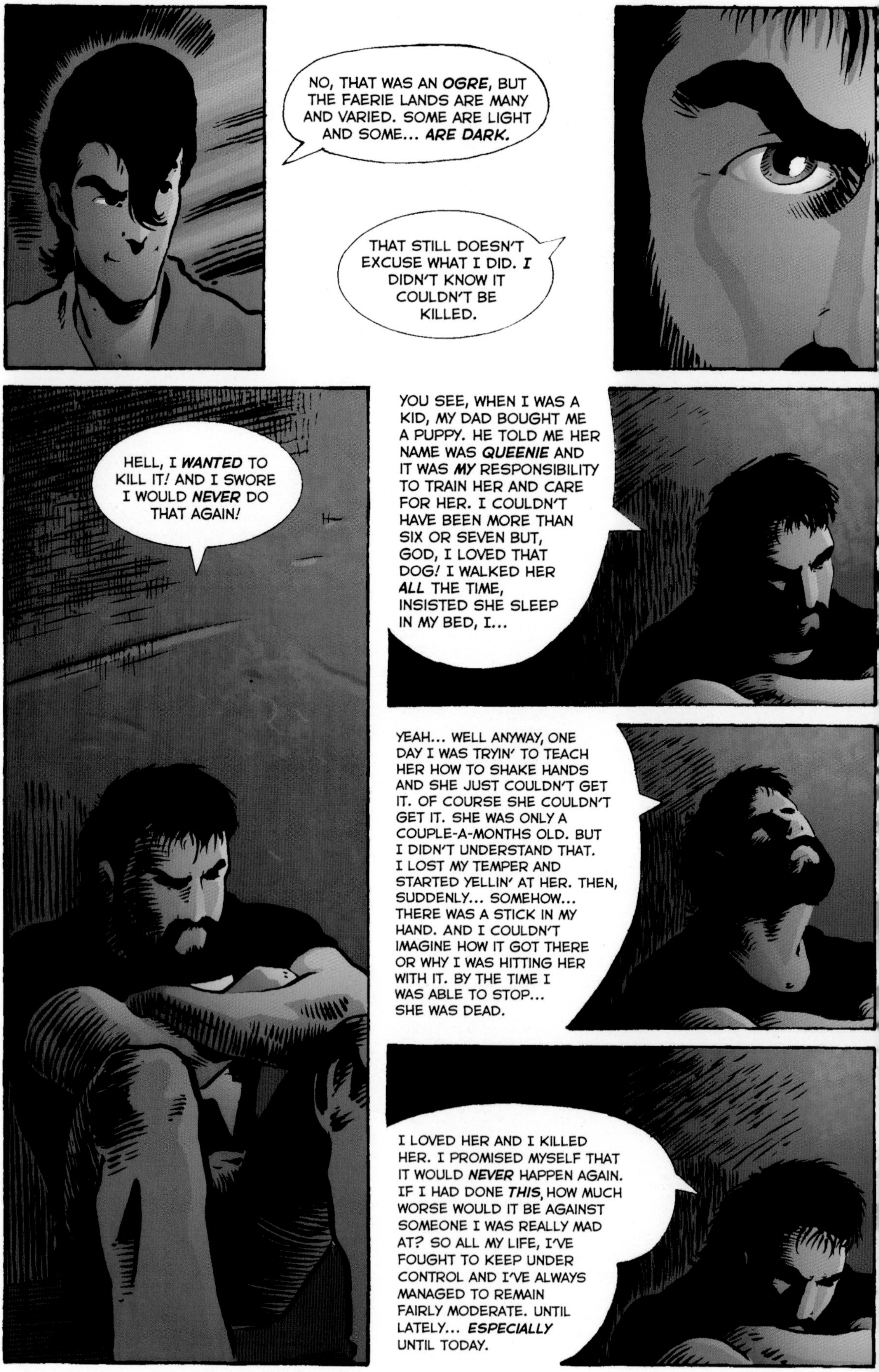
NO, THAT WAS AN OGRE, BUT THE FAERIE LANDS ARE MANY AND VARIED. SOME ARE LIGHT AND SOME... ARE DARK.
THAT STILL DOESN'T EXCUSE WHAT I DID. I DIDN'T KNOW IT COULDN'T BE KILLED.
HELL, I WANTED TO KILL IT! AND I SWORE I WOULD NEVER DO THAT AGAIN!
YOU SEE, WHEN I WAS A KID, MY DAD BOUGHT ME A PUPPY. HE TOLD ME HER NAME WAS QUEENIE AND IT WAS MY RESPONSIBILITY TO TRAIN HER AND CARE FOR HER. I COULDN'T HAVE BEEN MORE THAN SIX OR SEVEN BUT, GOD, I LOVED THAT DOG! I WALKED HER ALL THE TIME, INSISTED SHE SLEEP IN MY BED, I...
YEAH... WELL ANYWAY, ONE DAY I WAS TRYIN' TO TEACH HER HOW TO SHAKE HANDS AND SHE JUST COULDN'T GET IT. OF COURSE SHE COULDN'T GET IT. SHE WAS ONLY A COUPLE-A-MONTHS OLD. BUT I DIDN'T UNDERSTAND THAT. I LOST MY TEMPER AND STARTED YELLIN' AT HER. THEN, SUDDENLY... SOMEHOW... THERE WAS A STICK IN MY HAND. AND I COULDN'T IMAGINE HOW IT GOT THERE OR WHY I WAS HITTING HER WITH IT. BY THE TIME I WAS ABLE TO STOP... SHE WAS DEAD.
I LOVED HER AND I KILLED HER. I PROMISED MYSELF THAT IT WOULD NEVER HAPPEN AGAIN. IF I HAD DONE THIS, HOW MUCH WORSE WOULD IT BE AGAINST SOMEONE I WAS REALLY MAD AT? SO ALL MY LIFE, I'VE FOUGHT TO KEEP UNDER CONTROL AND I'VE ALWAYS MANAGED TO REMAIN FAIRLY MODERATE. UNTIL LATELY... ESPECIALLY UNTIL TODAY.

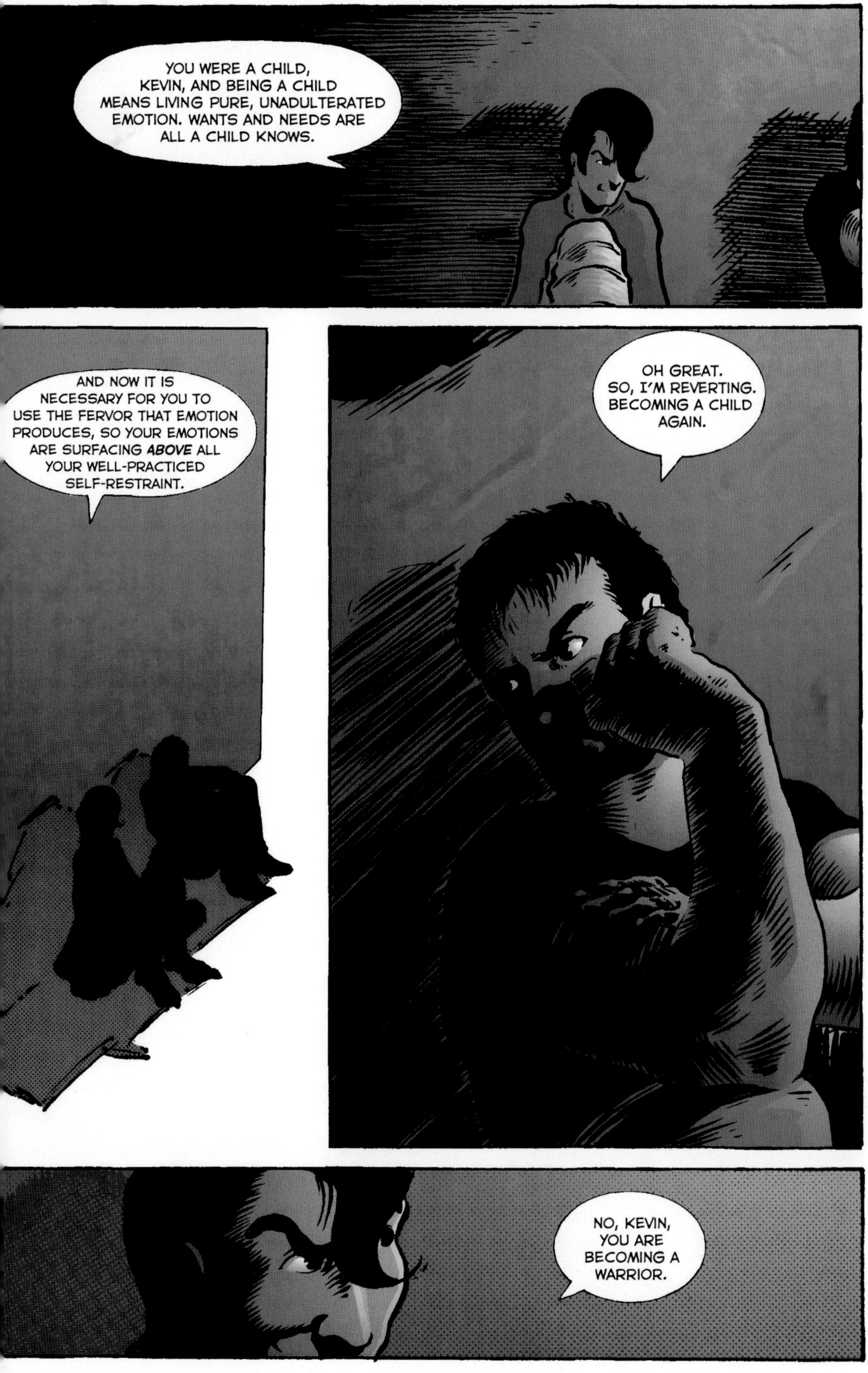
YOU WERE A CHILD, KEVIN, AND BEING A CHILD MEANS LIVING PURE, UNADULTERATED EMOTION. WANTS AND NEEDS ARE ALL A CHILD KNOWS.
AND NOW IT IS NECESSARY FOR YOU TO USE THE FERVOR THAT EMOTION PRODUCES, SO YOUR EMOTIONS ARE SURFACING *ABOVE* ALL YOUR WELL-PRACTICED SELF-RESTRAINT.
OH GREAT. SO, I'M REVERTING. BECOMING A CHILD AGAIN.
NO, KEVIN, YOU ARE BECOMING A WARRIOR.

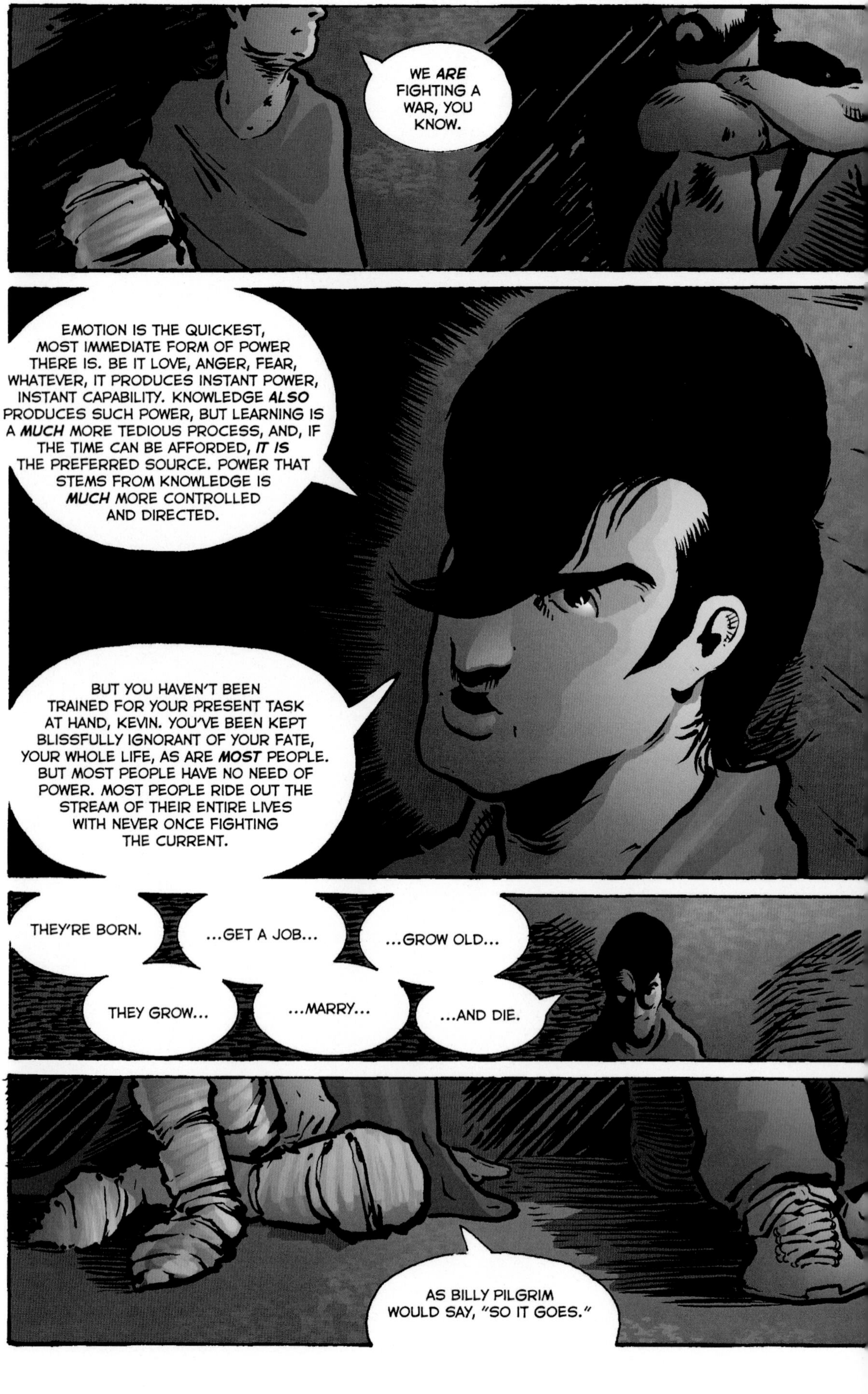
WE *ARE* FIGHTING A WAR, YOU KNOW.
EMOTION IS THE QUICKEST, MOST IMMEDIATE FORM OF POWER THERE IS. BE IT LOVE, ANGER, FEAR, WHATEVER, IT PRODUCES INSTANT POWER, INSTANT CAPABILITY. KNOWLEDGE *ALSO* PRODUCES SUCH POWER, BUT LEARNING IS A *MUCH* MORE TEDIOUS PROCESS, AND, IF THE TIME CAN BE AFFORDED, *IT IS* THE PREFERRED SOURCE. POWER THAT STEMS FROM KNOWLEDGE IS *MUCH* MORE CONTROLLED AND DIRECTED.
BUT YOU HAVEN'T BEEN TRAINED FOR YOUR PRESENT TASK AT HAND, KEVIN. YOU'VE BEEN KEPT BLISSFULLY IGNORANT OF YOUR FATE, YOUR WHOLE LIFE, AS ARE *MOST* PEOPLE. BUT MOST PEOPLE HAVE NO NEED OF POWER. MOST PEOPLE RIDE OUT THE STREAM OF THEIR ENTIRE LIVES WITH NEVER ONCE FIGHTING THE CURRENT.
THEY'RE BORN.
THEY GROW...
...GET A JOB...
...MARRY...
...GROW OLD...
...AND DIE.
AS BILLY PILGRIM WOULD SAY, "SO IT GOES."

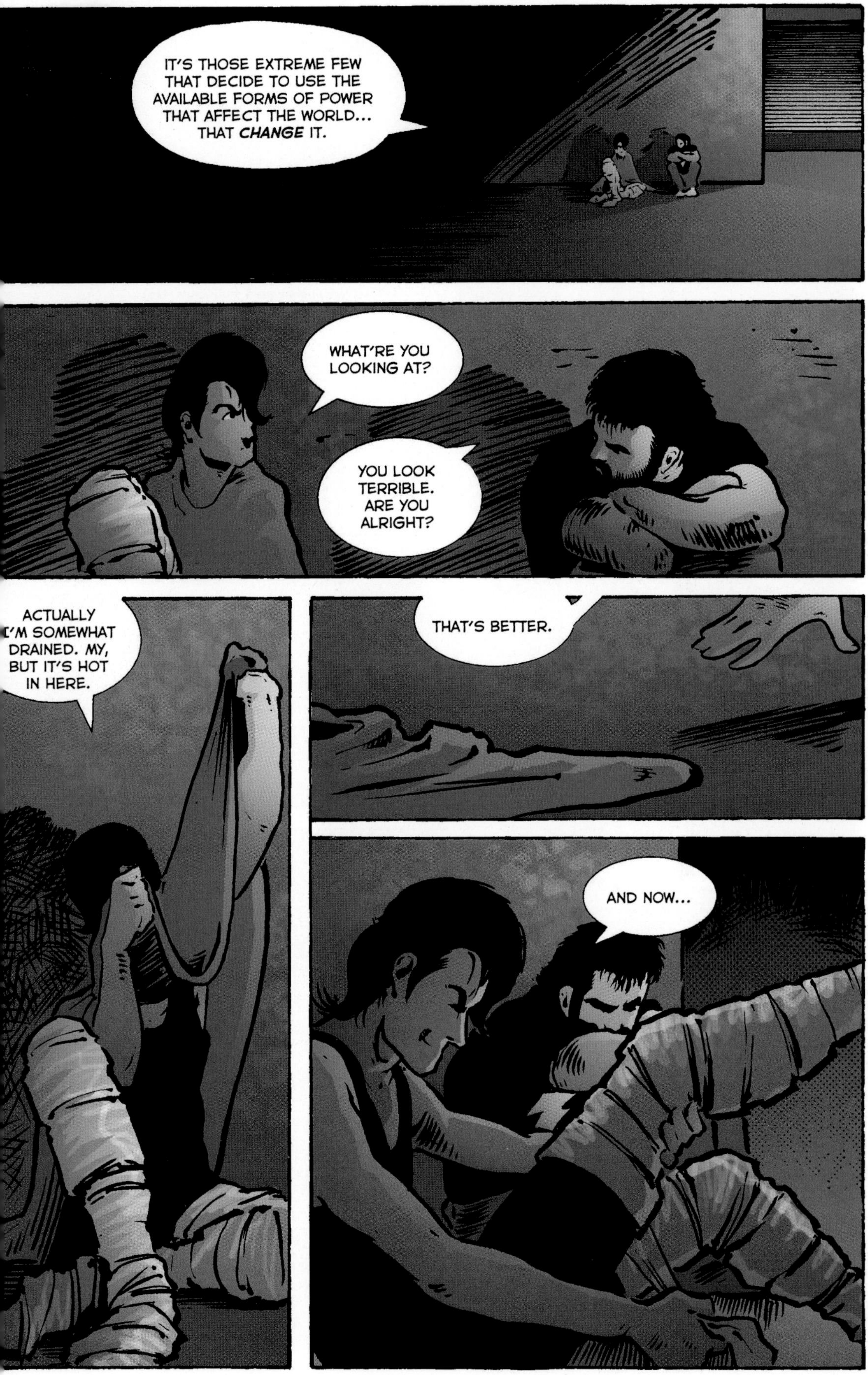
IT'S THOSE EXTREME FEW THAT DECIDE TO USE THE AVAILABLE FORMS OF POWER THAT AFFECT THE WORLD... THAT *CHANGE* IT.
WHAT'RE YOU LOOKING AT?
YOU LOOK TERRIBLE. ARE YOU ALRIGHT?
ACTUALLY I'M SOMEWHAT DRAINED. MY, BUT IT'S HOT IN HERE.
THAT'S BETTER.
AND NOW...

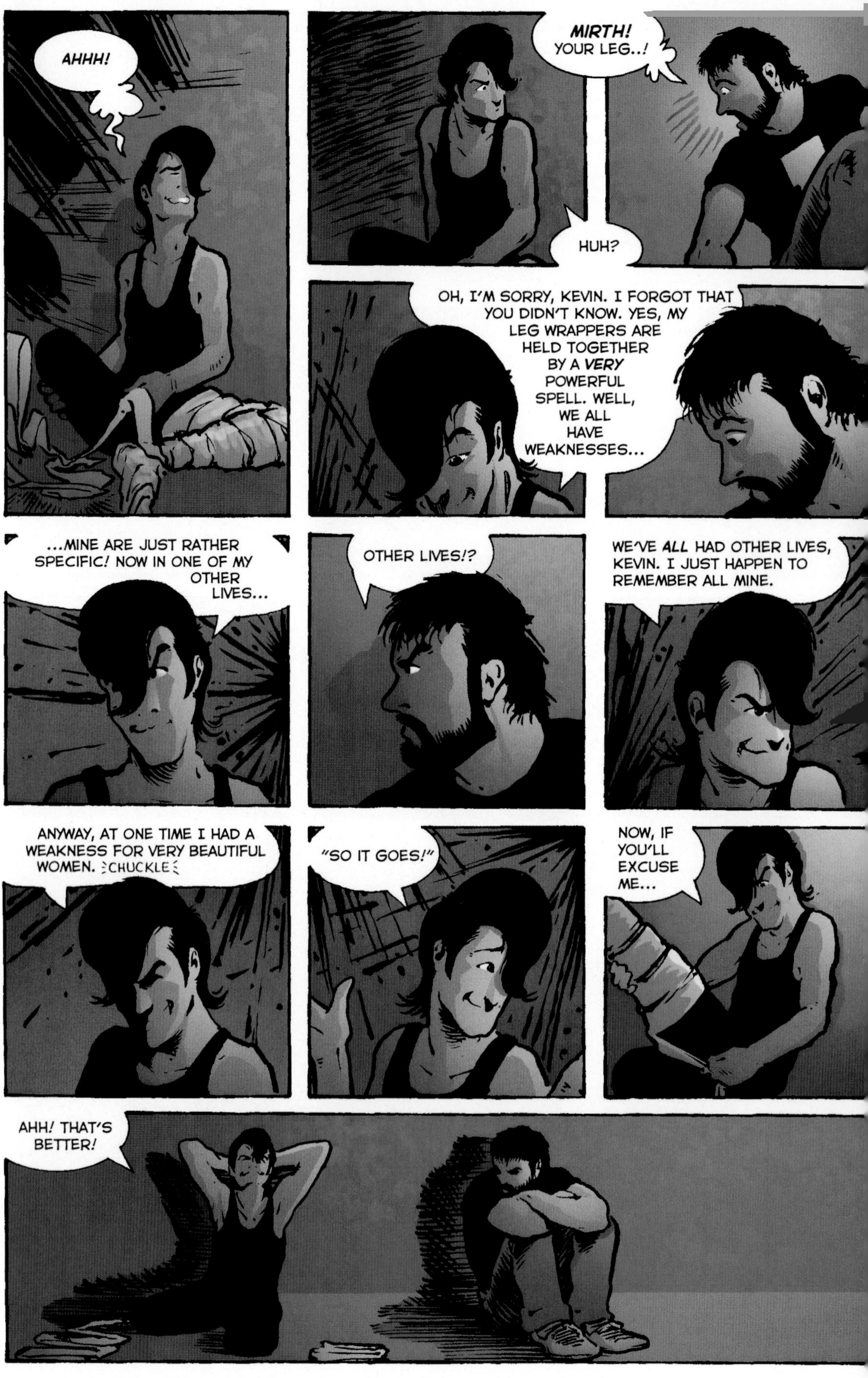
AHHH!
MIRTH! YOUR LEG..!
HUH?
OH, I'M SORRY, KEVIN. I FORGOT THAT YOU DIDN'T KNOW. YES, MY LEG WRAPPERS ARE HELD TOGETHER BY A VERY POWERFUL SPELL. WELL, WE ALL HAVE WEAKNESSES...
...MINE ARE JUST RATHER SPECIFIC! NOW IN ONE OF MY OTHER LIVES...
OTHER LIVES!?
WE'VE ALL HAD OTHER LIVES, KEVIN. I JUST HAPPEN TO REMEMBER ALL MINE.
ANYWAY, AT ONE TIME I HAD A WEAKNESS FOR VERY BEAUTIFUL WOMEN. CHUCKLE
"SO IT GOES!"
NOW, IF YOU'LL EXCUSE ME...
AHH! THAT'S BETTER!

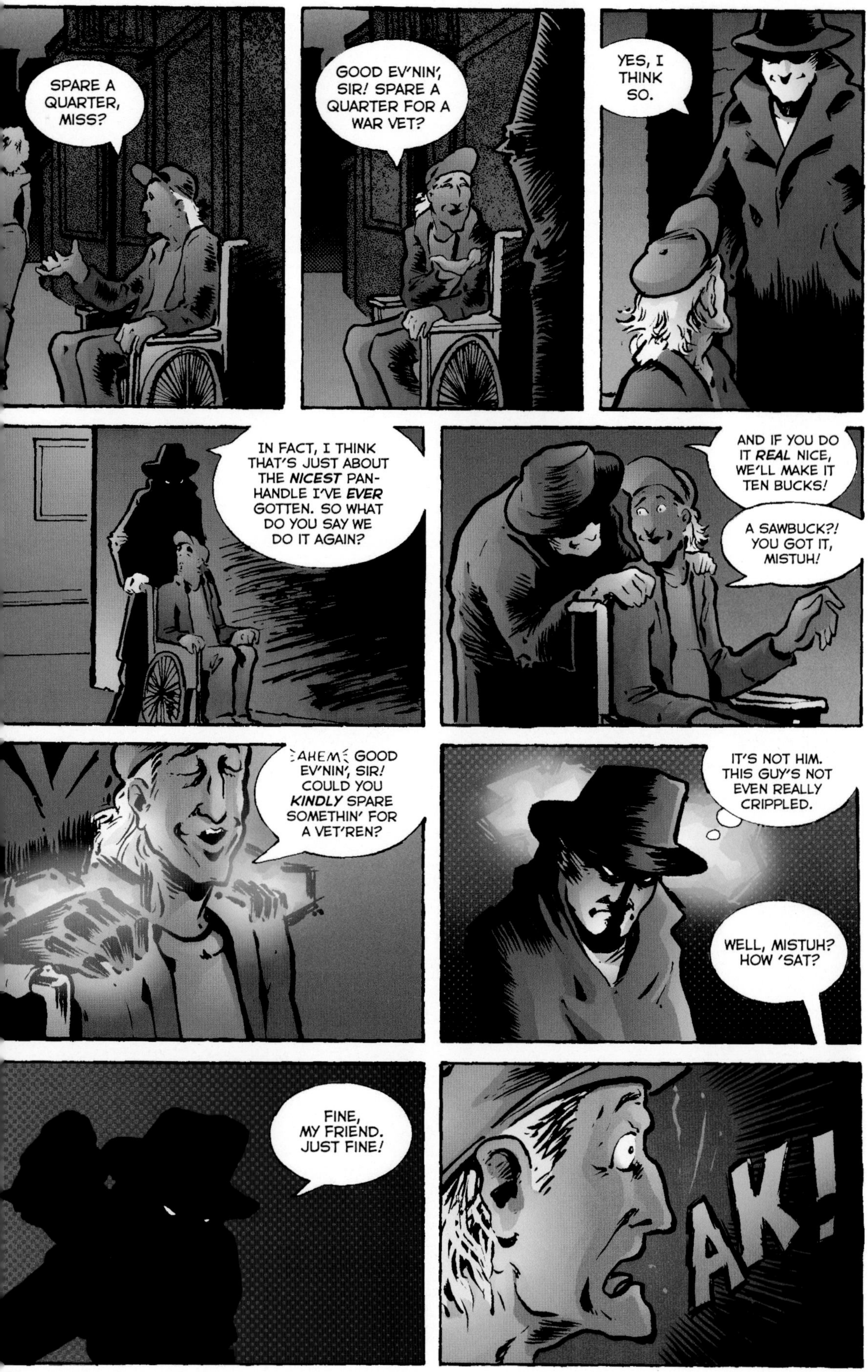
SPARE A QUARTER, MISS?
GOOD EV'NIN', SIR! SPARE A QUARTER FOR A WAR VET?
YES, I THINK SO.
IN FACT, I THINK THAT'S JUST ABOUT THE NICEST PAN-HANDLE I'VE EVER GOTTEN. SO WHAT DO YOU SAY WE DO IT AGAIN?
AND IF YOU DO IT REAL NICE, WE'LL MAKE IT TEN BUCKS!
A SAWBUCK?! YOU GOT IT, MISTUH!
AHEM GOOD EV'NIN', SIR! COULD YOU KINDLY SPARE SOMETHIN' FOR A VET'REN?
IT'S NOT HIM. THIS GUY'S NOT EVEN REALLY CRIPPLED.
WELL, MISTUH? HOW 'SAT?
FINE, MY FRIEND. JUST FINE!
AK!

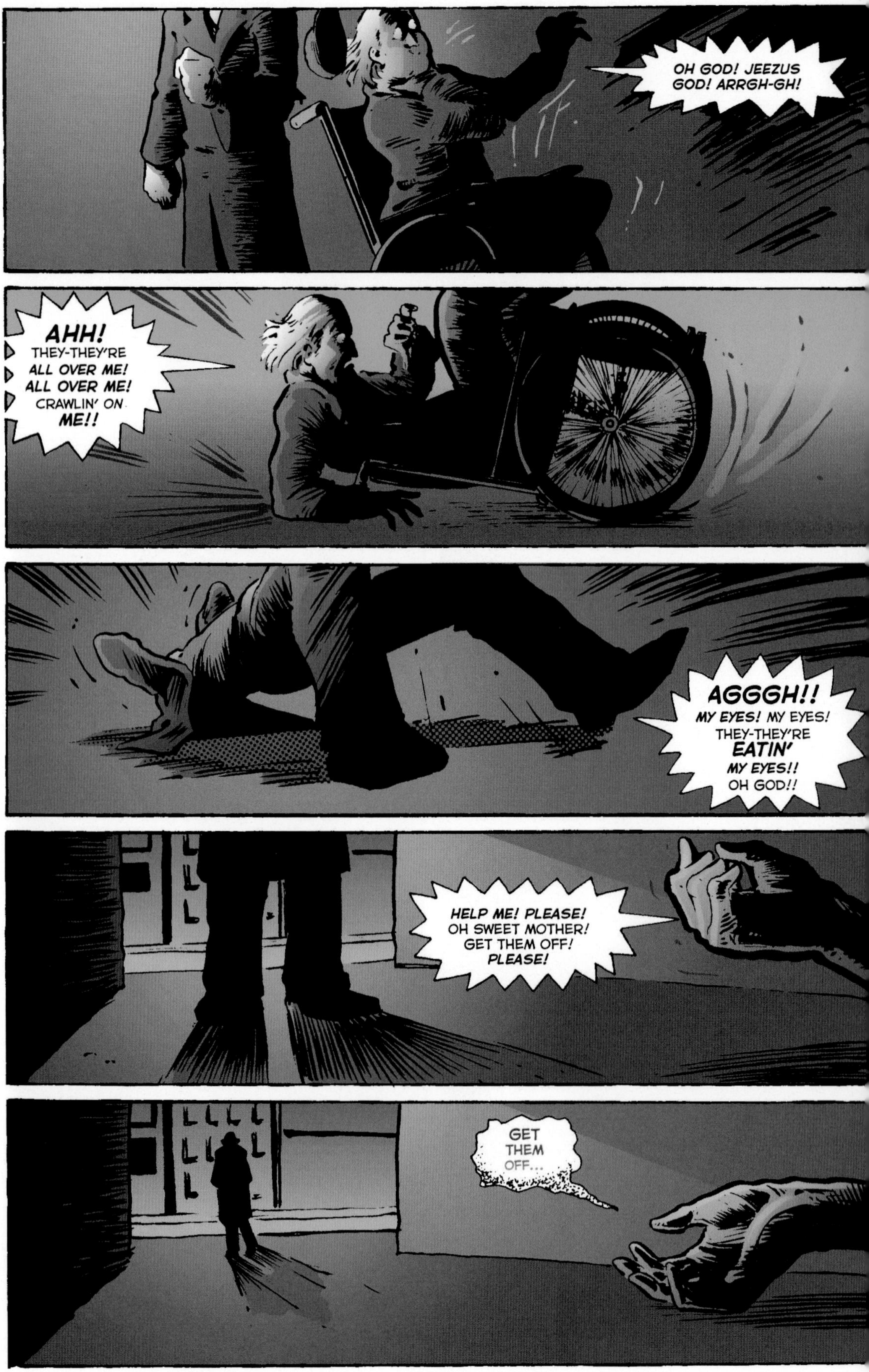
OH GOD! JEEZUS GOD! ARRGH-GH!
AHH! THEY-THEY'RE ALL OVER ME! ALL OVER ME! CRAWLIN' ON ME!!
AGGGH!! MY EYES! MY EYES! THEY-THEY'RE EATIN' MY EYES!! OH GOD!!
HELP ME! PLEASE! OH SWEET MOTHER! GET THEM OFF! PLEASE!
GET THEM OFF...

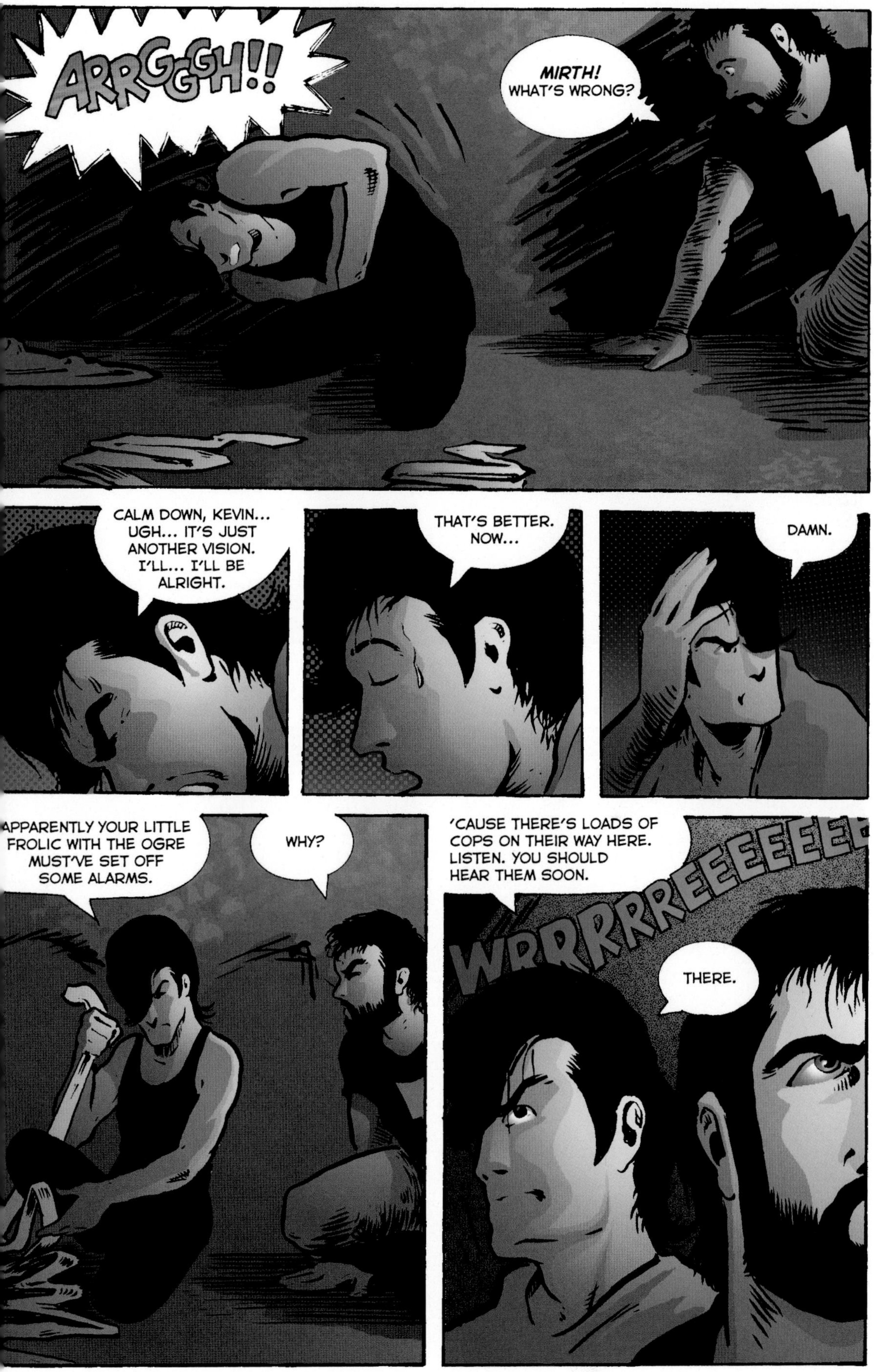
ARRGGGH!!
MIRTH! WHAT'S WRONG?
CALM DOWN, KEVIN... UGH... IT'S JUST ANOTHER VISION. I'LL... I'LL BE ALRIGHT.
THAT'S BETTER. NOW...
DAMN.
APPARENTLY YOUR LITTLE FROLIC WITH THE OGRE MUST'VE SET OFF SOME ALARMS.
WHY?
'CAUSE THERE'S LOADS OF COPS ON THEIR WAY HERE. LISTEN. YOU SHOULD HEAR THEM SOON.
WRRRRREEEEEEEE
THERE.

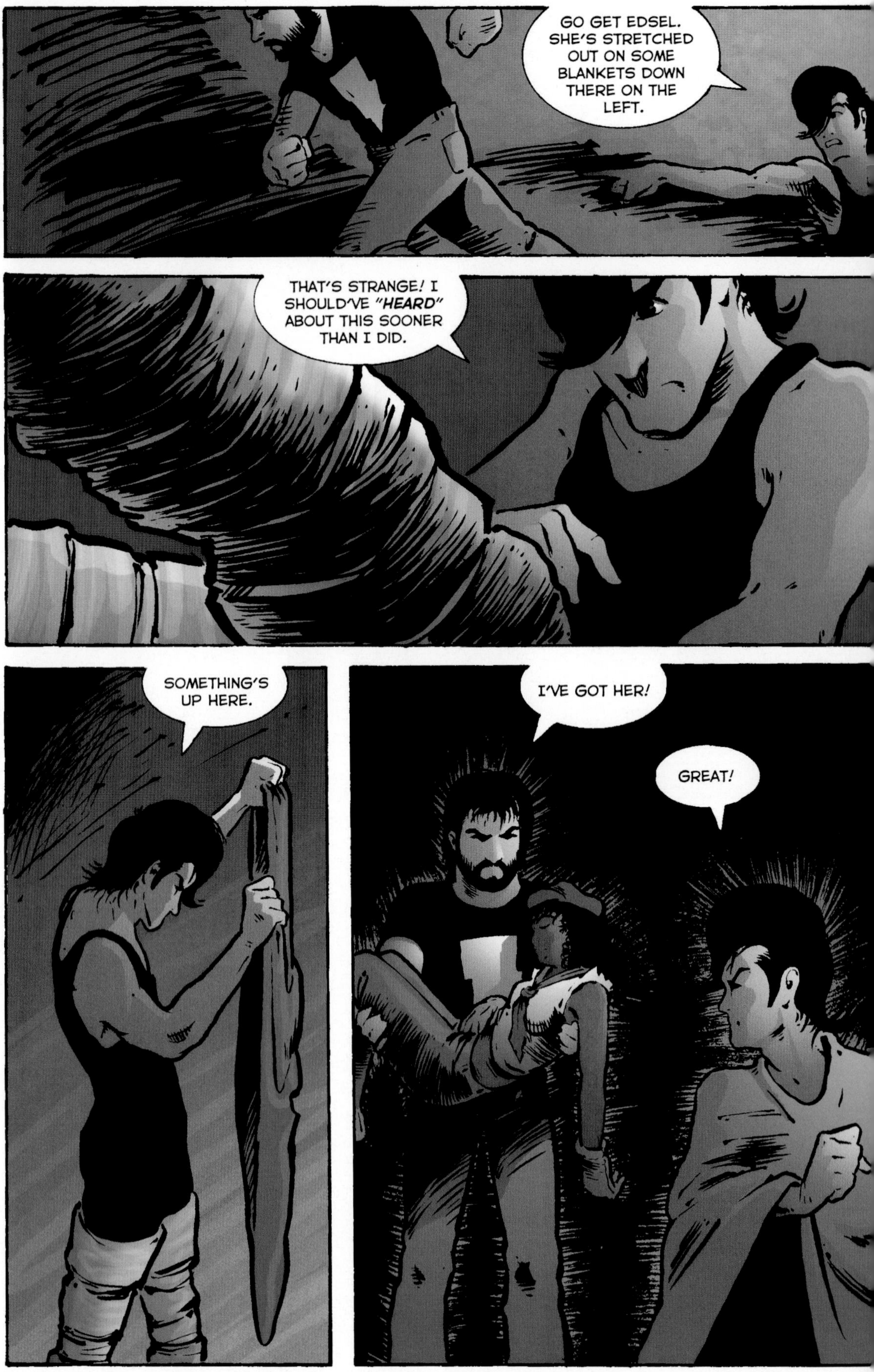
GO GET EDSEL. SHE'S STRETCHED OUT ON SOME BLANKETS DOWN THERE ON THE LEFT.
THAT'S STRANGE! I SHOULD'VE "***HEARD***" ABOUT THIS SOONER THAN I DID.
SOMETHING'S UP HERE.
I'VE GOT HER!
GREAT!

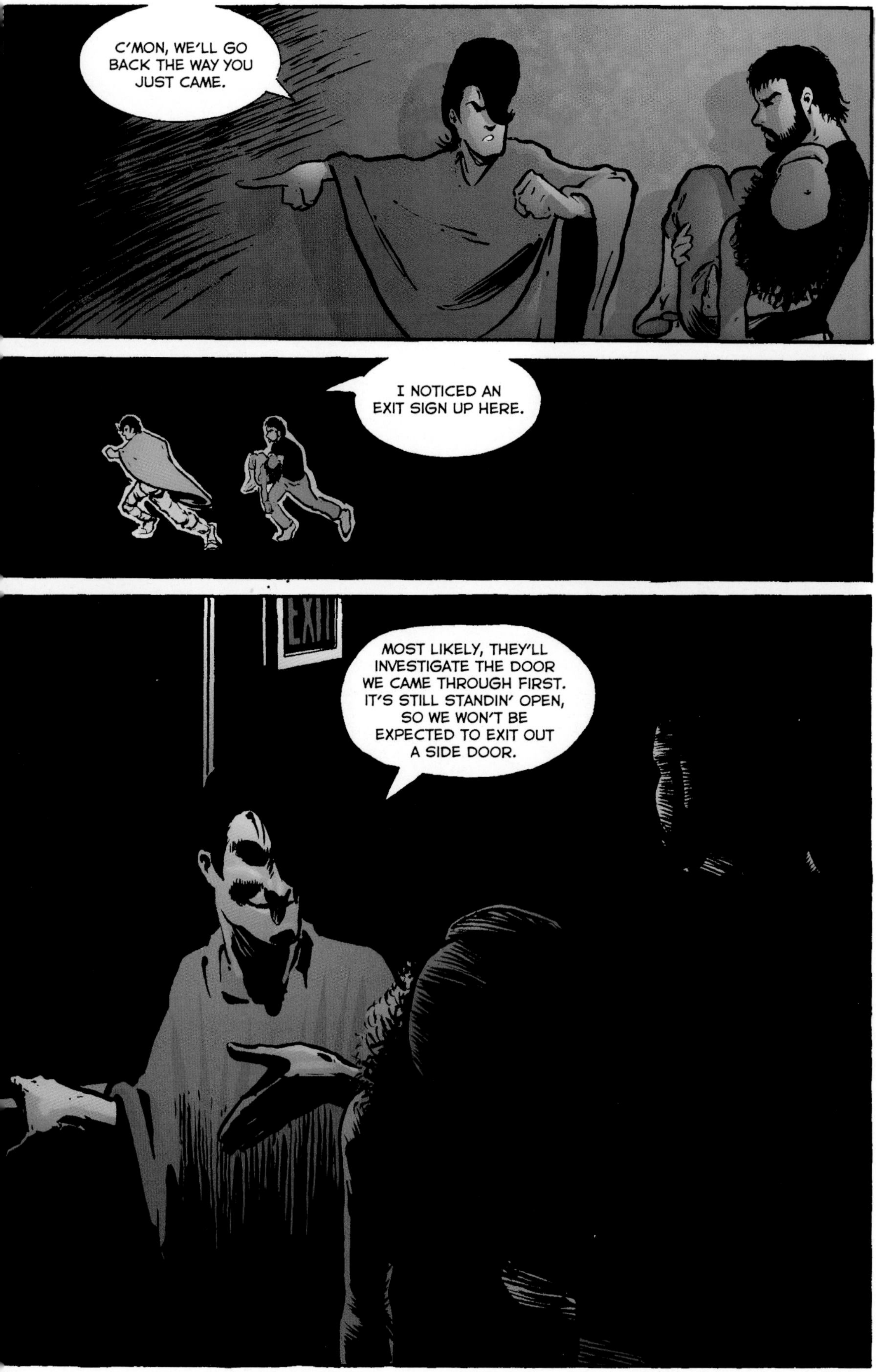
C'MON, WE'LL GO BACK THE WAY YOU JUST CAME.
I NOTICED AN EXIT SIGN UP HERE.
EXIT
MOST LIKELY, THEY'LL INVESTIGATE THE DOOR WE CAME THROUGH FIRST. IT'S STILL STANDIN' OPEN, SO WE WON'T BE EXPECTED TO EXIT OUT A SIDE DOOR.

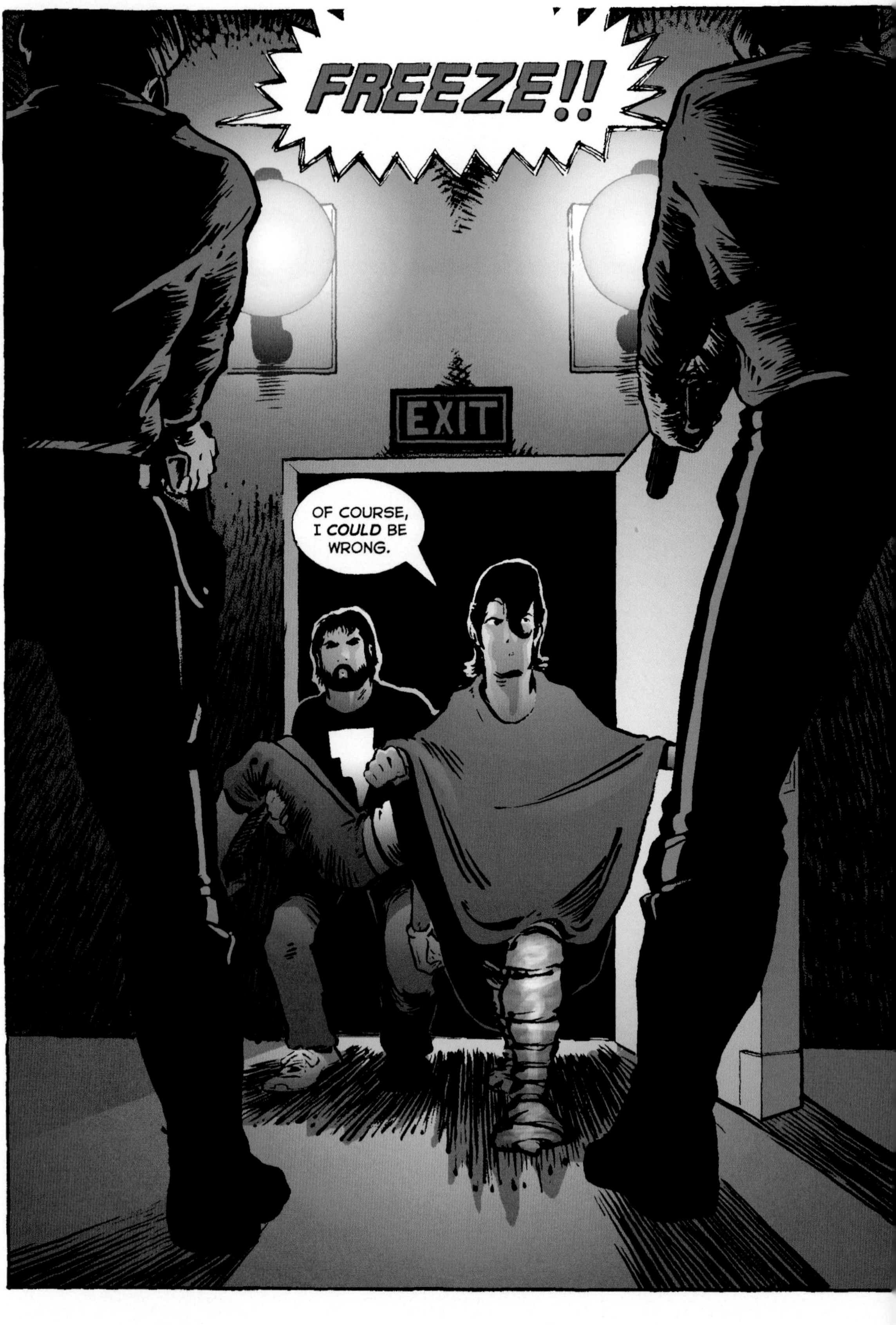
FREEZE!!
OF COURSE, I COULD BE WRONG.
EXIT

THE HERO DISCOVERED

MAGE

Chapter 05

Rosencrantz and
Guildenstern

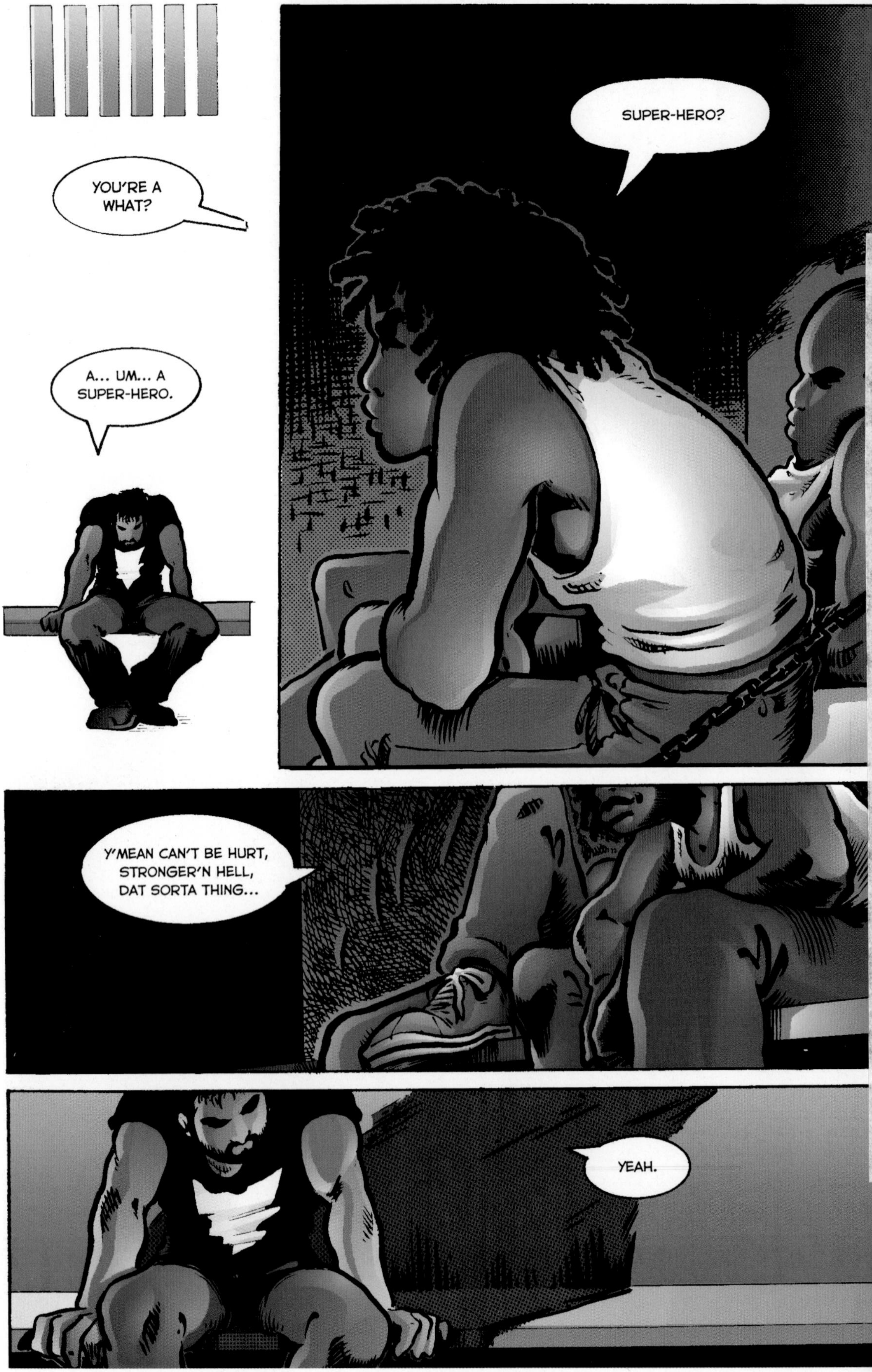
YOU'RE A WHAT?
SUPER-HERO?
A... UM... A SUPER-HERO.
Y'MEAN CAN'T BE HURT, STRONGER'N HELL, DAT SORTA THING...
YEAH.

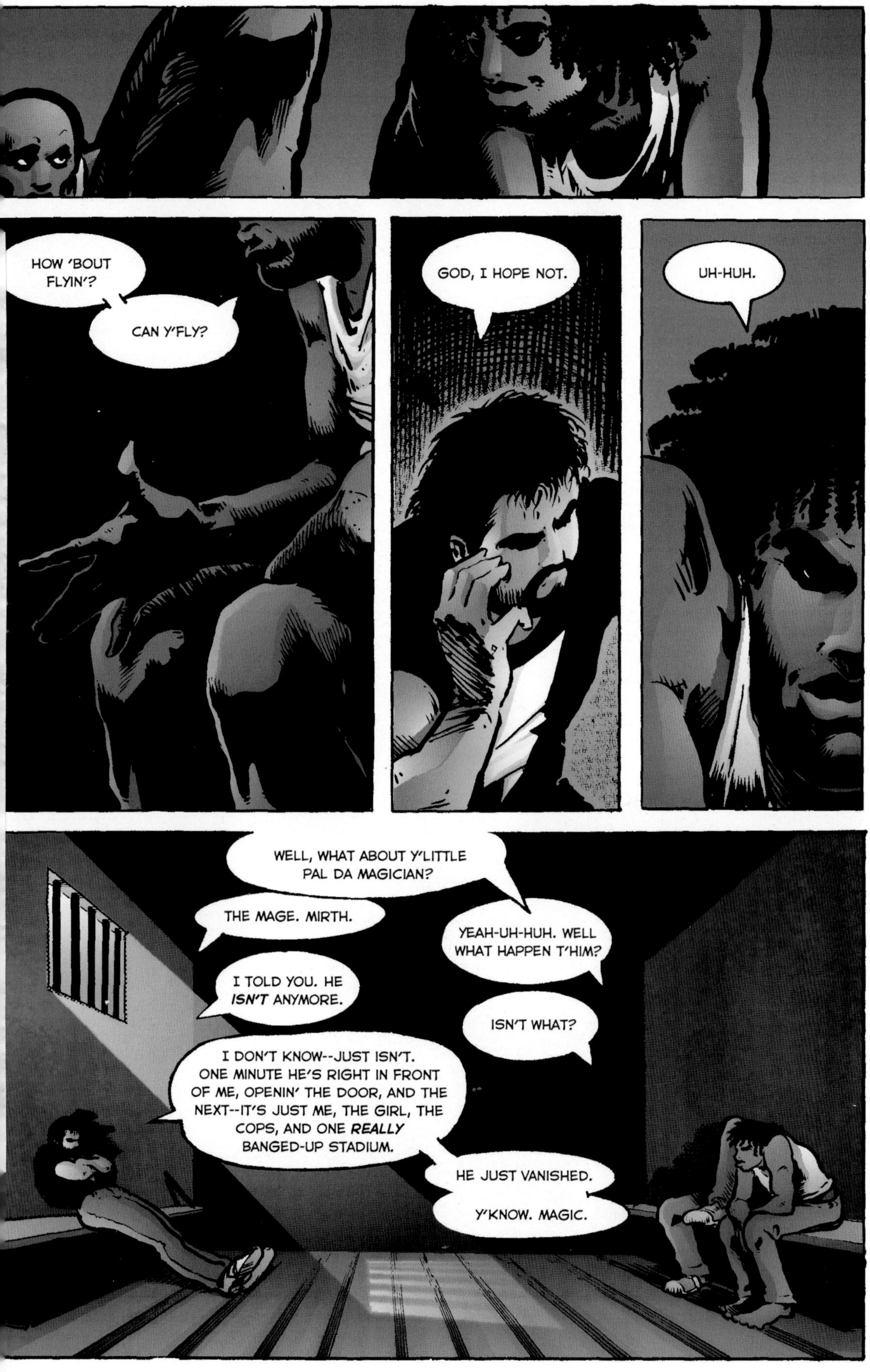
HOW 'BOUT FLYIN'?
CAN Y'FLY?
GOD, I HOPE NOT.
UH-HUH.
WELL, WHAT ABOUT Y'LITTLE PAL DA MAGICIAN?
THE MAGE. MIRTH.
YEAH-UH-HUH. WELL WHAT HAPPEN T'HIM?
I TOLD YOU. HE *ISN'T* ANYMORE.
ISN'T WHAT?
I DON'T KNOW--JUST ISN'T. ONE MINUTE HE'S RIGHT IN FRONT OF ME, OPENIN' THE DOOR, AND THE NEXT--IT'S JUST ME, THE GIRL, THE COPS, AND ONE *REALLY* BANGED-UP STADIUM.
HE JUST VANISHED.
Y'KNOW. MAGIC.

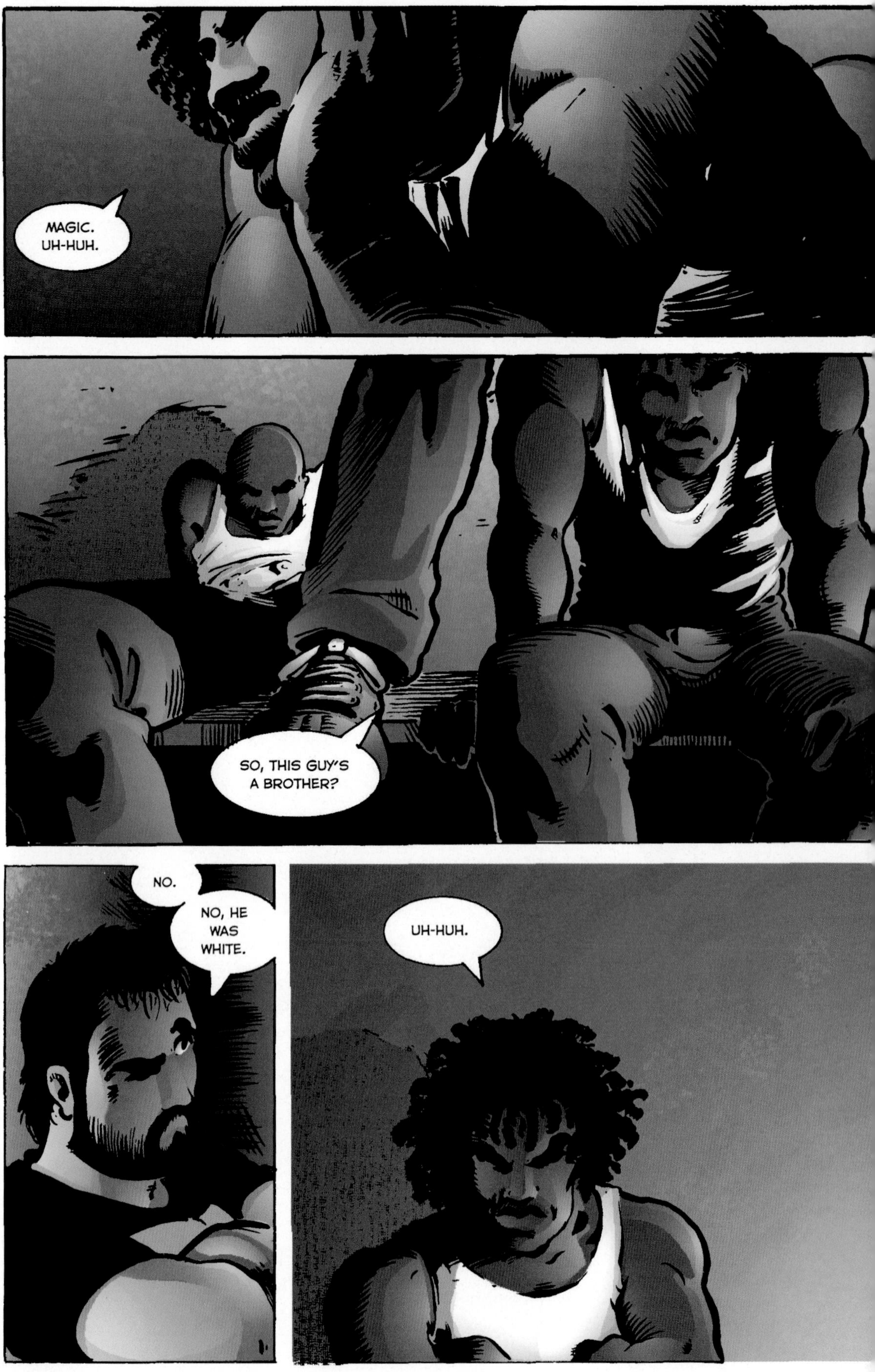
MAGIC.
UH-HUH.
SO, THIS GUY'S A BROTHER?
NO.
NO, HE WAS WHITE.
UH-HUH.

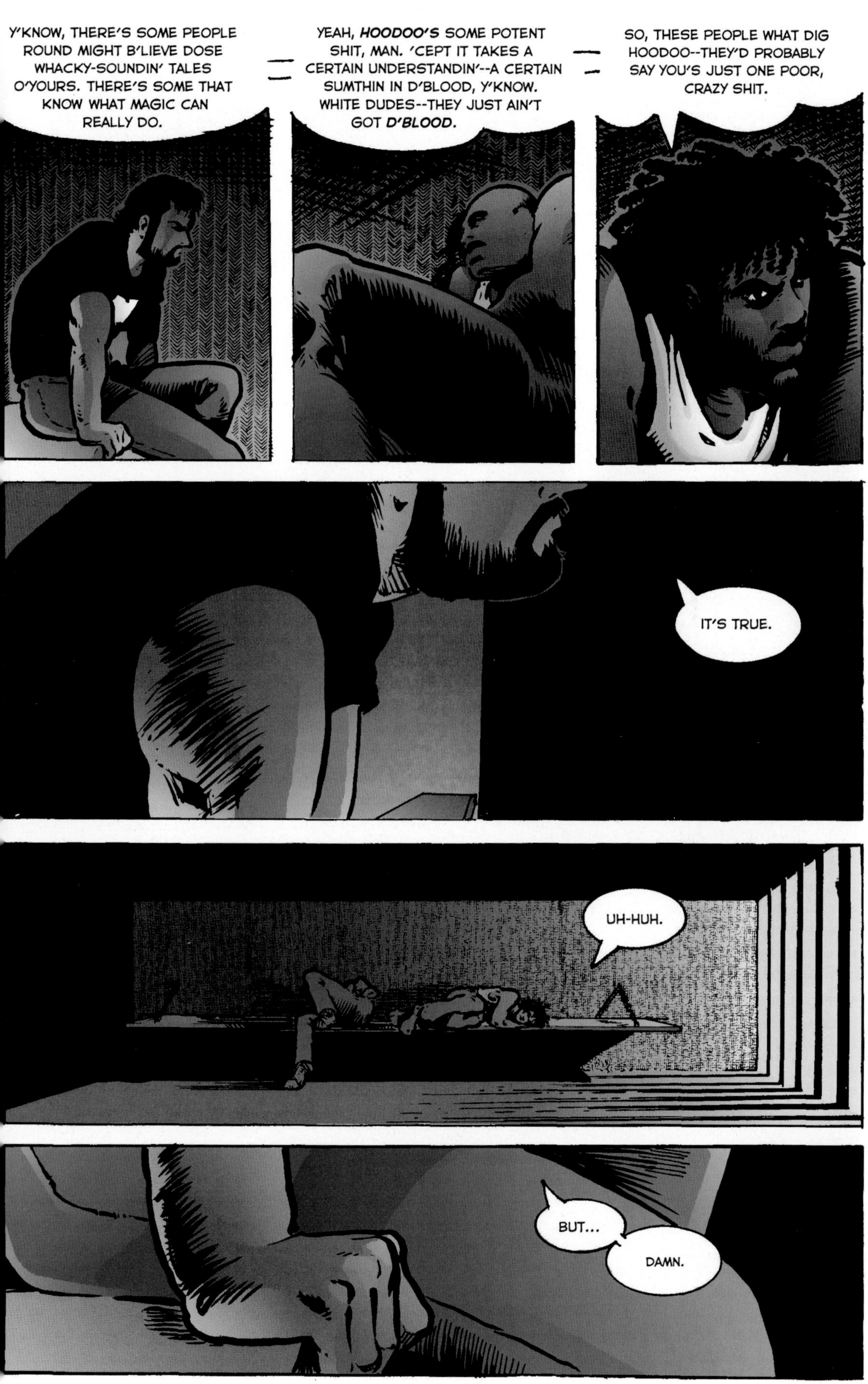
Y'KNOW, THERE'S SOME PEOPLE ROUND MIGHT B'LIEVE DOSE WHACKY-SOUNDIN' TALES O'YOURS. THERE'S SOME THAT KNOW WHAT MAGIC CAN REALLY DO.
YEAH, ***HOODOO'S*** SOME POTENT SHIT, MAN. 'CEPT IT TAKES A CERTAIN UNDERSTANDIN'--A CERTAIN SUMTHIN IN D'BLOOD, Y'KNOW. WHITE DUDES--THEY JUST AIN'T GOT ***D'BLOOD.***
SO, THESE PEOPLE WHAT DIG HOODOO--THEY'D PROBABLY SAY YOU'S JUST ONE POOR, CRAZY SHIT.
IT'S TRUE.
UH-HUH.
BUT...
DAMN.

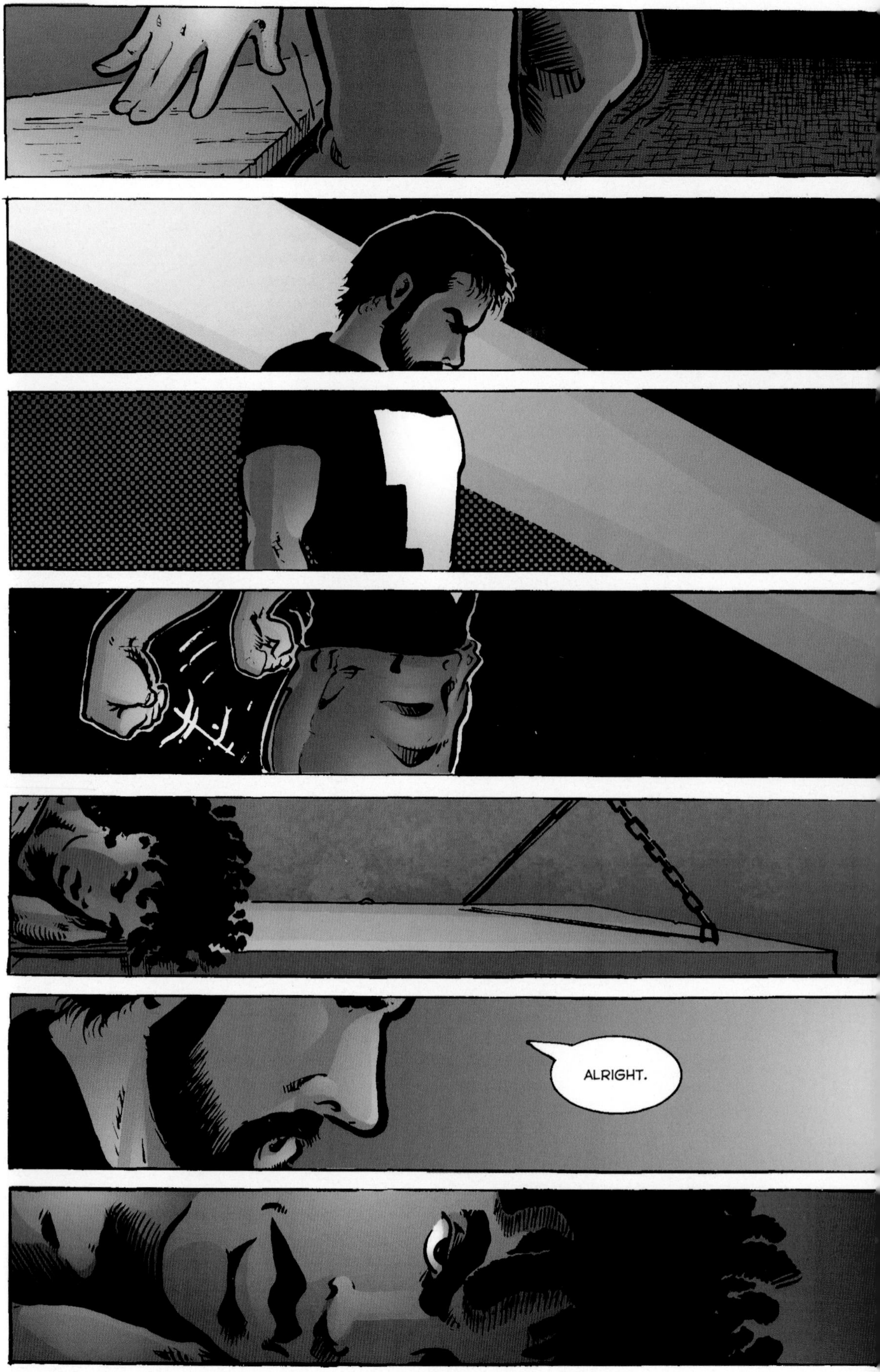
ALRIGHT.

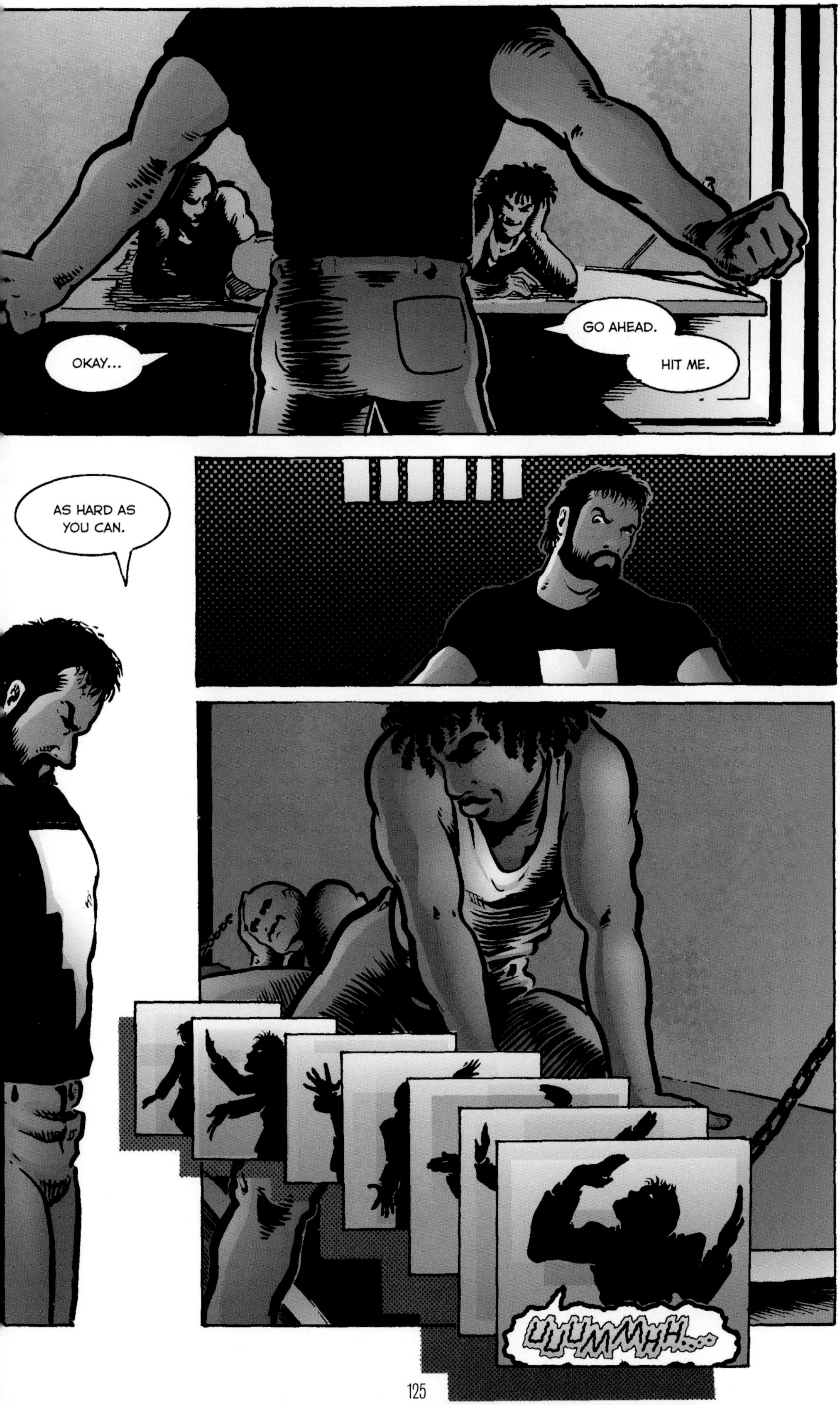
OKAY...
GO AHEAD.
HIT ME.
AS HARD AS YOU CAN.
UUUMMHH...

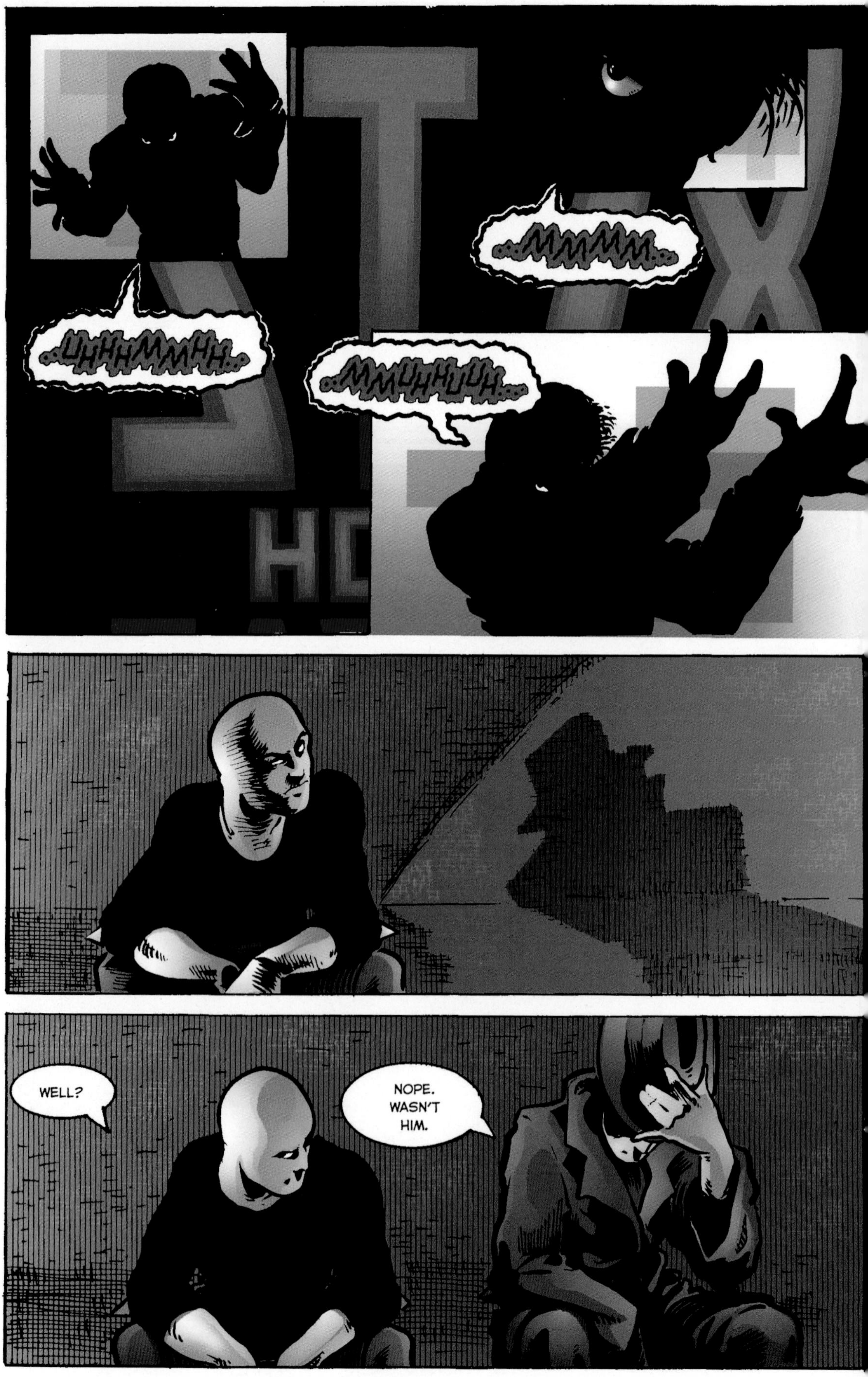
..UHHHMMHH..
..MMMM..
..MMUHHUUH...
WELL?
NOPE. WASN'T HIM.

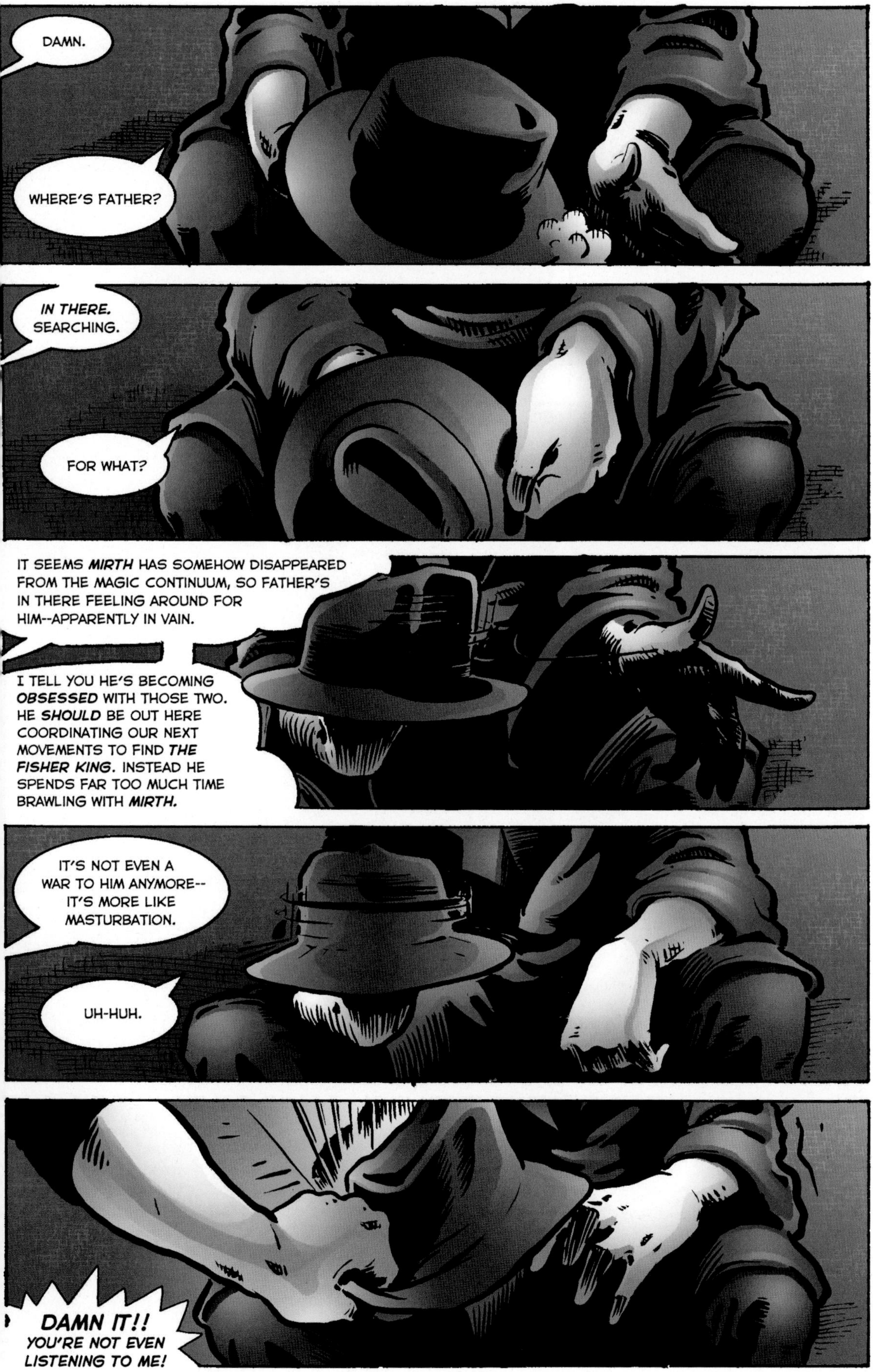
DAMN.
WHERE'S FATHER?
IN THERE. SEARCHING.
FOR WHAT?
IT SEEMS *MIRTH* HAS SOMEHOW DISAPPEARED FROM THE MAGIC CONTINUUM, SO FATHER'S IN THERE FEELING AROUND FOR HIM--APPARENTLY IN VAIN.
I TELL YOU HE'S BECOMING *OBSESSED* WITH THOSE TWO. HE *SHOULD* BE OUT HERE COORDINATING OUR NEXT MOVEMENTS TO FIND *THE FISHER KING*. INSTEAD HE SPENDS FAR TOO MUCH TIME BRAWLING WITH *MIRTH.*
IT'S NOT EVEN A WAR TO HIM ANYMORE-- IT'S MORE LIKE MASTURBATION.
UH-HUH.
DAMN IT!! YOU'RE NOT EVEN LISTENING TO ME!

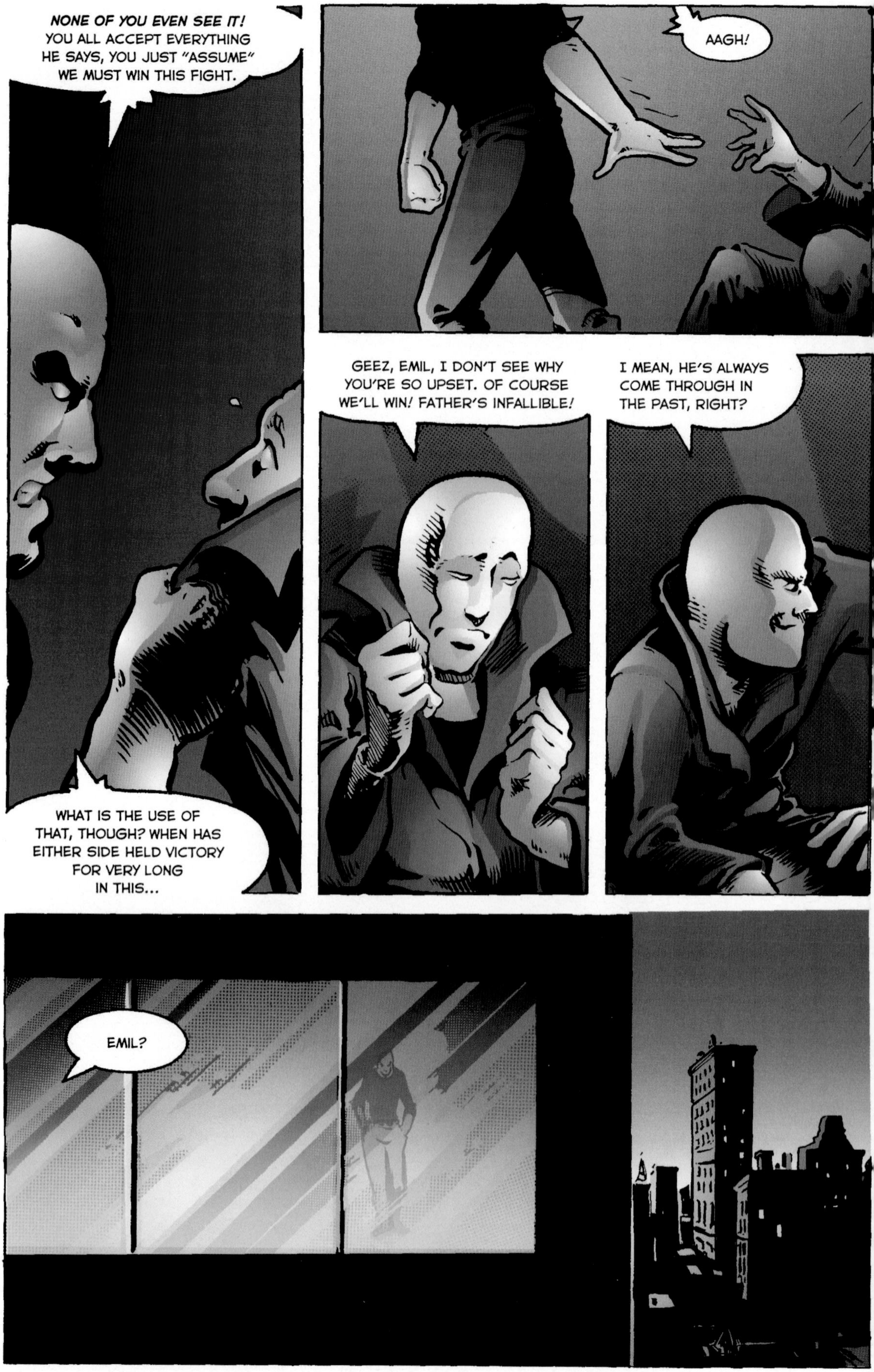
NONE OF YOU EVEN SEE IT! YOU ALL ACCEPT EVERYTHING HE SAYS, YOU JUST "ASSUME" WE MUST WIN THIS FIGHT.
WHAT IS THE USE OF THAT, THOUGH? WHEN HAS EITHER SIDE HELD VICTORY FOR VERY LONG IN THIS...
AAGH!
GEEZ, EMIL, I DON'T SEE WHY YOU'RE SO UPSET. OF COURSE WE'LL WIN! FATHER'S INFALLIBLE!
I MEAN, HE'S ALWAYS COME THROUGH IN THE PAST, RIGHT?
EMIL?

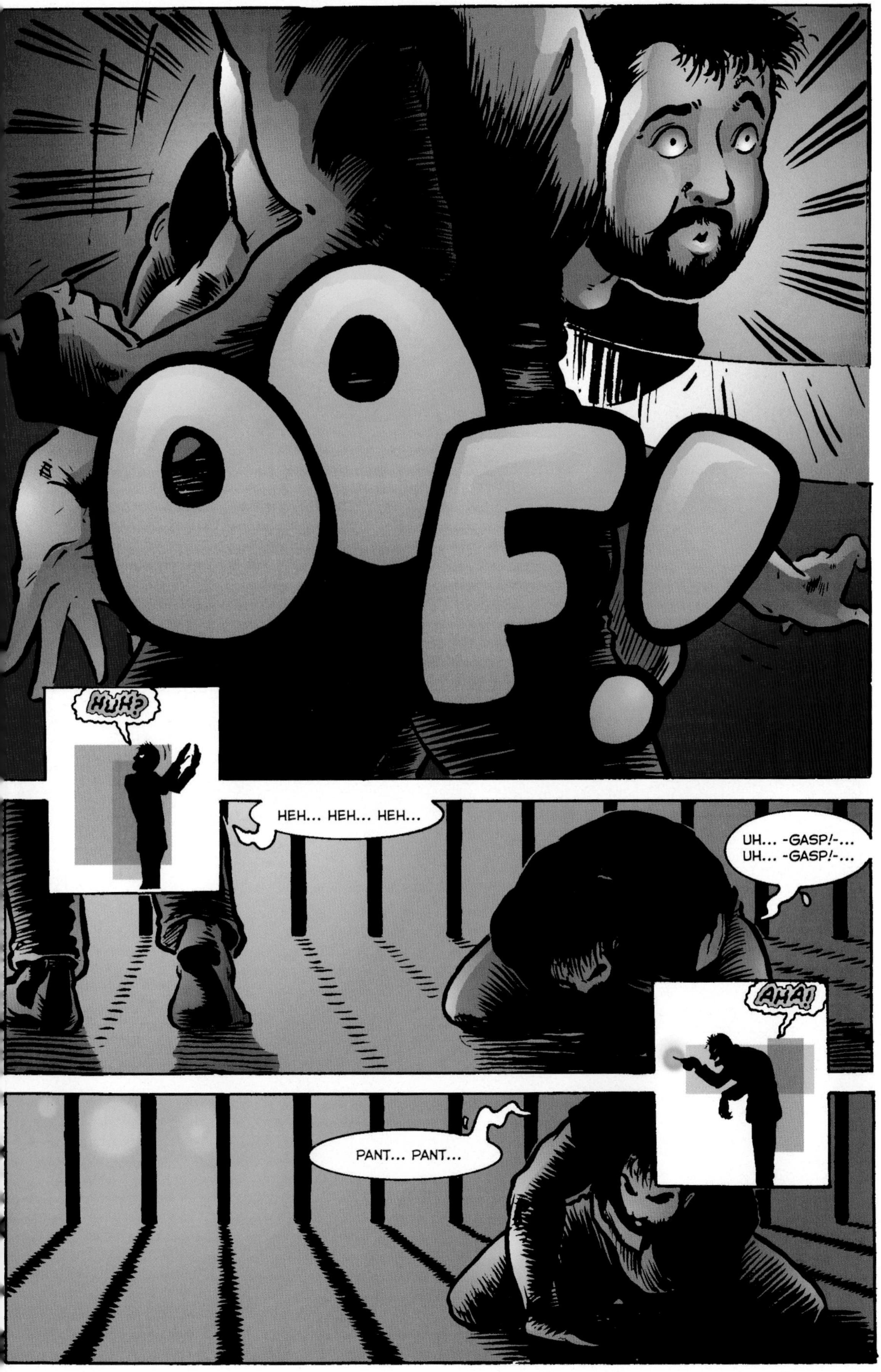
OOF!
HUH?
HEH... HEH... HEH...
UH... -GASP!-...
UH... -GASP!-...
AHA!
PANT... PANT...

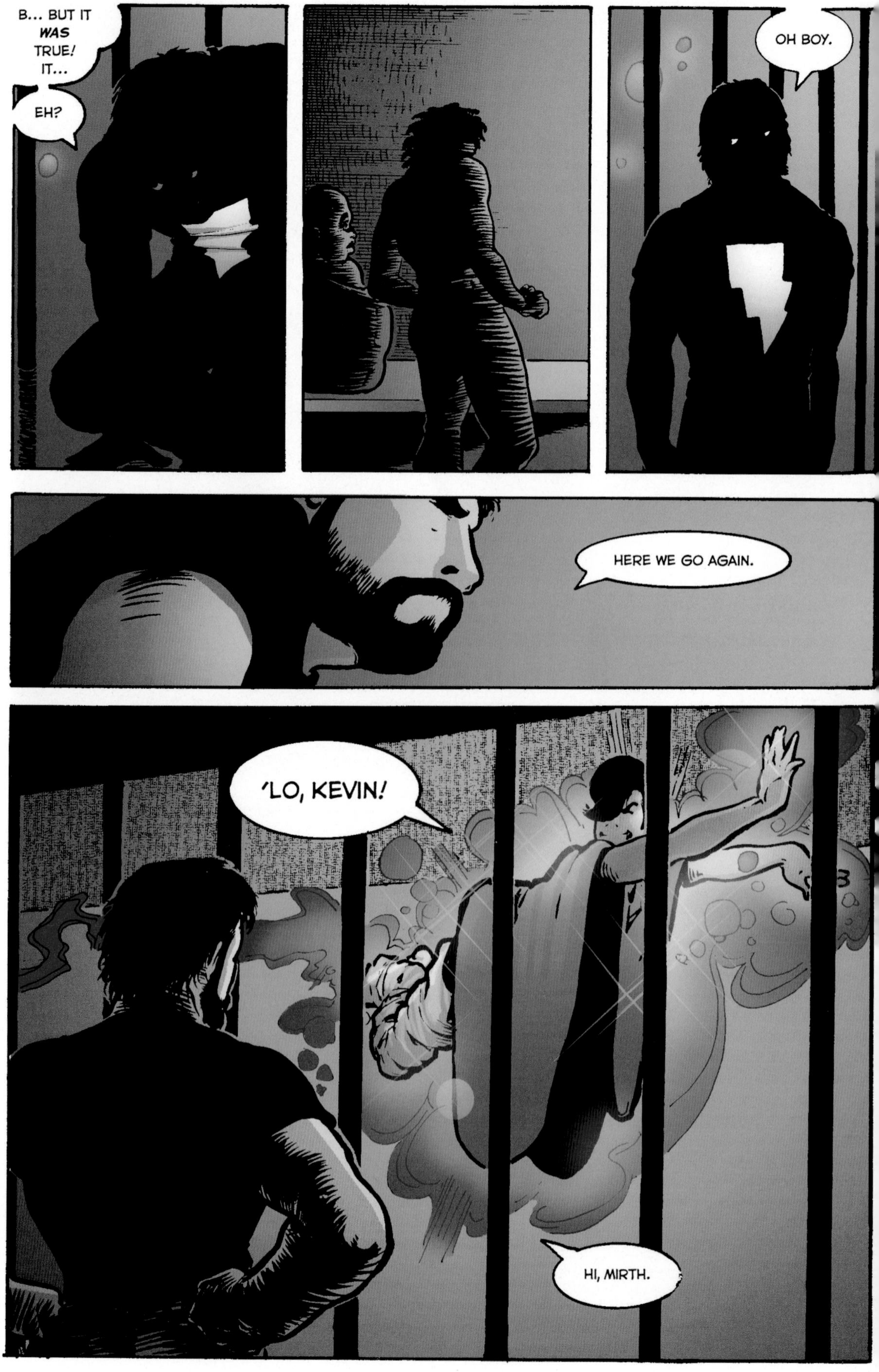
B... BUT IT WAS TRUE! IT...
EH?
OH BOY.
HERE WE GO AGAIN.
'LO, KEVIN!
HI, MIRTH.

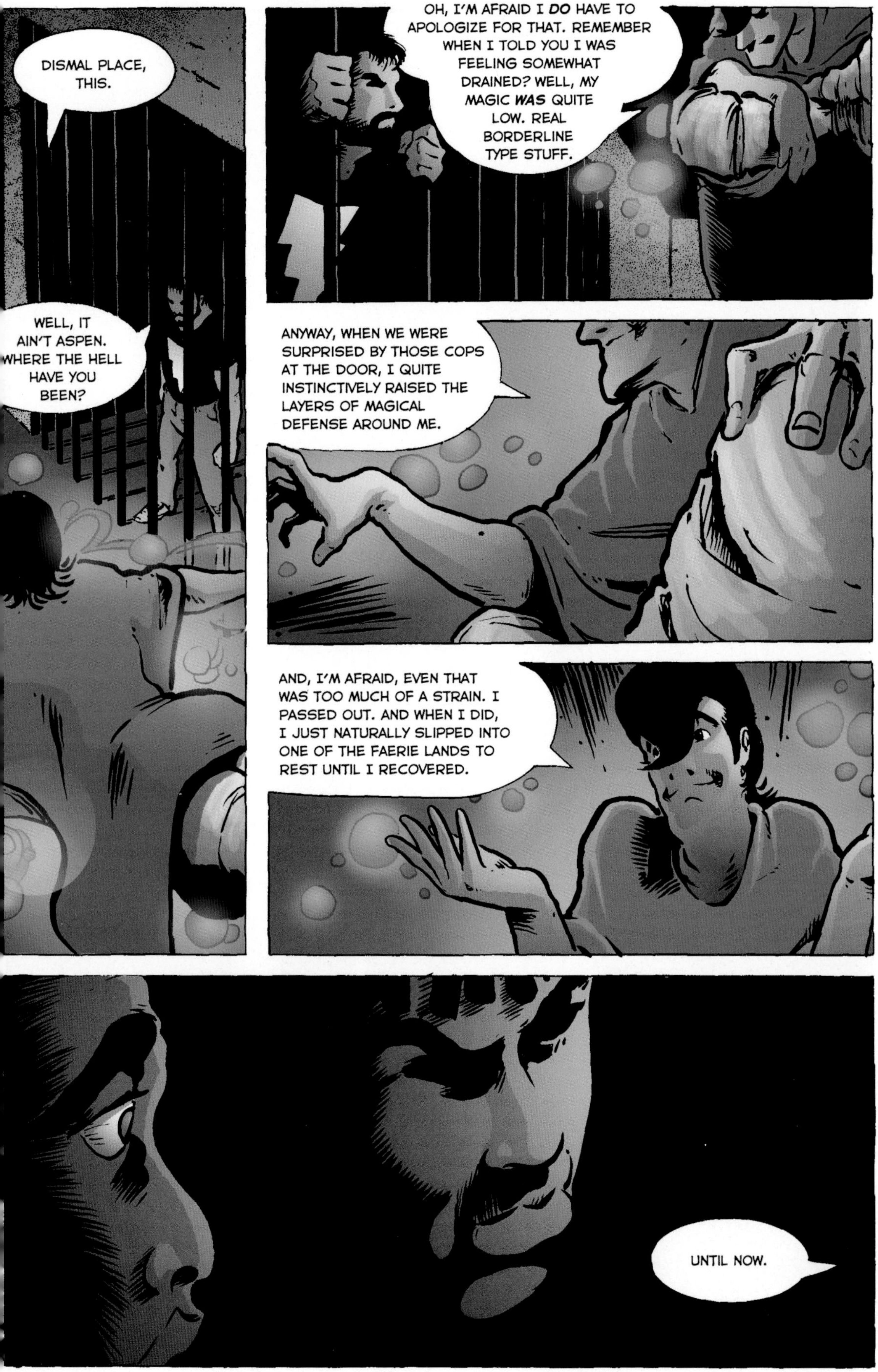
DISMAL PLACE, THIS.
OH, I'M AFRAID I DO HAVE TO APOLOGIZE FOR THAT. REMEMBER WHEN I TOLD YOU I WAS FEELING SOMEWHAT DRAINED? WELL, MY MAGIC WAS QUITE LOW. REAL BORDERLINE TYPE STUFF.
WELL, IT AIN'T ASPEN. WHERE THE HELL HAVE YOU BEEN?
ANYWAY, WHEN WE WERE SURPRISED BY THOSE COPS AT THE DOOR, I QUITE INSTINCTIVELY RAISED THE LAYERS OF MAGICAL DEFENSE AROUND ME.
AND, I'M AFRAID, EVEN THAT WAS TOO MUCH OF A STRAIN. I PASSED OUT. AND WHEN I DID, I JUST NATURALLY SLIPPED INTO ONE OF THE FAERIE LANDS TO REST UNTIL I RECOVERED.
UNTIL NOW.

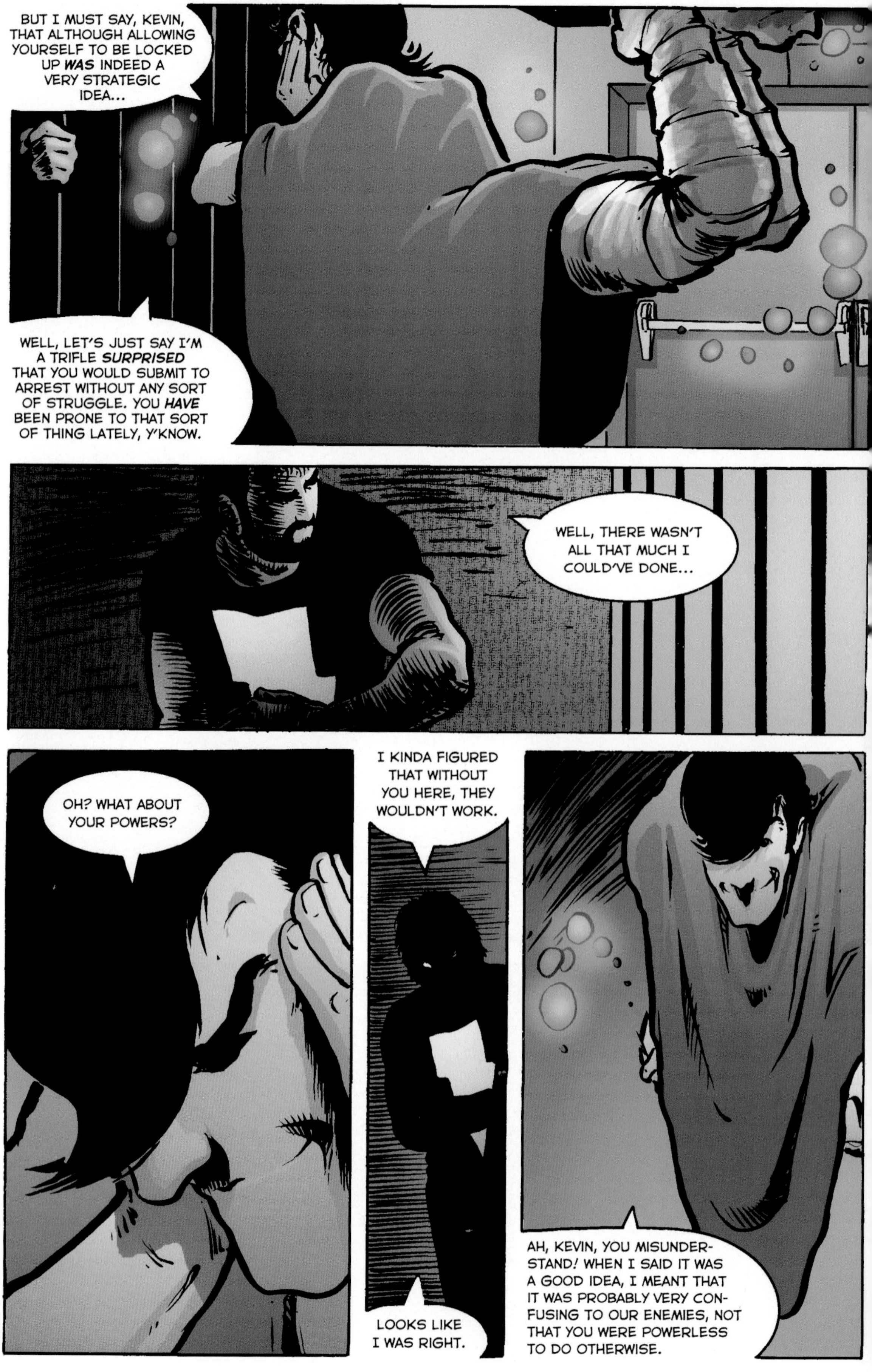
BUT I MUST SAY, KEVIN, THAT ALTHOUGH ALLOWING YOURSELF TO BE LOCKED UP WAS INDEED A VERY STRATEGIC IDEA...
WELL, LET'S JUST SAY I'M A TRIFLE SURPRISED THAT YOU WOULD SUBMIT TO ARREST WITHOUT ANY SORT OF STRUGGLE. YOU HAVE BEEN PRONE TO THAT SORT OF THING LATELY, Y'KNOW.
WELL, THERE WASN'T ALL THAT MUCH I COULD'VE DONE...
OH? WHAT ABOUT YOUR POWERS?
I KINDA FIGURED THAT WITHOUT YOU HERE, THEY WOULDN'T WORK.
LOOKS LIKE I WAS RIGHT.
AH, KEVIN, YOU MISUNDER-STAND! WHEN I SAID IT WAS A GOOD IDEA, I MEANT THAT IT WAS PROBABLY VERY CON-FUSING TO OUR ENEMIES, NOT THAT YOU WERE POWERLESS TO DO OTHERWISE.

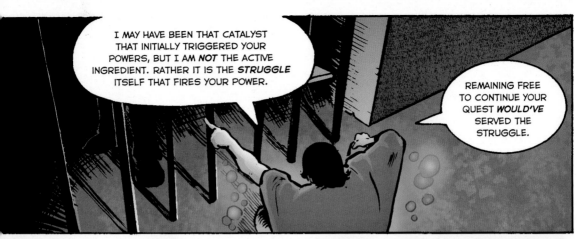

I MAY HAVE BEEN THAT CATALYST THAT INITIALLY TRIGGERED YOUR POWERS, BUT I AM *NOT* THE ACTIVE INGREDIENT. RATHER IT IS THE *STRUGGLE* ITSELF THAT FIRES YOUR POWER.

REMAINING FREE TO CONTINUE YOUR QUEST *WOULD'VE* SERVED THE STRUGGLE.

PROVING YOURSELF TO YOUR CELLMATES DID NOT.

BUT NOW THESE BARS STAND BETWEEN YOU AND YOUR TASK THAT AWAITS.

SO, TEAR THEM DOWN, KEVIN. USE YOUR STRENGTH.

THE STRUGGLE CALLS.

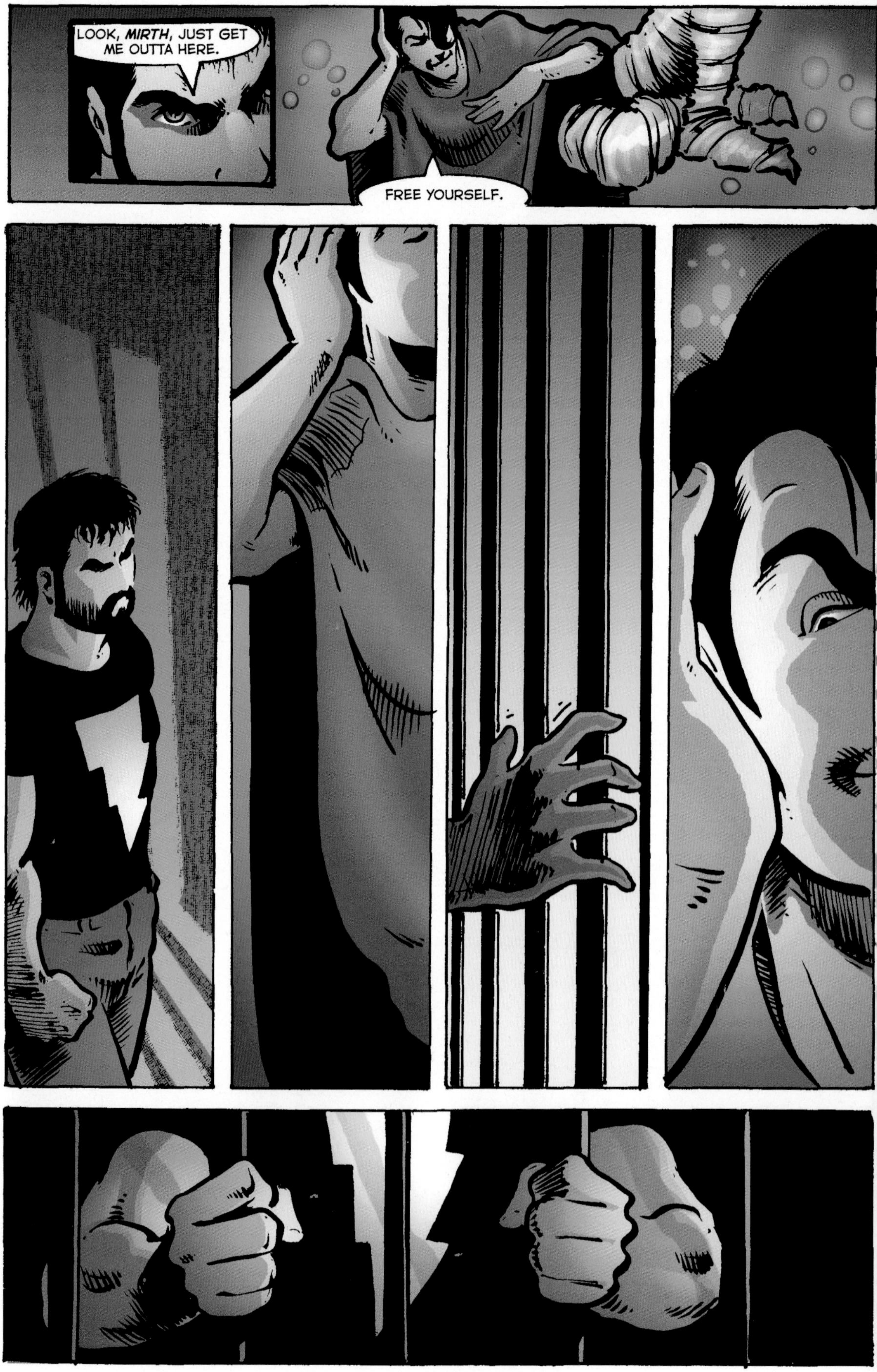
LOOK, *MIRTH*, JUST GET ME OUTTA HERE.
FREE YOURSELF.

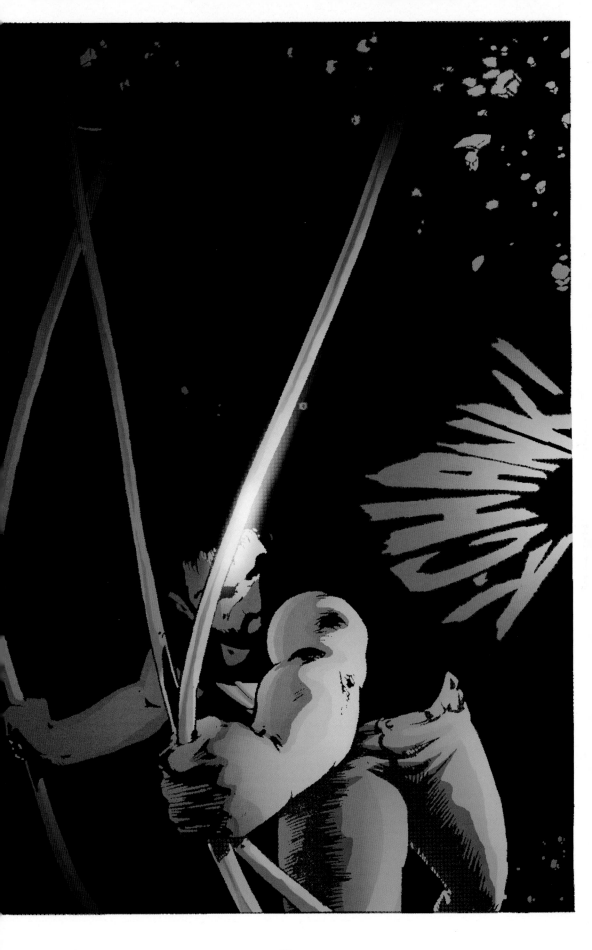

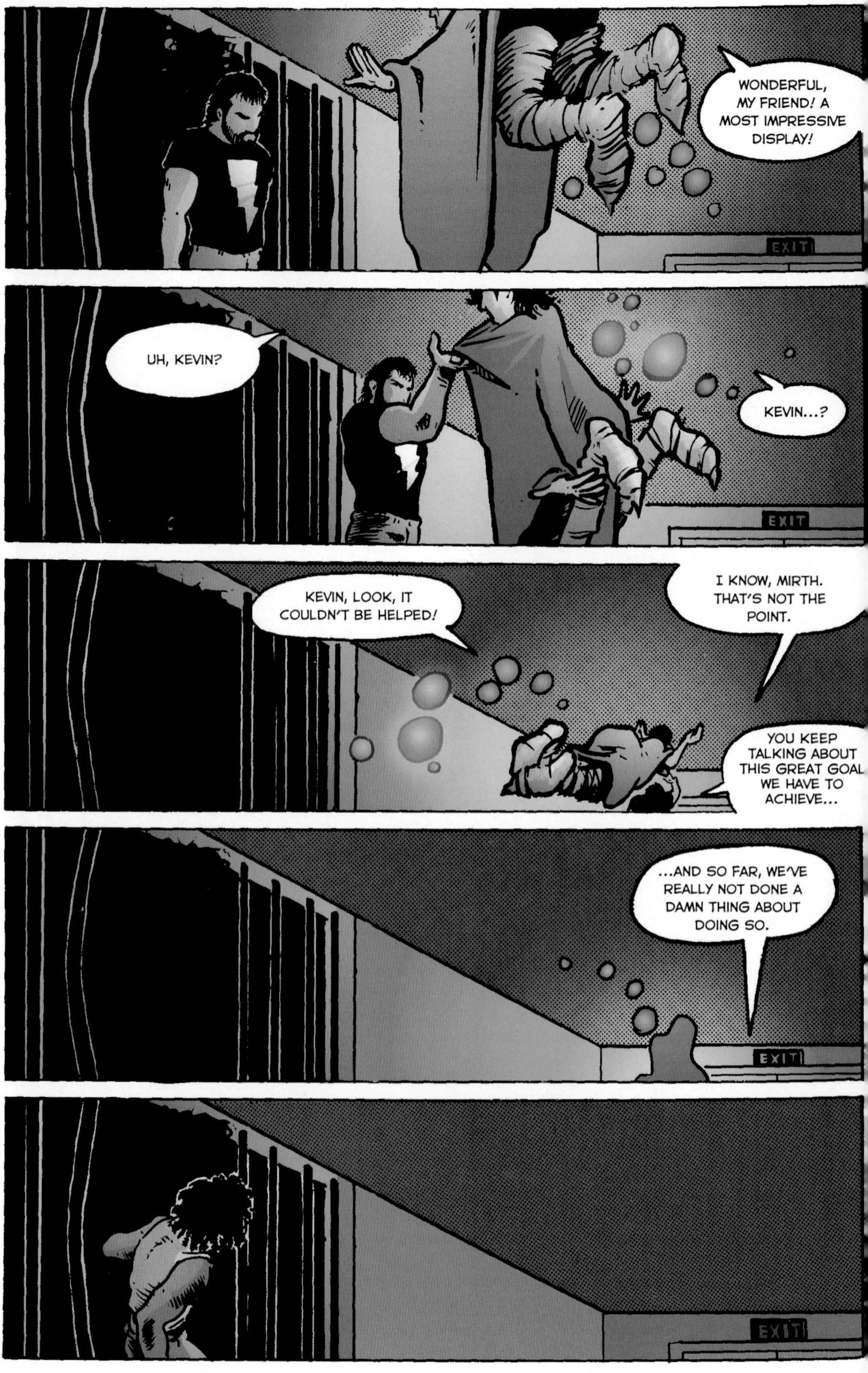
WONDERFUL, MY FRIEND! A MOST IMPRESSIVE DISPLAY!
EXIT
UH, KEVIN?
KEVIN...?
EXIT
KEVIN, LOOK, IT COULDN'T BE HELPED!
I KNOW, MIRTH. THAT'S NOT THE POINT.
YOU KEEP TALKING ABOUT THIS GREAT GOAL WE HAVE TO ACHIEVE...
...AND SO FAR, WE'VE REALLY NOT DONE A DAMN THING ABOUT DOING SO.
EXIT
EXIT

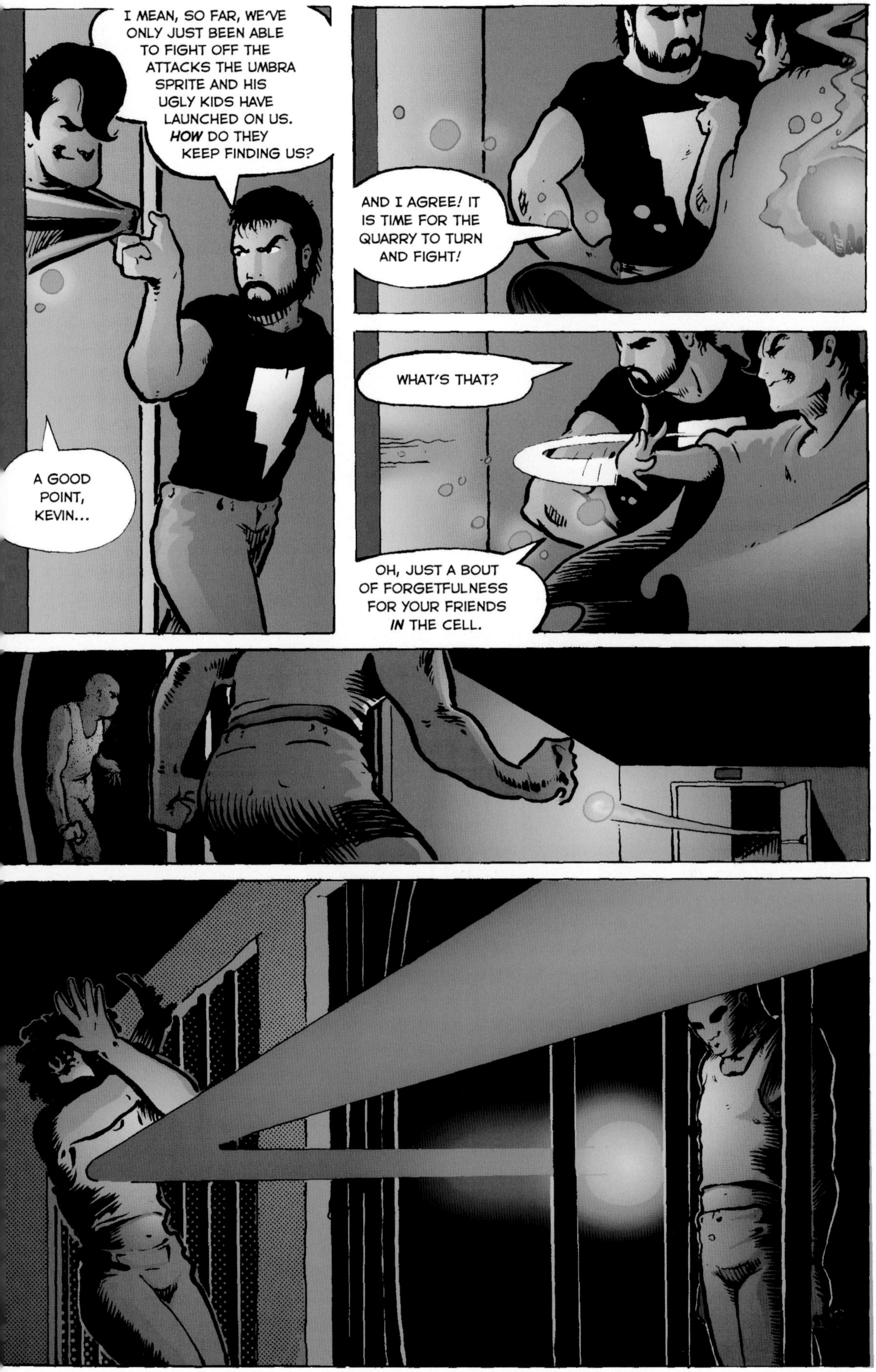

I MEAN, SO FAR, WE'VE ONLY JUST BEEN ABLE TO FIGHT OFF THE ATTACKS THE UMBRA SPRITE AND HIS UGLY KIDS HAVE LAUNCHED ON US. *HOW* DO THEY KEEP FINDING US?
A GOOD POINT, KEVIN...
AND I AGREE! IT IS TIME FOR THE QUARRY TO TURN AND FIGHT!
WHAT'S THAT?
OH, JUST A BOUT OF FORGETFULNESS FOR YOUR FRIENDS *IN* THE CELL.

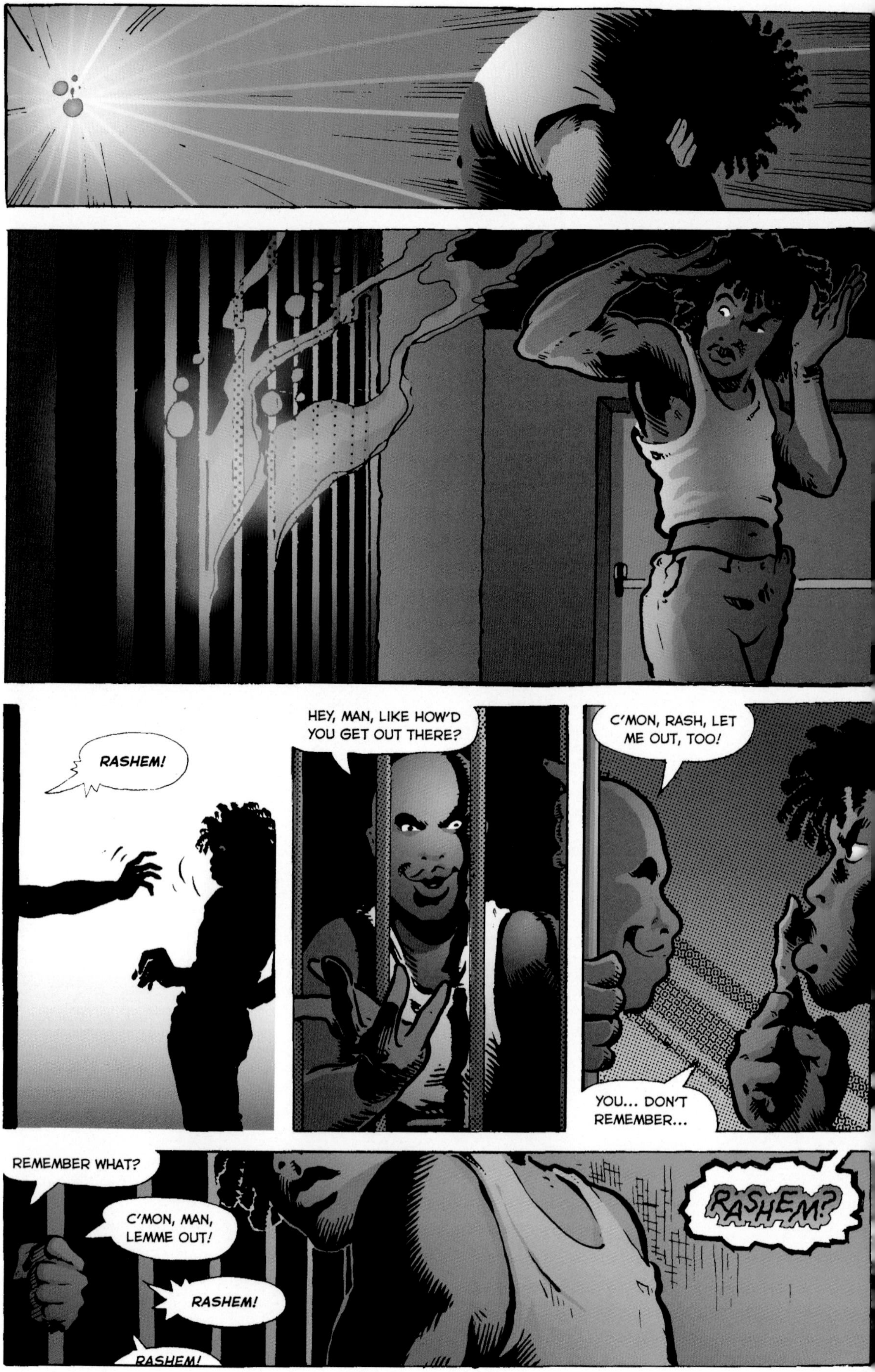
RASHEM!
HEY, MAN, LIKE HOW'D YOU GET OUT THERE?
C'MON, RASH, LET ME OUT, TOO!
YOU... DON'T REMEMBER...
REMEMBER WHAT?
C'MON, MAN, LEMME OUT!
RASHEM!
RASHEM!
RASHEM?

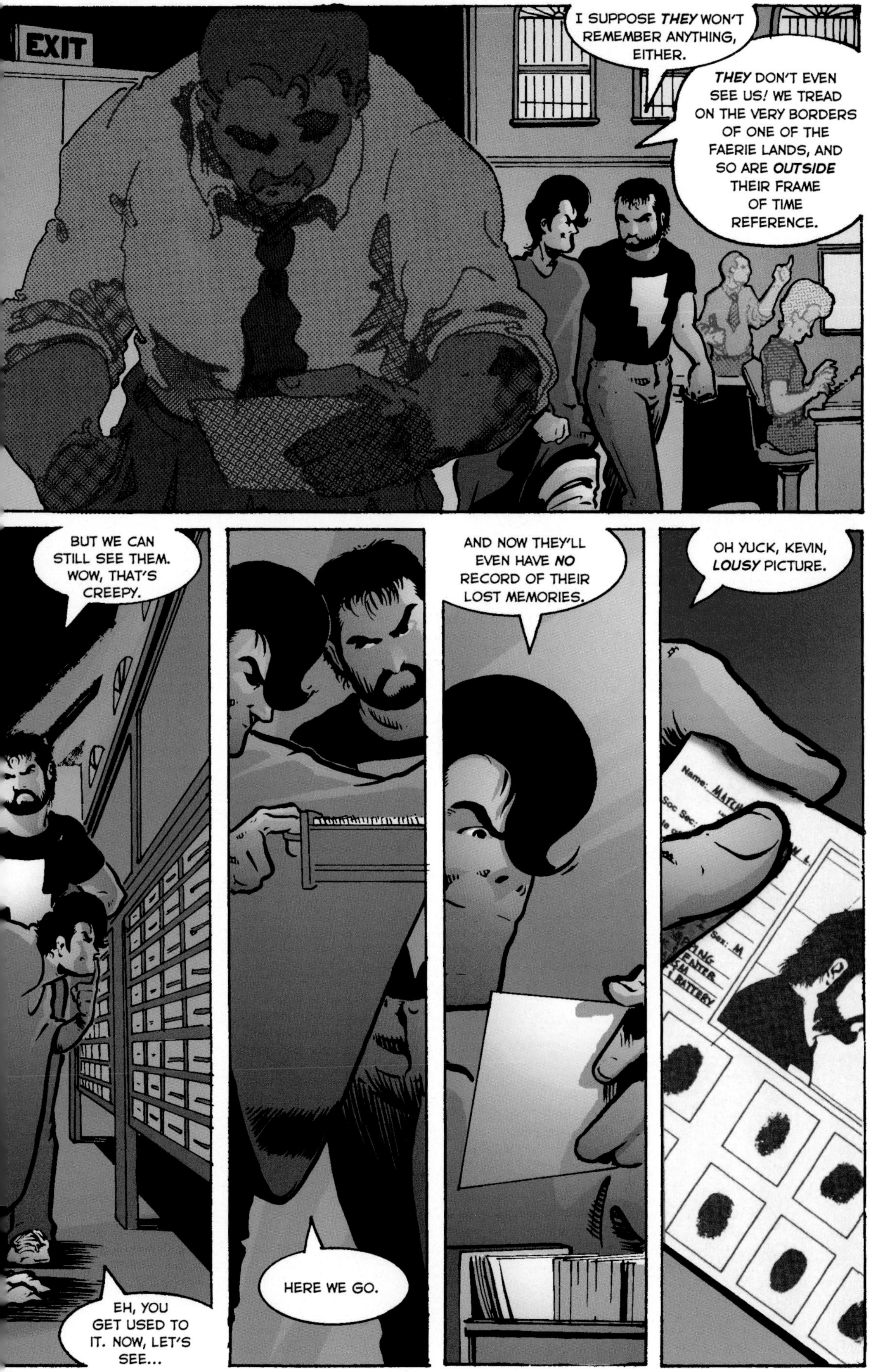
EXIT
I SUPPOSE THEY WON'T REMEMBER ANYTHING, EITHER.
THEY DON'T EVEN SEE US! WE TREAD ON THE VERY BORDERS OF ONE OF THE FAERIE LANDS, AND SO ARE OUTSIDE THEIR FRAME OF TIME REFERENCE.
BUT WE CAN STILL SEE THEM. WOW, THAT'S CREEPY.
EH, YOU GET USED TO IT. NOW, LET'S SEE...
HERE WE GO.
AND NOW THEY'LL EVEN HAVE NO RECORD OF THEIR LOST MEMORIES.
OH YUCK, KEVIN, LOUSY PICTURE.

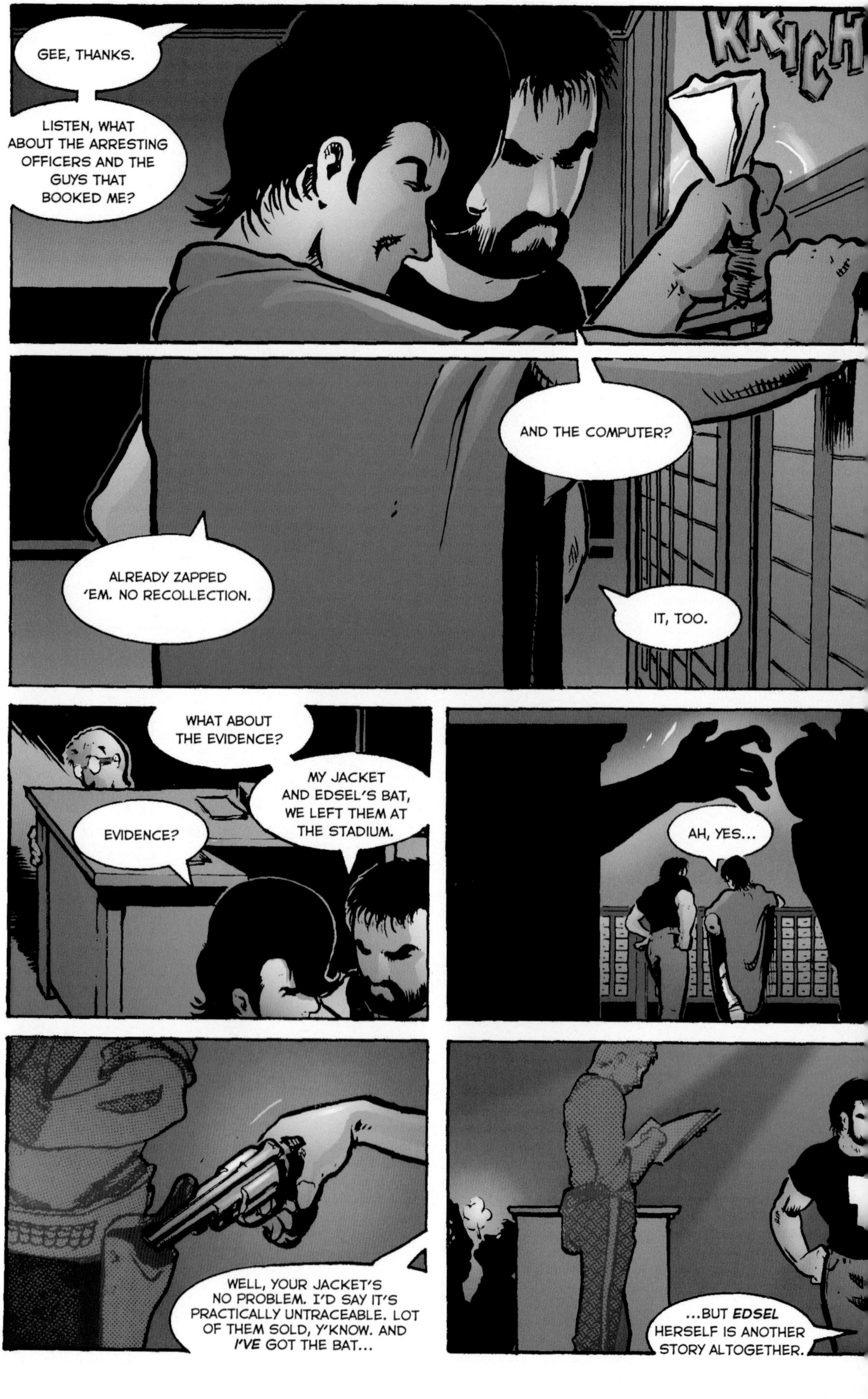

KRICH
GEE, THANKS.
LISTEN, WHAT ABOUT THE ARRESTING OFFICERS AND THE GUYS THAT BOOKED ME?
AND THE COMPUTER?
ALREADY ZAPPED 'EM. NO RECOLLECTION.
IT, TOO.
WHAT ABOUT THE EVIDENCE?
EVIDENCE?
MY JACKET AND EDSEL'S BAT, WE LEFT THEM AT THE STADIUM.
AH, YES...
WELL, YOUR JACKET'S NO PROBLEM. I'D SAY IT'S PRACTICALLY UNTRACEABLE. LOT OF THEM SOLD, Y'KNOW. AND *I'VE* GOT THE BAT...
...BUT *EDSEL* HERSELF IS ANOTHER STORY ALTOGETHER.

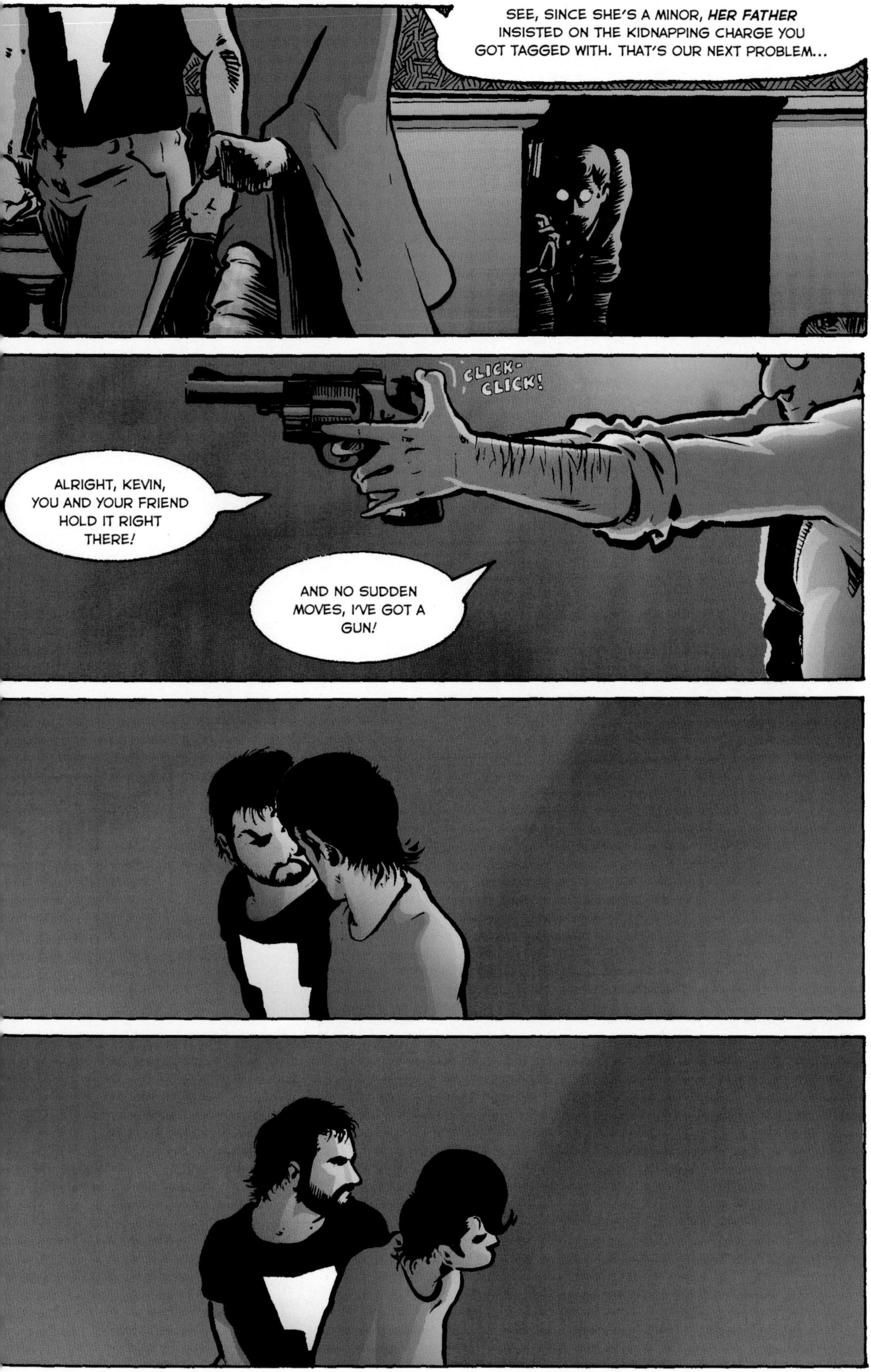
SEE, SINCE SHE'S A MINOR, ***HER FATHER*** INSISTED ON THE KIDNAPPING CHARGE YOU GOT TAGGED WITH. THAT'S OUR NEXT PROBLEM...
CLICK-CLICK!
ALRIGHT, KEVIN, YOU AND YOUR FRIEND HOLD IT RIGHT THERE!
AND NO SUDDEN MOVES, I'VE GOT A GUN!

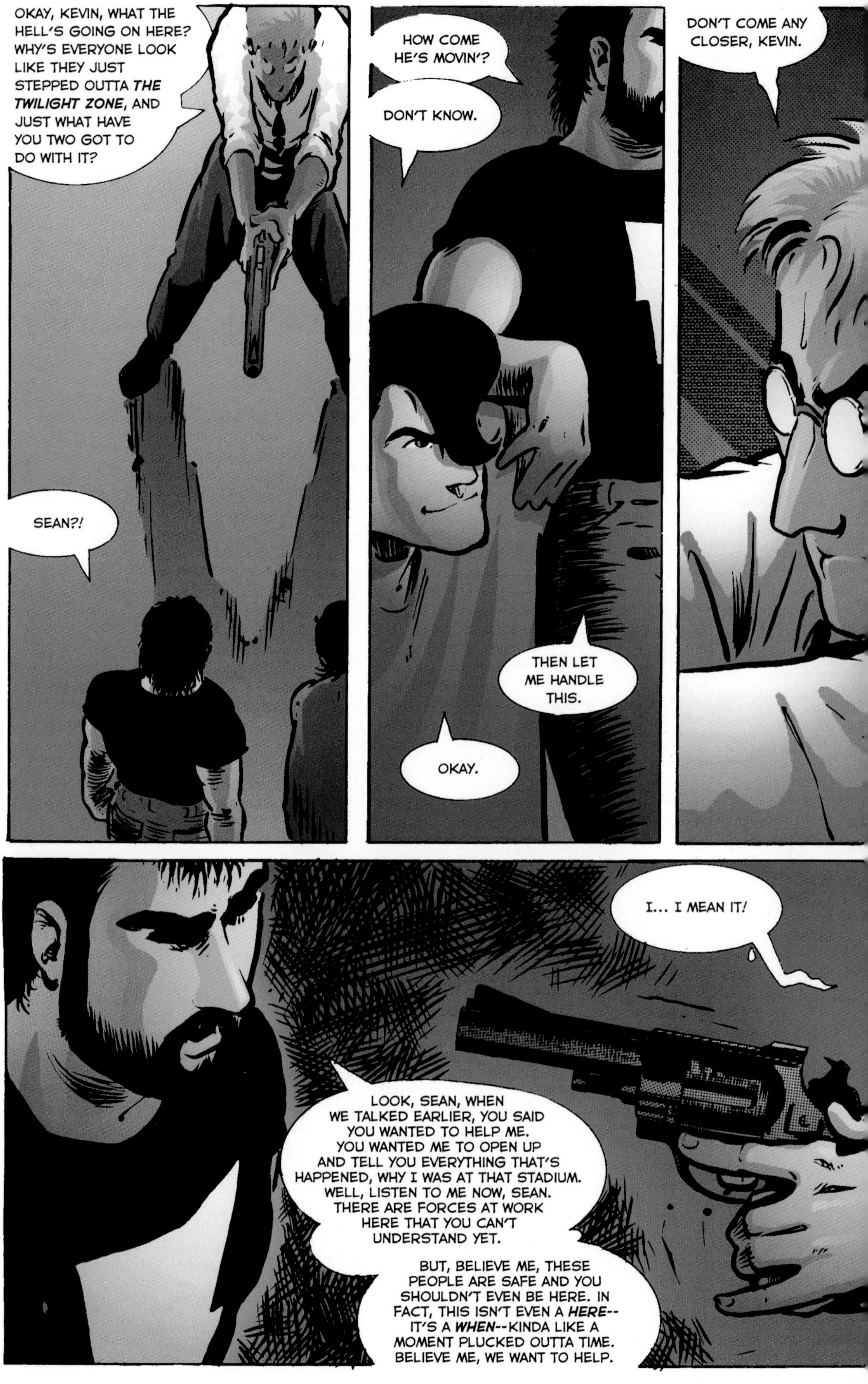
OKAY, KEVIN, WHAT THE HELL'S GOING ON HERE? WHY'S EVERYONE LOOK LIKE THEY JUST STEPPED OUTTA *THE TWILIGHT ZONE*, AND JUST WHAT HAVE YOU TWO GOT TO DO WITH IT?
SEAN?!
HOW COME HE'S MOVIN'?
DON'T KNOW.
THEN LET ME HANDLE THIS.
OKAY.
DON'T COME ANY CLOSER, KEVIN.
I... I MEAN IT!
LOOK, SEAN, WHEN WE TALKED EARLIER, YOU SAID YOU WANTED TO HELP ME. YOU WANTED ME TO OPEN UP AND TELL YOU EVERYTHING THAT'S HAPPENED, WHY I WAS AT THAT STADIUM. WELL, LISTEN TO ME NOW, SEAN. THERE ARE FORCES AT WORK HERE THAT YOU CAN'T UNDERSTAND YET.
BUT, BELIEVE ME, THESE PEOPLE ARE SAFE AND YOU SHOULDN'T EVEN BE HERE. IN FACT, THIS ISN'T EVEN A *HERE*--IT'S A *WHEN*--KINDA LIKE A MOMENT PLUCKED OUTTA TIME. BELIEVE ME, WE WANT TO HELP.

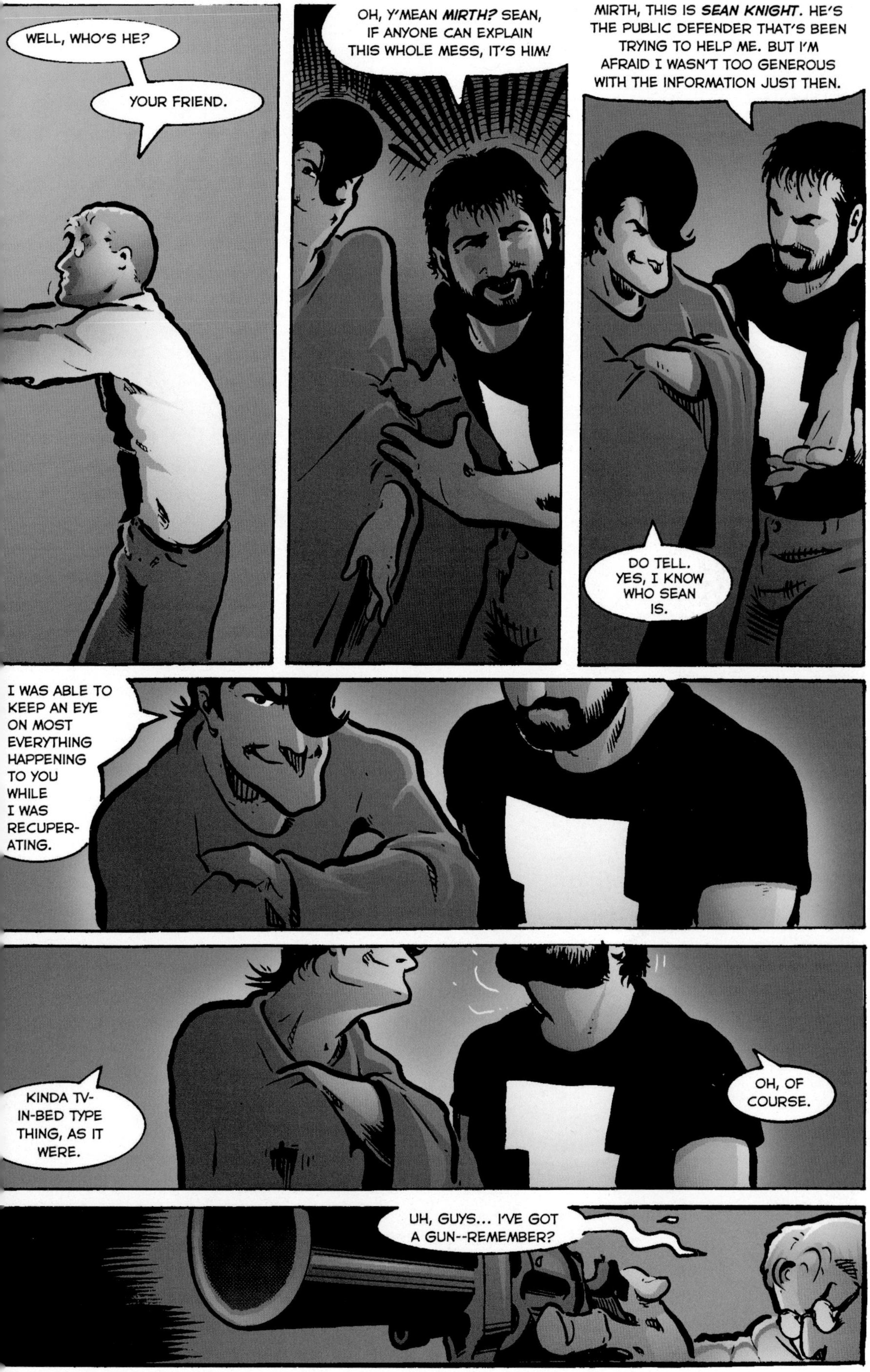
WELL, WHO'S HE?
YOUR FRIEND.
OH, Y'MEAN MIRTH? SEAN, IF ANYONE CAN EXPLAIN THIS WHOLE MESS, IT'S HIM!
MIRTH, THIS IS SEAN KNIGHT. HE'S THE PUBLIC DEFENDER THAT'S BEEN TRYING TO HELP ME. BUT I'M AFRAID I WASN'T TOO GENEROUS WITH THE INFORMATION JUST THEN.
DO TELL. YES, I KNOW WHO SEAN IS.
I WAS ABLE TO KEEP AN EYE ON MOST EVERYTHING HAPPENING TO YOU WHILE I WAS RECUPERATING.
KINDA TV-IN-BED TYPE THING, AS IT WERE.
OH, OF COURSE.
UH, GUYS... I'VE GOT A GUN--REMEMBER?

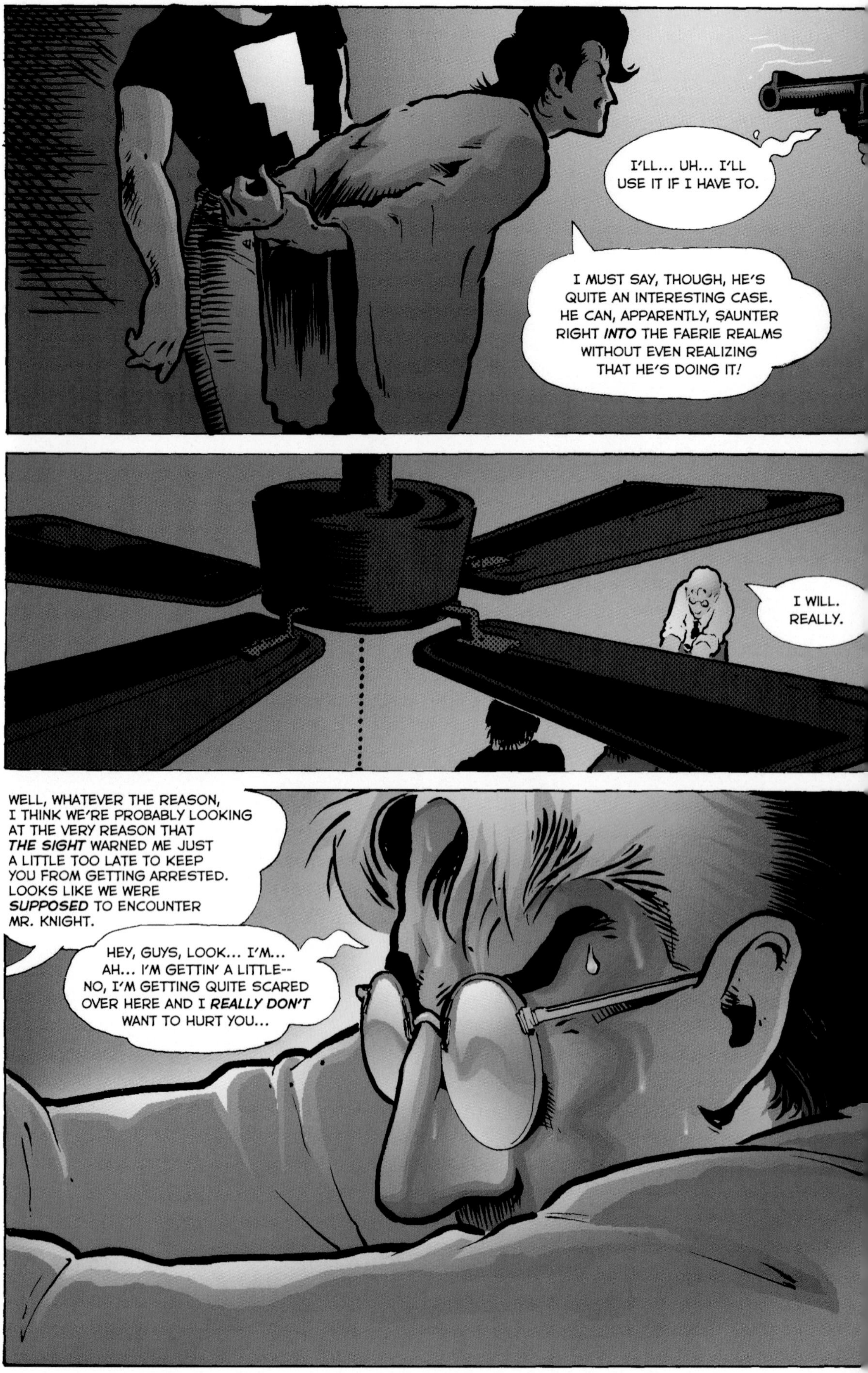
I'LL... UH... I'LL USE IT IF I HAVE TO.
I MUST SAY, THOUGH, HE'S QUITE AN INTERESTING CASE. HE CAN, APPARENTLY, SAUNTER RIGHT *INTO* THE FAERIE REALMS WITHOUT EVEN REALIZING THAT HE'S DOING IT!
I WILL. REALLY.
WELL, WHATEVER THE REASON, I THINK WE'RE PROBABLY LOOKING AT THE VERY REASON THAT *THE SIGHT* WARNED ME JUST A LITTLE TOO LATE TO KEEP YOU FROM GETTING ARRESTED. LOOKS LIKE WE WERE *SUPPOSED* TO ENCOUNTER MR. KNIGHT.
HEY, GUYS, LOOK... I'M... AH... I'M GETTIN' A LITTLE-- NO, I'M GETTING QUITE SCARED OVER HERE AND I *REALLY DON'T* WANT TO HURT YOU...

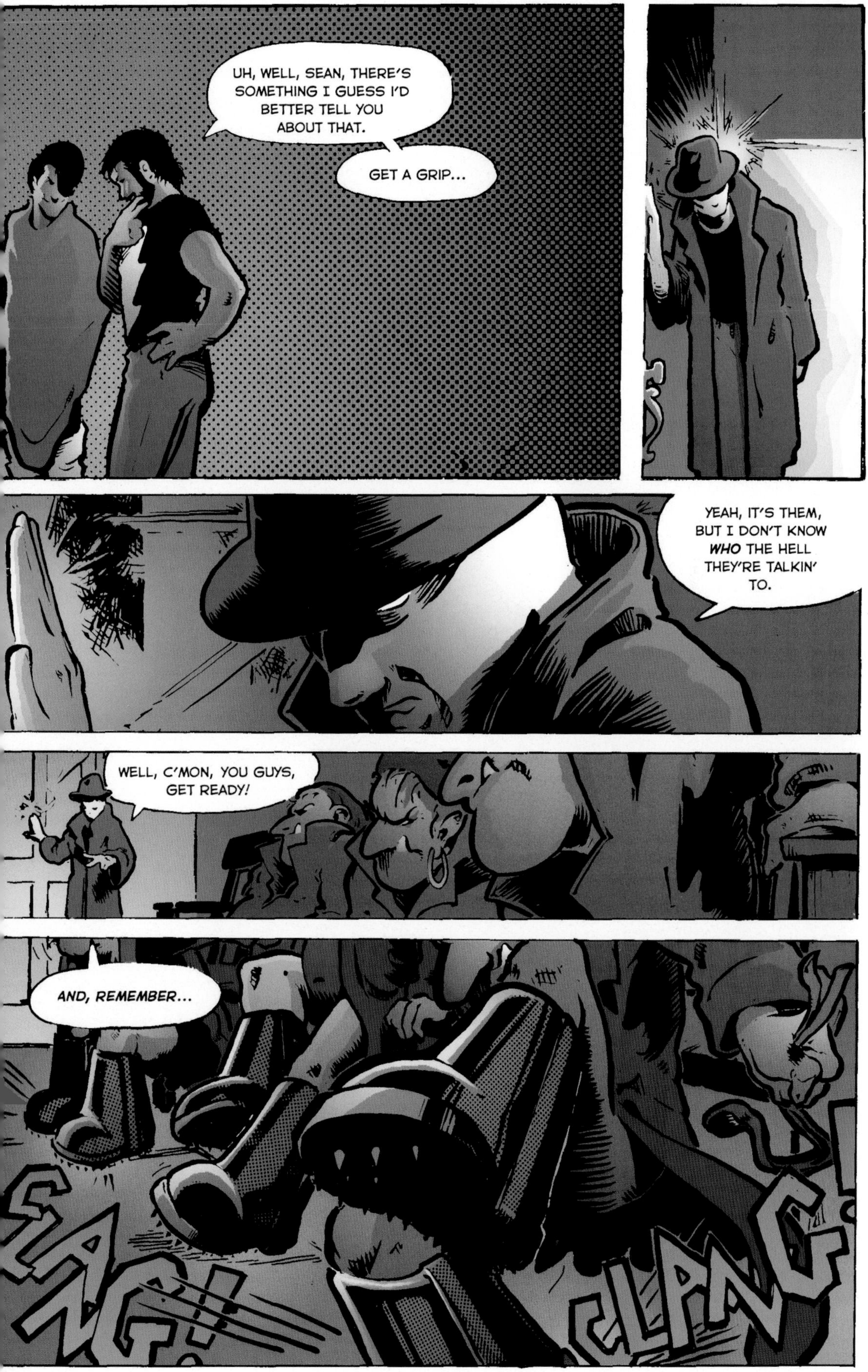
UH, WELL, SEAN, THERE'S SOMETHING I GUESS I'D BETTER TELL YOU ABOUT THAT.
GET A GRIP...
YEAH, IT'S THEM, BUT I DON'T KNOW *WHO* THE HELL THEY'RE TALKIN' TO.
WELL, C'MON, YOU GUYS, GET READY!
AND, REMEMBER...
CLANG!

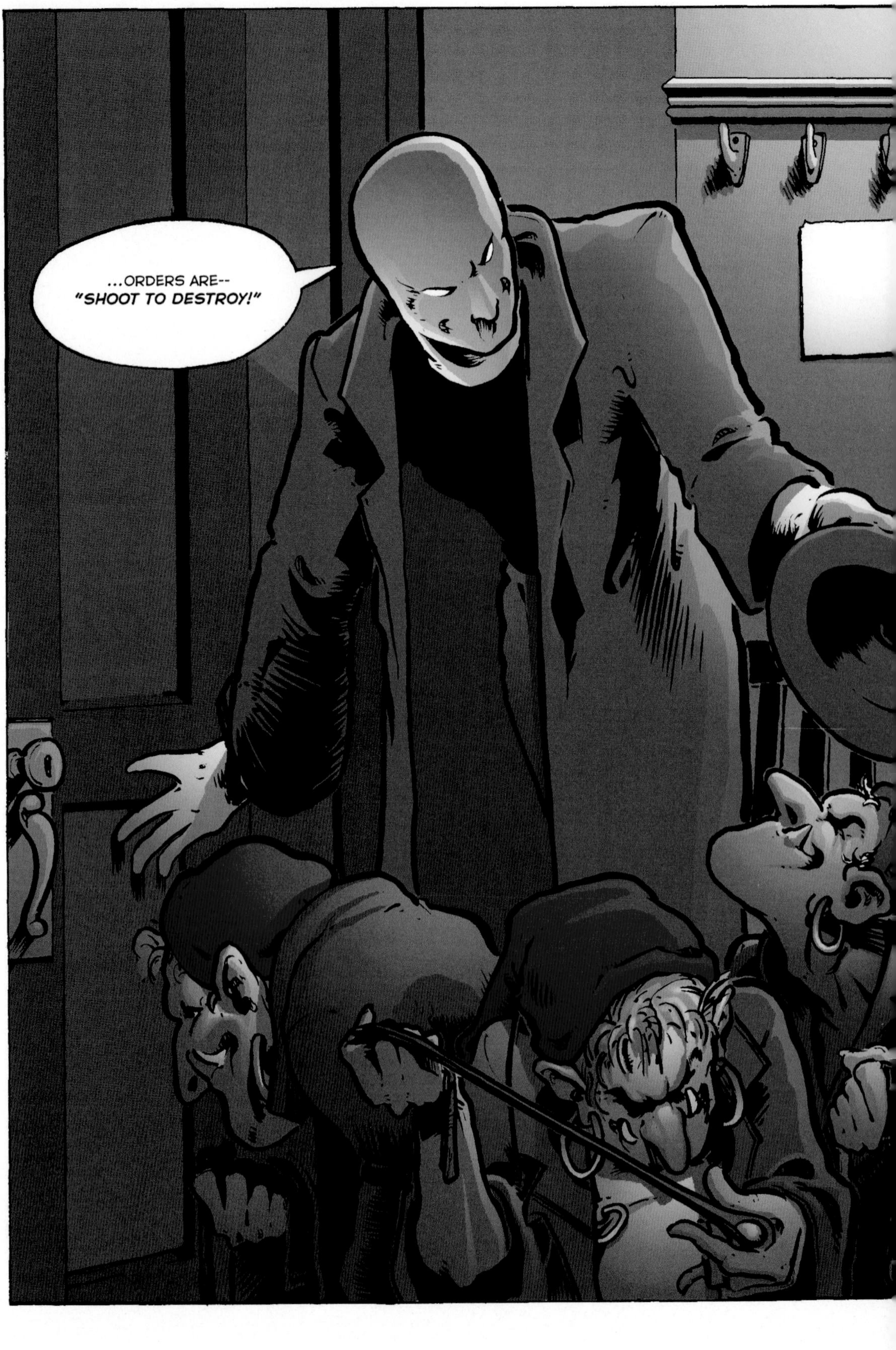
...ORDERS ARE--
"SHOOT TO DESTROY!"

THE HERO DISCOVERED

MAGE

Chapter 06

Alas, Poor Ghost

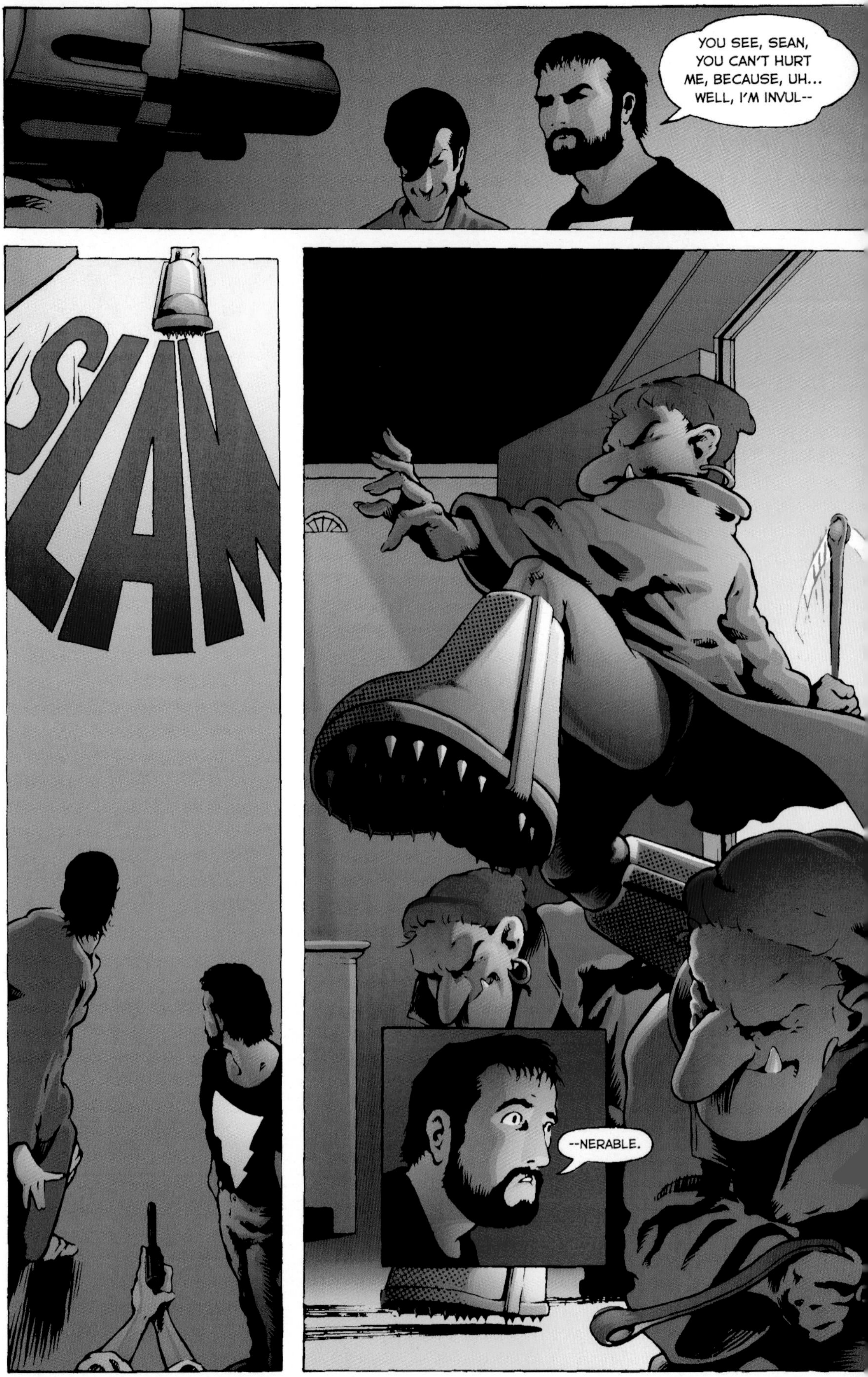
YOU SEE, SEAN, YOU CAN'T HURT ME, BECAUSE, UH... WELL, I'M INVUL--
SLAM
--NERABLE.

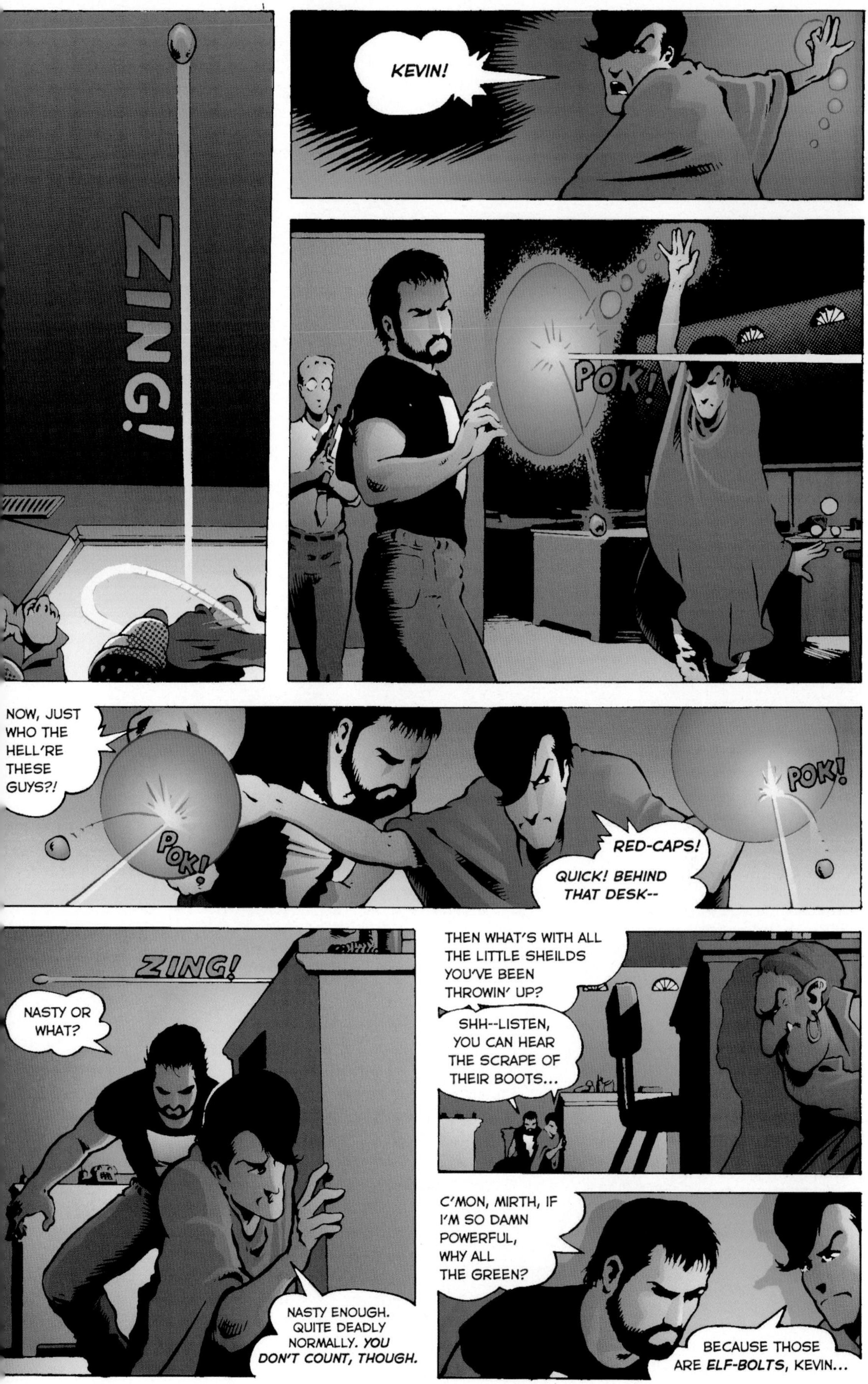
KEVIN!
ZING!
POK!
NOW, JUST WHO THE HELL'RE THESE GUYS?!
POK!
POK!
RED-CAPS!
QUICK! BEHIND THAT DESK--
ZING!
NASTY OR WHAT?
NASTY ENOUGH. QUITE DEADLY NORMALLY. *YOU DON'T COUNT, THOUGH.*
THEN WHAT'S WITH ALL THE LITTLE SHEILDS YOU'VE BEEN THROWIN' UP?
SHH--LISTEN, YOU CAN HEAR THE SCRAPE OF THEIR BOOTS...
C'MON, MIRTH, IF I'M SO DAMN POWERFUL, WHY ALL THE GREEN?
BECAUSE THOSE ARE *ELF-BOLTS*, KEVIN...

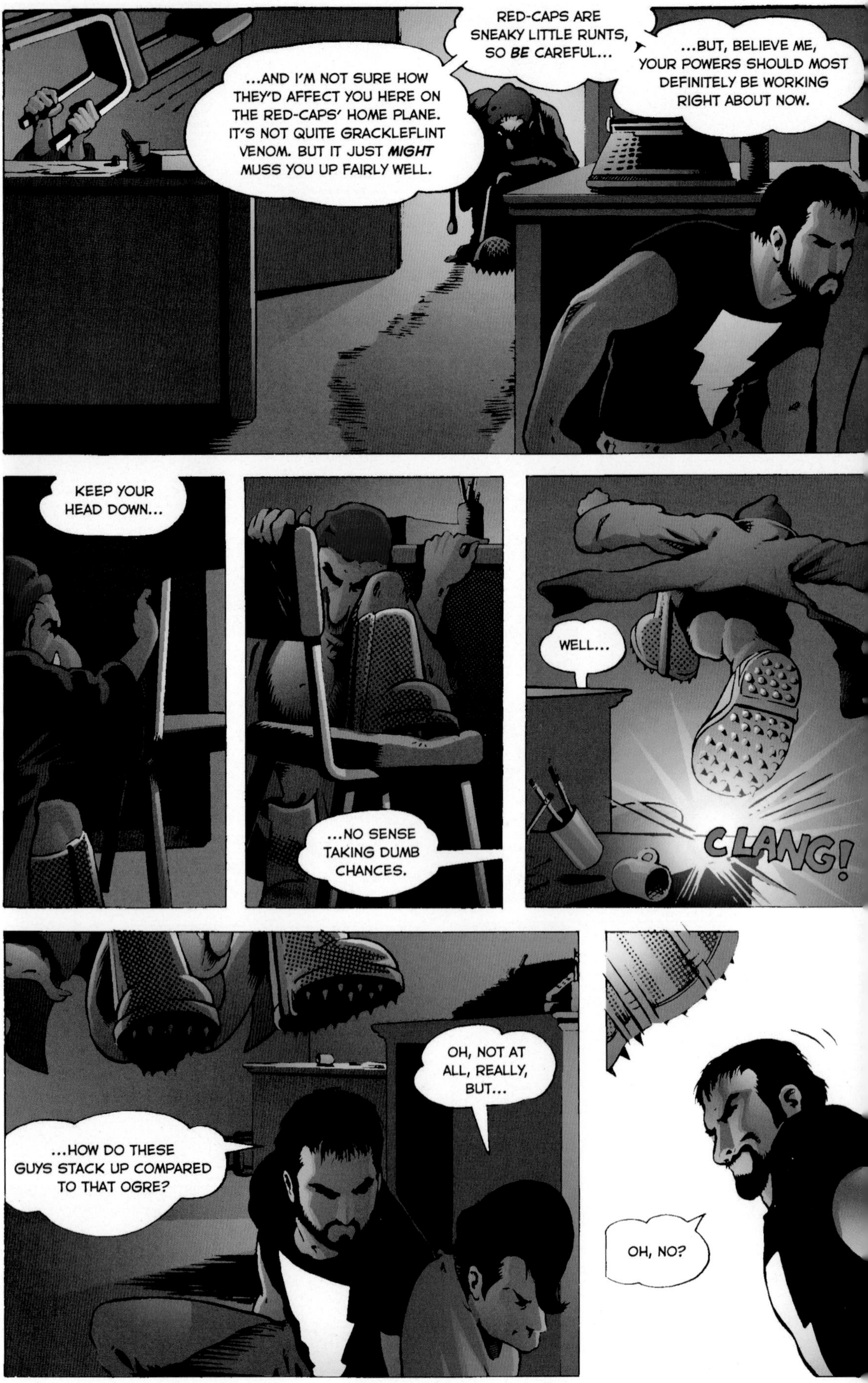
...AND I'M NOT SURE HOW THEY'D AFFECT YOU HERE ON THE RED-CAPS' HOME PLANE. IT'S NOT QUITE GRACKLEFLINT VENOM. BUT IT JUST *MIGHT* MUSS YOU UP FAIRLY WELL.
RED-CAPS ARE SNEAKY LITTLE RUNTS, SO *BE* CAREFUL...
...BUT, BELIEVE ME, YOUR POWERS SHOULD MOST DEFINITELY BE WORKING RIGHT ABOUT NOW.
KEEP YOUR HEAD DOWN...
...NO SENSE TAKING DUMB CHANCES.
WELL...
CLANG!
...HOW DO THESE GUYS STACK UP COMPARED TO THAT OGRE?
OH, NOT AT ALL, REALLY, BUT...
OH, NO?

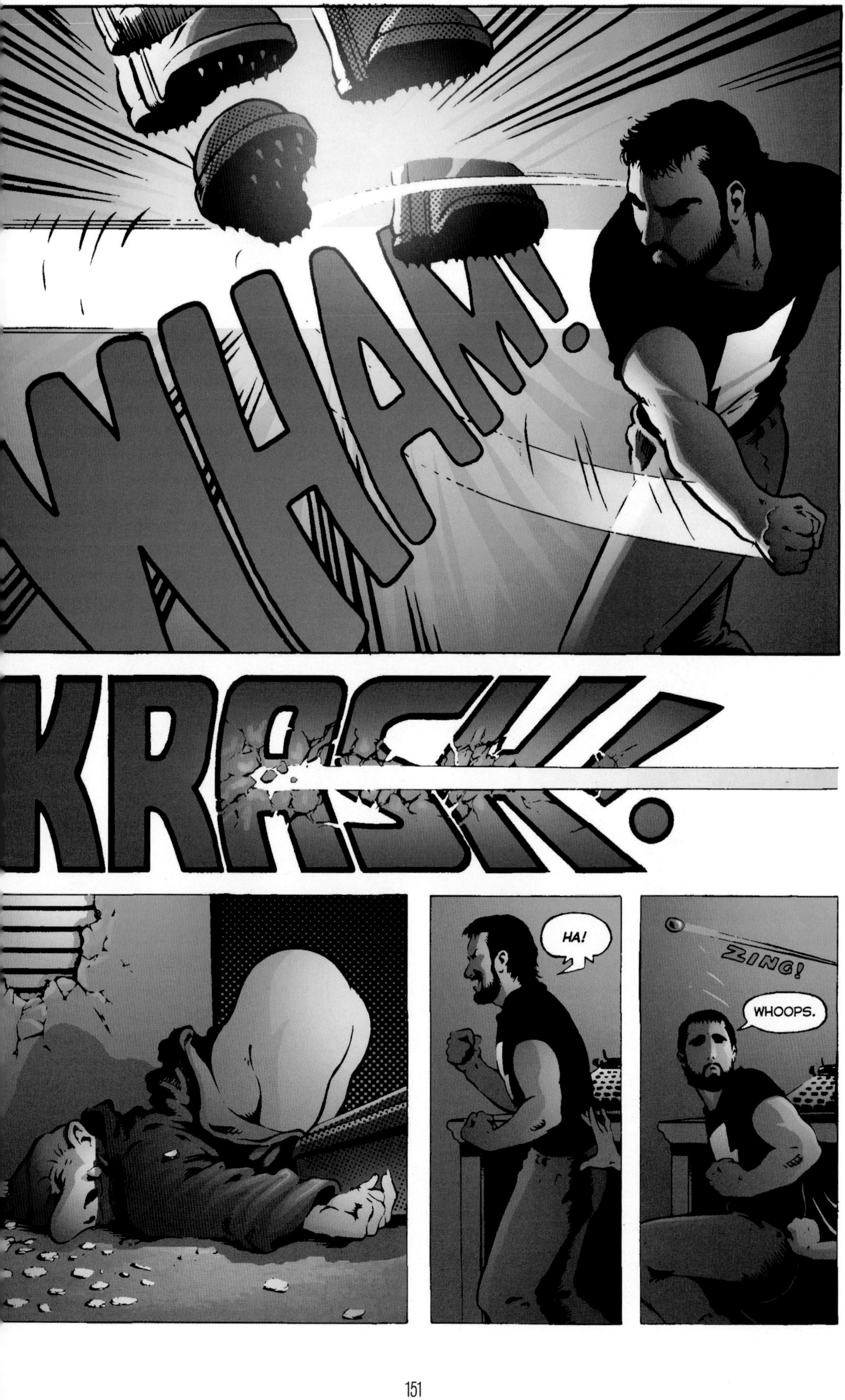
WHAM!
KRASH!
HA!
ZING!
WHOOPS.

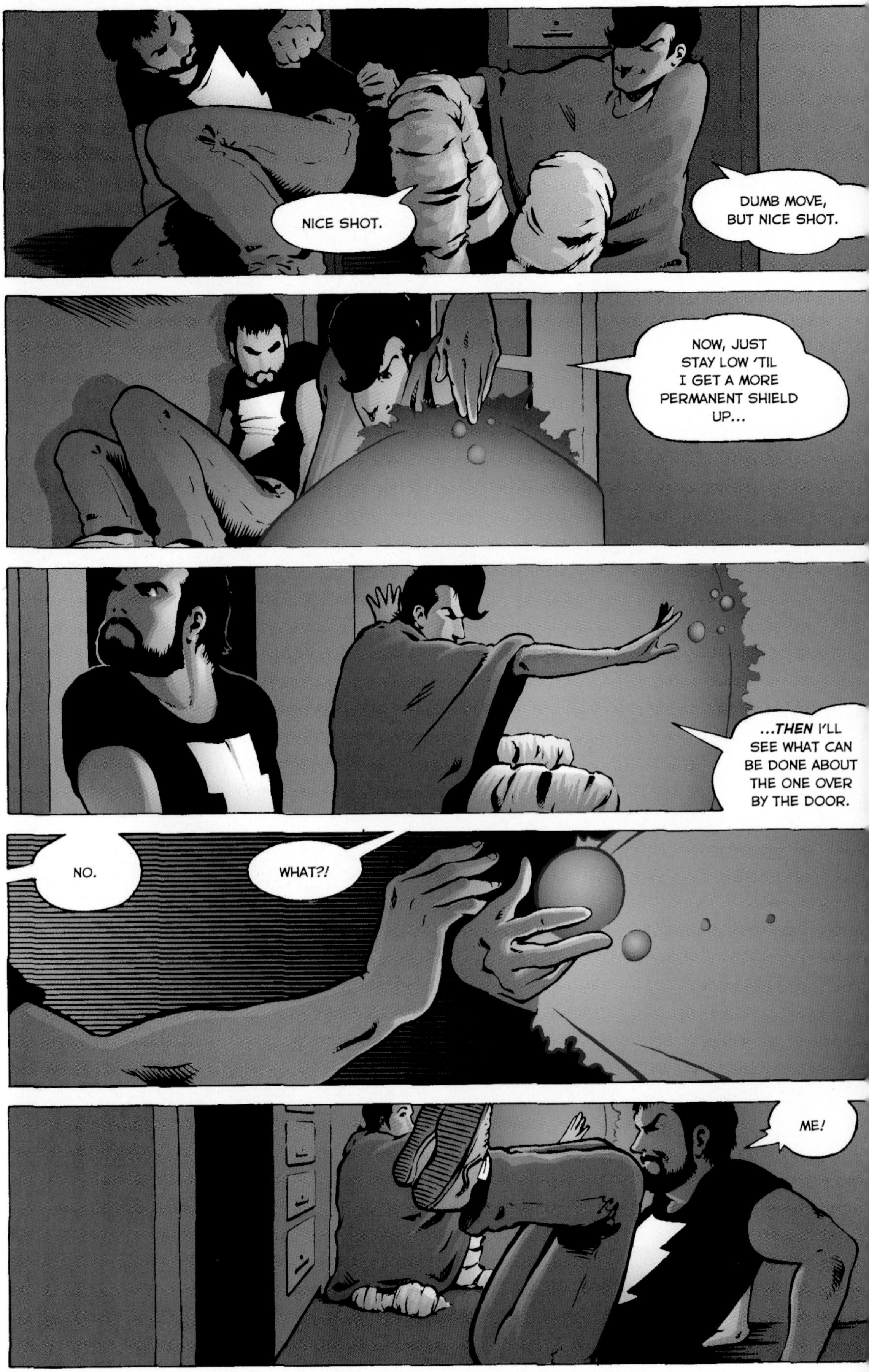
NICE SHOT.
DUMB MOVE, BUT NICE SHOT.
NOW, JUST STAY LOW 'TIL I GET A MORE PERMANENT SHIELD UP...
...THEN I'LL SEE WHAT CAN BE DONE ABOUT THE ONE OVER BY THE DOOR.
NO.
WHAT?!
ME!

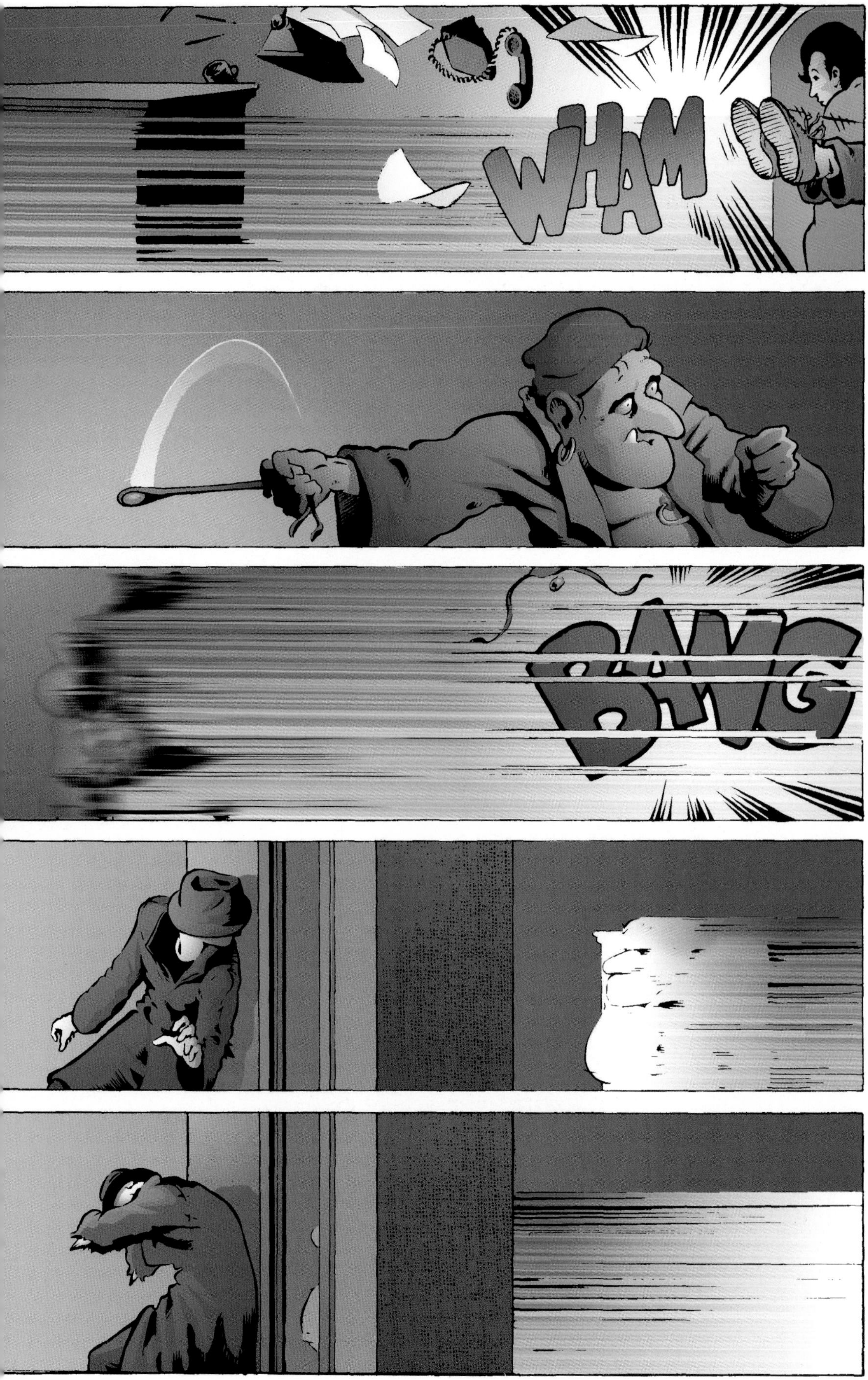
WHAM
BANG

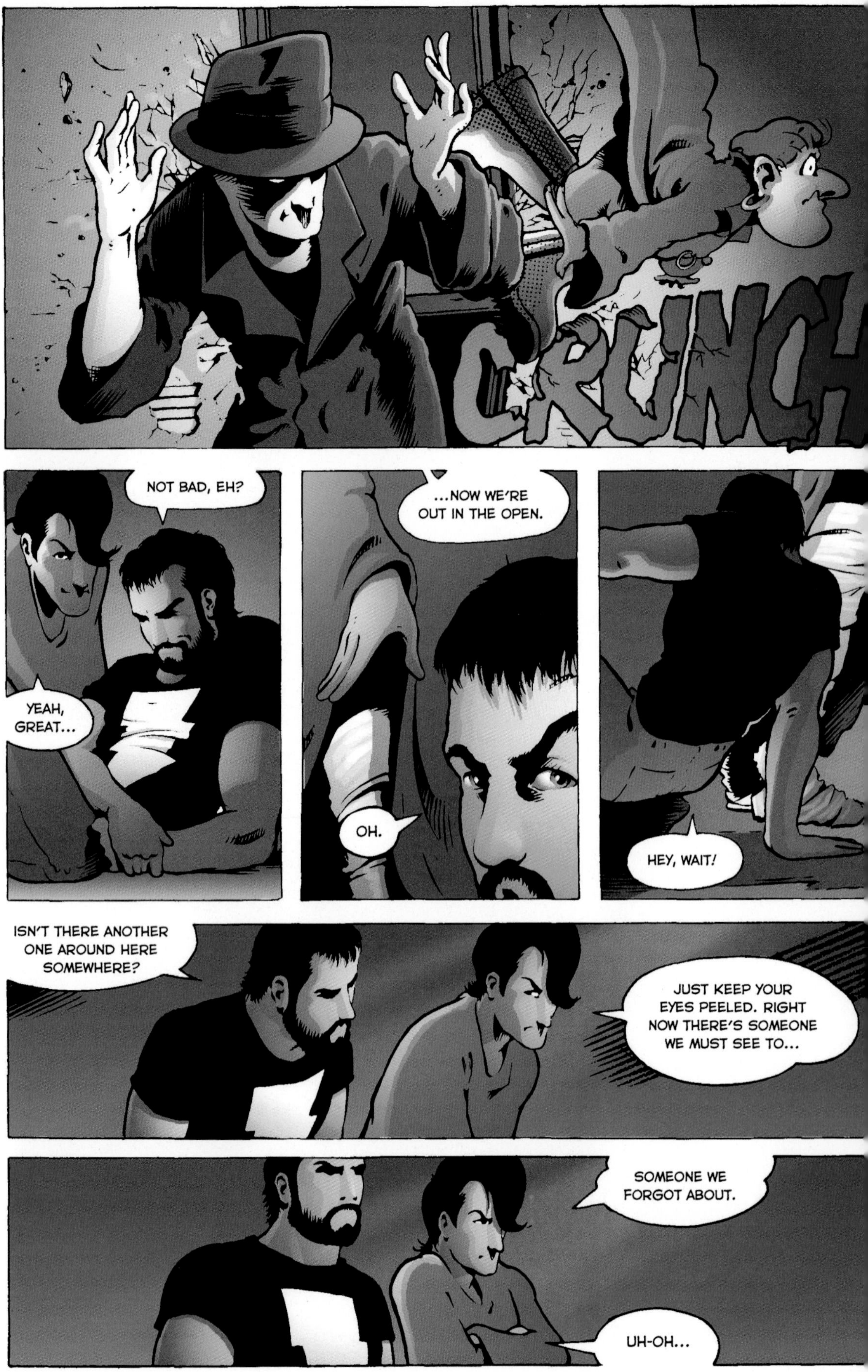
CRUNCH
NOT BAD, EH?
YEAH, GREAT...
...NOW WE'RE OUT IN THE OPEN.
OH.
HEY, WAIT!
ISN'T THERE ANOTHER ONE AROUND HERE SOMEWHERE?
JUST KEEP YOUR EYES PEELED. RIGHT NOW THERE'S SOMEONE WE MUST SEE TO...
SOMEONE WE FORGOT ABOUT.
UH-OH...

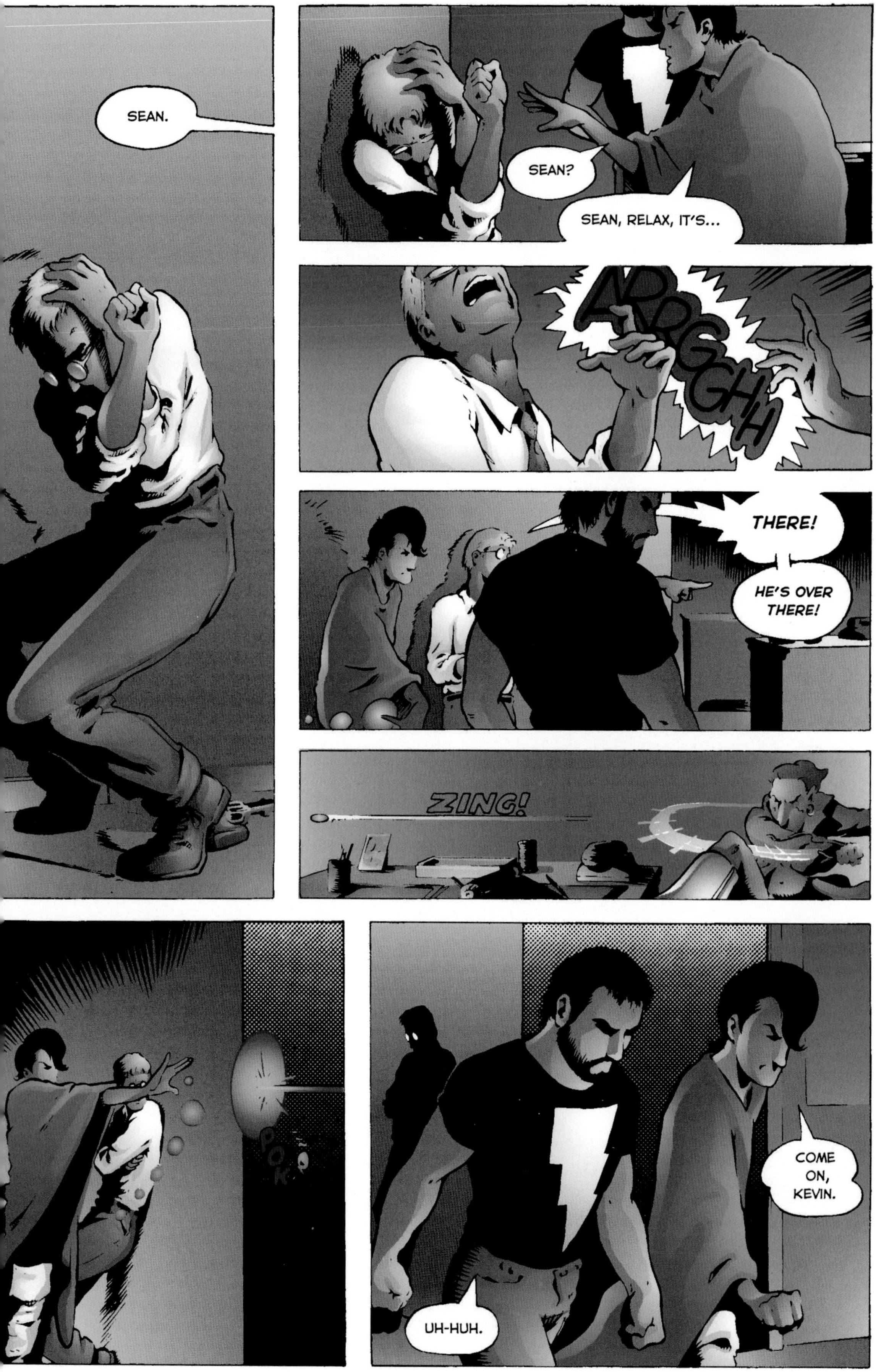
SEAN.
SEAN?
SEAN, RELAX, IT'S...
ARRGGHH
THERE!
HE'S OVER THERE!
ZING!
POK
COME ON, KEVIN.
UH-HUH.

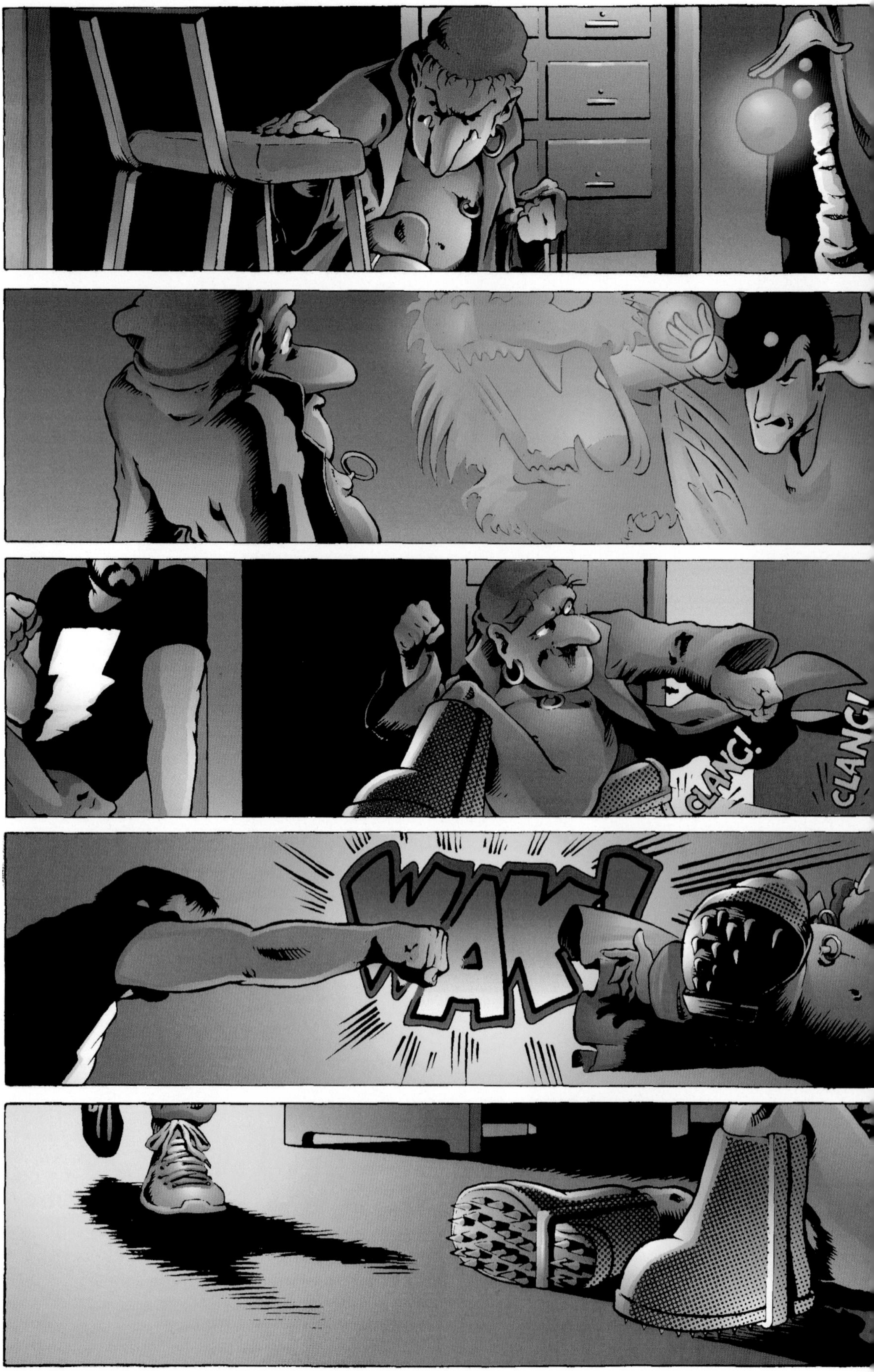
CLANG!
CLANG!
WAK!

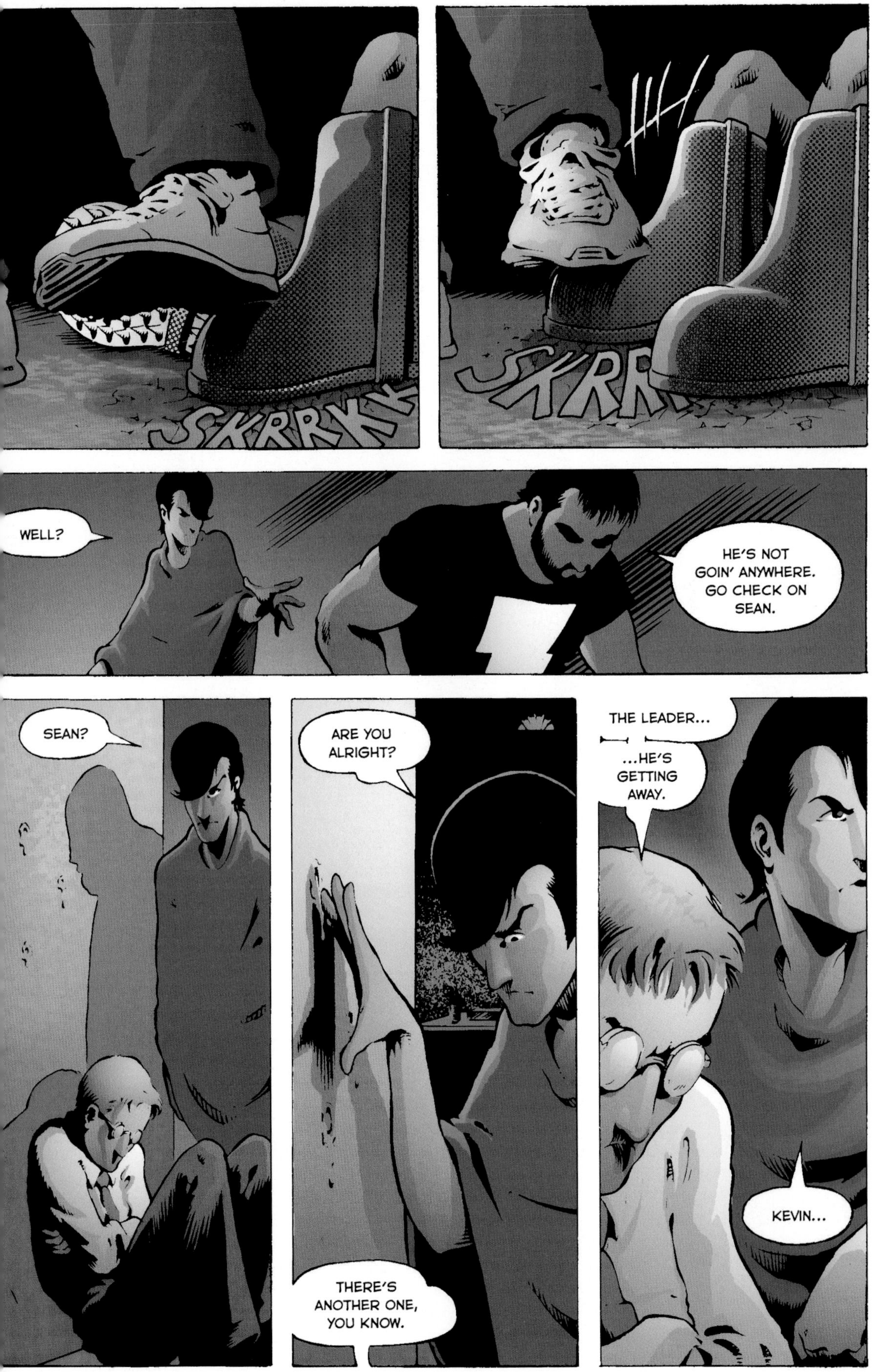
SKRRKK
SKRR
WELL?
HE'S NOT GOIN' ANYWHERE. GO CHECK ON SEAN.
SEAN?
ARE YOU ALRIGHT?
THERE'S ANOTHER ONE, YOU KNOW.
THE LEADER...
...HE'S GETTING AWAY.
KEVIN...

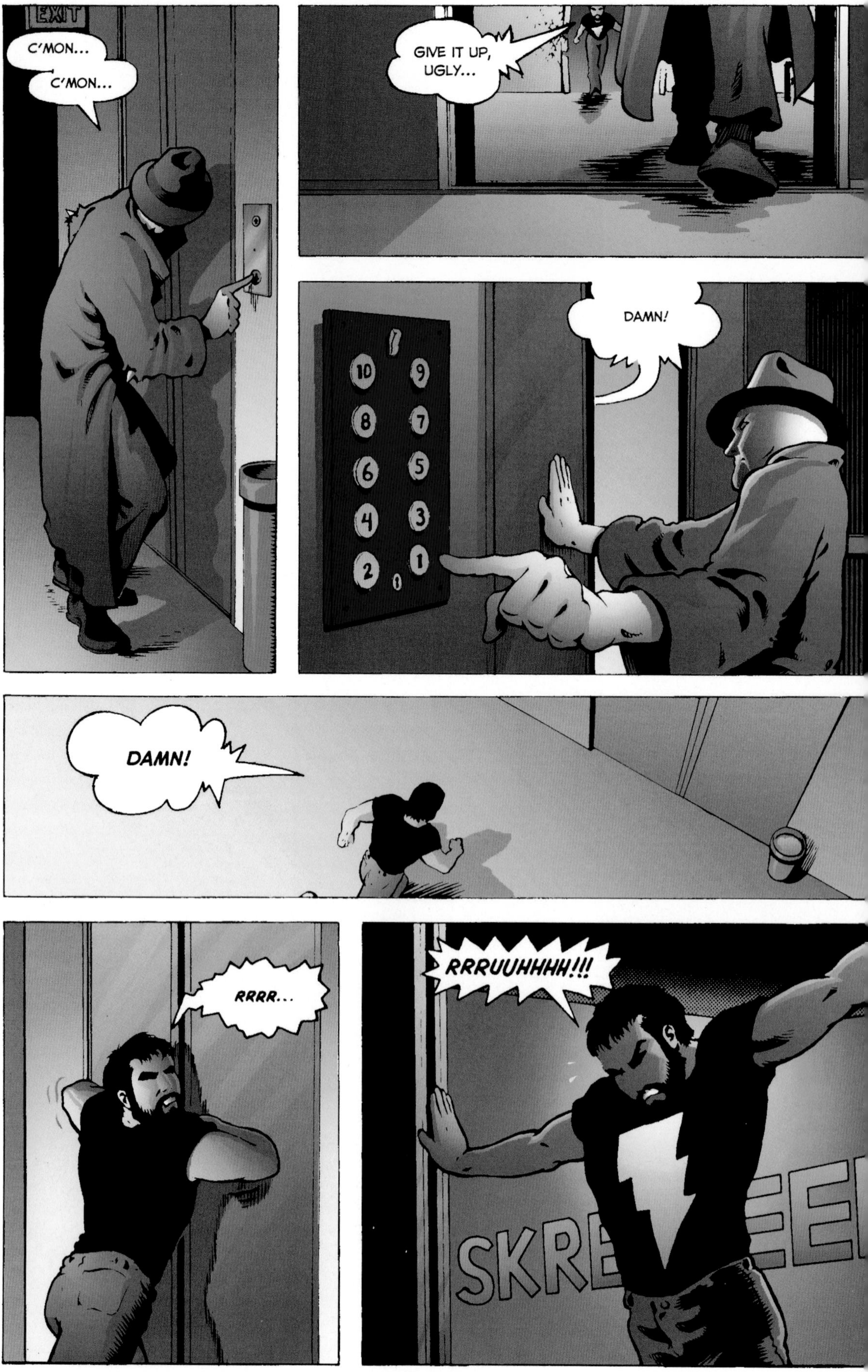
C'MON...
C'MON...
GIVE IT UP, UGLY...
DAMN!
DAMN!
RRRR...
RRRUUHHHH!!!
SKRE

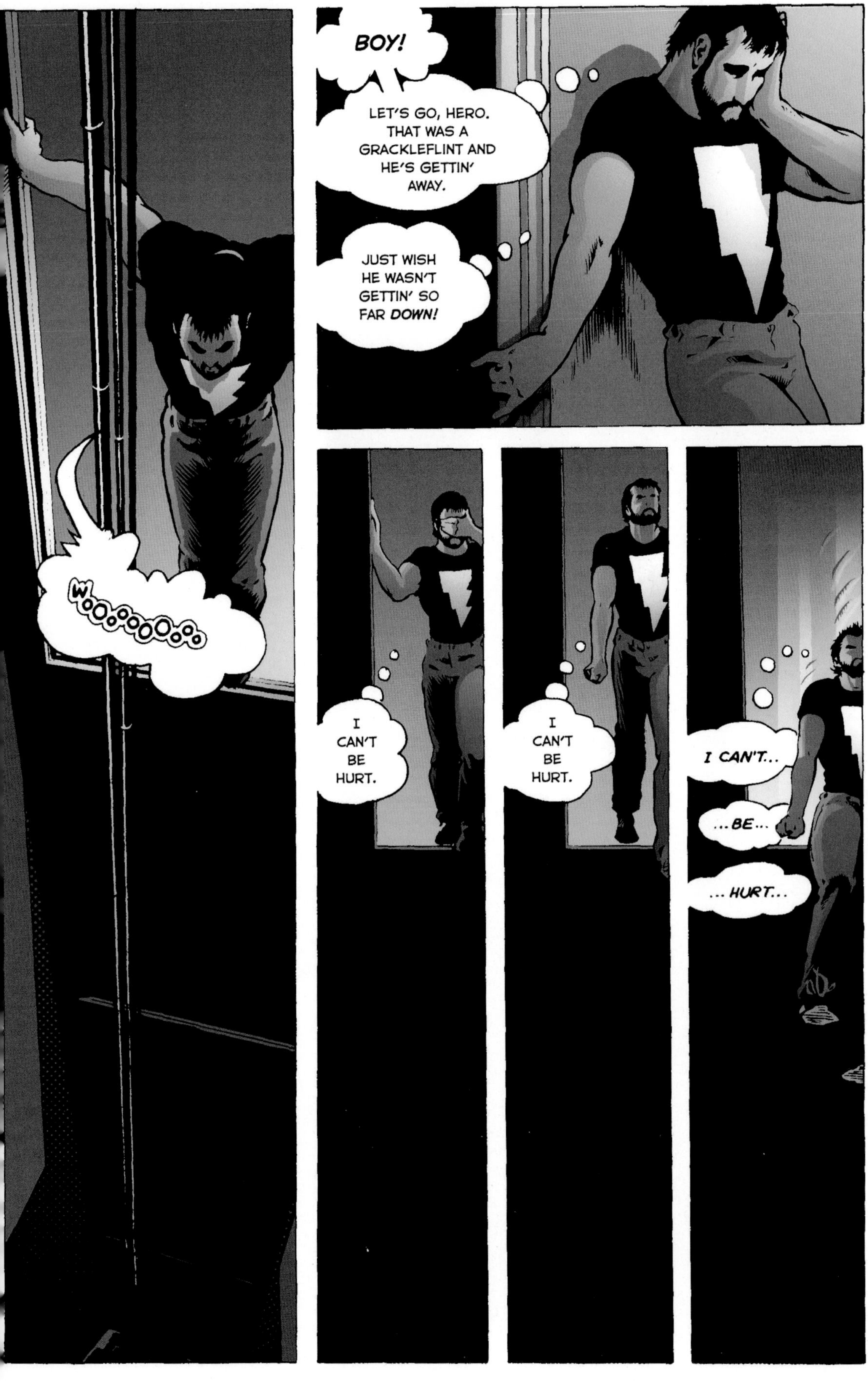
WoOoOoOoOoOo
BOY!
LET'S GO, HERO. THAT WAS A GRACKLEFLINT AND HE'S GETTIN' AWAY.
JUST WISH HE WASN'T GETTIN' SO FAR DOWN!
I CAN'T BE HURT.
I CAN'T BE HURT.
I CAN'T...
...BE...
...HURT...

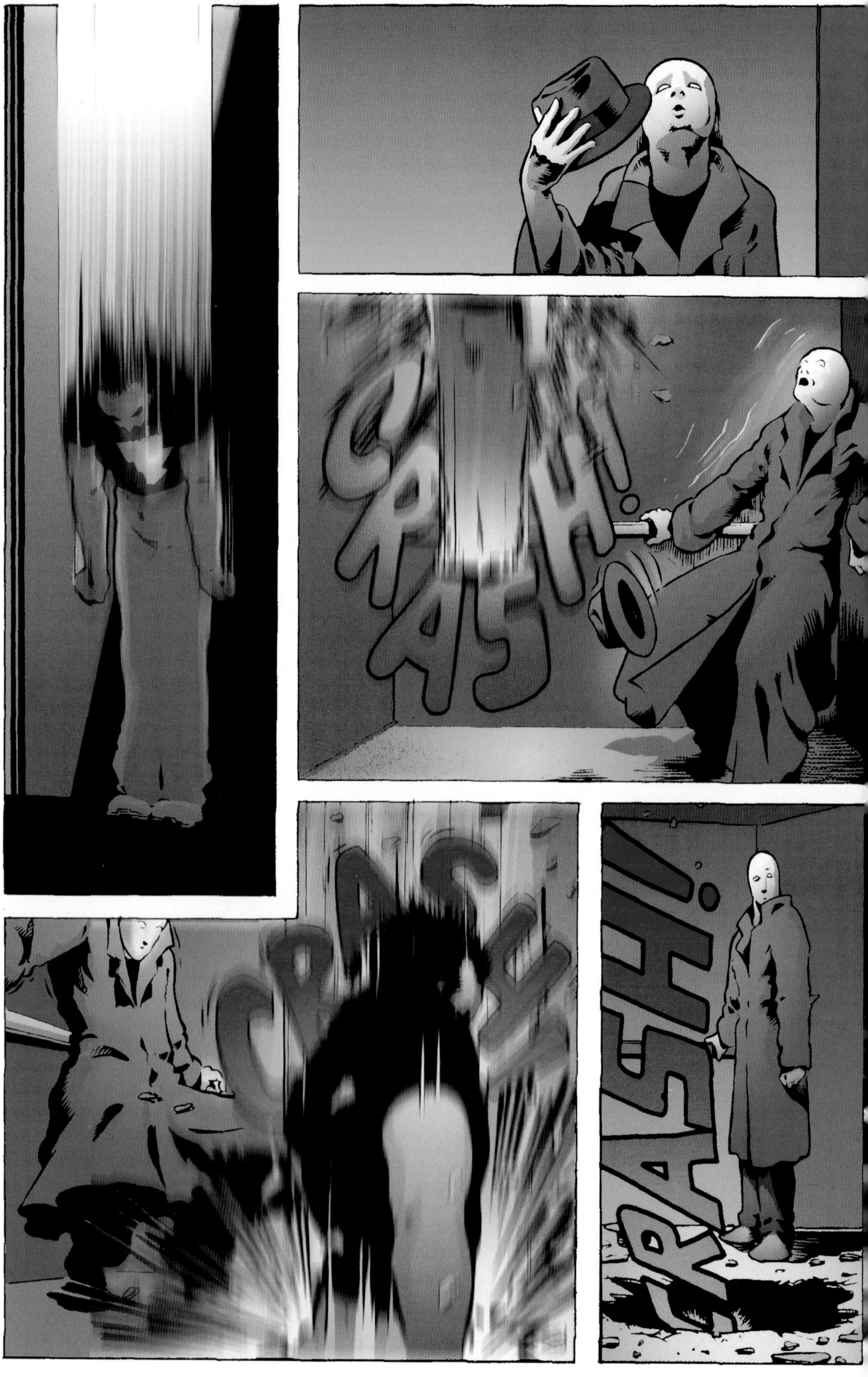
CRASH!
CRASH!
CRASH!

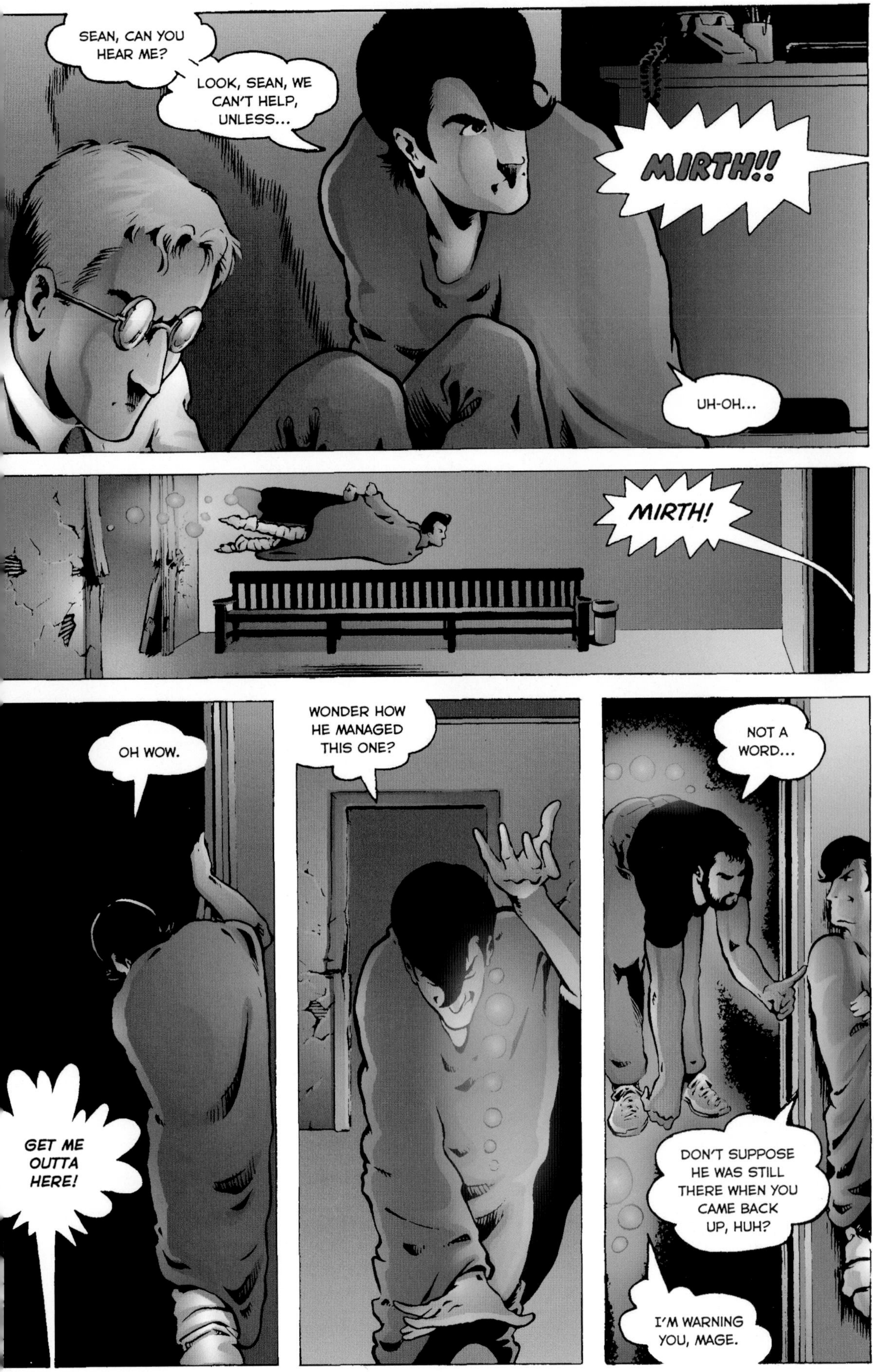
SEAN, CAN YOU HEAR ME?
LOOK, SEAN, WE CAN'T HELP, UNLESS...
MIRTH!!
UH-OH...
MIRTH!
OH WOW.
GET ME OUTTA HERE!
WONDER HOW HE MANAGED THIS ONE?
NOT A WORD...
DON'T SUPPOSE HE WAS STILL THERE WHEN YOU CAME BACK UP, HUH?
I'M WARNING YOU, MAGE.

...JUST DIDN'T STOP TO THINK ABOUT IT.

WELL, A COURAGEOUS TRY, AT LEAST.

YOU GUYS...

...GET ME OUTTA THIS PLACE...

...NOW!

OKAY, *SEAN*. WE'RE LEAVING. JUST RELAX AND WALK. I'LL TAKE CARE OF THE REST.

TRAVELLING THROUGH THE FAERIE REALMS IS ACTUALLY QUITE SIMPLE, BUT IT'S ALSO MARVELOUSLY SUBTLE, AND, AS YOU JUST SAW, SOMETIMES DANGEROUS.

I KNOW YOU'RE VERY CONFUSED, BUT WE'LL TRY TO CLEAR THINGS UP FOR YOU, STARTING WITH HOW YOU GOT HERE...

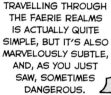

...YOU SEE, *SEAN*, I THINK YOU'RE *DEAD*.

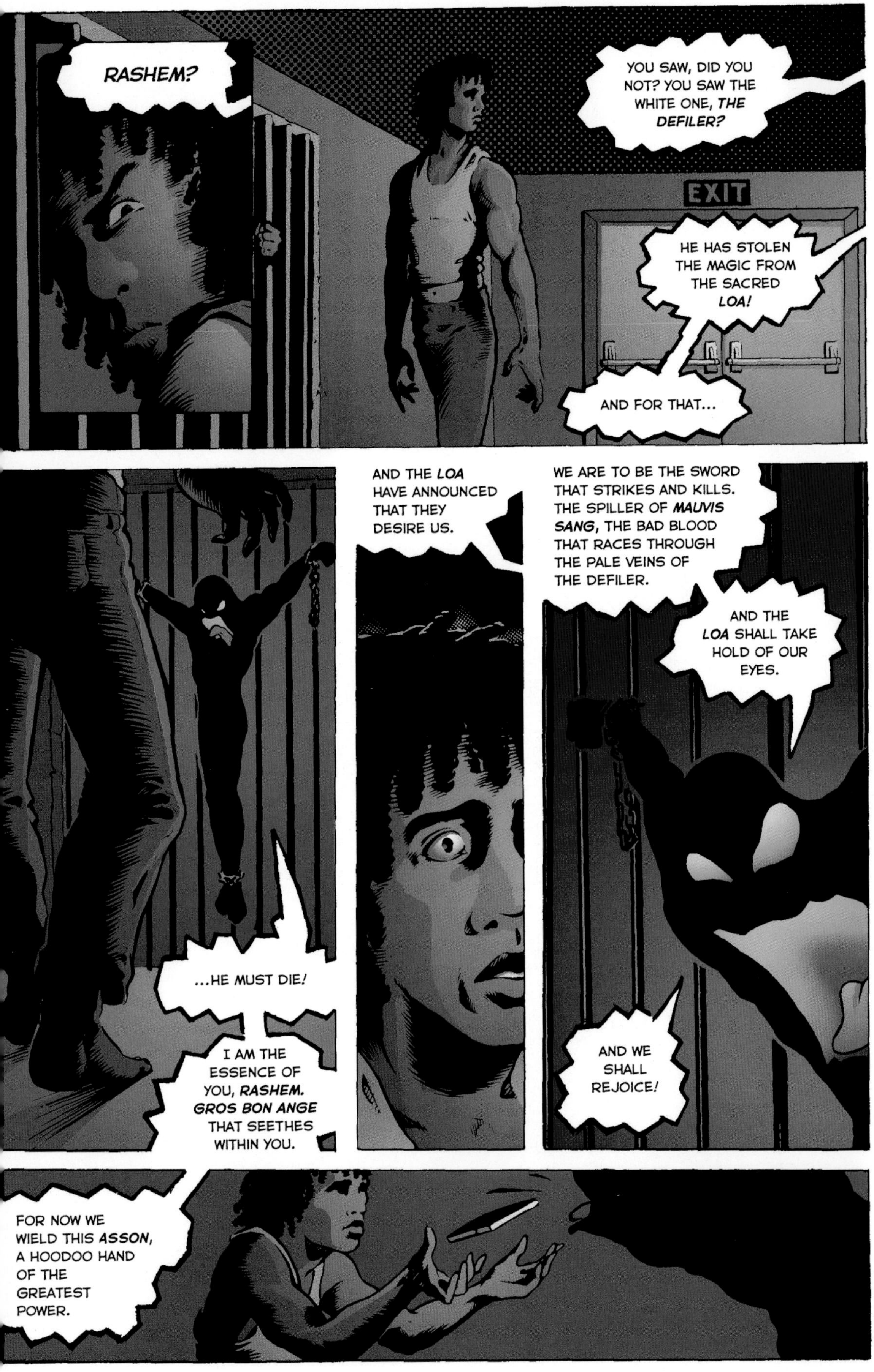
RASHEM?
YOU SAW, DID YOU NOT? YOU SAW THE WHITE ONE, THE DEFILER?
HE HAS STOLEN THE MAGIC FROM THE SACRED LOA!
AND FOR THAT...
...HE MUST DIE!
I AM THE ESSENCE OF YOU, RASHEM. GROS BON ANGE THAT SEETHES WITHIN YOU.
AND THE LOA HAVE ANNOUNCED THAT THEY DESIRE US.
WE ARE TO BE THE SWORD THAT STRIKES AND KILLS. THE SPILLER OF MAUVIS SANG, THE BAD BLOOD THAT RACES THROUGH THE PALE VEINS OF THE DEFILER.
AND THE LOA SHALL TAKE HOLD OF OUR EYES.
AND WE SHALL REJOICE!
FOR NOW WE WIELD THIS ASSON, A HOODOO HAND OF THE GREATEST POWER.
EXIT

ITS SPITTLE IS DEATH.

THE HAIRY ONE IS BEYOND YOUR GRASP, THOUGH, AND WILL SEEK TO PROTECT THE FOUL MAGICIAN.

LOOK TO STRIKE AT HIM THROUGH THE *JEUNESSE* SLUT YOU WILL SEE JOIN THEM.

DOUBLE LUCKY ARE WE, *RASHEM*.

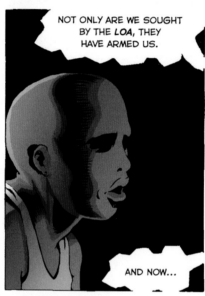

NOT ONLY ARE WE SOUGHT BY THE *LOA*, THEY HAVE ARMED US.

AND NOW...

FZZZ

...LO, THEY GRANT US A COMPANION.

SEEK THEM AT MIDDAY, WHEN THEY CAST NO SHADOW.

LET *BARON SAMEDI* FEAST ON THEIR BONES.

FAREWELL, *RASHEM*, MY LOVE.

WHAT IS IT?

LOOKS LIKE A STAPLE GUN.

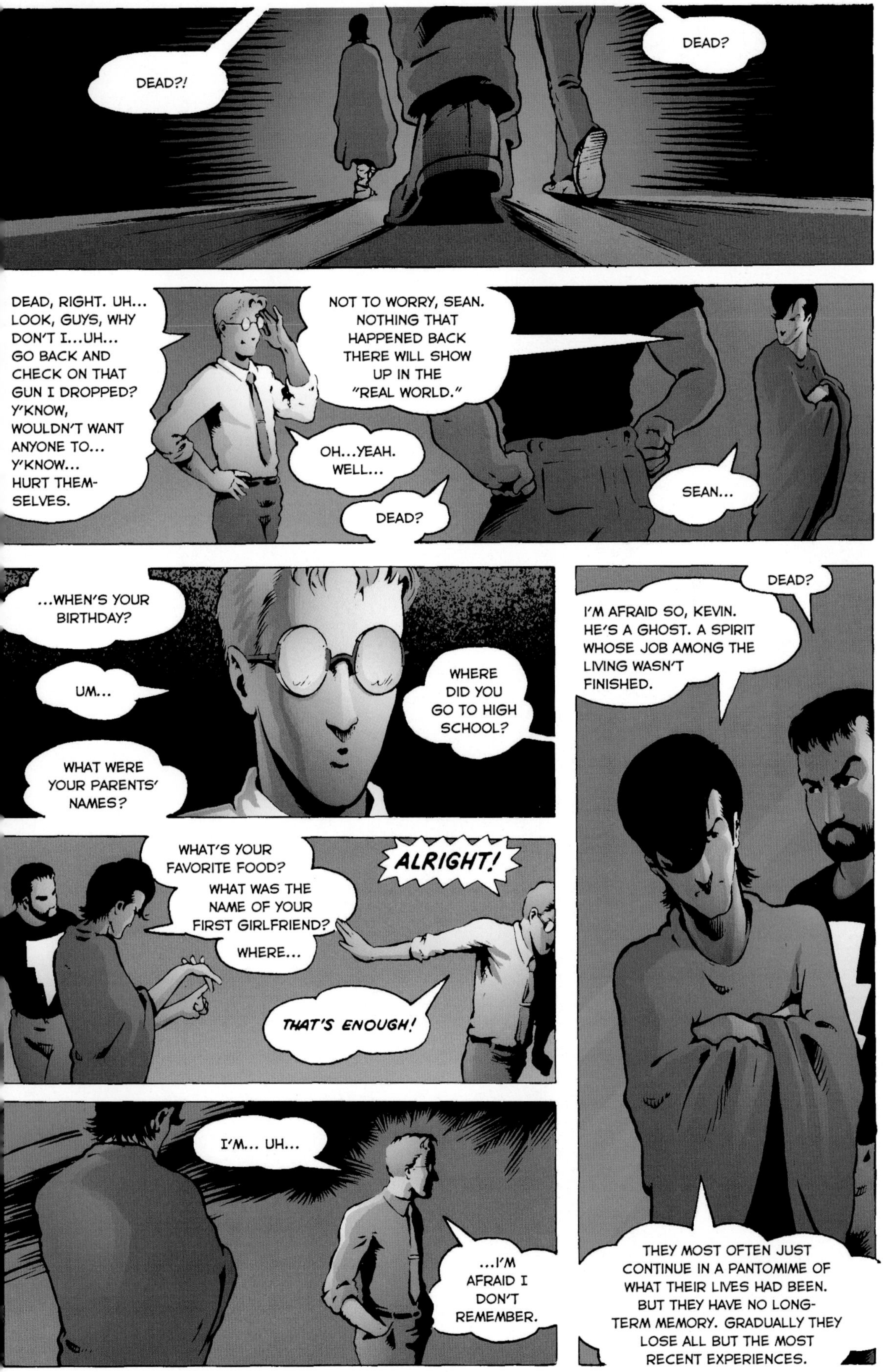
DEAD?!
DEAD?
DEAD, RIGHT. UH... LOOK, GUYS, WHY DON'T I...UH... GO BACK AND CHECK ON THAT GUN I DROPPED? Y'KNOW, WOULDN'T WANT ANYONE TO... Y'KNOW... HURT THEM-SELVES.
NOT TO WORRY, SEAN. NOTHING THAT HAPPENED BACK THERE WILL SHOW UP IN THE "REAL WORLD."
OH...YEAH. WELL...
DEAD?
SEAN...
...WHEN'S YOUR BIRTHDAY?
UM...
WHERE DID YOU GO TO HIGH SCHOOL?
WHAT WERE YOUR PARENTS' NAMES?
WHAT'S YOUR FAVORITE FOOD?
WHAT WAS THE NAME OF YOUR FIRST GIRLFRIEND?
WHERE...
ALRIGHT!
THAT'S ENOUGH!
I'M... UH...
...I'M AFRAID I DON'T REMEMBER.
DEAD?
I'M AFRAID SO, KEVIN. HE'S A GHOST. A SPIRIT WHOSE JOB AMONG THE LIVING WASN'T FINISHED.
THEY MOST OFTEN JUST CONTINUE IN A PANTOMIME OF WHAT THEIR LIVES HAD BEEN. BUT THEY HAVE NO LONG-TERM MEMORY. GRADUALLY THEY LOSE ALL BUT THE MOST RECENT EXPERIENCES.

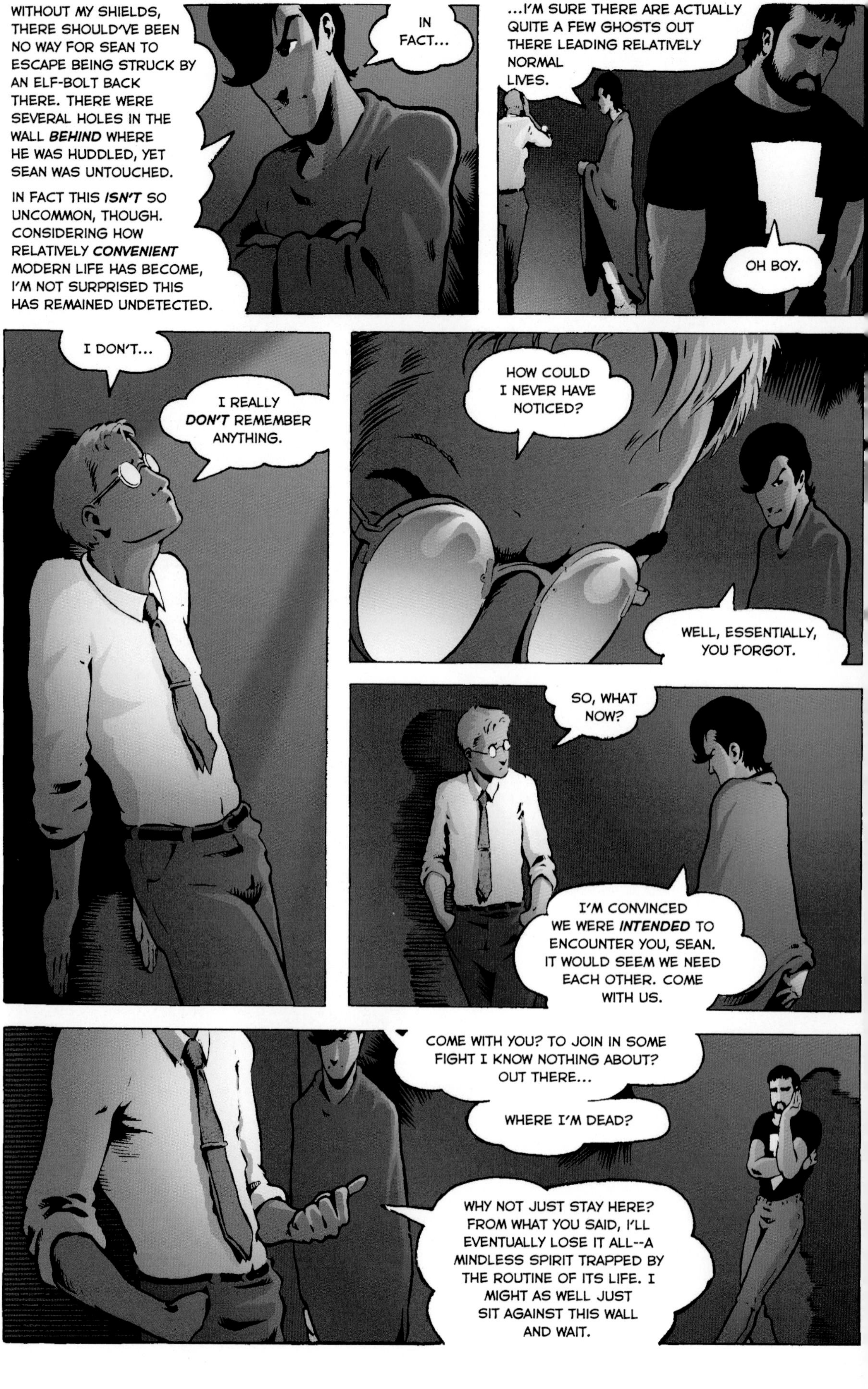
WITHOUT MY SHIELDS, THERE SHOULD'VE BEEN NO WAY FOR SEAN TO ESCAPE BEING STRUCK BY AN ELF-BOLT BACK THERE. THERE WERE SEVERAL HOLES IN THE WALL *BEHIND* WHERE HE WAS HUDDLED, YET SEAN WAS UNTOUCHED.
IN FACT THIS *ISN'T* SO UNCOMMON, THOUGH. CONSIDERING HOW RELATIVELY *CONVENIENT* MODERN LIFE HAS BECOME, I'M NOT SURPRISED THIS HAS REMAINED UNDETECTED.
IN FACT...
...I'M SURE THERE ARE ACTUALLY QUITE A FEW GHOSTS OUT THERE LEADING RELATIVELY NORMAL LIVES.
OH BOY.
I DON'T...
I REALLY *DON'T* REMEMBER ANYTHING.
HOW COULD I NEVER HAVE NOTICED?
WELL, ESSENTIALLY, YOU FORGOT.
SO, WHAT NOW?
I'M CONVINCED WE WERE *INTENDED* TO ENCOUNTER YOU, SEAN. IT WOULD SEEM WE NEED EACH OTHER. COME WITH US.
COME WITH YOU? TO JOIN IN SOME FIGHT I KNOW NOTHING ABOUT? OUT THERE...
WHERE I'M DEAD?
WHY NOT JUST STAY HERE? FROM WHAT YOU SAID, I'LL EVENTUALLY LOSE IT ALL--A MINDLESS SPIRIT TRAPPED BY THE ROUTINE OF ITS LIFE. I MIGHT AS WELL JUST SIT AGAINST THIS WALL AND WAIT.

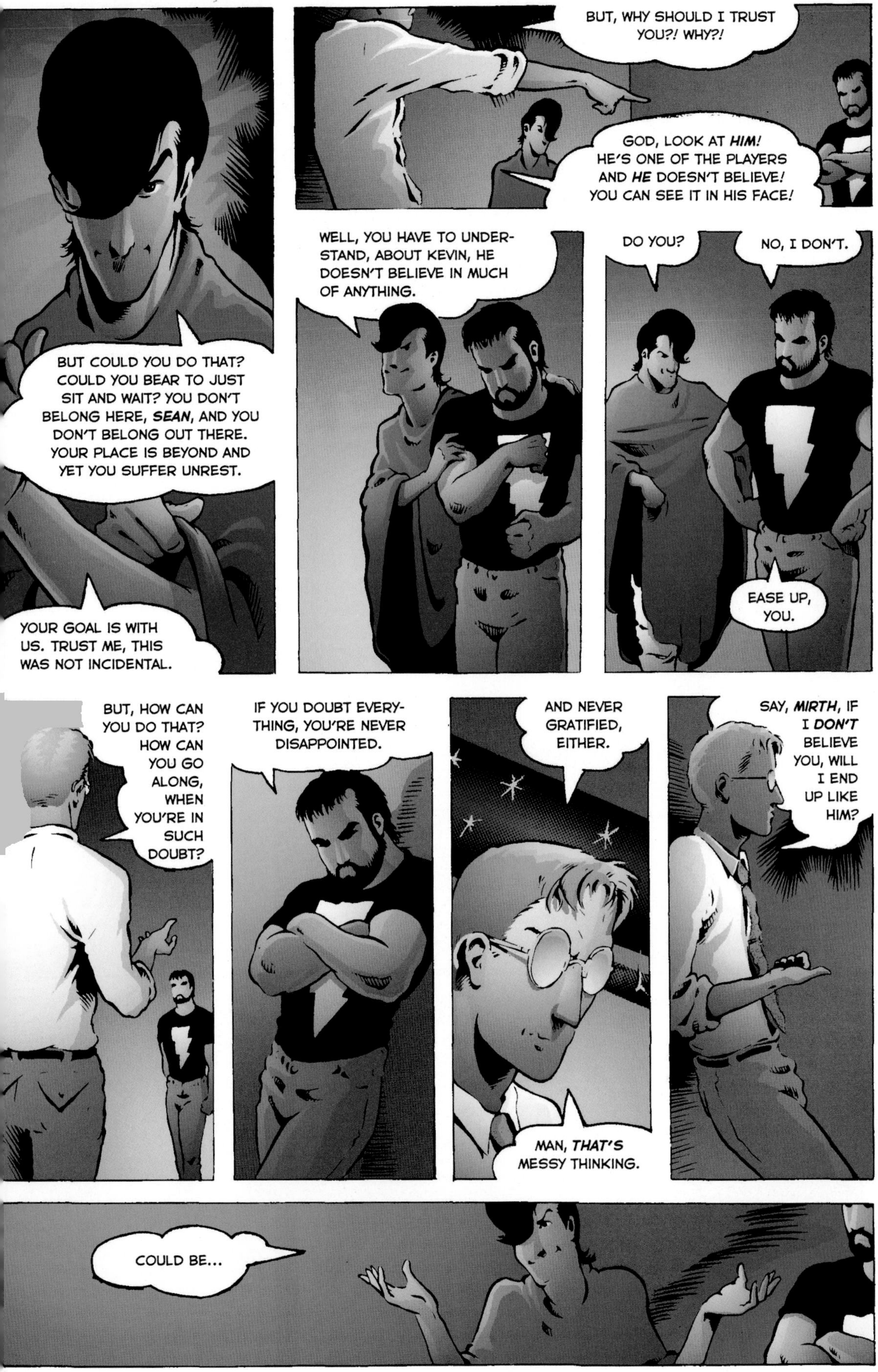

BUT COULD YOU DO THAT? COULD YOU BEAR TO JUST SIT AND WAIT? YOU DON'T BELONG HERE, **SEAN**, AND YOU DON'T BELONG OUT THERE. YOUR PLACE IS BEYOND AND YET YOU SUFFER UNREST.
YOUR GOAL IS WITH US. TRUST ME, THIS WAS NOT INCIDENTAL.
BUT, WHY SHOULD I TRUST YOU?! WHY?!
GOD, LOOK AT **HIM!** HE'S ONE OF THE PLAYERS AND **HE** DOESN'T BELIEVE! YOU CAN SEE IT IN HIS FACE!
WELL, YOU HAVE TO UNDERSTAND, ABOUT KEVIN, HE DOESN'T BELIEVE IN MUCH OF ANYTHING.
DO YOU?
NO, I DON'T.
EASE UP, YOU.
BUT, HOW CAN YOU DO THAT? HOW CAN YOU GO ALONG, WHEN YOU'RE IN SUCH DOUBT?
IF YOU DOUBT EVERYTHING, YOU'RE NEVER DISAPPOINTED.
AND NEVER GRATIFIED, EITHER.
MAN, **THAT'S** MESSY THINKING.
SAY, **MIRTH**, IF I **DON'T** BELIEVE YOU, WILL I END UP LIKE HIM?
COULD BE...

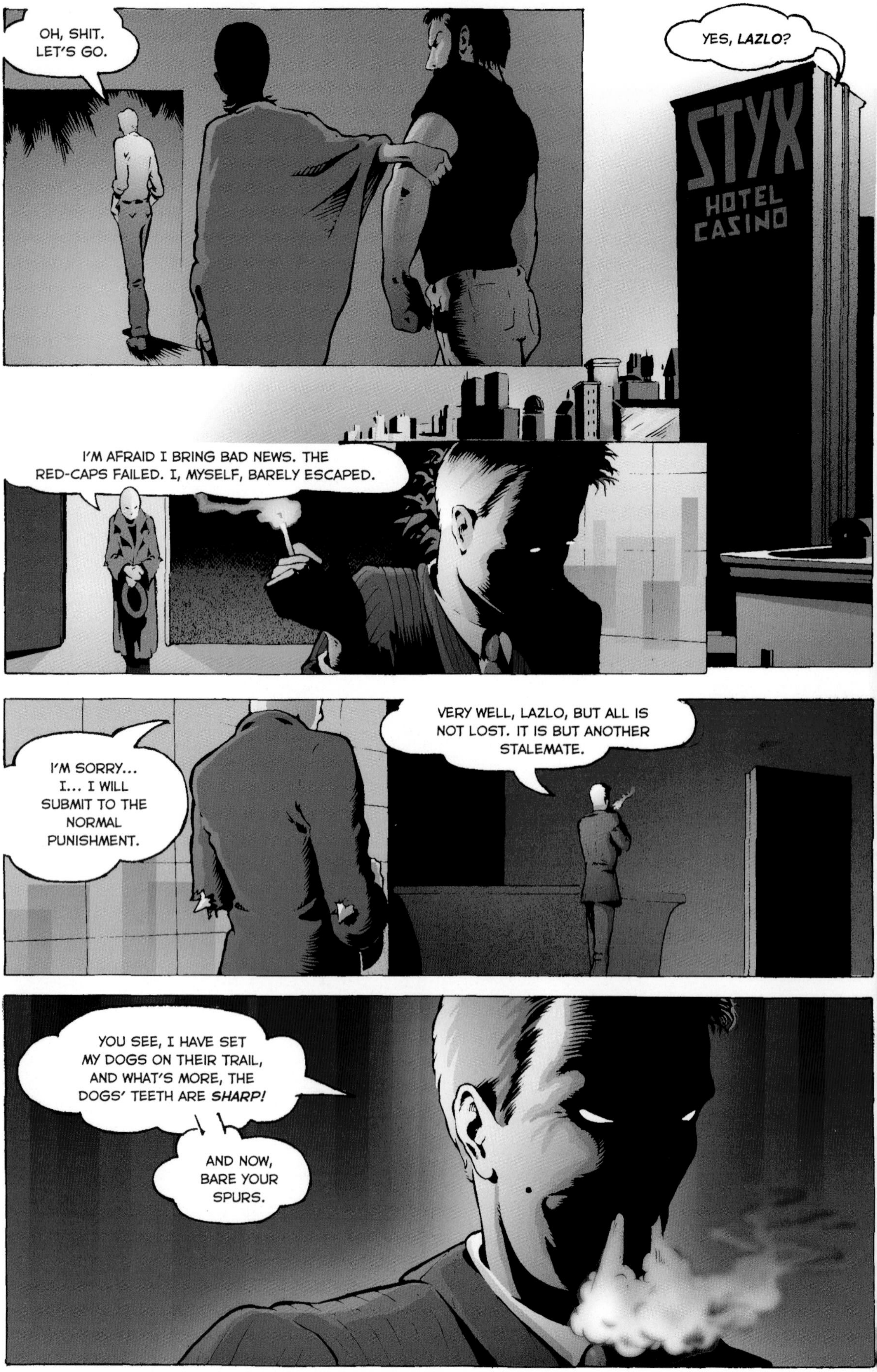
OH, SHIT. LET'S GO.
YES, LAZLO?
STYX HOTEL CASINO
I'M AFRAID I BRING BAD NEWS. THE RED-CAPS FAILED. I, MYSELF, BARELY ESCAPED.
I'M SORRY... I... I WILL SUBMIT TO THE NORMAL PUNISHMENT.
VERY WELL, LAZLO, BUT ALL IS NOT LOST. IT IS BUT ANOTHER STALEMATE.
YOU SEE, I HAVE SET MY DOGS ON THEIR TRAIL, AND WHAT'S MORE, THE DOGS' TEETH ARE SHARP!
AND NOW, BARE YOUR SPURS.

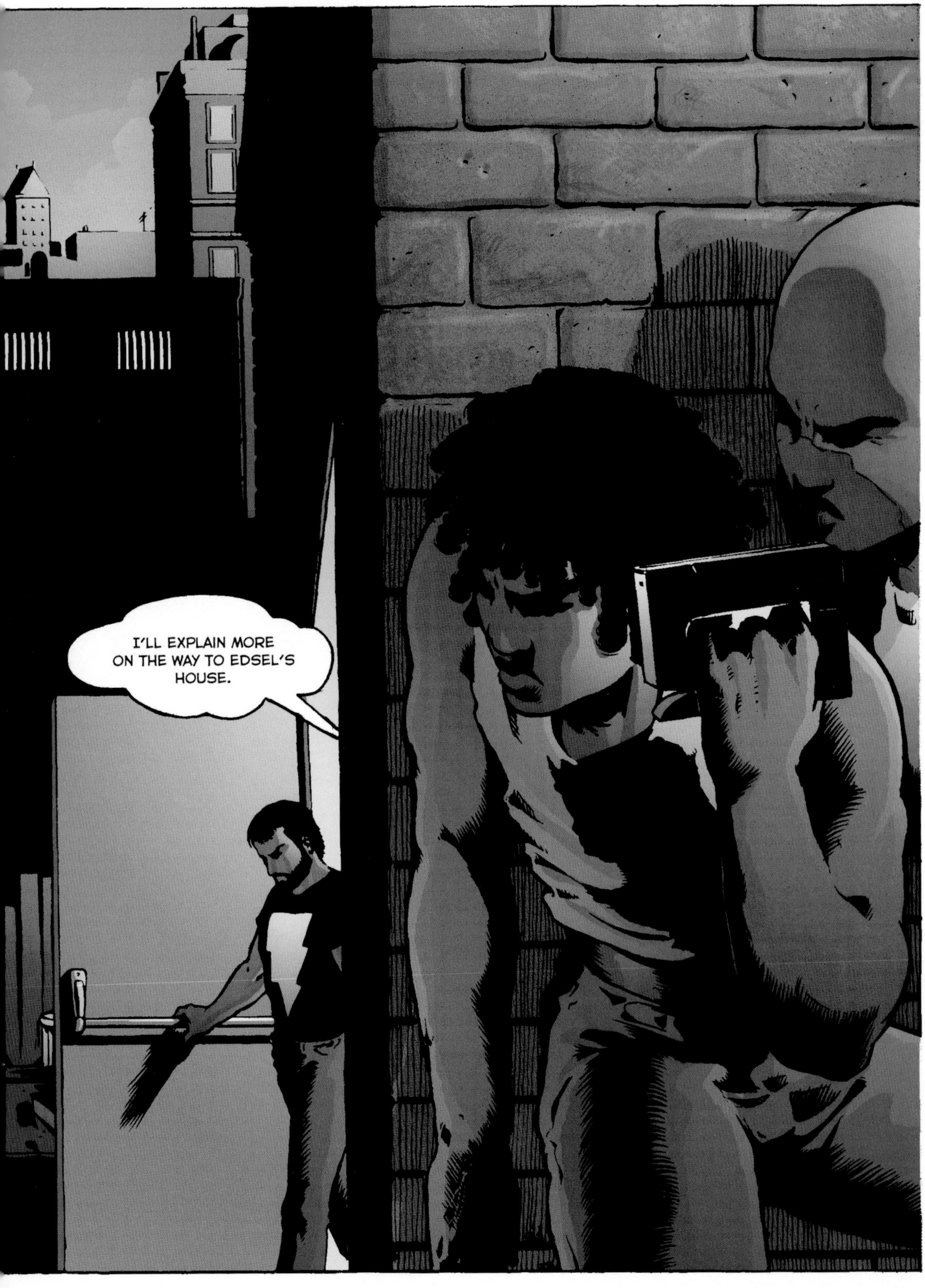
I'LL EXPLAIN MORE ON THE WAY TO EDSEL'S HOUSE.

THE HERO DISCOVERED

MAGE

Chapter 07

Lady, Shall I Lie In Your Lap?

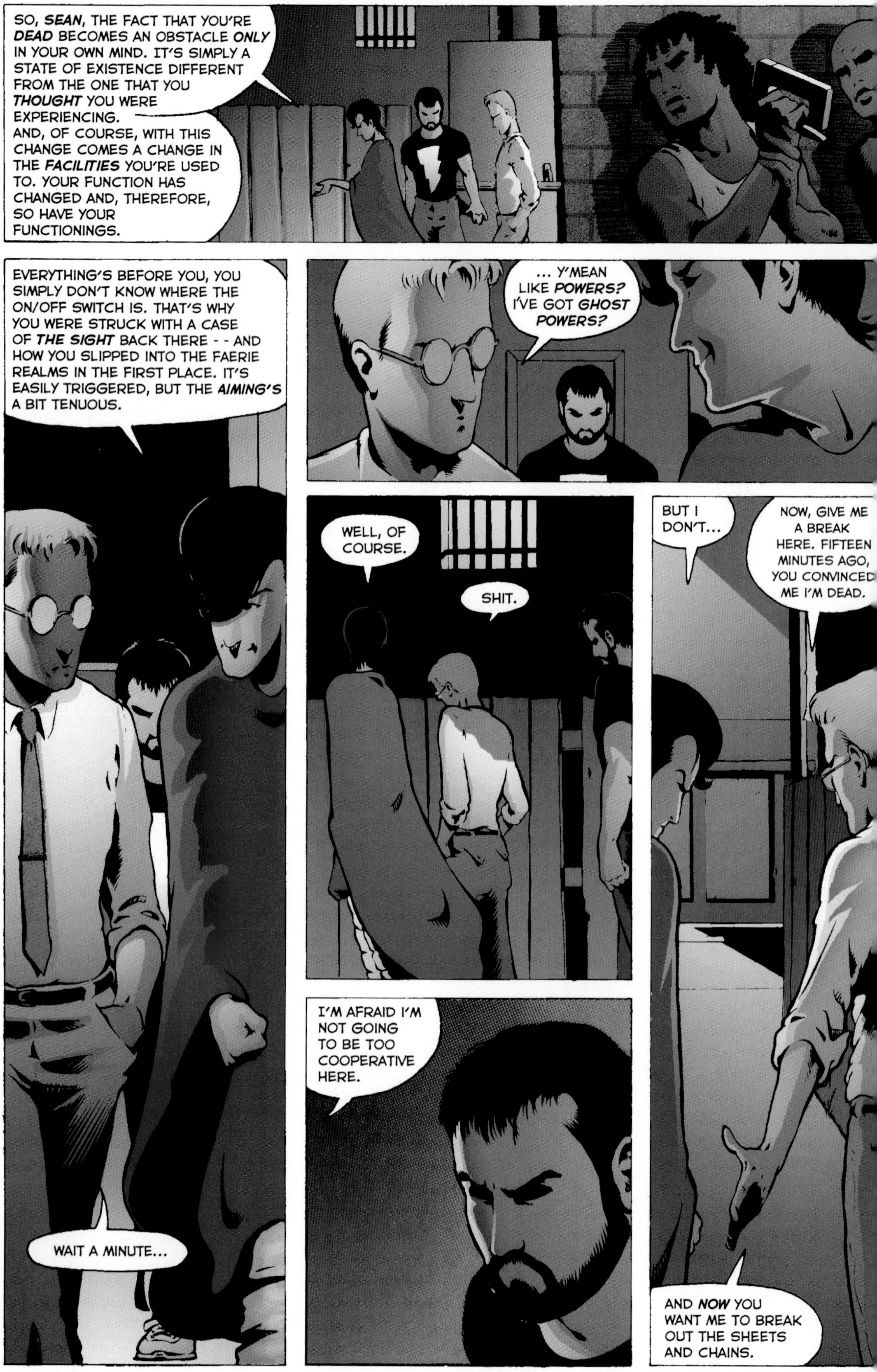
SO, SEAN, THE FACT THAT YOU'RE DEAD BECOMES AN OBSTACLE ONLY IN YOUR OWN MIND. IT'S SIMPLY A STATE OF EXISTENCE DIFFERENT FROM THE ONE THAT YOU THOUGHT YOU WERE EXPERIENCING.
AND, OF COURSE, WITH THIS CHANGE COMES A CHANGE IN THE FACILITIES YOU'RE USED TO. YOUR FUNCTION HAS CHANGED AND, THEREFORE, SO HAVE YOUR FUNCTIONINGS.
EVERYTHING'S BEFORE YOU, YOU SIMPLY DON'T KNOW WHERE THE ON/OFF SWITCH IS. THAT'S WHY YOU WERE STRUCK WITH A CASE OF THE SIGHT BACK THERE - - AND HOW YOU SLIPPED INTO THE FAERIE REALMS IN THE FIRST PLACE. IT'S EASILY TRIGGERED, BUT THE AIMING'S A BIT TENUOUS.
WAIT A MINUTE...
... Y'MEAN LIKE POWERS? I'VE GOT GHOST POWERS?
WELL, OF COURSE.
SHIT.
I'M AFRAID I'M NOT GOING TO BE TOO COOPERATIVE HERE.
BUT I DON'T...
NOW, GIVE ME A BREAK HERE. FIFTEEN MINUTES AGO, YOU CONVINCED ME I'M DEAD.
AND NOW YOU WANT ME TO BREAK OUT THE SHEETS AND CHAINS.

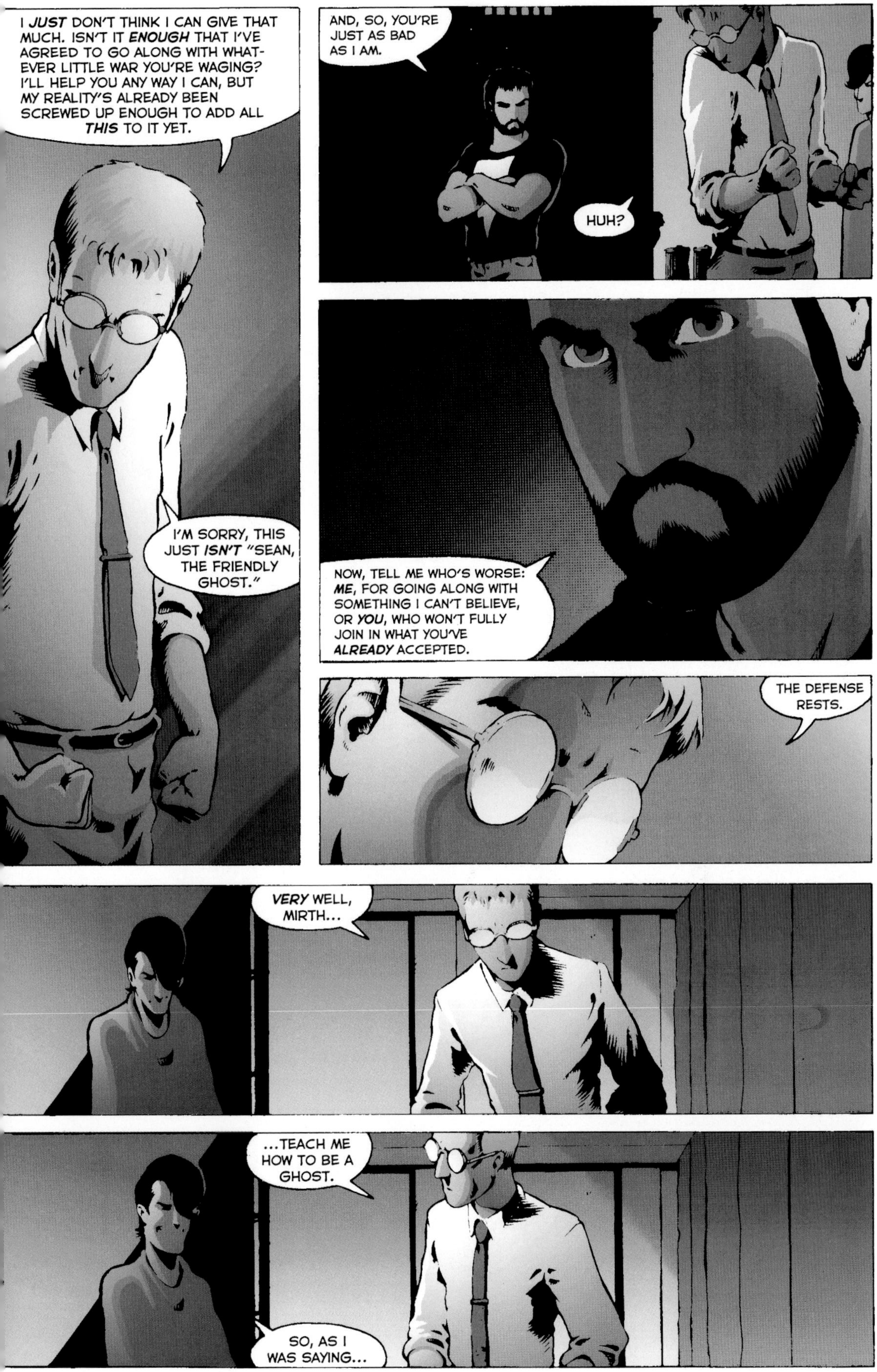
I JUST DON'T THINK I CAN GIVE THAT MUCH. ISN'T IT ENOUGH THAT I'VE AGREED TO GO ALONG WITH WHAT-EVER LITTLE WAR YOU'RE WAGING? I'LL HELP YOU ANY WAY I CAN, BUT MY REALITY'S ALREADY BEEN SCREWED UP ENOUGH TO ADD ALL THIS TO IT YET.
I'M SORRY, THIS JUST ISN'T "SEAN, THE FRIENDLY GHOST."
AND, SO, YOU'RE JUST AS BAD AS I AM.
HUH?
NOW, TELL ME WHO'S WORSE: ME, FOR GOING ALONG WITH SOMETHING I CAN'T BELIEVE, OR YOU, WHO WON'T FULLY JOIN IN WHAT YOU'VE ALREADY ACCEPTED.
THE DEFENSE RESTS.
VERY WELL, MIRTH...
...TEACH ME HOW TO BE A GHOST.
SO, AS I WAS SAYING...

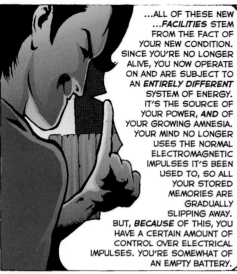

...ALL OF THESE NEW ...*FACILITIES* STEM FROM THE FACT OF YOUR NEW CONDITION. SINCE YOU'RE NO LONGER ALIVE, YOU NOW OPERATE ON AND ARE SUBJECT TO AN *ENTIRELY DIFFERENT* SYSTEM OF ENERGY. IT'S THE SOURCE OF YOUR POWER, *AND* OF YOUR GROWING AMNESIA. YOUR MIND NO LONGER USES THE NORMAL ELECTROMAGNETIC IMPULSES IT'S BEEN USED TO, SO ALL YOUR STORED MEMORIES ARE GRADUALLY SLIPPING AWAY. BUT, *BECAUSE* OF THIS, YOU HAVE A CERTAIN AMOUNT OF CONTROL OVER ELECTRICAL IMPULSES. YOU'RE SOMEWHAT OF AN EMPTY BATTERY.

EARLIER, I SAID THAT YOUR PLACE WAS NEITHER HERE NOR THERE, BUT SOMEWHERE BEYOND. UNTIL YOU REACH THAT GOAL, YOU ARE FREE TO TRAVEL AMONG THE OTHER LAYERS AT WILL.

IN SHORT, YOU'RE *INTANGIBLE...* IF YOU SO DESIRE.

NOW, COME ON, GIVE IT A TRY. THE TRICK IS TO REACH. AFTER ALL, YOU'RE NOT WHERE YOU WANT TO BE.

ARE YOU?

SEE? NOTHING TO IT.

NOW, TAKE IT OUT.

...DOES THIS GET EASIER? OR IS IT THE *VERY DIFFICULTY* THAT FIRES YOUR DISBELIEF?

IV'E GOT *NO HOPE* OF CONTROL, COUNSELOR. MY NEW *"FACILITIES"* OCCUR WHETHER I LIKE IT OR NOT. *THEY* DECIDE WHEN AND WHERE.

YES...WELL, YOUR CONTROL CAN ONLY IMPROVE.

BELIEVE ME...

TELL ME, KEVIN...

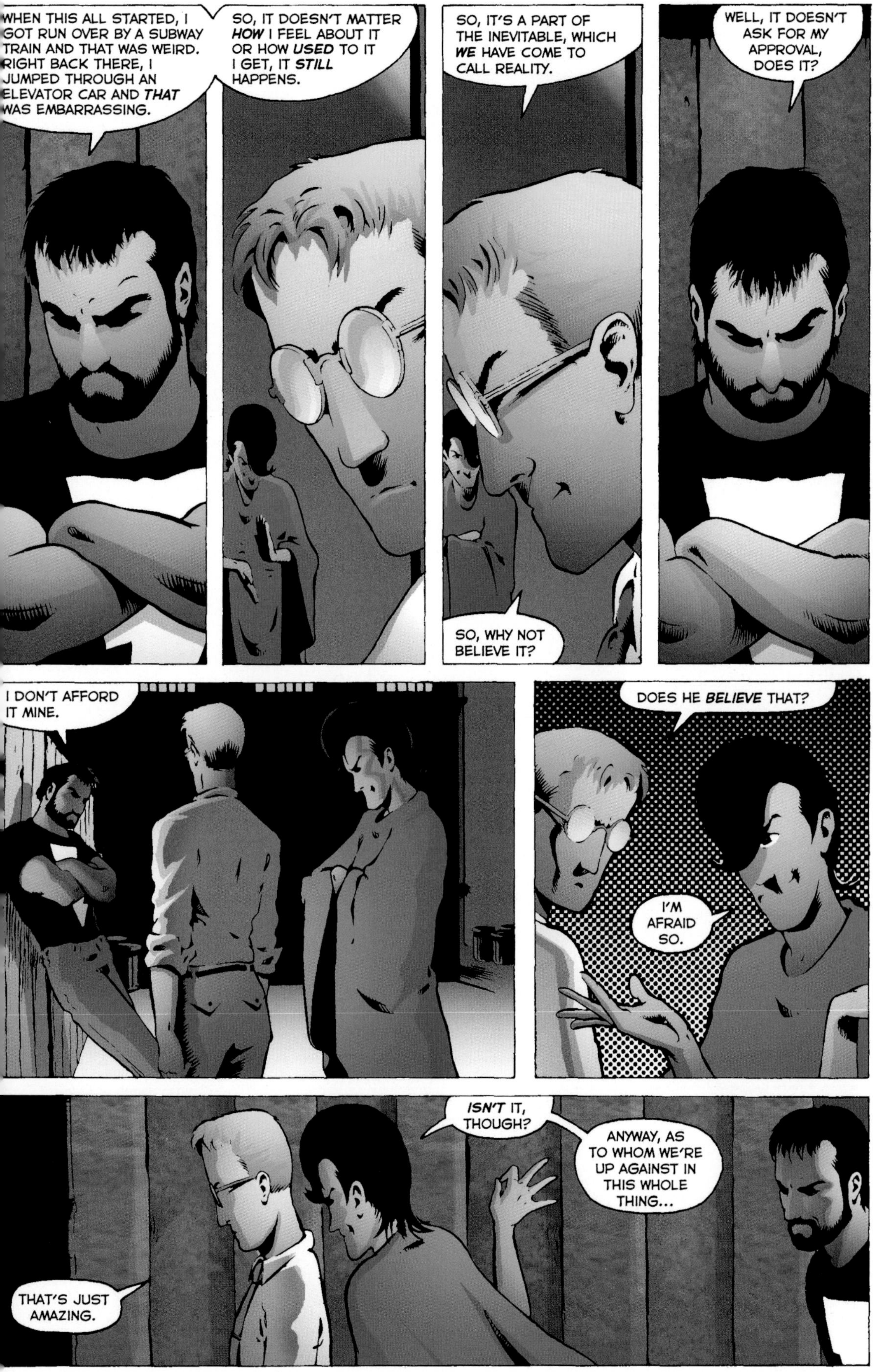
WHEN THIS ALL STARTED, I GOT RUN OVER BY A SUBWAY TRAIN AND THAT WAS WEIRD. RIGHT BACK THERE, I JUMPED THROUGH AN ELEVATOR CAR AND THAT WAS EMBARRASSING.
SO, IT DOESN'T MATTER HOW I FEEL ABOUT IT OR HOW USED TO IT I GET, IT STILL HAPPENS.
SO, IT'S A PART OF THE INEVITABLE, WHICH WE HAVE COME TO CALL REALITY.
SO, WHY NOT BELIEVE IT?
WELL, IT DOESN'T ASK FOR MY APPROVAL, DOES IT?
I DON'T AFFORD IT MINE.
DOES HE BELIEVE THAT?
I'M AFRAID SO.
THAT'S JUST AMAZING.
ISN'T IT, THOUGH?
ANYWAY, AS TO WHOM WE'RE UP AGAINST IN THIS WHOLE THING...

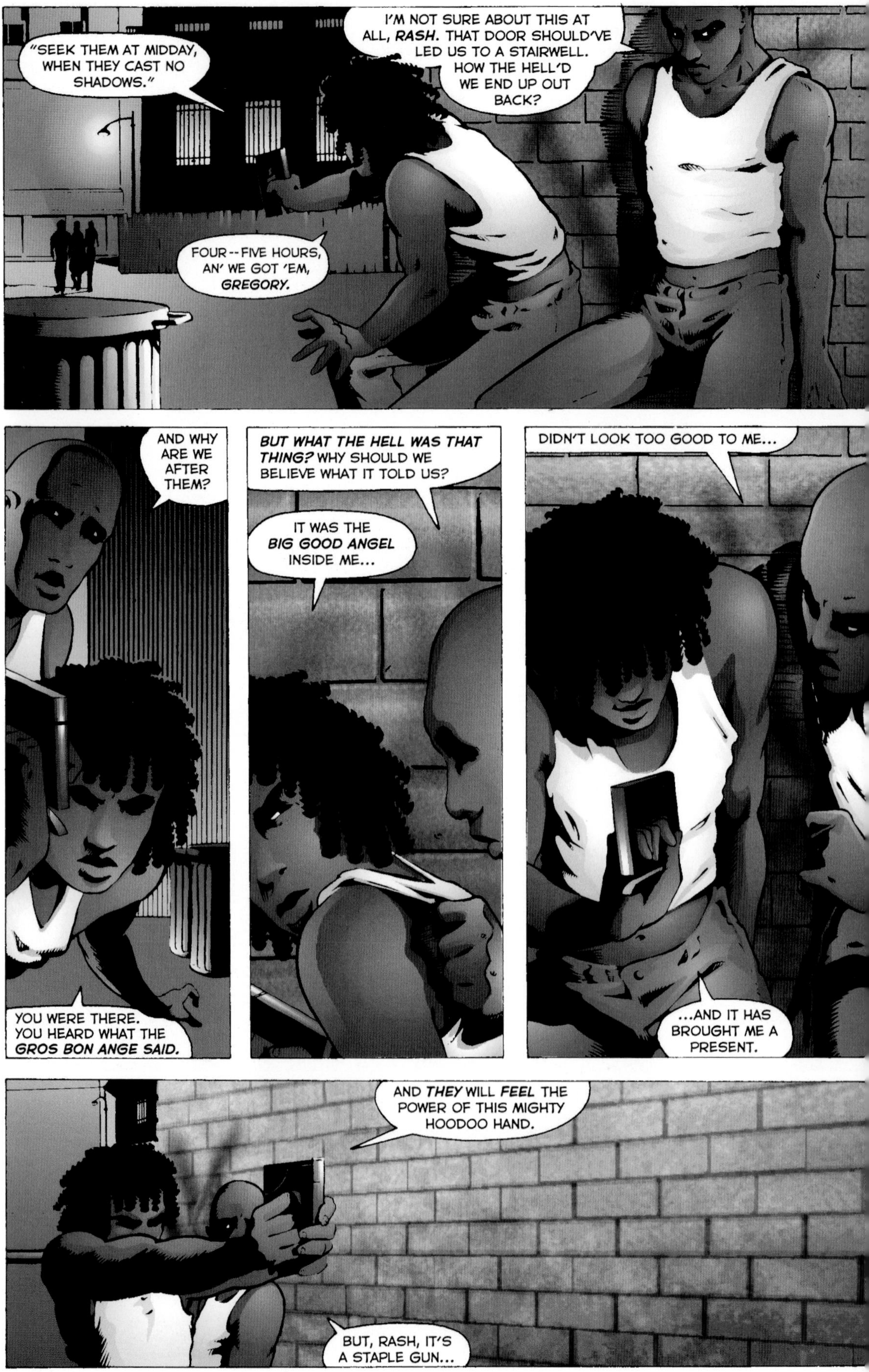
"SEEK THEM AT MIDDAY, WHEN THEY CAST NO SHADOWS."
I'M NOT SURE ABOUT THIS AT ALL, RASH. THAT DOOR SHOULD'VE LED US TO A STAIRWELL. HOW THE HELL'D WE END UP OUT BACK?
FOUR--FIVE HOURS, AN' WE GOT 'EM, GREGORY.
AND WHY ARE WE AFTER THEM?
YOU WERE THERE. YOU HEARD WHAT THE GROS BON ANGE SAID.
BUT WHAT THE HELL WAS THAT THING? WHY SHOULD WE BELIEVE WHAT IT TOLD US?
IT WAS THE BIG GOOD ANGEL INSIDE ME...
DIDN'T LOOK TOO GOOD TO ME...
...AND IT HAS BROUGHT ME A PRESENT.
AND THEY WILL FEEL THE POWER OF THIS MIGHTY HOODOO HAND.
BUT, RASH, IT'S A STAPLE GUN...

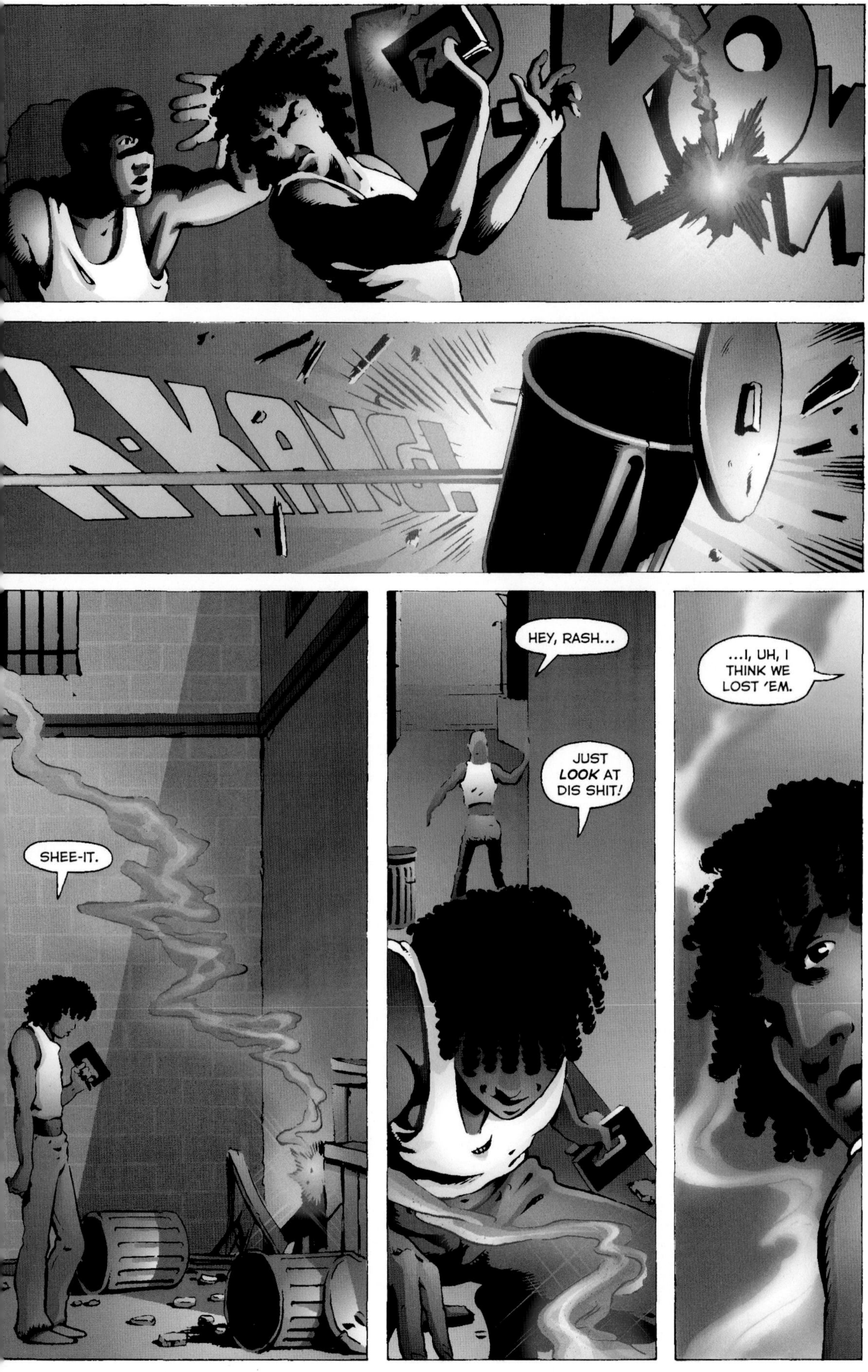
P-KOW
K-KANG!
SHEE-IT.
HEY, RASH...
JUST LOOK AT DIS SHIT!
...I, UH, I THINK WE LOST 'EM.

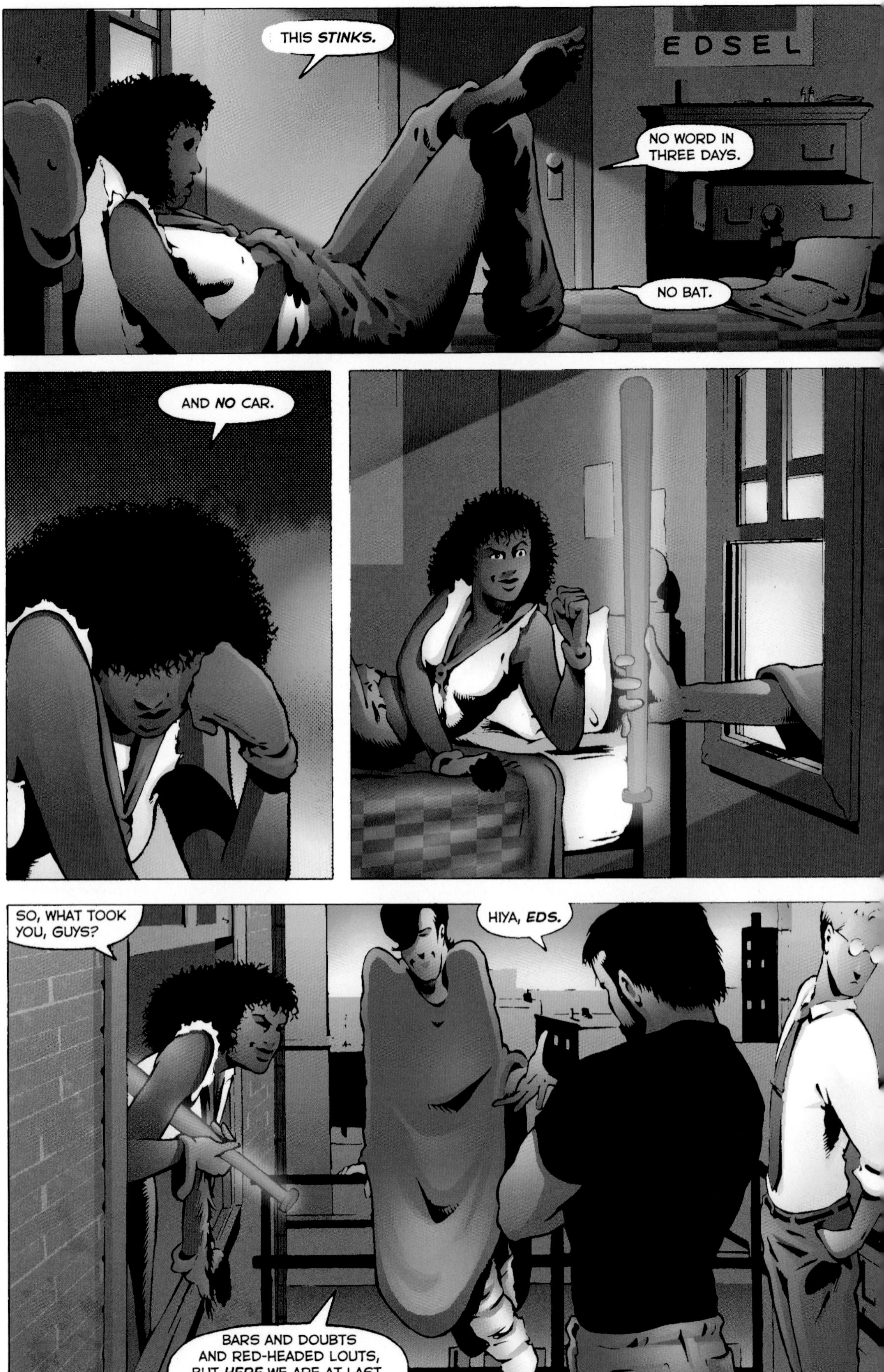
THIS STINKS.
NO WORD IN THREE DAYS.
NO BAT.
AND NO CAR.
SO, WHAT TOOK YOU, GUYS?
HIYA, EDS.
BARS AND DOUBTS AND RED-HEADED LOUTS, BUT HERE WE ARE AT LAST.

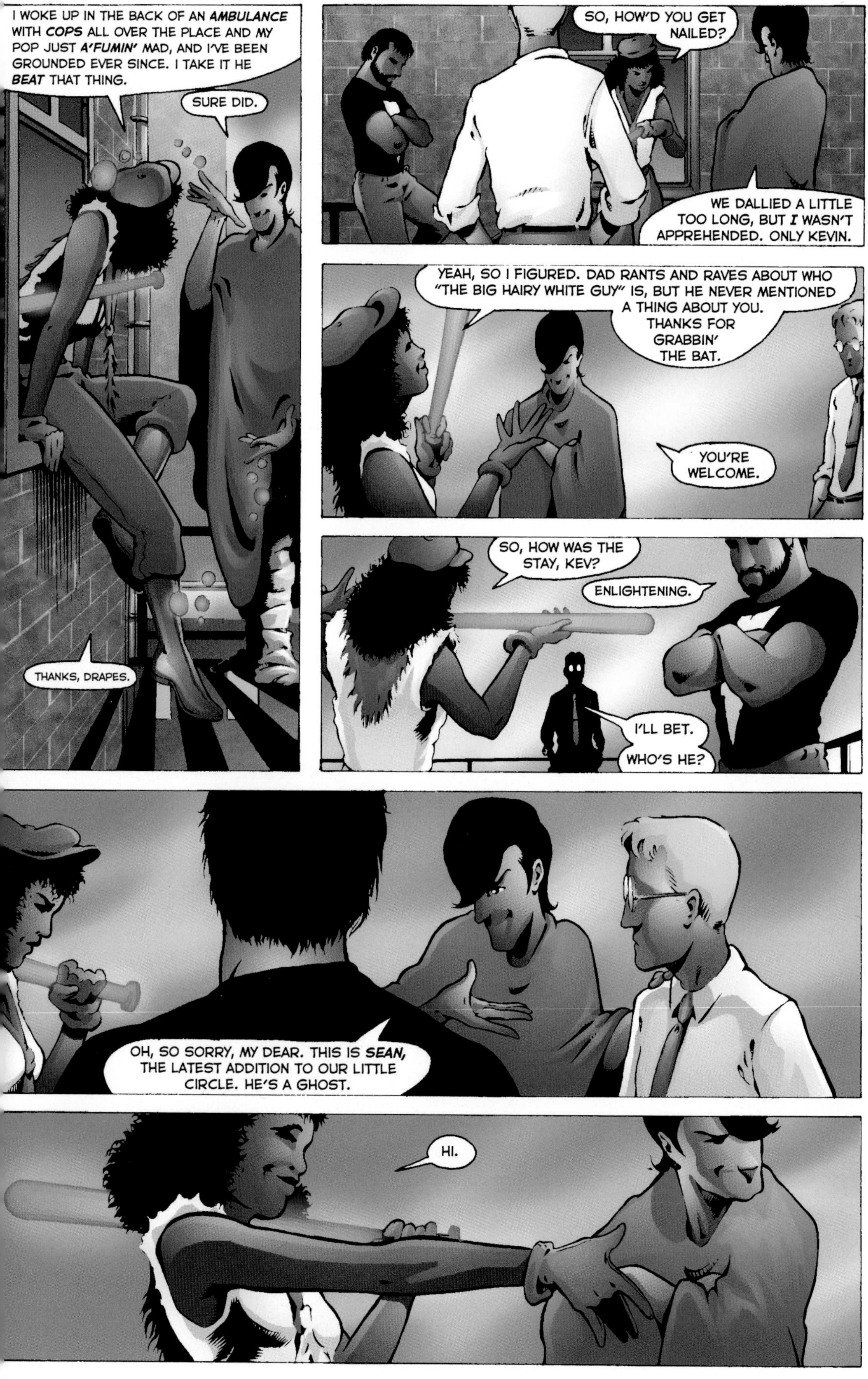
I WOKE UP IN THE BACK OF AN AMBULANCE WITH COPS ALL OVER THE PLACE AND MY POP JUST A'FUMIN' MAD, AND I'VE BEEN GROUNDED EVER SINCE. I TAKE IT HE BEAT THAT THING.
SURE DID.
THANKS, DRAPES.
SO, HOW'D YOU GET NAILED?
WE DALLIED A LITTLE TOO LONG, BUT I WASN'T APPREHENDED. ONLY KEVIN.
YEAH, SO I FIGURED. DAD RANTS AND RAVES ABOUT WHO "THE BIG HAIRY WHITE GUY" IS, BUT HE NEVER MENTIONED A THING ABOUT YOU. THANKS FOR GRABBIN' THE BAT.
YOU'RE WELCOME.
SO, HOW WAS THE STAY, KEV?
ENLIGHTENING.
I'LL BET.
WHO'S HE?
OH, SO SORRY, MY DEAR. THIS IS SEAN, THE LATEST ADDITION TO OUR LITTLE CIRCLE. HE'S A GHOST.
HI.

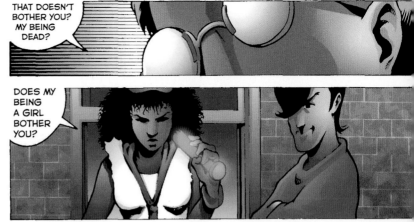

THAT DOESN'T BOTHER YOU? MY BEING DEAD?

DOES MY BEING A GIRL BOTHER YOU?

NO, OF *COURSE* NOT.

IT'S ONLY WHAT YOU ARE, MAN. NOTHIN' YOU CAN CHANGE. I MEAN, SO YOU'RE A GHOST? *MIRTH'S* THE *WORLD-MAGE.* KEVIN'S...

...A...

...HERO!

WELL, YES, YOUNG LADY, THAT'S A VERY CUTE LITTLE ARGUMENT, AND NO DOUBT TRUE...

LISTEN, SPOOK, I JUMPED ON AN *OGRE'S* BACK WITH ONLY THIS IN MY HANDS...

...BUT THEY ARE STILL ALIVE, NOW AREN'T THEY?

...SO DON'T FEED ME ALL THESE DEATH HANG-UPS. WE'VE *ALL* LOOKED DEATH SQUARE IN THE EYES LATELY. WE'RE NOT AFRAID.

SPEAKING OF WHICH, HOW'S YOUR DAD KEEP YOU UNDER WRAPS? LOCK YOU IN?

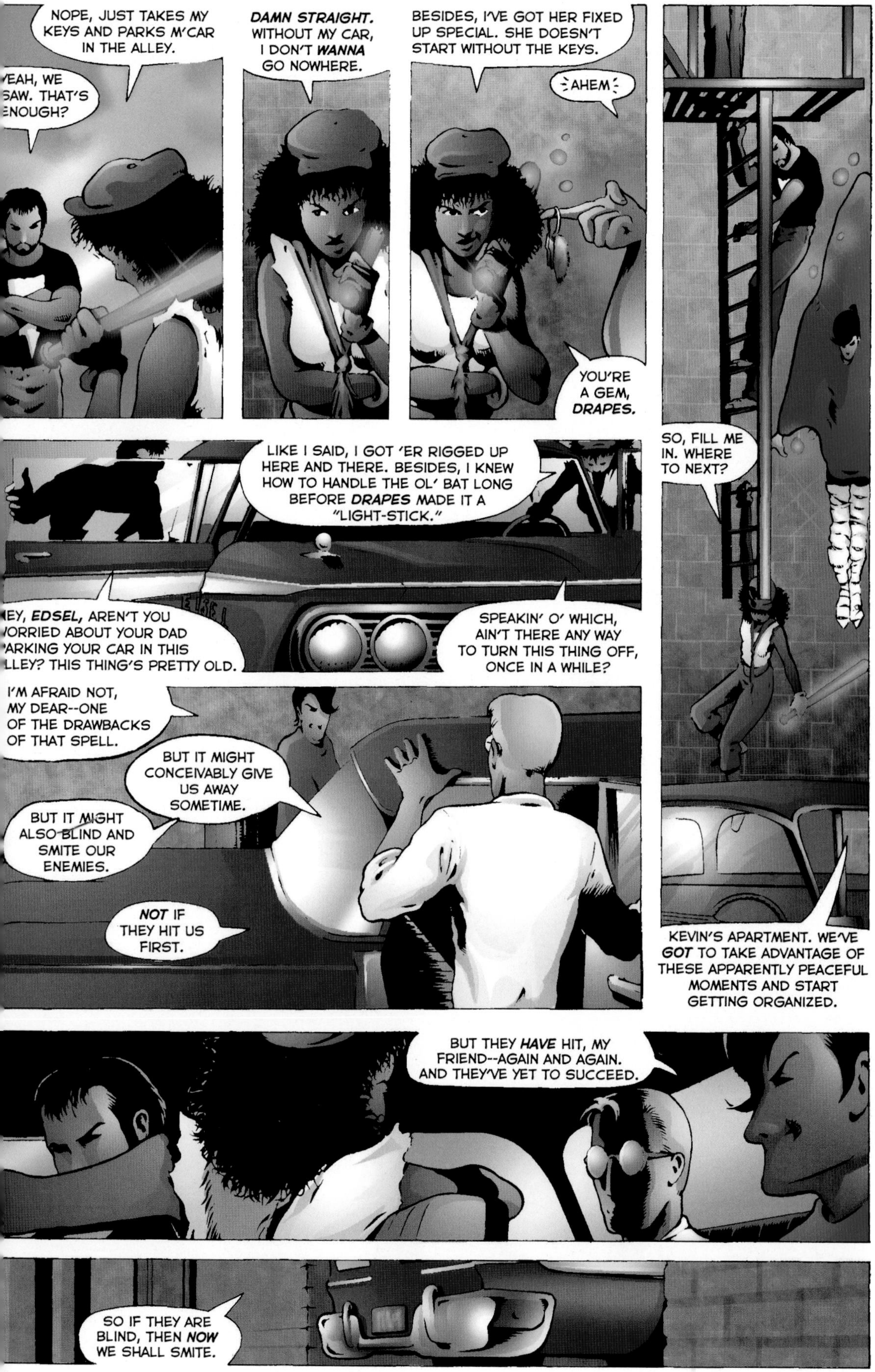
NOPE, JUST TAKES MY KEYS AND PARKS M'CAR IN THE ALLEY.
EAH, WE SAW. THAT'S ENOUGH?
DAMN STRAIGHT. WITHOUT MY CAR, I DON'T WANNA GO NOWHERE.
BESIDES, I'VE GOT HER FIXED UP SPECIAL. SHE DOESN'T START WITHOUT THE KEYS.
AHEM
YOU'RE A GEM, DRAPES.
EY, EDSEL, AREN'T YOU ORRIED ABOUT YOUR DAD ARKING YOUR CAR IN THIS LLEY? THIS THING'S PRETTY OLD.
LIKE I SAID, I GOT 'ER RIGGED UP HERE AND THERE. BESIDES, I KNEW HOW TO HANDLE THE OL' BAT LONG BEFORE DRAPES MADE IT A "LIGHT-STICK."
SPEAKIN' O' WHICH, AIN'T THERE ANY WAY TO TURN THIS THING OFF, ONCE IN A WHILE?
I'M AFRAID NOT, MY DEAR--ONE OF THE DRAWBACKS OF THAT SPELL.
BUT IT MIGHT CONCEIVABLY GIVE US AWAY SOMETIME.
BUT IT MIGHT ALSO BLIND AND SMITE OUR ENEMIES.
NOT IF THEY HIT US FIRST.
SO, FILL ME IN. WHERE TO NEXT?
KEVIN'S APARTMENT. WE'VE GOT TO TAKE ADVANTAGE OF THESE APPARENTLY PEACEFUL MOMENTS AND START GETTING ORGANIZED.
BUT THEY HAVE HIT, MY FRIEND--AGAIN AND AGAIN. AND THEY'VE YET TO SUCCEED.
SO IF THEY ARE BLIND, THEN NOW WE SHALL SMITE.

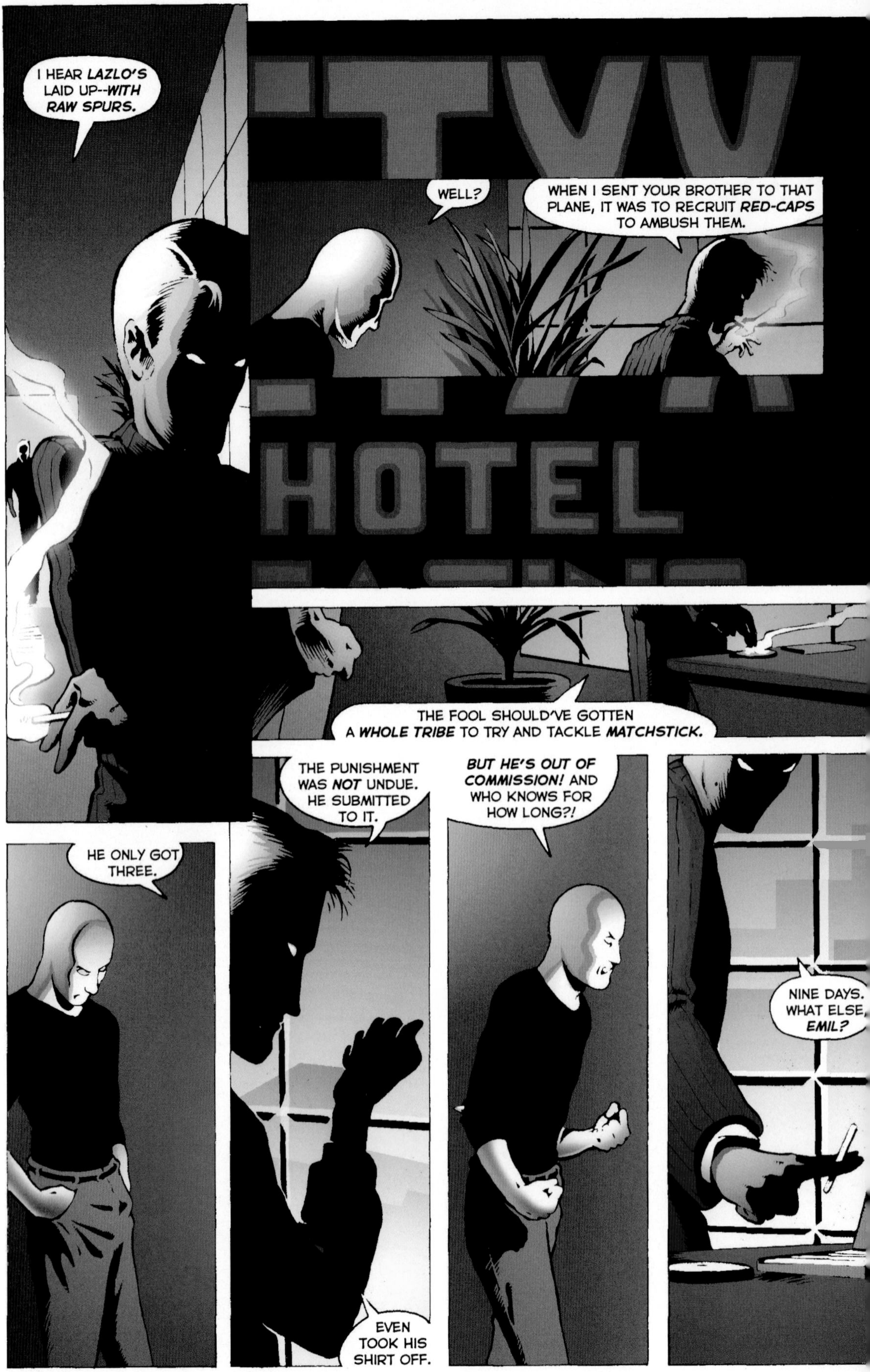
I HEAR LAZLO'S LAID UP--WITH RAW SPURS.
WELL?
WHEN I SENT YOUR BROTHER TO THAT PLANE, IT WAS TO RECRUIT RED-CAPS TO AMBUSH THEM.
HOTEL
THE FOOL SHOULD'VE GOTTEN A WHOLE TRIBE TO TRY AND TACKLE MATCHSTICK.
HE ONLY GOT THREE.
THE PUNISHMENT WAS NOT UNDUE. HE SUBMITTED TO IT.
EVEN TOOK HIS SHIRT OFF.
BUT HE'S OUT OF COMMISSION! AND WHO KNOWS FOR HOW LONG?!
NINE DAYS. WHAT ELSE, EMIL?

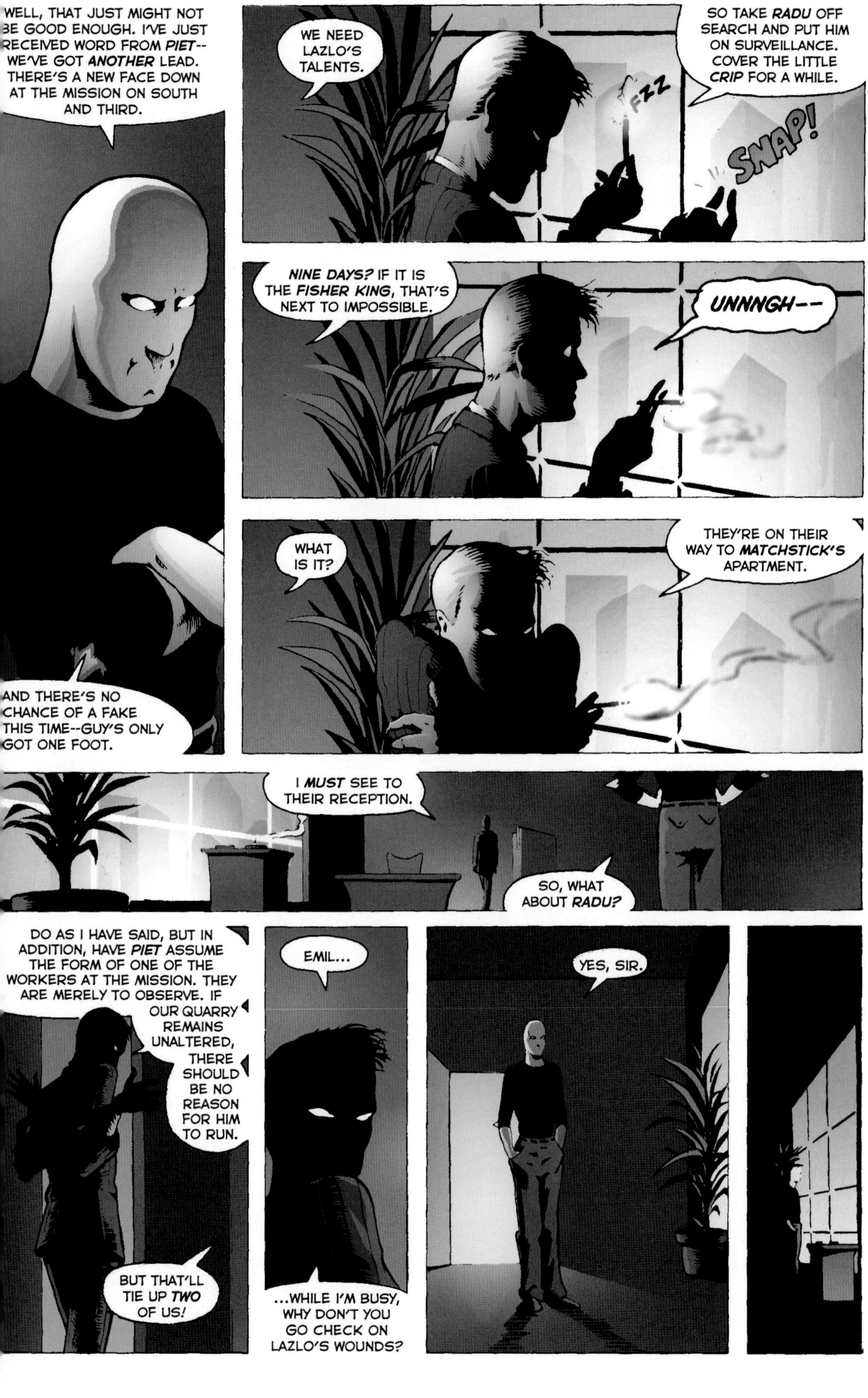
WELL, THAT JUST MIGHT NOT BE GOOD ENOUGH. I'VE JUST RECEIVED WORD FROM PIET-- WE'VE GOT ANOTHER LEAD. THERE'S A NEW FACE DOWN AT THE MISSION ON SOUTH AND THIRD.
WE NEED LAZLO'S TALENTS.
FZZ
SO TAKE RADU OFF SEARCH AND PUT HIM ON SURVEILLANCE. COVER THE LITTLE CRIP FOR A WHILE.
SNAP!
NINE DAYS? IF IT IS THE FISHER KING, THAT'S NEXT TO IMPOSSIBLE.
UNNNGH--
AND THERE'S NO CHANCE OF A FAKE THIS TIME--GUY'S ONLY GOT ONE FOOT.
WHAT IS IT?
THEY'RE ON THEIR WAY TO MATCHSTICK'S APARTMENT.
I MUST SEE TO THEIR RECEPTION.
SO, WHAT ABOUT RADU?
DO AS I HAVE SAID, BUT IN ADDITION, HAVE PIET ASSUME THE FORM OF ONE OF THE WORKERS AT THE MISSION. THEY ARE MERELY TO OBSERVE. IF OUR QUARRY REMAINS UNALTERED, THERE SHOULD BE NO REASON FOR HIM TO RUN.
BUT THAT'LL TIE UP TWO OF US!
EMIL...
...WHILE I'M BUSY, WHY DON'T YOU GO CHECK ON LAZLO'S WOUNDS?
YES, SIR.

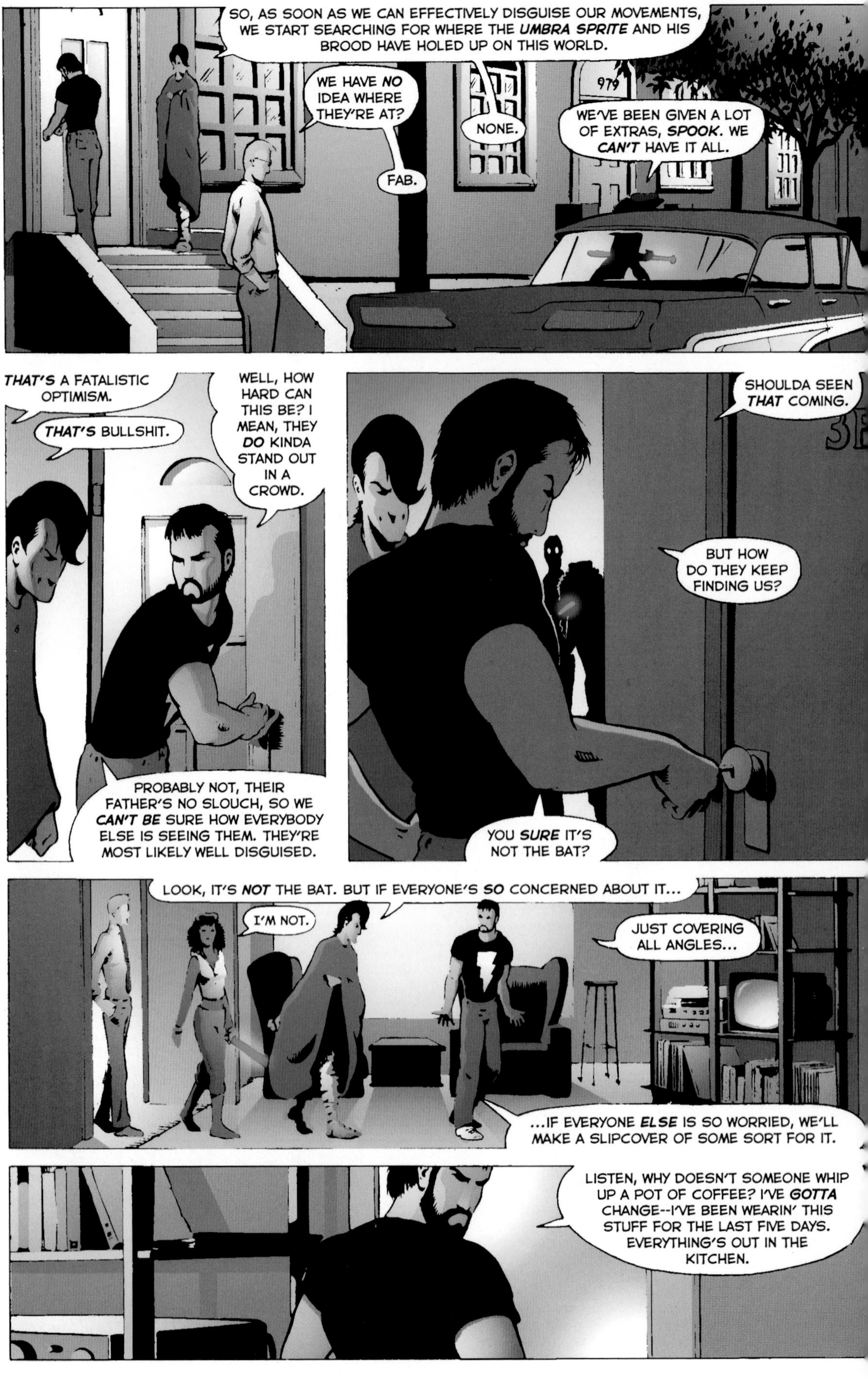
SO, AS SOON AS WE CAN EFFECTIVELY DISGUISE OUR MOVEMENTS, WE START SEARCHING FOR WHERE THE UMBRA SPRITE AND HIS BROOD HAVE HOLED UP ON THIS WORLD.
WE HAVE NO IDEA WHERE THEY'RE AT?
NONE.
FAB.
979
WE'VE BEEN GIVEN A LOT OF EXTRAS, SPOOK. WE CAN'T HAVE IT ALL.
THAT'S A FATALISTIC OPTIMISM.
THAT'S BULLSHIT.
WELL, HOW HARD CAN THIS BE? I MEAN, THEY DO KINDA STAND OUT IN A CROWD.
PROBABLY NOT, THEIR FATHER'S NO SLOUCH, SO WE CAN'T BE SURE HOW EVERYBODY ELSE IS SEEING THEM. THEY'RE MOST LIKELY WELL DISGUISED.
SHOULDA SEEN THAT COMING.
BUT HOW DO THEY KEEP FINDING US?
YOU SURE IT'S NOT THE BAT?
LOOK, IT'S NOT THE BAT. BUT IF EVERYONE'S SO CONCERNED ABOUT IT...
I'M NOT.
JUST COVERING ALL ANGLES...
...IF EVERYONE ELSE IS SO WORRIED, WE'LL MAKE A SLIPCOVER OF SOME SORT FOR IT.
LISTEN, WHY DOESN'T SOMEONE WHIP UP A POT OF COFFEE? I'VE GOTTA CHANGE--I'VE BEEN WEARIN' THIS STUFF FOR THE LAST FIVE DAYS. EVERYTHING'S OUT IN THE KITCHEN.

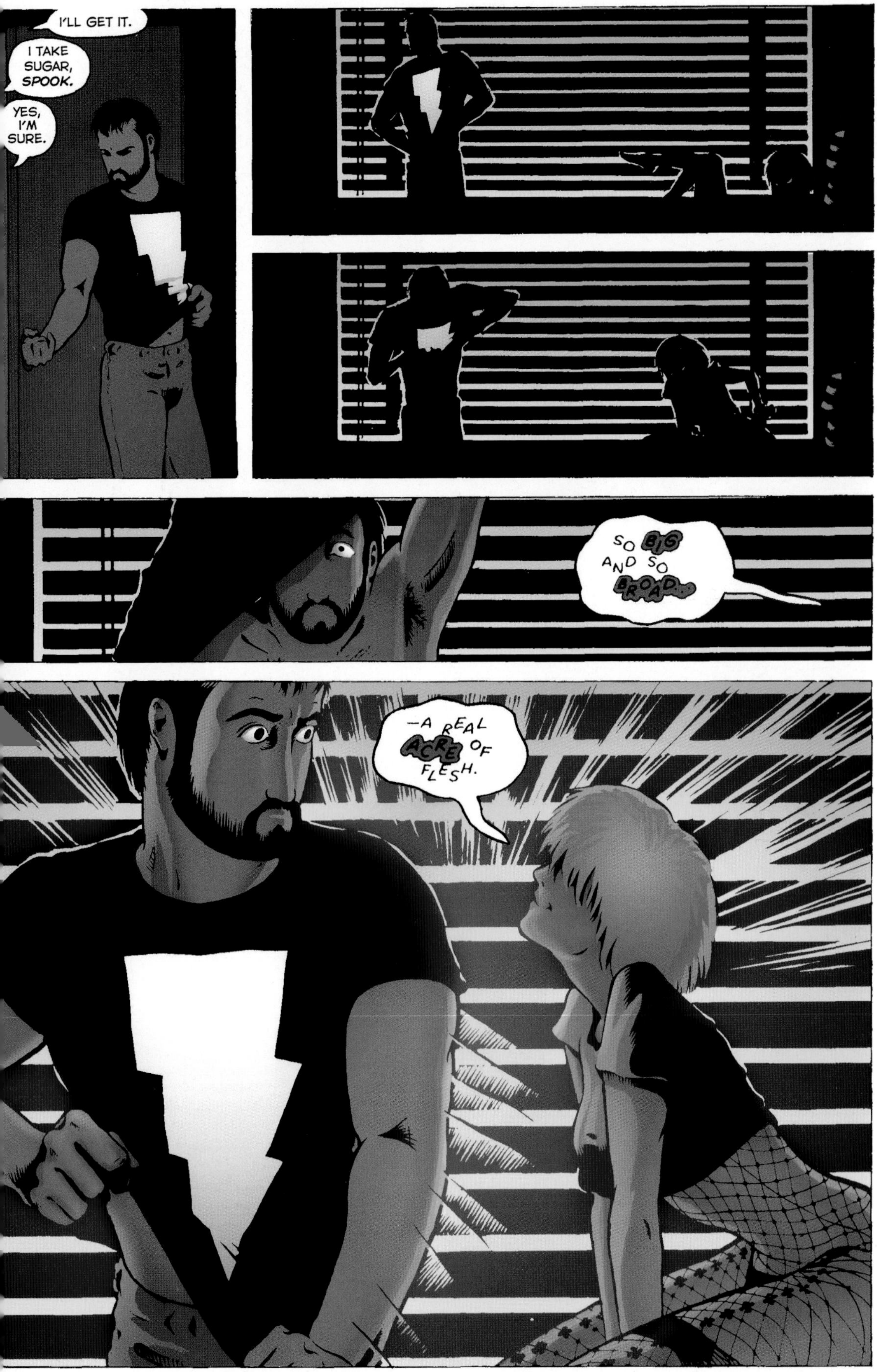
I'LL GET IT.
I TAKE SUGAR, SPOOK.
YES, I'M SURE.
SO BIG AND SO BROAD...
—A REAL ACRE OF FLESH.

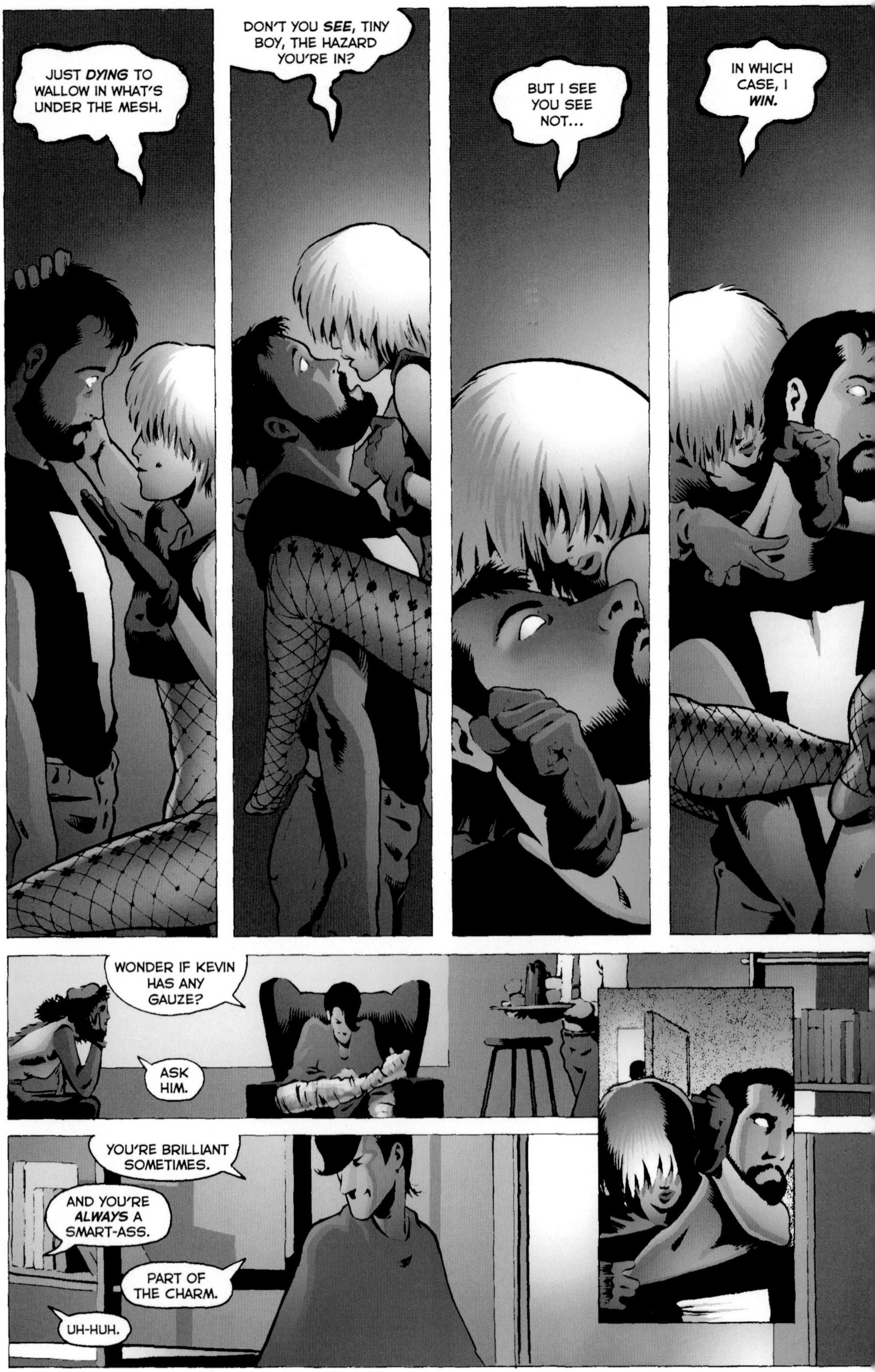
JUST DYING TO WALLOW IN WHAT'S UNDER THE MESH.
DON'T YOU SEE, TINY BOY, THE HAZARD YOU'RE IN?
BUT I SEE YOU SEE NOT...
IN WHICH CASE, I WIN.
WONDER IF KEVIN HAS ANY GAUZE?
ASK HIM.
YOU'RE BRILLIANT SOMETIMES.
AND YOU'RE ALWAYS A SMART-ASS.
PART OF THE CHARM.
UH-HUH.

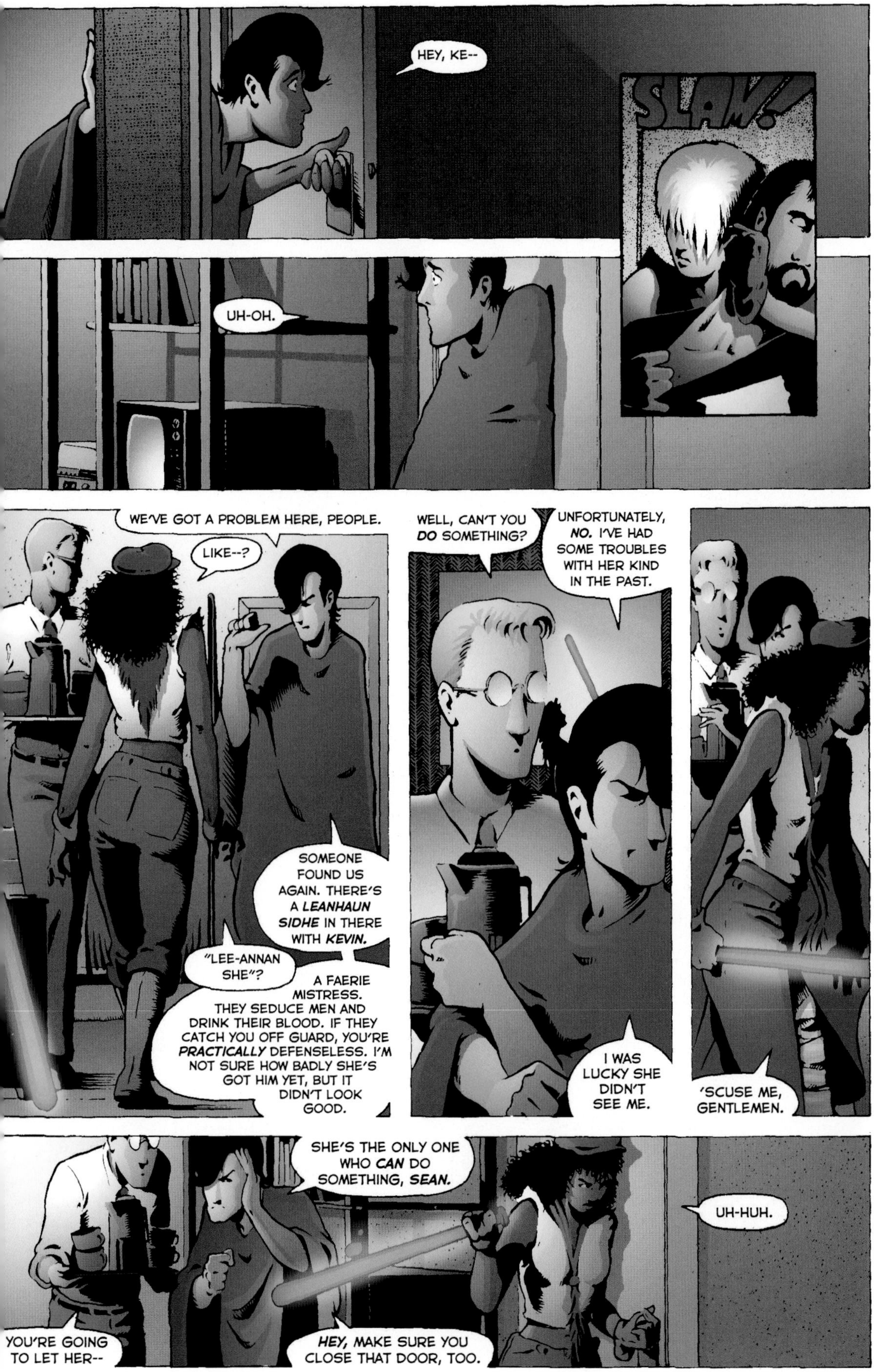
HEY, KE--
SLAM!
UH-OH.
WE'VE GOT A PROBLEM HERE, PEOPLE.
LIKE--?
SOMEONE FOUND US AGAIN. THERE'S A LEANHAUN SIDHE IN THERE WITH KEVIN.
"LEE-ANNAN SHE"?
A FAERIE MISTRESS. THEY SEDUCE MEN AND DRINK THEIR BLOOD. IF THEY CATCH YOU OFF GUARD, YOU'RE PRACTICALLY DEFENSELESS. I'M NOT SURE HOW BADLY SHE'S GOT HIM YET, BUT IT DIDN'T LOOK GOOD.
WELL, CAN'T YOU DO SOMETHING?
UNFORTUNATELY, NO. I'VE HAD SOME TROUBLES WITH HER KIND IN THE PAST.
I WAS LUCKY SHE DIDN'T SEE ME.
'SCUSE ME, GENTLEMEN.
YOU'RE GOING TO LET HER--
SHE'S THE ONLY ONE WHO CAN DO SOMETHING, SEAN.
HEY, MAKE SURE YOU CLOSE THAT DOOR, TOO.
UH-HUH.

UHNN-GH...

MMP!

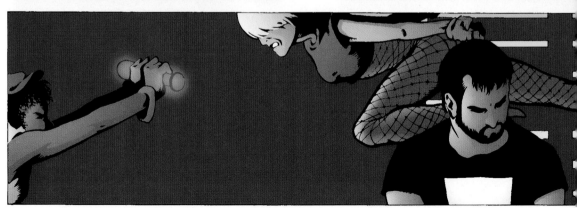

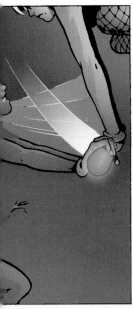

SO, A MISSY JUMPS IN WITH WEAPON AND SPUNK

TO SAVE HIM BY WHOM THEY ARE LED.

SO, WE'LL SEE HOW HE LIKES YOU, YOU MEDDLESOME PUNK,

WITH YOUR FACE NOW *ALL MANGLED AND RED.*

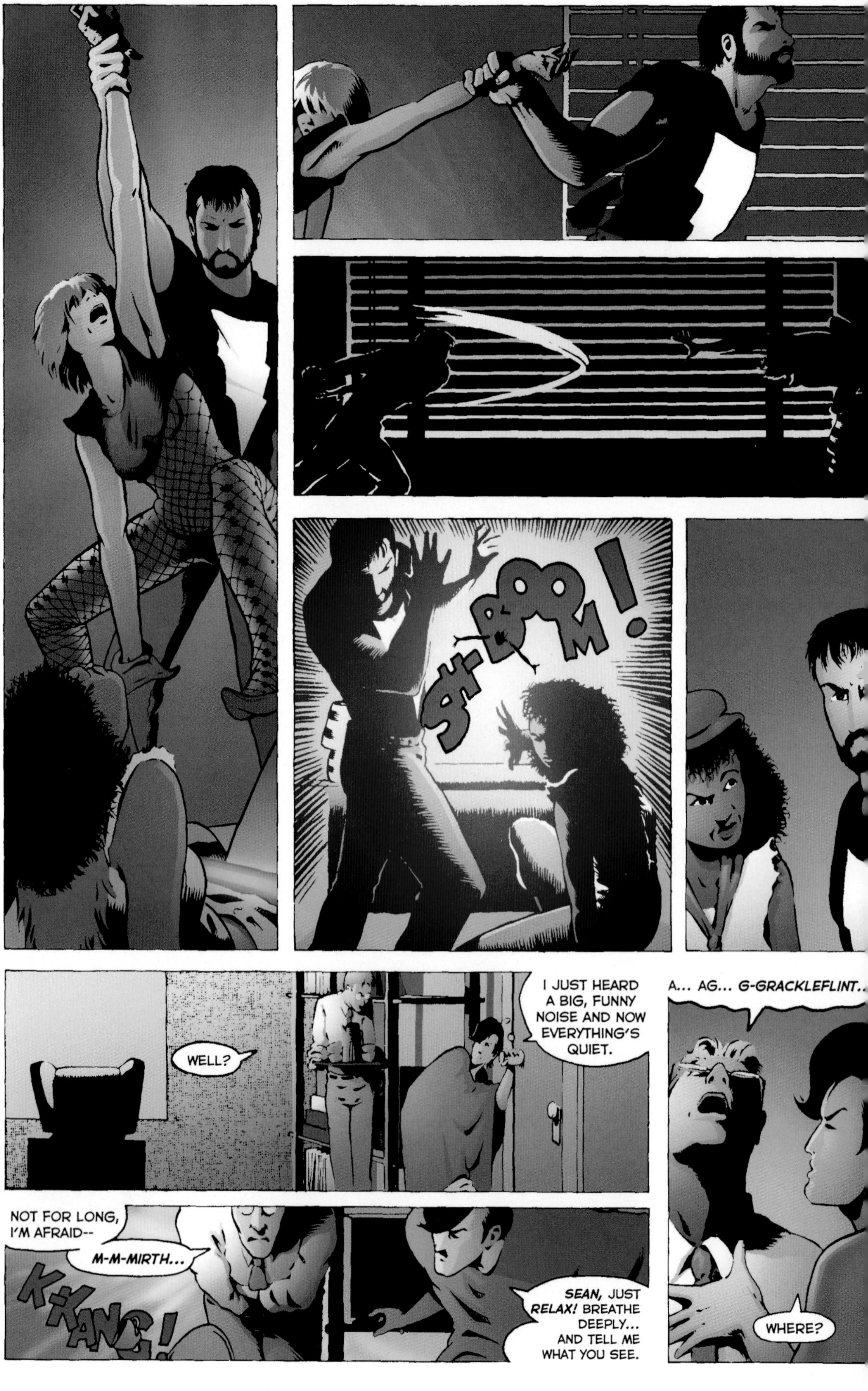

SH-BOOM!
WELL?
I JUST HEARD A BIG, FUNNY NOISE AND NOW EVERYTHING'S QUIET.
A... AG... G-GRACKLEFLINT...
NOT FOR LONG, I'M AFRAID--
M-M-MIRTH...
K-KANG!
SEAN, JUST RELAX! BREATHE DEEPLY... AND TELL ME WHAT YOU SEE.
WHERE?

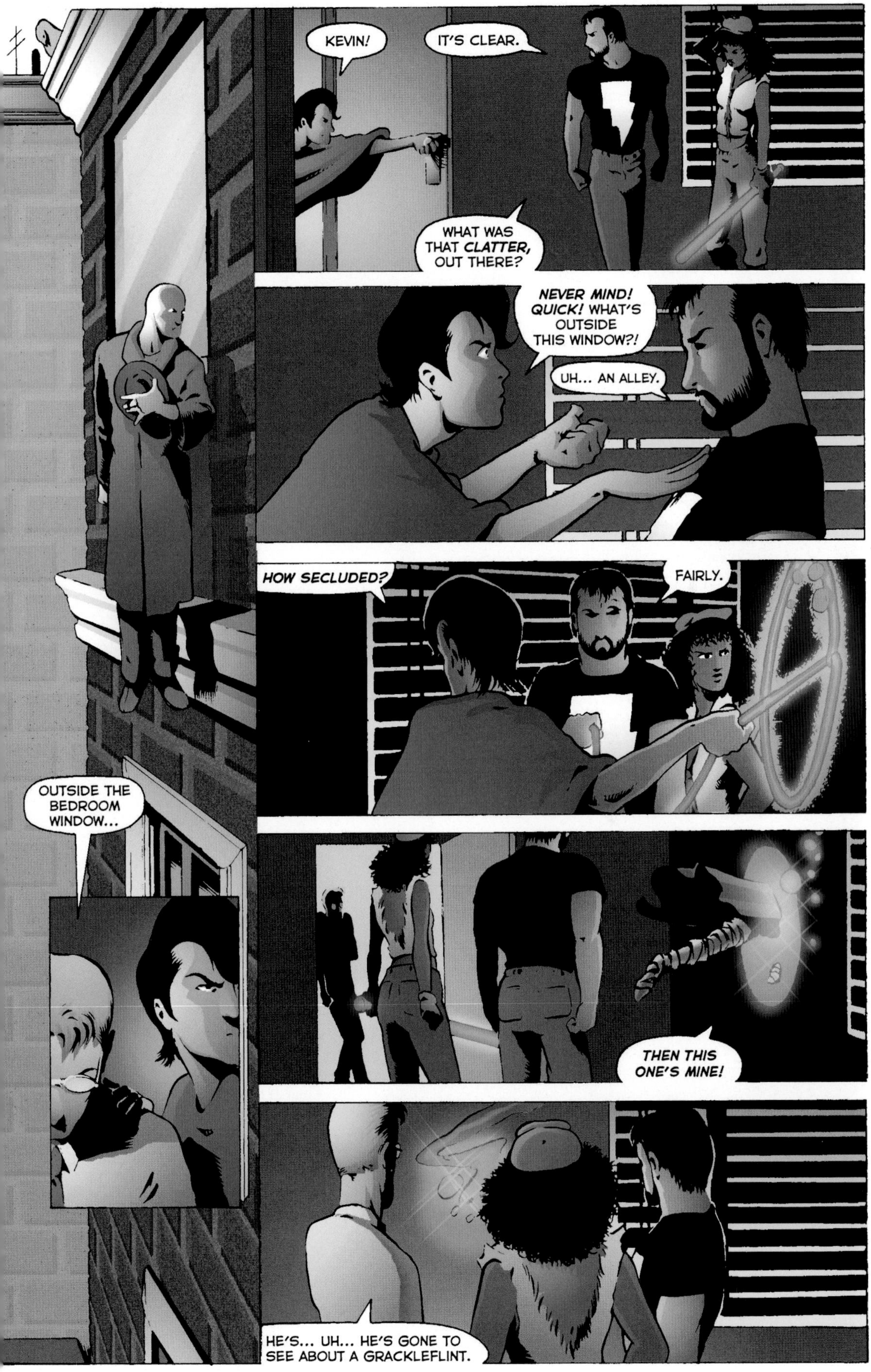
KEVIN!
IT'S CLEAR.
WHAT WAS THAT *CLATTER,* OUT THERE?
NEVER MIND! QUICK! WHAT'S OUTSIDE THIS WINDOW?!
UH... AN ALLEY.
HOW SECLUDED?
FAIRLY.
THEN THIS ONE'S MINE!
HE'S... UH... HE'S GONE TO SEE ABOUT A GRACKLEFLINT.
OUTSIDE THE BEDROOM WINDOW...

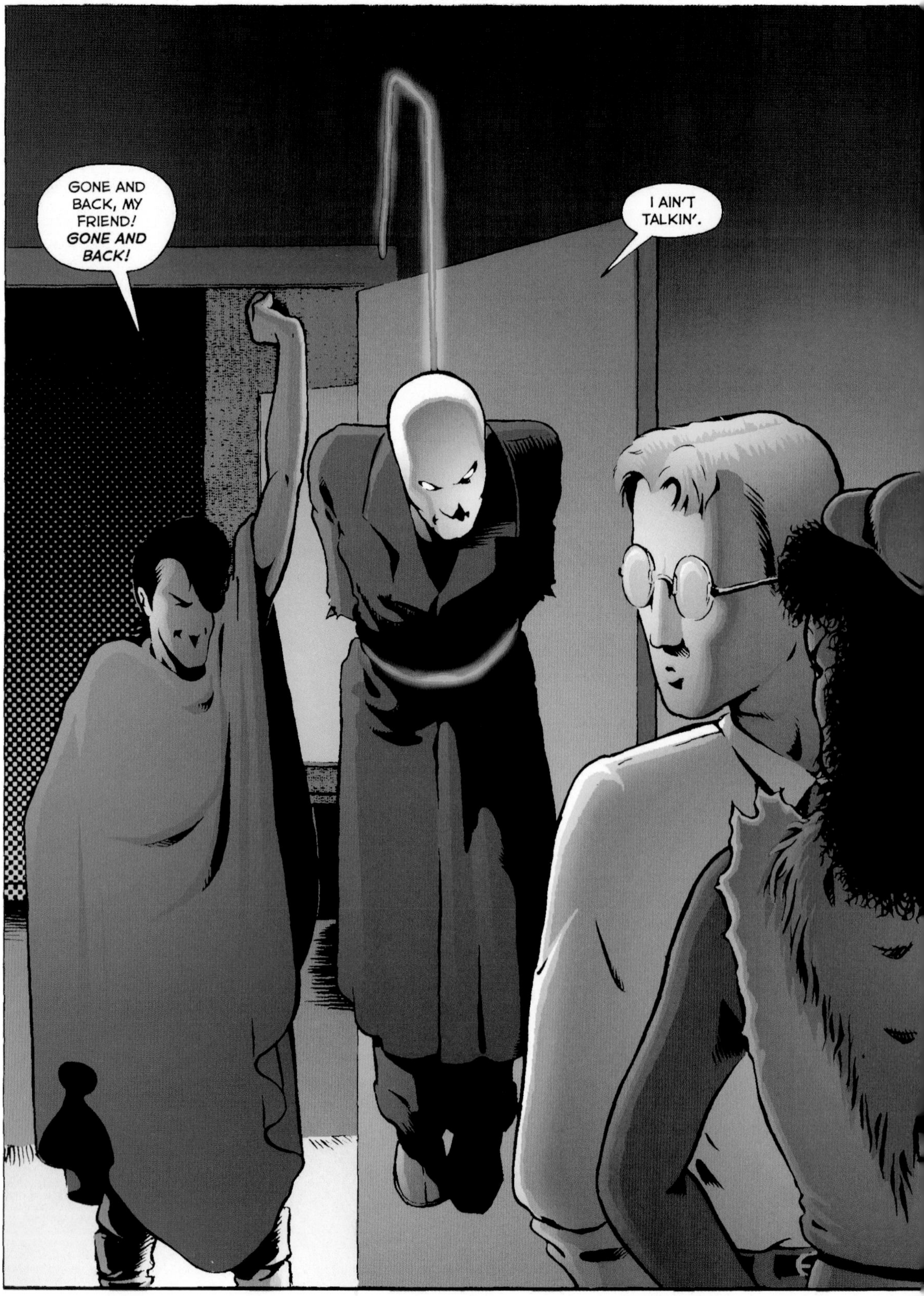
GONE AND BACK, MY FRIEND! *GONE AND BACK!*
I AIN'T TALKIN'.

THE HERO DISCOVERED

MAGE

Chapter 08

Against A Sea Of Troubles

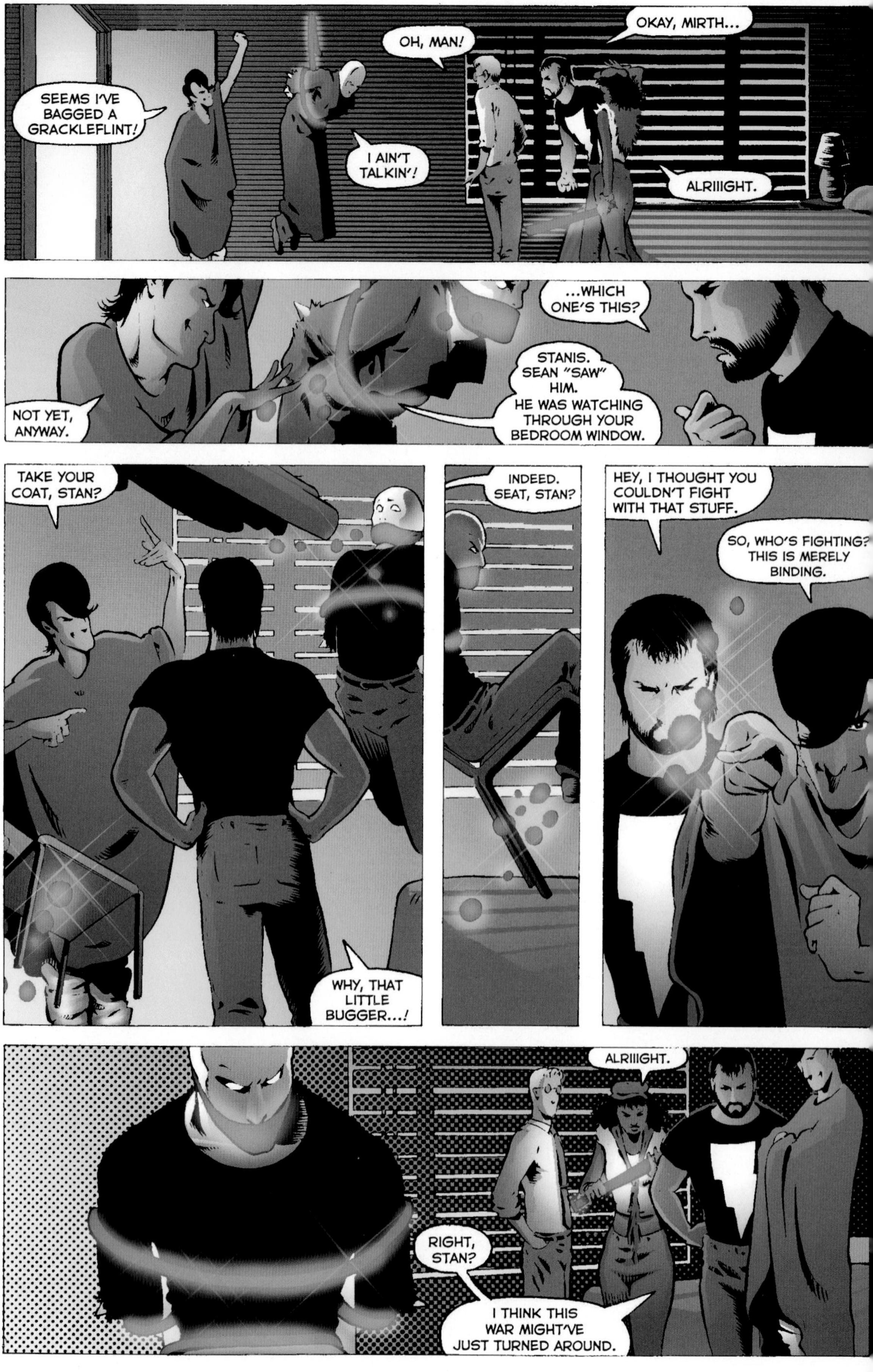
SEEMS I'VE BAGGED A GRACKLEFLINT!
OH, MAN!
I AIN'T TALKIN'!
OKAY, MIRTH...
ALRIIIGHT.
NOT YET, ANYWAY.
...WHICH ONE'S THIS?
STANIS. SEAN "SAW" HIM. HE WAS WATCHING THROUGH YOUR BEDROOM WINDOW.
TAKE YOUR COAT, STAN?
WHY, THAT LITTLE BUGGER...!
INDEED. SEAT, STAN?
HEY, I THOUGHT YOU COULDN'T FIGHT WITH THAT STUFF.
SO, WHO'S FIGHTING? THIS IS MERELY BINDING.
ALRIIIGHT.
RIGHT, STAN?
I THINK THIS WAR MIGHT'VE JUST TURNED AROUND.

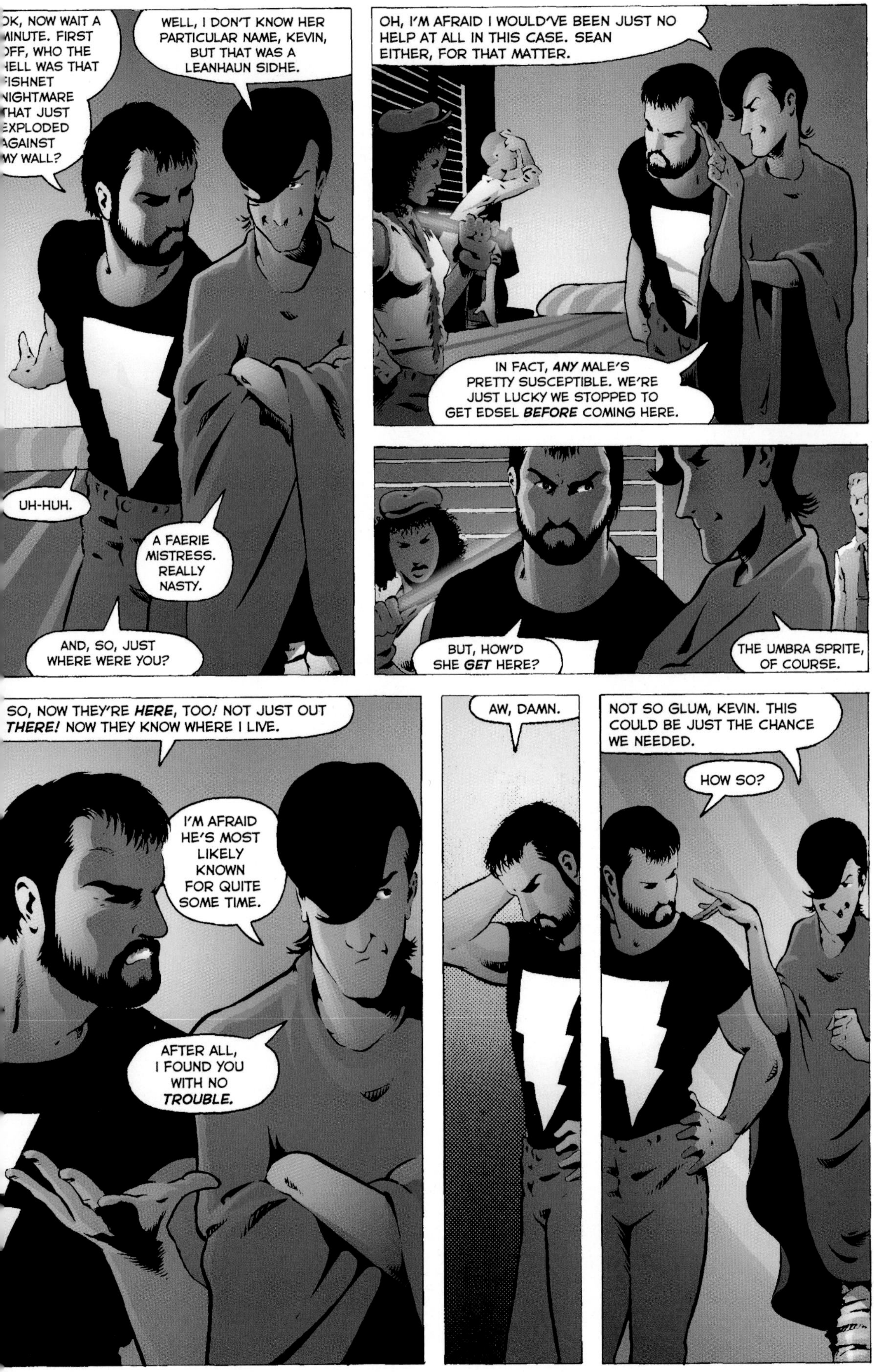
OK, NOW WAIT A MINUTE. FIRST OFF, WHO THE HELL WAS THAT FISHNET NIGHTMARE THAT JUST EXPLODED AGAINST MY WALL?
WELL, I DON'T KNOW HER PARTICULAR NAME, KEVIN, BUT THAT WAS A LEANHAUN SIDHE.
UH-HUH.
A FAERIE MISTRESS. REALLY NASTY.
AND, SO, JUST WHERE WERE YOU?
OH, I'M AFRAID I WOULD'VE BEEN JUST NO HELP AT ALL IN THIS CASE. SEAN EITHER, FOR THAT MATTER.
IN FACT, *ANY* MALE'S PRETTY SUSCEPTIBLE. WE'RE JUST LUCKY WE STOPPED TO GET EDSEL *BEFORE* COMING HERE.
BUT, HOW'D SHE *GET* HERE?
THE UMBRA SPRITE, OF COURSE.
SO, NOW THEY'RE *HERE*, TOO! NOT JUST OUT *THERE!* NOW THEY KNOW WHERE I LIVE.
I'M AFRAID HE'S MOST LIKELY KNOWN FOR QUITE SOME TIME.
AFTER ALL, I FOUND YOU WITH NO *TROUBLE.*
AW, DAMN.
NOT SO GLUM, KEVIN. THIS COULD BE JUST THE CHANCE WE NEEDED.
HOW SO?

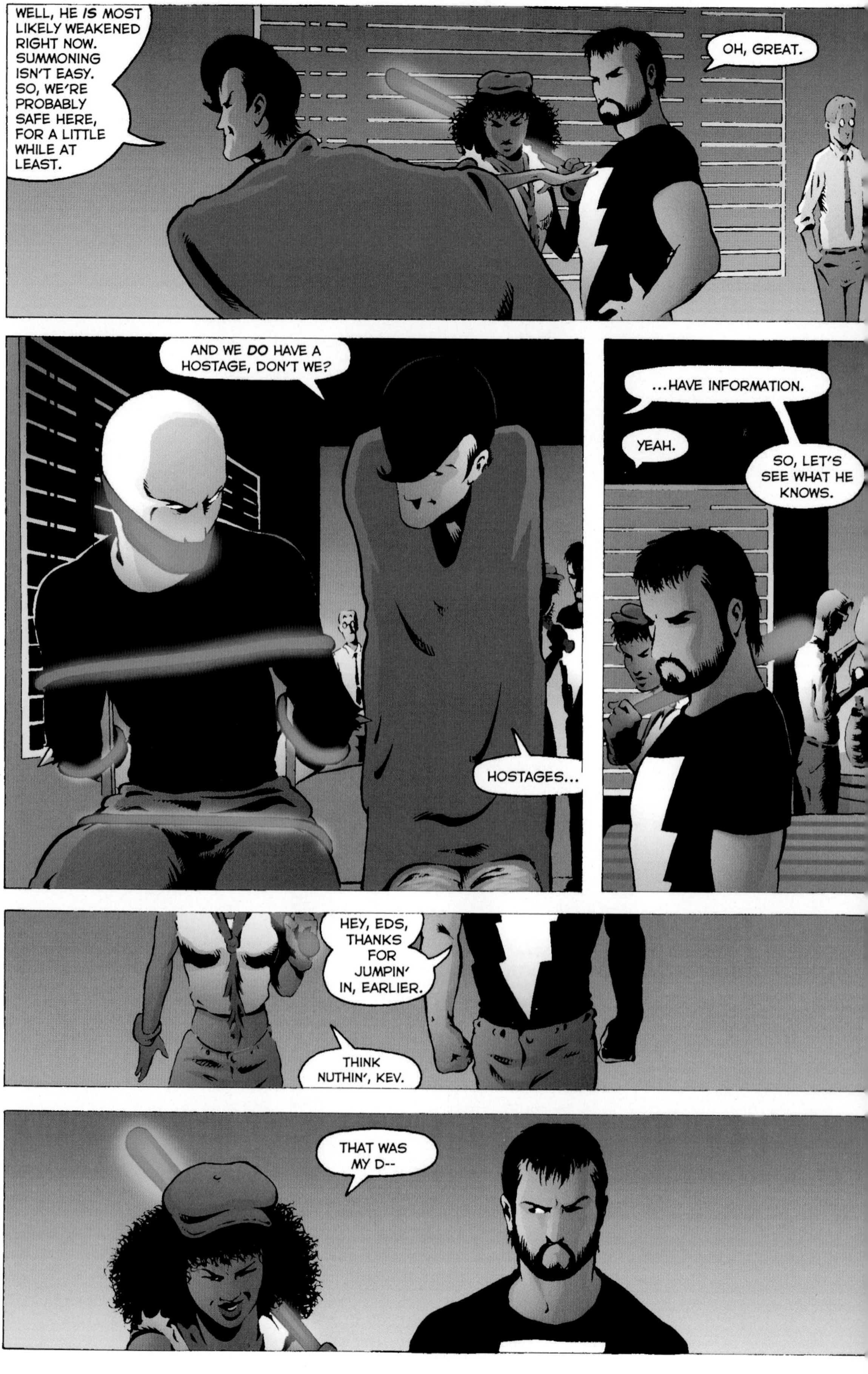
WELL, HE IS MOST LIKELY WEAKENED RIGHT NOW. SUMMONING ISN'T EASY. SO, WE'RE PROBABLY SAFE HERE, FOR A LITTLE WHILE AT LEAST.
OH, GREAT.
AND WE DO HAVE A HOSTAGE, DON'T WE?
HOSTAGES...
...HAVE INFORMATION.
YEAH.
SO, LET'S SEE WHAT HE KNOWS.
HEY, EDS, THANKS FOR JUMPIN' IN, EARLIER.
THINK NUTHIN', KEV.
THAT WAS MY D--

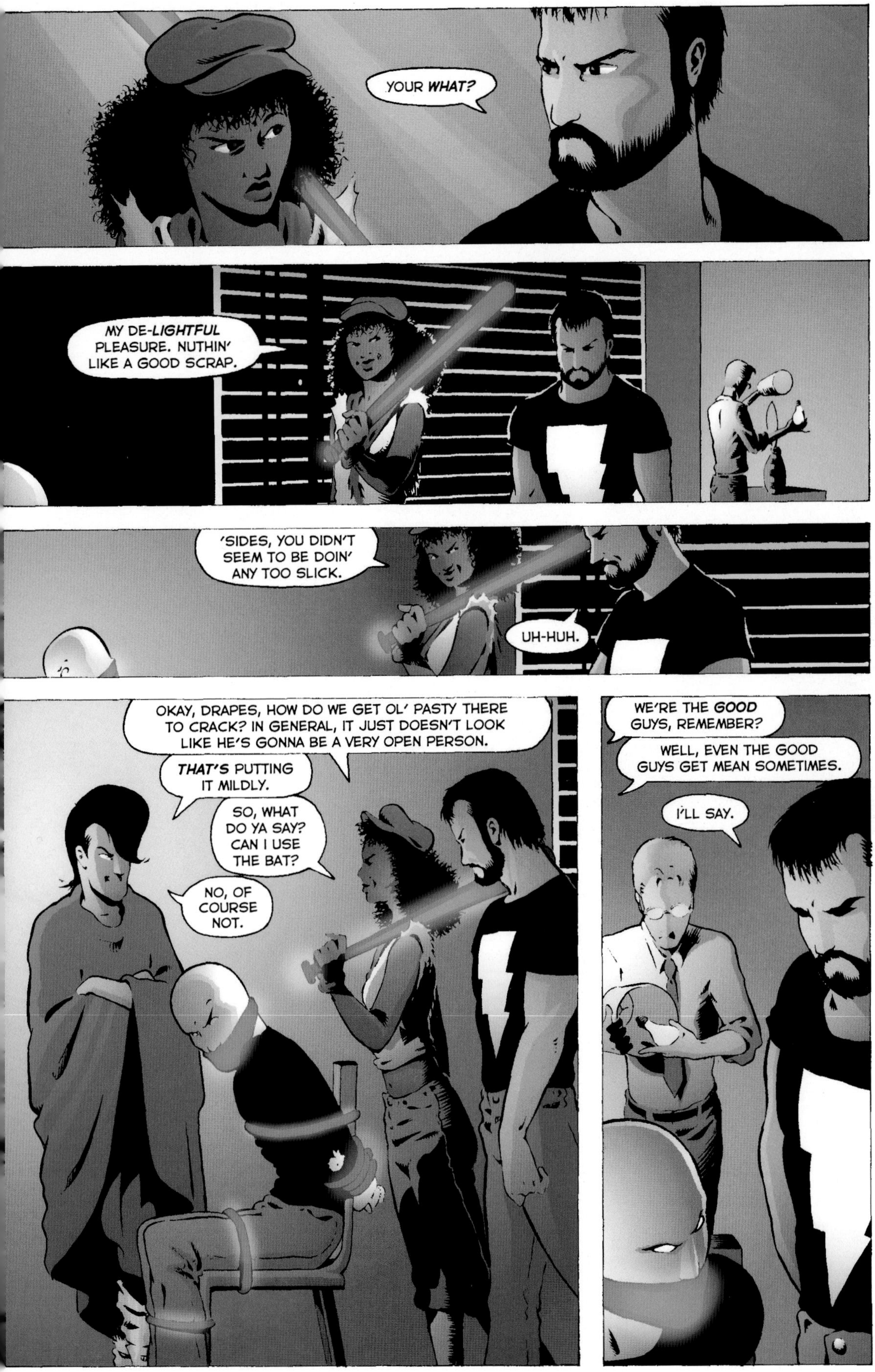
YOUR WHAT?
MY DE-LIGHTFUL PLEASURE. NUTHIN' LIKE A GOOD SCRAP.
'SIDES, YOU DIDN'T SEEM TO BE DOIN' ANY TOO SLICK.
UH-HUH.
OKAY, DRAPES, HOW DO WE GET OL' PASTY THERE TO CRACK? IN GENERAL, IT JUST DOESN'T LOOK LIKE HE'S GONNA BE A VERY OPEN PERSON.
THAT'S PUTTING IT MILDLY.
SO, WHAT DO YA SAY? CAN I USE THE BAT?
NO, OF COURSE NOT.
WE'RE THE GOOD GUYS, REMEMBER?
WELL, EVEN THE GOOD GUYS GET MEAN SOMETIMES.
I'LL SAY.

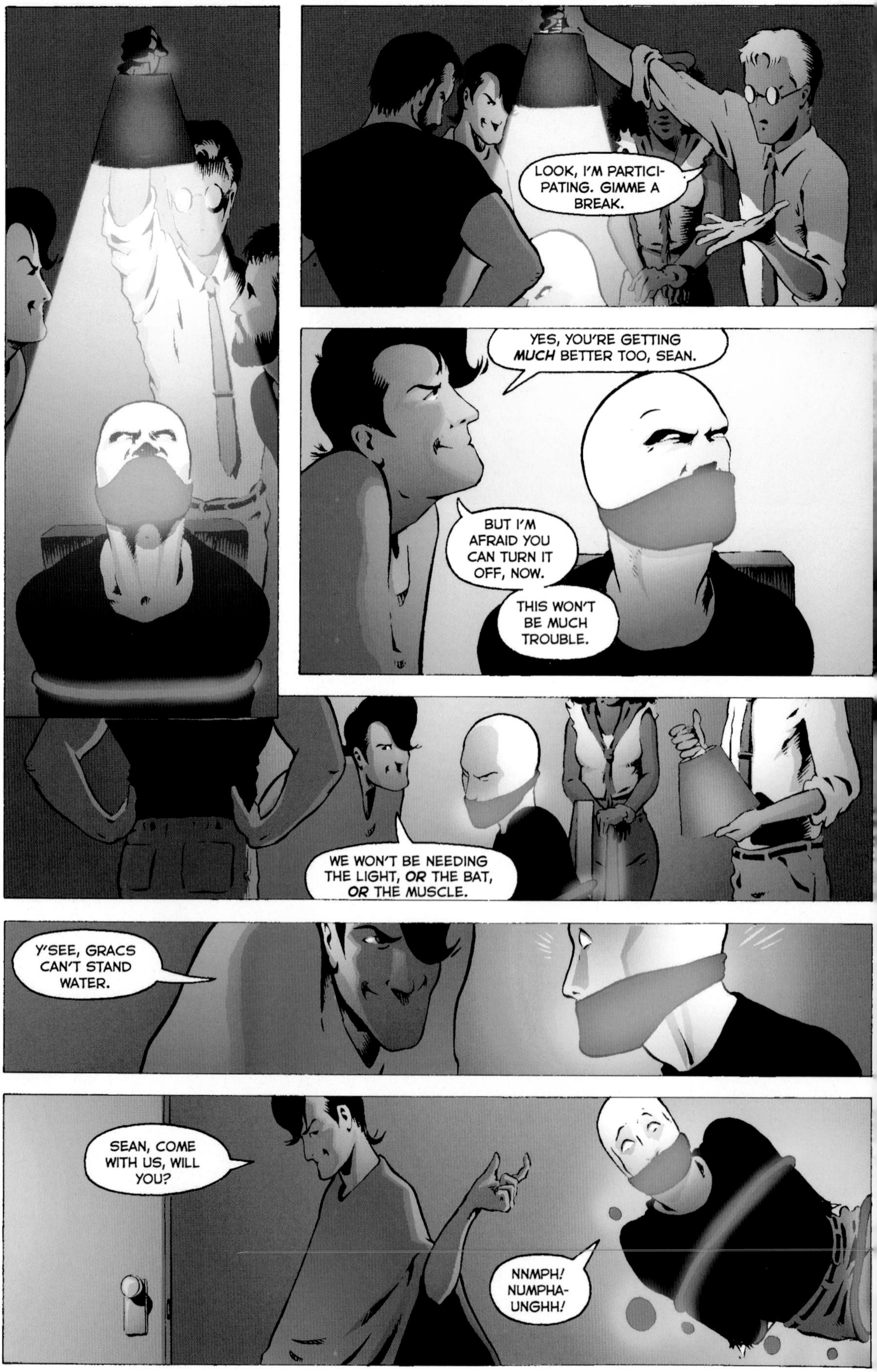

LOOK, I'M PARTICI-PATING. GIMME A BREAK.
YES, YOU'RE GETTING *MUCH* BETTER TOO, SEAN.
BUT I'M AFRAID YOU CAN TURN IT OFF, NOW.
THIS WON'T BE MUCH TROUBLE.
WE WON'T BE NEEDING THE LIGHT, *OR* THE BAT, *OR* THE MUSCLE.
Y'SEE, GRACS CAN'T STAND WATER.
SEAN, COME WITH US, WILL YOU?
NNMPH! NUMPHA-UNGHH!

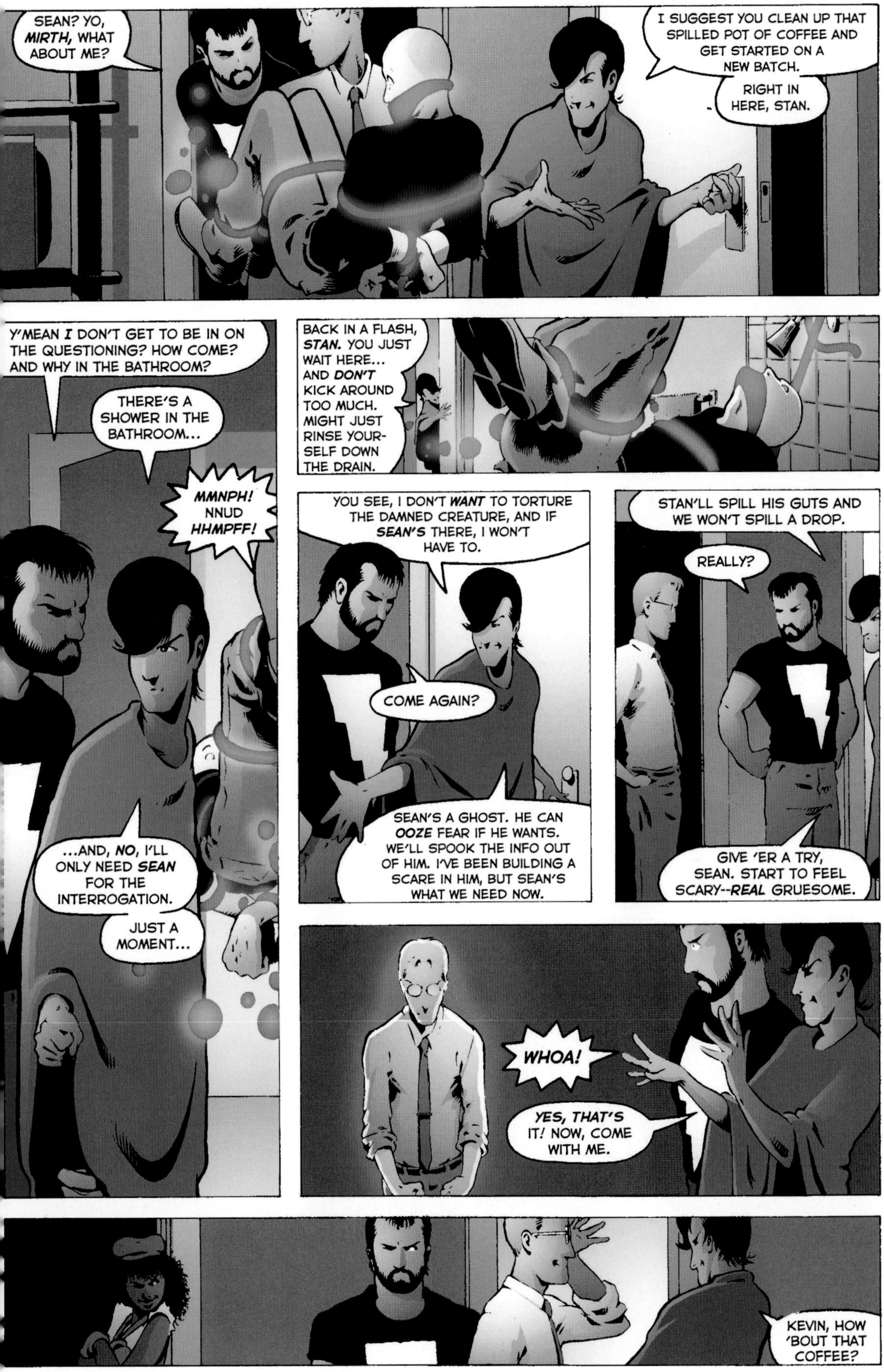
SEAN? YO, MIRTH, WHAT ABOUT ME?
I SUGGEST YOU CLEAN UP THAT SPILLED POT OF COFFEE AND GET STARTED ON A NEW BATCH.
RIGHT IN HERE, STAN.
Y'MEAN I DON'T GET TO BE IN ON THE QUESTIONING? HOW COME? AND WHY IN THE BATHROOM?
THERE'S A SHOWER IN THE BATHROOM...
MMNPH! NNUD HHMPFF!
...AND, NO, I'LL ONLY NEED SEAN FOR THE INTERROGATION.
JUST A MOMENT...
BACK IN A FLASH, STAN. YOU JUST WAIT HERE... AND DON'T KICK AROUND TOO MUCH. MIGHT JUST RINSE YOURSELF DOWN THE DRAIN.
YOU SEE, I DON'T WANT TO TORTURE THE DAMNED CREATURE, AND IF SEAN'S THERE, I WON'T HAVE TO.
COME AGAIN?
SEAN'S A GHOST. HE CAN OOZE FEAR IF HE WANTS. WE'LL SPOOK THE INFO OUT OF HIM. I'VE BEEN BUILDING A SCARE IN HIM, BUT SEAN'S WHAT WE NEED NOW.
STAN'LL SPILL HIS GUTS AND WE WON'T SPILL A DROP.
REALLY?
GIVE 'ER A TRY, SEAN. START TO FEEL SCARY--REAL GRUESOME.
WHOA!
YES, THAT'S IT! NOW, COME WITH ME.
KEVIN, HOW 'BOUT THAT COFFEE?

HELLO, STAN.

READY TO PLAY?

THE GAME'S *"HYDROQUIZ"!* EACH WRONG ANSWER RESULTS IN A QUICK SPRINKLE OF PROGRESSIVE LENGTH. (WINNERS RECEIVE A SPIEGEL CATALOGUE.)

HOW'S HE FIND US, STAN?

PISS OFF, MAGE, MATCHSTICK DOESN'T *KNOW* YET, *DOES* HE? OTHERWISE, YOU'D LET HIM *BE* HERE. YOU'RE STILL WITHOUT YOUR LEADER, *AREN'T* YOU?

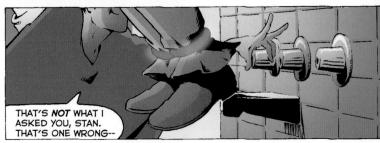

THAT'S *NOT* WHAT I ASKED YOU, STAN. THAT'S ONE WRONG--

rr-UGGHH!

...YOU *REALLY* SHOULDN'T HAVE TRIED THAT.

I'M AFRAID SEAN'S MAD AT YOU NOW.

HEH! HEH! OH MY, STAN. OH, MY...MY... MY...

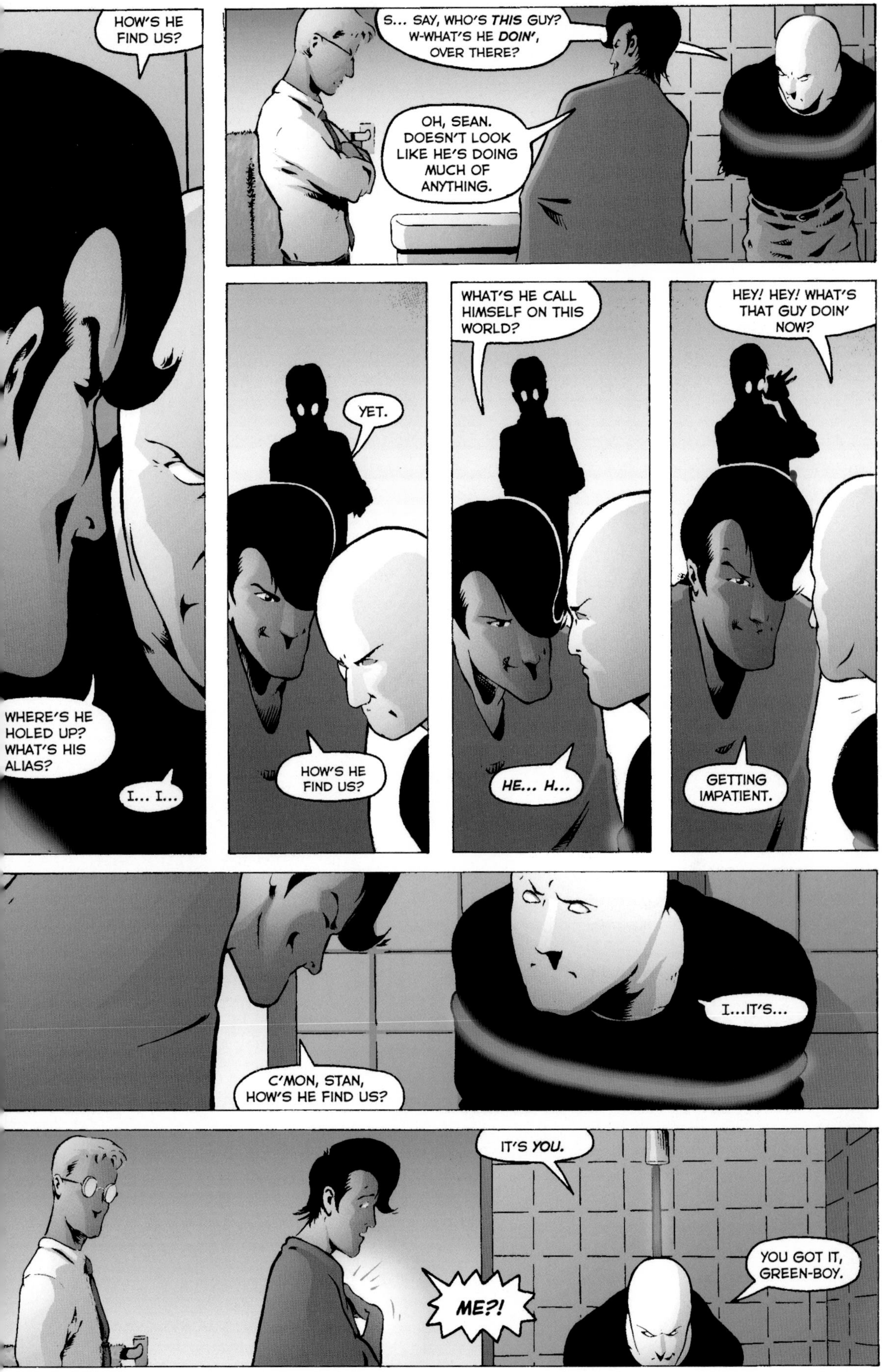
HOW'S HE FIND US?
S... SAY, WHO'S *THIS* GUY? W-WHAT'S HE *DOIN'*, OVER THERE?
OH, SEAN. DOESN'T LOOK LIKE HE'S DOING MUCH OF ANYTHING.
WHERE'S HE HOLED UP? WHAT'S HIS ALIAS?
I... I...
YET.
HOW'S HE FIND US?
WHAT'S HE CALL HIMSELF ON THIS WORLD?
HE... H...
HEY! HEY! WHAT'S THAT GUY DOIN' NOW?
GETTING IMPATIENT.
I...IT'S...
C'MON, STAN, HOW'S HE FIND US?
IT'S *YOU.*
ME?!
YOU GOT IT, GREEN-BOY.

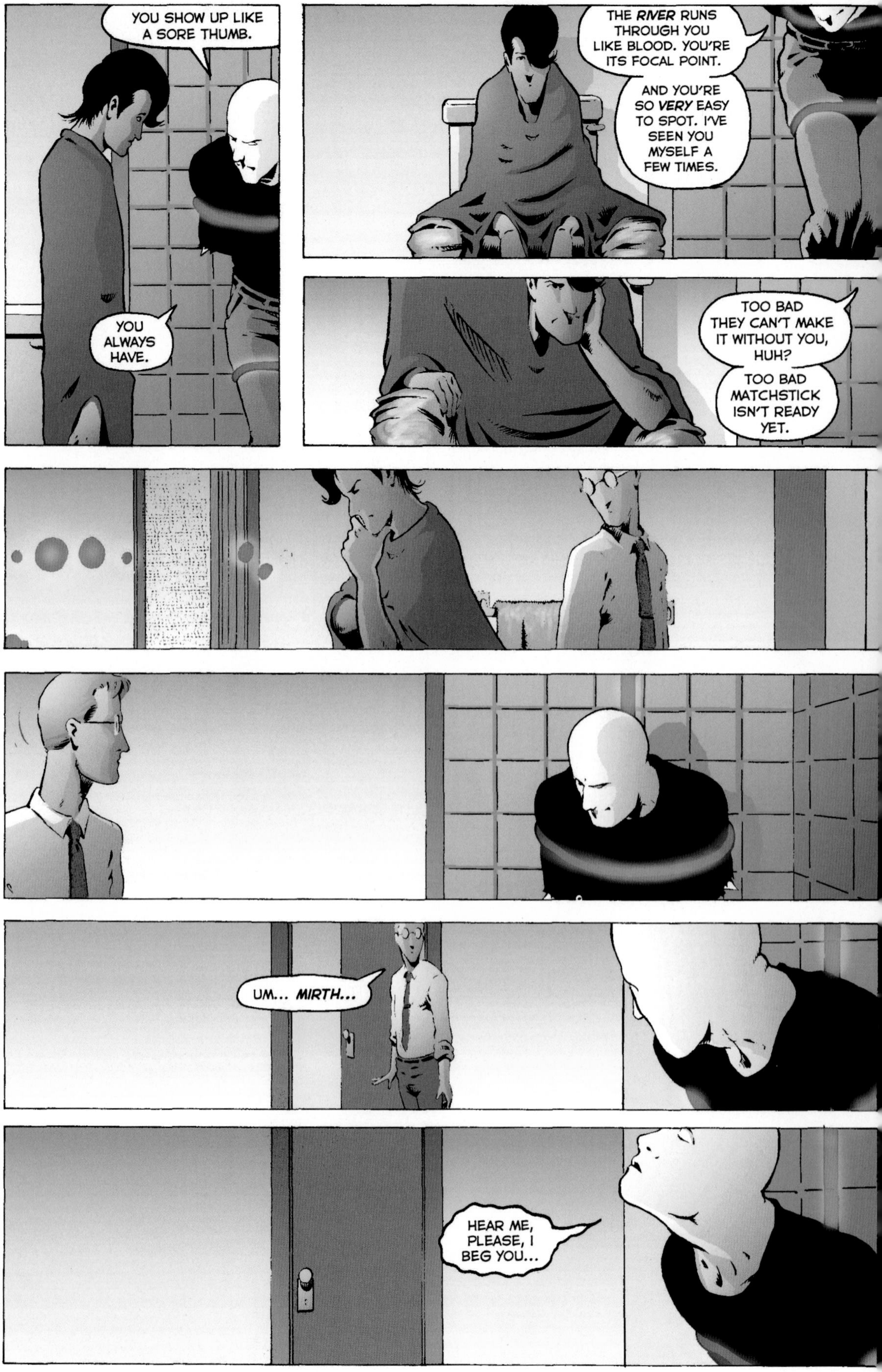
YOU SHOW UP LIKE A SORE THUMB.
YOU ALWAYS HAVE.
THE *RIVER* RUNS THROUGH YOU LIKE BLOOD. YOU'RE ITS FOCAL POINT.
AND YOU'RE SO *VERY* EASY TO SPOT. I'VE SEEN YOU MYSELF A FEW TIMES.
TOO BAD THEY CAN'T MAKE IT WITHOUT YOU, HUH?
TOO BAD MATCHSTICK ISN'T READY YET.
UM... *MIRTH*...
HEAR ME, PLEASE, I BEG YOU...

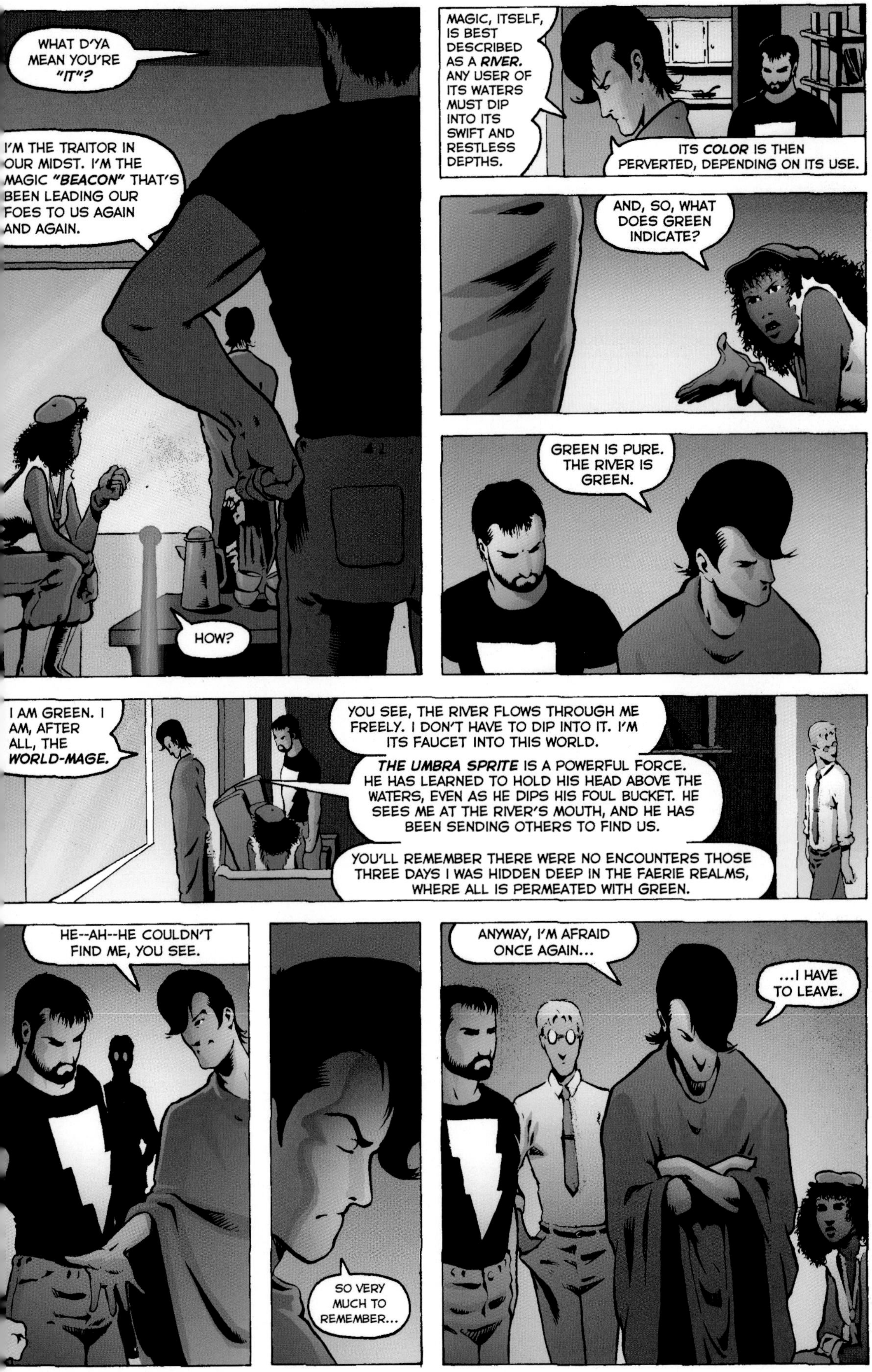
WHAT D'YA MEAN YOU'RE "IT"?
I'M THE TRAITOR IN OUR MIDST. I'M THE MAGIC "BEACON" THAT'S BEEN LEADING OUR FOES TO US AGAIN AND AGAIN.
HOW?
MAGIC, ITSELF, IS BEST DESCRIBED AS A RIVER. ANY USER OF ITS WATERS MUST DIP INTO ITS SWIFT AND RESTLESS DEPTHS.
ITS COLOR IS THEN PERVERTED, DEPENDING ON ITS USE.
AND, SO, WHAT DOES GREEN INDICATE?
GREEN IS PURE. THE RIVER IS GREEN.
I AM GREEN. I AM, AFTER ALL, THE WORLD-MAGE.
YOU SEE, THE RIVER FLOWS THROUGH ME FREELY. I DON'T HAVE TO DIP INTO IT. I'M ITS FAUCET INTO THIS WORLD.
THE UMBRA SPRITE IS A POWERFUL FORCE. HE HAS LEARNED TO HOLD HIS HEAD ABOVE THE WATERS, EVEN AS HE DIPS HIS FOUL BUCKET. HE SEES ME AT THE RIVER'S MOUTH, AND HE HAS BEEN SENDING OTHERS TO FIND US.
YOU'LL REMEMBER THERE WERE NO ENCOUNTERS THOSE THREE DAYS I WAS HIDDEN DEEP IN THE FAERIE REALMS, WHERE ALL IS PERMEATED WITH GREEN.
HE--AH--HE COULDN'T FIND ME, YOU SEE.
SO VERY MUCH TO REMEMBER...
ANYWAY, I'M AFRAID ONCE AGAIN...
...I HAVE TO LEAVE.

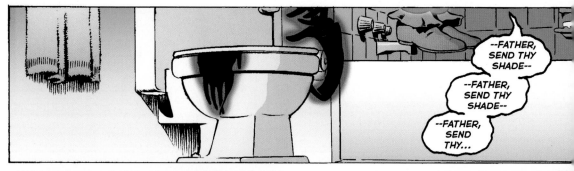

--FATHER, SEND THY SHADE--

--FATHER, SEND THY SHADE--

--FATHER, SEND THY...

THANK YOU, BEAUTIFUL DARKNESS...

SOMETIMES I *STILL* FEEL THE BLINDING GREEN THAT THE *ETERNAL KNAVE* STRUCK ME WITH...

...AND IT REMINDS ME THAT THERE, *AGAIN,* IT WAS FOR YOUR SAKE THAT I CAME INTO HIS PRESENCE.

AND, OF COURSE, YOU MUST ALSO BEAR THE PAIN OF DIMINUTION.

YES, FATHER.

DAMN YOU, STANIS.

KNOW YOU NOT HOW IT WILL *PAIN* ME TO TOUCH HIS ROPES?

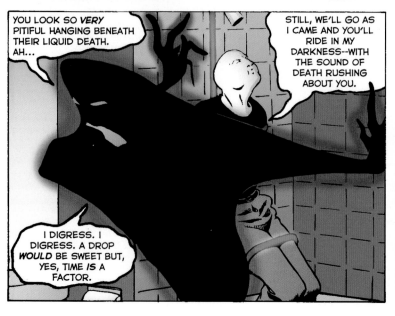

YOU LOOK SO *VERY* PITIFUL HANGING BENEATH THEIR LIQUID DEATH. AH...

STILL, WE'LL GO AS I CAME AND YOU'LL RIDE IN MY DARKNESS--WITH THE SOUND OF DEATH RUSHING ABOUT YOU.

I DIGRESS. I DIGRESS. A DROP *WOULD* BE SWEET BUT, YES, TIME *IS* A FACTOR.

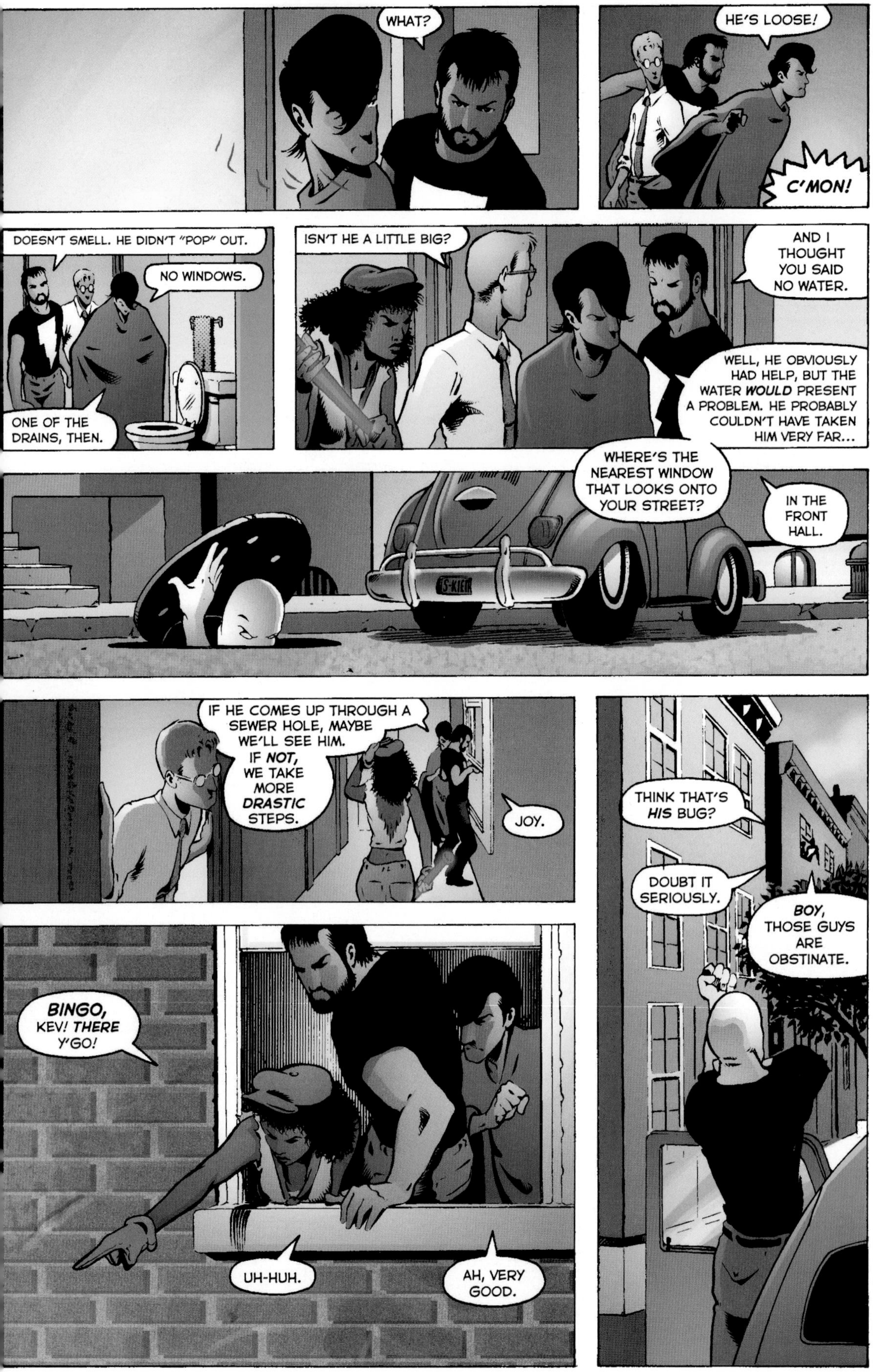
WHAT?
HE'S LOOSE!
C'MON!
DOESN'T SMELL. HE DIDN'T "POP" OUT.
NO WINDOWS.
ONE OF THE DRAINS, THEN.
ISN'T HE A LITTLE BIG?
AND I THOUGHT YOU SAID NO WATER.
WELL, HE OBVIOUSLY HAD HELP, BUT THE WATER *WOULD* PRESENT A PROBLEM. HE PROBABLY COULDN'T HAVE TAKEN HIM VERY FAR...
WHERE'S THE NEAREST WINDOW THAT LOOKS ONTO YOUR STREET?
IN THE FRONT HALL.
S-KIER
IF HE COMES UP THROUGH A SEWER HOLE, MAYBE WE'LL SEE HIM. IF *NOT,* WE TAKE MORE *DRASTIC* STEPS.
JOY.
THINK THAT'S *HIS* BUG?
DOUBT IT SERIOUSLY.
BOY, THOSE GUYS ARE OBSTINATE.
BINGO, KEV! *THERE* Y'GO!
UH-HUH.
AH, VERY GOOD.

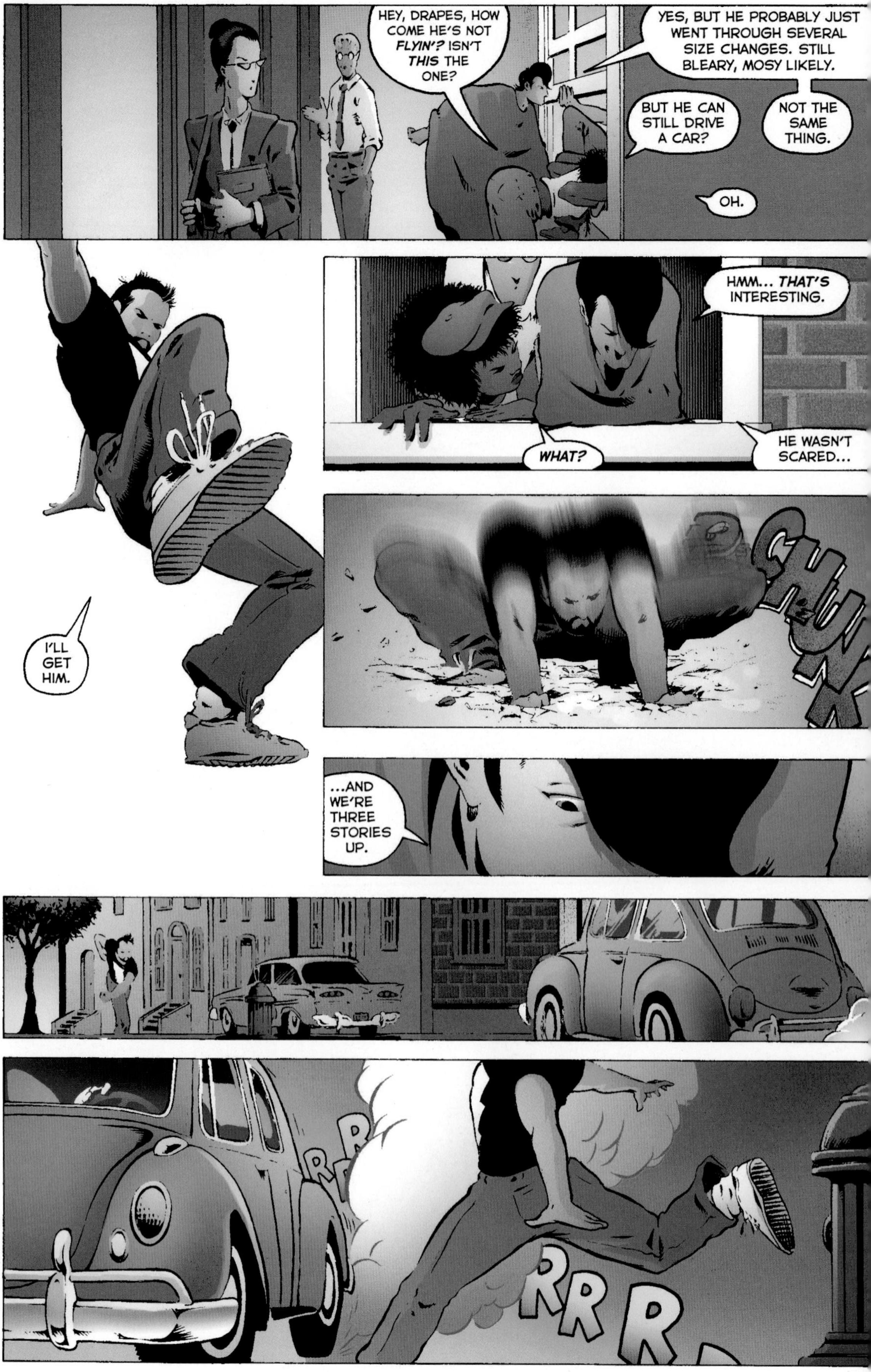
HEY, DRAPES, HOW COME HE'S NOT *FLYIN'?* ISN'T *THIS* THE ONE?
YES, BUT HE PROBABLY JUST WENT THROUGH SEVERAL SIZE CHANGES. STILL BLEARY, MOSY LIKELY.
BUT HE CAN STILL DRIVE A CAR?
NOT THE SAME THING.
OH.
HMM... *THAT'S* INTERESTING.
WHAT?
HE WASN'T SCARED...
I'LL GET HIM.
CHUNK
...AND WE'RE THREE STORIES UP.
RRR
RRR

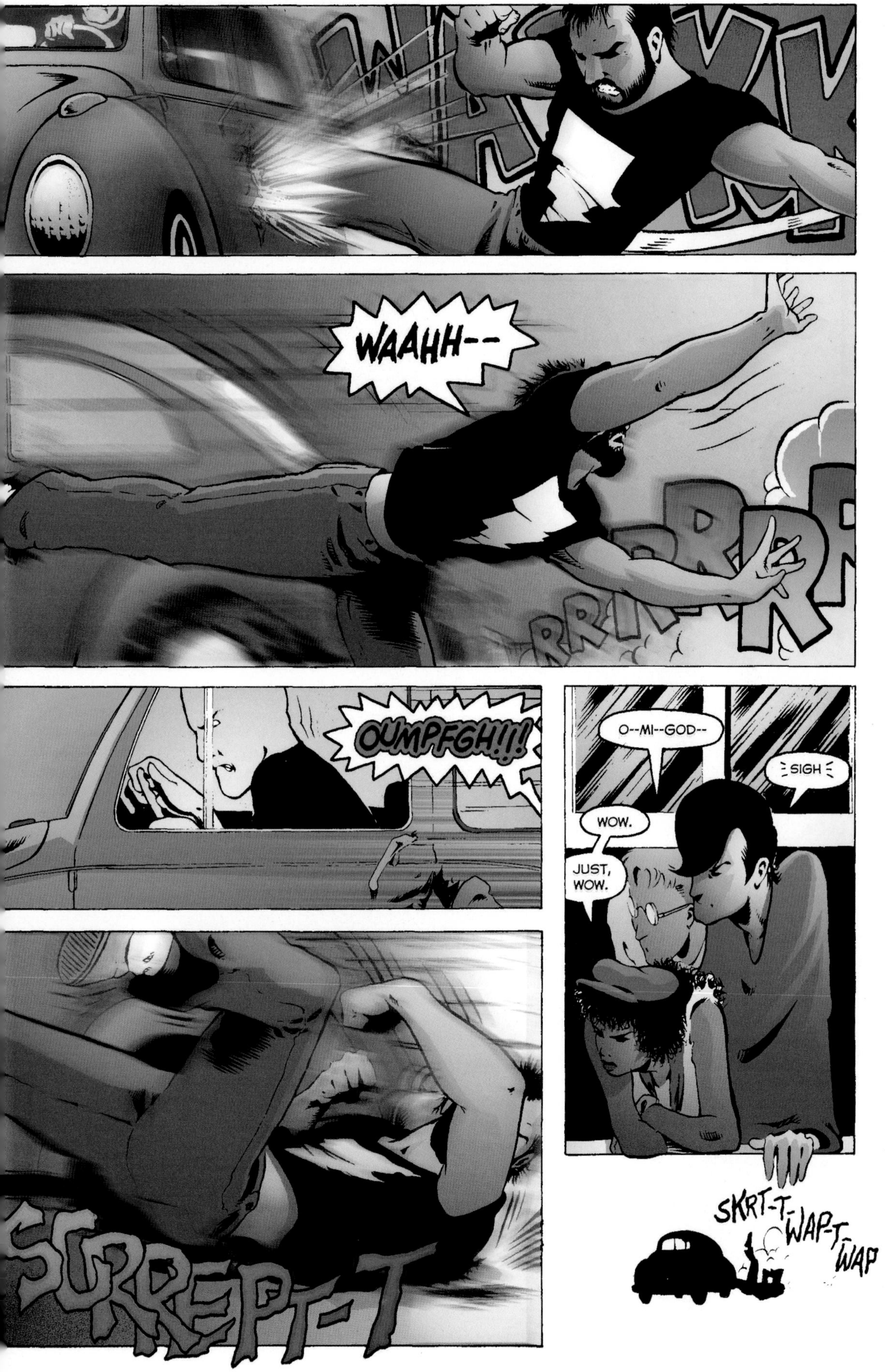
WAAHH--
OUMPFGH!!!
O--MI--GOD--
SIGH
WOW.
JUST, WOW.
SCRREPT-T
SKRT-T-WAP-T-WAP

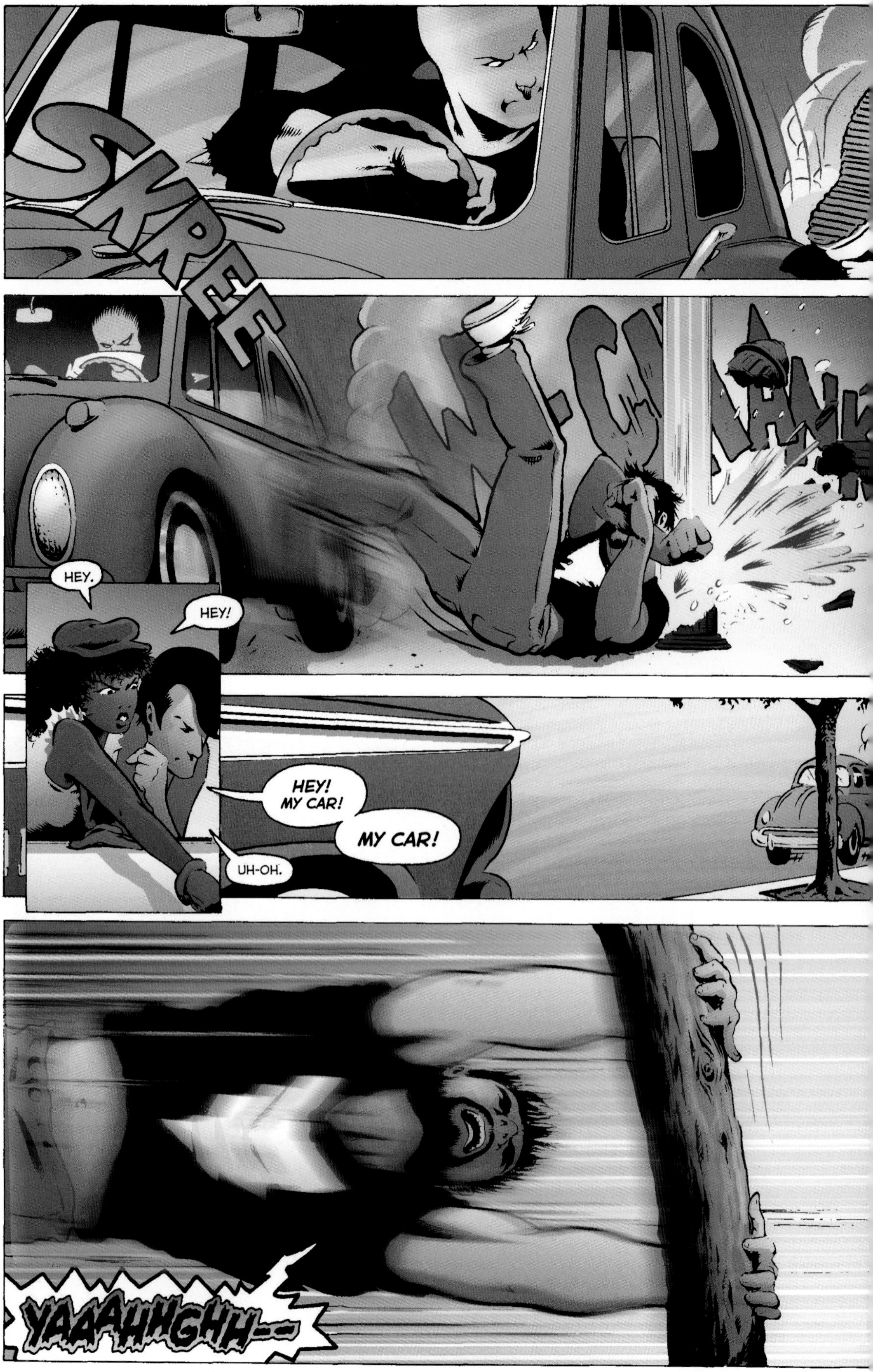
SKREE
HEY.
HEY!
HEY!
MY CAR!
MY CAR!
UH-OH.
YAAHHGHH--

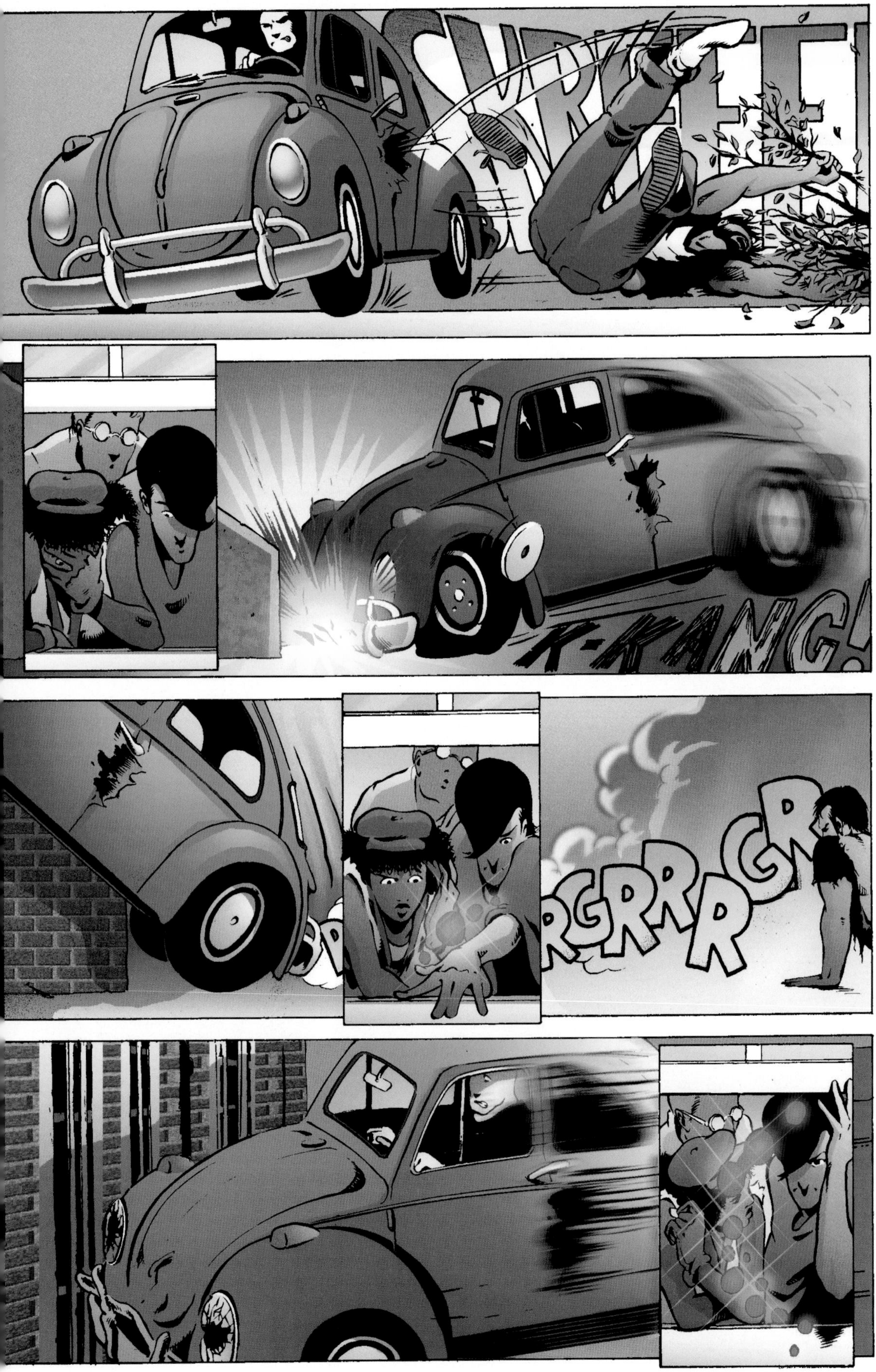
K-KANG!

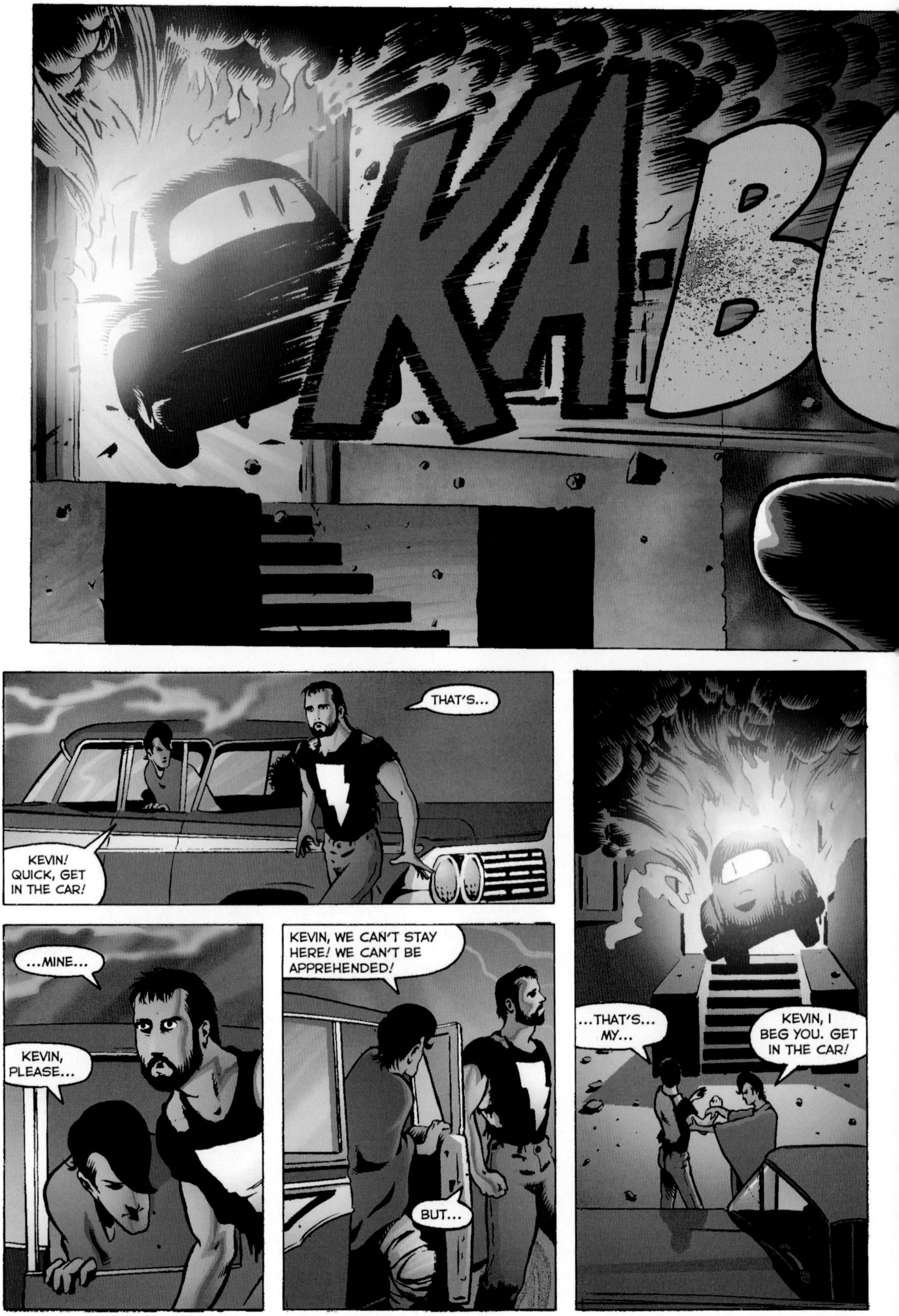
KA-BO
THAT'S...
KEVIN! QUICK, GET IN THE CAR!
...MINE...
KEVIN, PLEASE...
KEVIN, WE CAN'T STAY HERE! WE CAN'T BE APPREHENDED!
BUT...
...THAT'S... MY...
KEVIN, I BEG YOU. GET IN THE CAR!

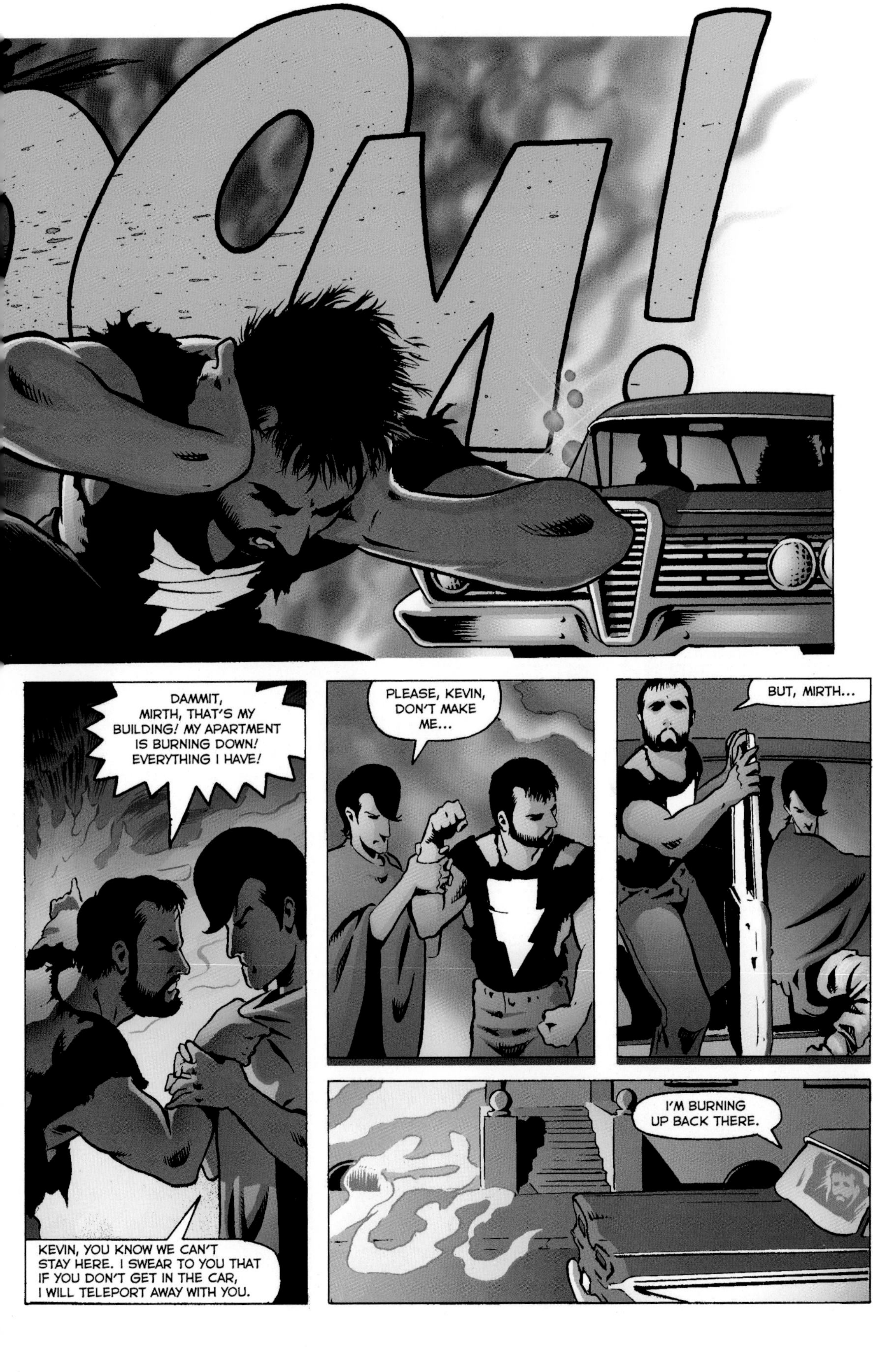

DAMMIT, MIRTH, THAT'S MY BUILDING! MY APARTMENT IS BURNING DOWN! EVERYTHING I HAVE!
KEVIN, YOU KNOW WE CAN'T STAY HERE. I SWEAR TO YOU THAT IF YOU DON'T GET IN THE CAR, I WILL TELEPORT AWAY WITH YOU.
PLEASE, KEVIN, DON'T MAKE ME...
BUT, MIRTH...
I'M BURNING UP BACK THERE.

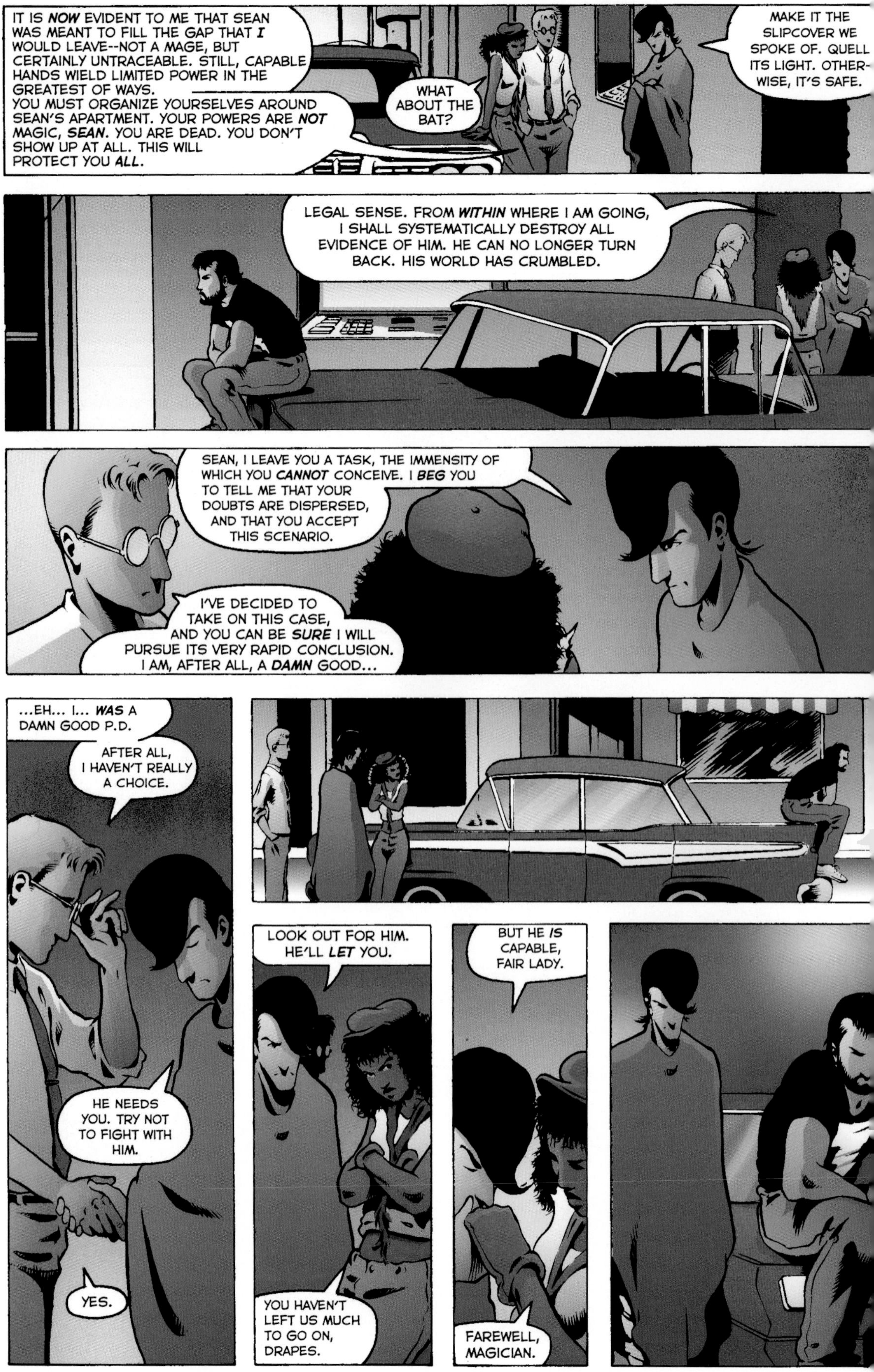
IT IS NOW EVIDENT TO ME THAT SEAN WAS MEANT TO FILL THE GAP THAT I WOULD LEAVE--NOT A MAGE, BUT CERTAINLY UNTRACEABLE. STILL, CAPABLE HANDS WIELD LIMITED POWER IN THE GREATEST OF WAYS.
YOU MUST ORGANIZE YOURSELVES AROUND SEAN'S APARTMENT. YOUR POWERS ARE NOT MAGIC, SEAN. YOU ARE DEAD. YOU DON'T SHOW UP AT ALL. THIS WILL PROTECT YOU ALL.
WHAT ABOUT THE BAT?
MAKE IT THE SLIPCOVER WE SPOKE OF. QUELL ITS LIGHT. OTHERWISE, IT'S SAFE.
LEGAL SENSE. FROM WITHIN WHERE I AM GOING, I SHALL SYSTEMATICALLY DESTROY ALL EVIDENCE OF HIM. HE CAN NO LONGER TURN BACK. HIS WORLD HAS CRUMBLED.
SEAN, I LEAVE YOU A TASK, THE IMMENSITY OF WHICH YOU CANNOT CONCEIVE. I BEG YOU TO TELL ME THAT YOUR DOUBTS ARE DISPERSED, AND THAT YOU ACCEPT THIS SCENARIO.
I'VE DECIDED TO TAKE ON THIS CASE, AND YOU CAN BE SURE I WILL PURSUE ITS VERY RAPID CONCLUSION. I AM, AFTER ALL, A DAMN GOOD...
...EH... I... WAS A DAMN GOOD P.D.
AFTER ALL, I HAVEN'T REALLY A CHOICE.
HE NEEDS YOU. TRY NOT TO FIGHT WITH HIM.
YES.
LOOK OUT FOR HIM. HE'LL LET YOU.
YOU HAVEN'T LEFT US MUCH TO GO ON, DRAPES.
BUT HE IS CAPABLE, FAIR LADY.
FAREWELL, MAGICIAN.

IT CERTAINLY WAS A VOLATILE EXPLOSION.

I HEAR YOU.

YOU MEAN IT HAD "HELP."

YEAH. IT'S THE UMBRA SPRITE.

OF COURSE.

YOU UNDERSTAND WHY I HAVE TO LEAVE.

YEAH. WHERE, AGAIN?

INSIDE THIS COMPUTER LINE I BECOME *AS ONE* WITH THE MACHINE.

ENTOMBED. UNTRACEABLE.

I *CAN* LEAVE YOU THIS, THOUGH. YOU CAN USE IT TO CONTACT ME-- AT *ANY* SUCH TERMINAL.

PROBABLY NOT A GOOD IDEA TO USE IT TOO OFTEN.

UH-HUH.

THE CODE WORD'S *MAGE.*

CUTE.

I *STILL* DON'T BELIEVE ANY OF THIS SHIT YET.

MONEY ANY TIME

YOU WILL.

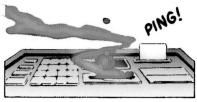

PING!

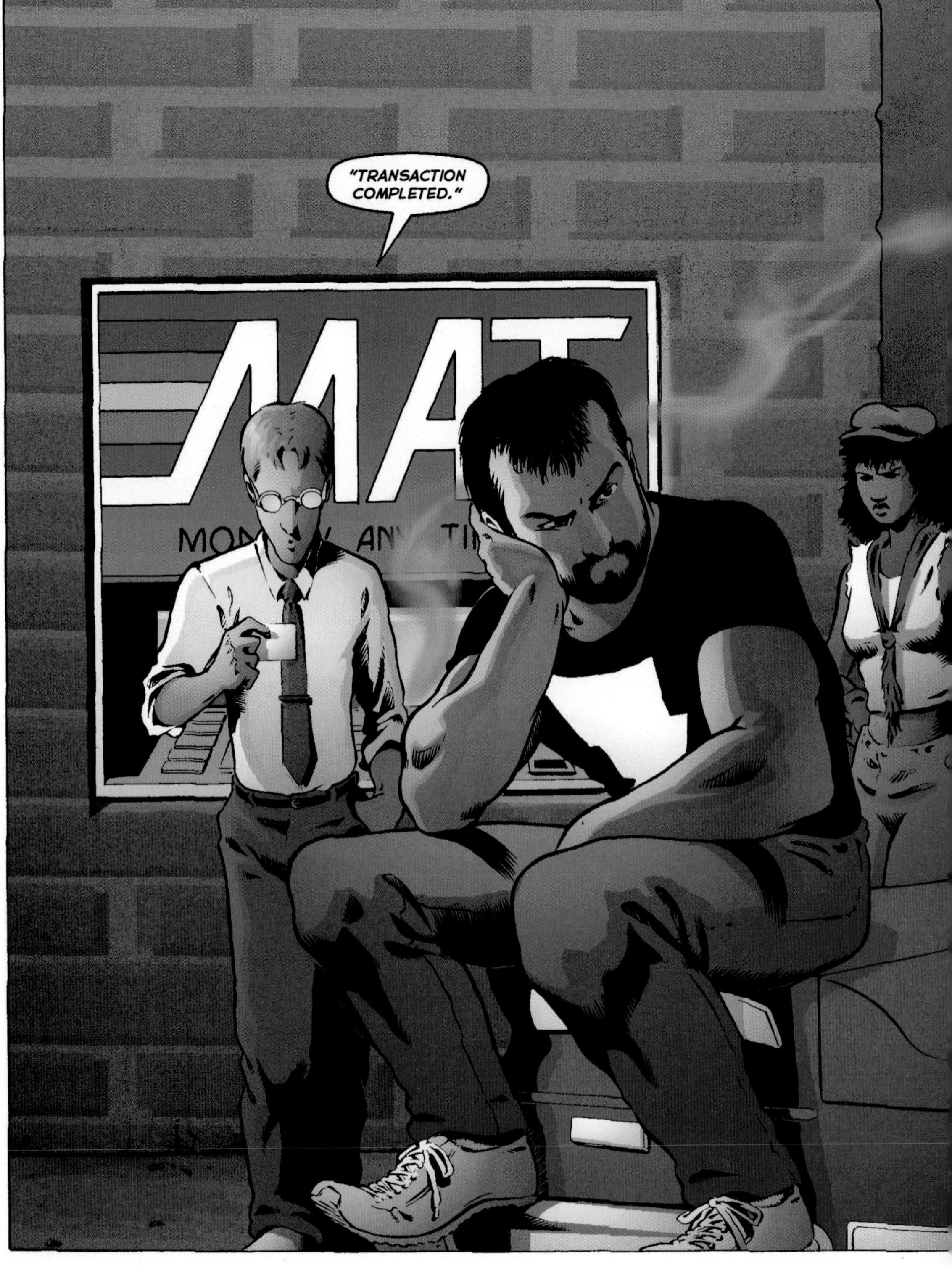
"TRANSACTION COMPLETED."
MAT

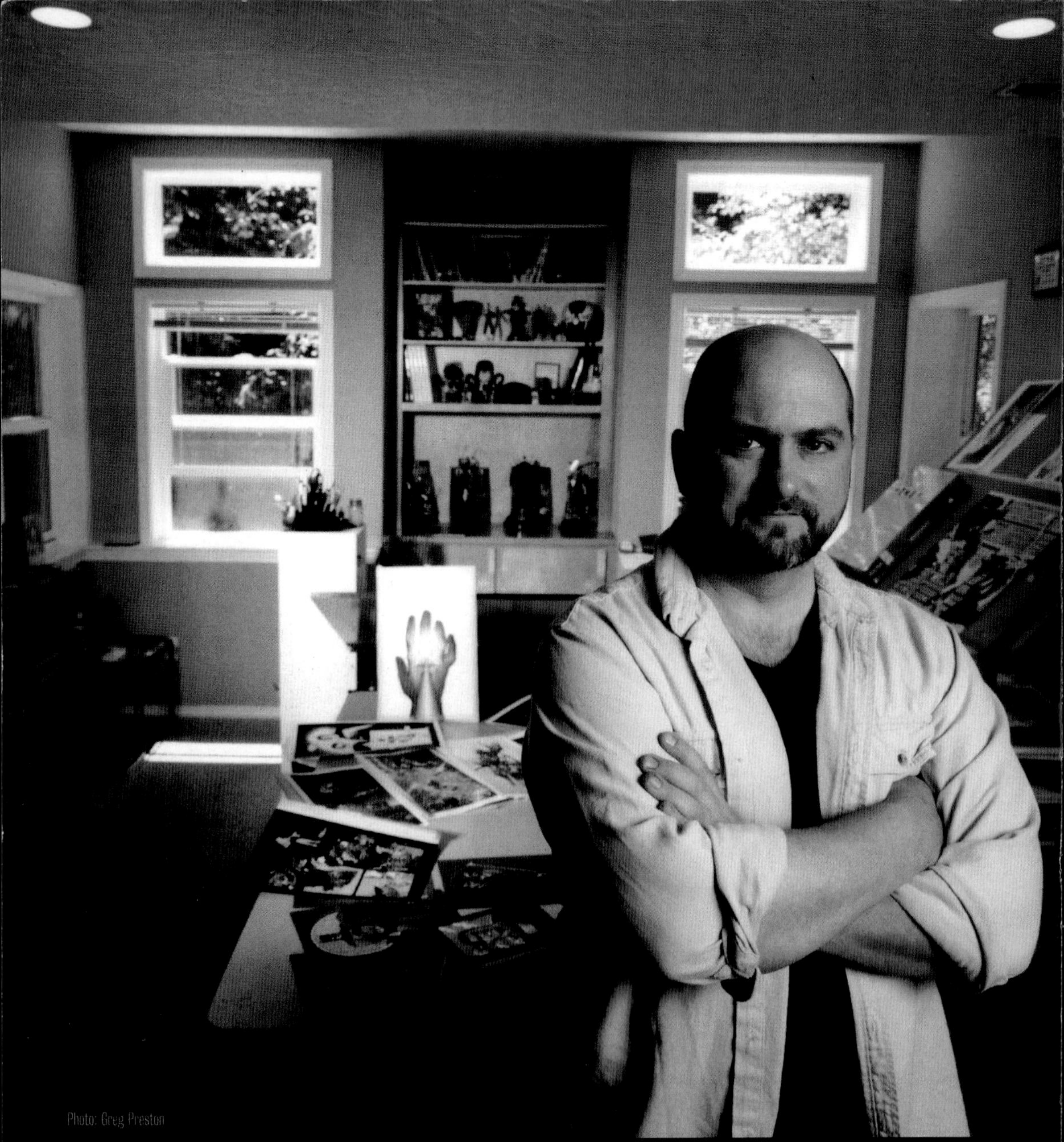

Photo: Greg Preston

MATT WAGNER has been a pioneer of the independent comics scene for over thirty years. His first published work was a short story that would introduce one of comicdom's earliest and most respected creator-owned characters—the mastermind assassin, GRENDEL. Shortly after this, he began work on his most personal work, the epic fantasy trilogy, MAGE. Known for his character-driven stories and an obvious love of world history and mythologies, Matt has also worked on a variety of established characters over the course of his career. These projects include extensive work on BATMAN for DC COMICS as well as two BATMAN/GRENDEL crossover events and TRINITY, a best-selling prestige series starring Superman, Batman and Wonder Woman. Renowned for his skills as both a writer and an artist, Matt's other mainstream work includes: SANDMAN MYSTERY THEATRE, DR. MID-NITE, GREEN ARROW, MADAME XANADU, ZORRO, THE GREEN HORNET, THE SHADOW and a 75th anniversary relaunch of Will Eisner's iconic character, THE SPIRIT. He recently teamed with renowned film-maker Quentin Tarantino to co-craft and write a DJANGO/ZORRO crossover series. In 2017, Matt finally returned to write and draw the long-awaited conclusion to his MAGE trilogy, THE HERO DENIED. He lives with his family in Oregon.